KERRY J DONOVAN

ON THE WING

VINCI
BOOKS

The Ryan Kaine series by Kerry J Donovan

To the real Melanie Archer, who deserves all the good fortune coming to her. Be strong, be safe, be happy.

Vinci Books

vinci-books.com

Published by Vinci Books Ltd in 2025

1

Printed and bound in Great Britain by Clays Ltd, Elcograf S.p.A.

Chapter One

Monday 12th April - Melanie Archer

Shower Facilities, HMP Falston Manor, Derbyshire, England

A thumping, grinding blow. Back of the head.

Flashes of bright light. Fog.

White tiles, wet and harsh, raced up. Smacked Mel in the face. Another blow, a kick. Heavy shoes, the toecaps cracked bone. Her bone. Bones.

"You're gonna die, bitch!" a voice hissed in her ear.

"The killer's going down." A different voice, angry.

Oh God!

Someone laughed.

"Don't need no money for this. Do it for free, me."

Another kick landed.

1

Added to the pain.

"I'll have your share, then."

"Fuck off. What's mine's mine."

Agony.

Wall to wall.

Floor to floor.

Total, encompassing. Nothing but agony.

Head, eyes, jaw, ribs, stomach. Every movement screamed pain. The ribs hurt more on the left side.

Why?

Darkness enclosed her.

Someone whimpered, cried. High-pitched and feeble. Mel felt the sounds inside and outside her head. Another groan, this one louder.

Her cries.

Her whimpers.

What's happening?

She tried to open both eyes, but only the left lid reacted, letting in the searing agony of bright, white light. Too bright, too much to suffer. She squeezed her lid closed and the ache lessened. But not by much.

Sunny? It's sunny?

The sun gave out no heat. Her skin was cold. Sweaty cold. Clammy. Somewhere close by, water splashed. Dripped. The sound echoed off hard, reflective surfaces.

The shower block.

Another kick, to the back, this one barely noticed. Hardly even felt.

Relax, Mel. Let it end. End now.

Shouts.

Raised voices.

Female voices. High-pitched, but sharp and guttural.

She stopped talking again, breathing deeply through her mouth, panting.

"Do you need a break? Would you like a cuppa?"

She nodded. "Y-Yes. Yes, please."

"Kitchen's that way, right?" Danny pointed through the door he'd already used twice. "Through the hall?"

"Yes. H-How did you know that?"

"I'm a good guesser. Come on."

Danny stood, closed the gap between them, and held out his hand. She looked up at him and hesitated a moment before taking it in a firm grip. He helped her up and released her hand only when certain she wouldn't topple over.

"Before we go, can you tell me where the man took your husband?"

"They've gone to the office. Vadik said Robbie needed to be at work on time as normal. Something about ... nothing could interfere with the exchange. Whatever that means. As I said, I don't really have much of an ... involvement with the business. I really don't know what they were talking about, but ..." She paused and sighed.

"But?"

Her eyes locked with Danny's for the longest time since he'd burst in to the house.

"There was something ... I don't know. Something strange about the way Robbie acted."

"Strange? In what way?"

"Well, he kept telling me how sorry he was. How everything was all his fault."

"Because you were attacked?"

"No ... yes. Well, sort of. But it was more than that. The way Robbie and Vadik acted together. It was almost as though they knew each other before we were taken hostage."

Danny nodded but didn't know what to say. The whole situation kept getting stranger, more complicated. He needed to dig deeper, but Marian looked about ready to collapse onto the sofa again and he'd promised her a cuppa.

"How long does it normally take your husband to get to work?"

"This time of the day, over an hour." She hugged the giraffe tighter. "Traffic can be terrible."

"Are you expecting a call when they arrive? I mean, is this Vadik character going to check in with Nemeth?"

Marian Prentiss shrugged. "I-I have no idea. They didn't mention a call. Vadik just told Nemeth to guard me until they got back this afternoon. Told him to keep his hands off me, too. The pig looked disappointed, but promised to do as he was told." She shuddered, probably at the thought of spending most of the day alone in the house with the bastard who'd done so much damage to her already.

Danny nodded. They had time. Maybe not long, but hopefully enough.

"So, are you ready for that cuppa?"

She nodded.

"Okay, let's go."

He took her hand again and led her through to the kitchen, trying to block her view of the splodge he'd left behind the staircase, but she stopped and took a long look at the man who'd attacked her.

"Sorry for messing up your décor, but I imagine the tiles will scrub clean."

She shook her head carefully. "I haven't started in the hall yet. The house is still a work in progress. The entrance is horrible. It looks like a mausoleum. We've been decorating, room by room, from the top down. My God, you don't think I designed this monstrosity, do you?"

Danny shook his head. "Of course not."

It wasn't the first time he'd been proven wrong that day, and he didn't mind lying to hide yet another mistake.

"If I was wearing shoes and not these slippers," she said, lifting her foot, "I'd go over there and kick the filthy turd's head in some more."

"And I'd do nothing to stop you," Danny said, delighted to be telling the truth once more.

He wasn't the least bit shocked by her language. Nemeth deserved every scrap of her anger.

Marian took over and led the way into a bright, modern kitchen.

"Tea or coffee?" she asked, filling the kettle from a chromed tap that looked as though it might have cost Danny a week's pay. The kitchen was an understated blend of creams and greys, with the occasional burst of sunshine yellow. Minimalist modern. Airy. Nice.

"Coffee, please. Did you design the kitchen?"

She smiled beneath the nose splint. "I did. You like it?"

"I do. It's sleek. Elegant."

"Thank you. That's what I was going for."

Danny made his way to the full-length French doors overlooking the manicured gardens. If he'd craned his neck hard enough, he might have been able to spot where he'd spent part of the night.

He watched Marian's reflection as she fussed over the brewing process. In her kitchen, doing normal things, she seemed to draw out of herself. It relaxed her and made her more composed.

After setting aside the coffee pot, she turned and leaned her back against the counter.

"Thanks for giving me time," she said. "Now, where was I?"

Danny grimaced. "Upstairs in bed, struggling to breathe."

Grab your copy...
vinci-books.com/onthehunt

About Kerry J Donovan

#1 International Best-seller with *Ryan Kaine: On the Run*, Kerry was born in Dublin. He currently lives with Margaret in a bungalow in Nottinghamshire. He has three children and four grandchildren.

Kerry earned a first-class honours degree in Human Biology and has a PhD in Sport and Exercise Sciences. A former scientific advisor to The Office of the Deputy Prime Minister, he helped UK emergency first-responders prepare for chemical attacks in the wake of 9/11. He is also a former furniture designer/maker.

kerryjdonovan.com

In the distance, way off, an alarm bell rang. Too far away. No safety there. No help.

Mel lay on her side, curled into a foetal ball. That much, she could tell. The unforgiving surface she lay on—stiff, cold, gritty—it smelled of urine, caustic bleach, and … decay.

Another blow, this one to her head.

She retched. Gagged. Vomited.

Blackness rushed up to swallow her and end the pain.

Please.

End it.

Darkness closed in. Restful darkness. Peace.

Thank you, God. Thank …

––––––––

QUIET PEACEFULNESS.

Softness. Scratchy softness.

Murmured voices in the distance, talking in subdued tones over the tinny music expelled from a radio. Mel didn't recognise the song, but it was gentle, relaxing. She smiled—or tried to. Her lips were swollen and split. Pain, the stinging pain of lemon juice driven into a cut, shocked her fully awake.

Mel lay on her back. The rough grit of tile and grout beneath her had been exchanged for the firm, intermittent lumpiness of an old, heavily used mattress. The smell had changed, too. From urine and corrosive bleach, to lemons and something else. Something sharp.

Starched sheets tucked in around and over her.

She tried to lift her head, but it was heavy, far too heavy, as though a concrete block was pressing against her forehead.

Her heartbeat thumped loud inside a throbbing head. Pounding. Adding to the cluster of pain.

She tried to swallow, but her mouth was too dry.

Mel moved her tongue, trying to generate some spit, some moisture. The tongue found a hole. A gap where her upper front tooth used to be. No pain though. An old injury. One of many. Years old. Nearly a decade. The missing front tooth had been replaced by a ceramic implant. A perfect match to the original in shape and colour, but not in feel.

In the gap, something sharp—the implant's metallic head protruding from her gum—cut the tip of her tongue. Made it bleed. The blood seeped into her mouth, tasted of old pennies.

She swallowed. Gagged. Swallowed again. Coughed.

Fresh, exquisite pain blazed through her side. The jagged edge of a rib bit deep. She yelped.

The distant conversation stopped. Footsteps approached. Heels clicked on a hard floor.

Metal rattled. Keys on a chain.

"Try not to move," a sharp voice ordered

"What?"

"You have two broken ribs, a fractured wrist, multiple contusions, and a suspected concussion," the woman said. Her voice was cool and unemotional, but carried the rasping burr of a long-term smoker. Her breath stank of cigarettes. "Try not to move. Wouldn't want those ribs to pierce a lung."

"Where … Where am …"

"The infirmary."

"Where?"

Hesitation, an intake of breath.

"You don't know where you are? Can you tell me your name?"

"Sorry? What?"

"You took a few blows to the head. What's your name?"

Mel swallowed, blood mixed with saliva.

"Mel … Melanie Archer."

"Good. Do you know where you are, in general terms?"

She tried to nod but, again, her head refused to move. Pain knifed through her neck, behind her eyes, running between the temples, pulsing along with the rapid beat of her heart. Her neck seemed pinned in place, as though held in a vice. Something restricted her movement, stopped her from dipping her chin. A neck brace. Mel recognised its softly restrictive force. She'd worn one before. Long ago.

"F-Falston," she answered, "Falston Manor?" Her voice sounded as dry and cracked as the other woman's, but Mel had never smoked a cigarette in her life.

Wouldn't have dreamed of it. *He* wouldn't have allowed it.

"Yes, that's right. Your memory's unimpaired. That's good," the woman said, but didn't seem particularly relieved. "Means we won't need to send you for a scan. Paperwork for a transfer on medical grounds can be a nightmare. Expensive, too."

Mel tried opening her eyes again, but her lids wouldn't move. The right was being held in place by something soft but unforgiving—bandages. The lids of her left eye were stuck, gummed together.

"Oh God, I-I can't see." Even though she fought the panic, Mel's voice rose in pitch and volume.

"Calm down, Archer. Far as I can tell, there's nothing wrong with your vision. Heavy swelling and a deep laceration to the right side of your face needed bandages. I'll clear the left in a second. Hold still." The last words were barked in an order. One that expected obedience. An order Mel intended to obey.

Footsteps clicked again. Moving away.

In the near-silence that followed, broken only by the ticking of a clock and the tinny music, the seconds stretched into minutes. Mel tried to stay calm, keep her breathing shallow and slow. Panic wouldn't help. She'd learned that the hard way, over the long years.

Think.

Plan.

Stay calm and subservient on the outside, cool and determined on the inside. The only way to survive.

How much damage had they done? What could she move?

Head? No, the neck brace handled that.

Hands and arms? She could make a fist with her left hand, but when she tried moving the fingers of her right, a fireball of pain exploded. Broken. Probably at the wrist. Again, not for the first time.

Hips, knees, and ankles? All moved normally, and without excessive discomfort.

Now for the important part, the one kept for last, the chest and stomach.

Mel moved slowly, testing each area gently by tensing and relaxing the necessary muscle groups.

Broken ribs were a given. She already knew that, and the bones would heal. Doctors didn't bandage damaged ribs anymore. Not worth the time or effort. Pain would restrict movement well enough, and the patient needed to breathe. But what about her stomach?

Mel held her breath and tensed her abdomen. Sore, bruised, but not seriously. In the past, she'd suffered worse, much worse. The current damage was superficial. Damage to the belly didn't matter. No chance of her ever being pregnant again. *He'd* seen to that seventeen, no, eighteen years ago.

Oh God. Little Bella.

Gone, and without having a chance at any sort of a life.

Bella would be doing her A-levels this year. She'd have been smart, like her mother, but more worldly wise. Better prepared for what life could throw at her. Mel would have seen to that. Bella would have had none of the naïve ignorance of her teenage mother, and absolutely none of her father's cunning evil or *his* brutishness.

Tears formed behind gummy, gritty eyes.

She would have protected little Bella from *his* scheming, *his* anger. Mel would have done anything to save her daughter from the fear and the misery.

So many years of guilt and suffering had led to … where? Her Majesty's Prison, Falston Manor.

Overcrowded cells and strip searches.

Inmates.

Why? What had she done?

Nothing.

Why wouldn't anyone believe her? It wasn't fair. Life wasn't fair. It never had been.

Returning footsteps broke through Mel's drift into self-pity.

"By the way," the woman with the gravelly voice said, "I'm Dr Milliner, the Chief Medical Officer here. You might remember me from your orientation."

Orientation?

Ritual humiliation, more like.

It started before Mel had even arrived.

Blurred, fractured memories crawled through her head, unwanted. An hour-long ride in a prison van with blacked-

7

out windows. Sitting handcuffed on a bench seat, safety belt around her lap. Two more luckless, whey-faced prisoners on the bench to her left. One—fat and brassy with hair bleached at the tips and a ring through her nose—kept leering at Mel, licking her lips and blowing kisses. The other —pale, skinny, terrified, hair cut in an angular bob and no more than a teenager—cried throughout the journey and bit her nails to the nubs.

Normally, inmates were allowed to wear their own clothes, but the guards deemed Mel's too expensive, too eye-catching. They stripped her, gave her a faded, green track-suit, three sizes too big, a couple of T-shirts, and plain, cotton underwear.

The so-called medical exam was cursory and performed by a wizen-faced, fifty-something woman. She had short, grey hair, horn-rimmed glasses, washed-out brown eyes, and a sneer. Presumably the owner of the raspy voice and the harsh bedside manner, Dr Milliner.

For the exam, Milliner asked a few general health ques-tions, ticked the answers on a form attached to a clipboard, and made Mel sign it. No stethoscope to the chest, no blood pressure test, nothing "hands-on".

Medical over, the real horror began.

How long ago was that? Two weeks? Three?

The days blurred. They merged into one long, indeter-minate routine, interspersed with threats and intimidation, leading to … here.

Metal scraped on a hard surface close to Mel's head. It made her jump. Plastic rustled and crumpled. A vacuum-sealed bag popped open. The lid of a plastic bottle clicked, its seal broken. Liquid poured into a container.

"This will feel cold," Dr Milliner said, her voice close,

her breath still reeking. "Nothing but distilled water to clean your eye. Keep it closed until I'm done."

Cool liquid from a cotton-wool swab soaked her lid. The cold water ran down the side of her face and pooled in her ear. Tickled. The doctor's touch was more gentle than expected. A dry swab dabbed away the excess liquid and, two firm swipes later, Milliner pulled away from the bed, taking the smell of stale cigarettes with her.

"Okay, try now."

Mel opened her eye, closed it against the sharp, white light, and took a shallow breath. She opened the lid again, blinked two, three times, and waited.

Slowly, the fuzzy pictures coalesced. The blurry images sharpened, but didn't clear fully.

The hatchet-faced Dr Milliner pressed the tips of her fingers to Mel's bandaged head and held up a brown-stained index finger.

"Follow my finger. Don't move your head."

The hazy digit moved left and right, up and down. Mel followed it as best she could, keeping her head still. The migraine flared when she looked up and to the left. She winced and groaned but said nothing.

Milliner pulled away.

"You'll have a headache for a while. If it gets any worse I might be able to prescribe some ibuprofen." She paused, reading the time from her wristwatch. "Paperwork to do. I'll be back to check on you shortly, maybe remove that neck brace. Meanwhile, try to get some rest."

The doctor spun on a low-heeled shoe and marched away. Her footsteps clicked on the tiled floor once again, and the keychain attached to her belt jangled. She paused at one of only two doors in the three-bed ward, selected a key from the bundle, and turned it in the lock. She left the ward without looking back.

"Paperwork? Really. Smoke break, more like," Mel mumbled, struggling to form the words with damaged lips.

Someone turned off the radio. Apart from the continuous ticking of the cheap wall clock, the room fell silent. For the first time since entering Falston Manor, Melanie Archer felt safe.

But how long would it last?

Chapter Two

Monday 12th April - Melanie Archer

Health Care Centre, HMP Falston Manor, Derbyshire, England

True to her word, Dr Milliner returned from completing her "paperwork" smelling even more of used cigarettes than when she'd left. With nothing in the way of small talk, she checked the grip strength in Mel's good hand, before removing the neck brace and helping her sit up in bed.

"Thank you, doctor."

"Hmm. Just doing my job. Nurse Stephens will be here later. She's on her rounds right now or she'd be looking after you instead of me. Drink?"

"Yes … please."

The doctor took a covered jug from the bedside cabinet and poured water into a plastic cup. She removed a bent straw from a wrapper and dropped it into the cup before placing it on the bedside cabinet, within easy reach of Mel's left hand.

Mel took the cup and sucked hard on the straw. Water had never tasted better. It even seemed to make the thumping migraine fade a little. She drained the cup and asked for more.

"Take it easy on the water, Archer. You won't be able to use the loo on your own for a while, and I don't empty bedpans."

"But I'm thirsty."

"Understandable," Milliner said, nodding. "You lost a fair amount of blood. Not so much you needed a transfusion, though. But probably enough to account for the dry mouth."

Milliner stood back, appraising her patient.

"CM Thatcher will be here to take your statement soon."

Mel's tender stomach clenched automatically at the mere mention of the prison's most hated officer, Custodial Manager Marcus Thatcher. She winced.

Milliner arched an unplucked eyebrow. "You've met CM Thatcher?"

Mel nodded, unable to speak for fear of bursting into tears.

"Thought so," she said quietly. "He doesn't take long to introduce himself to the pretty ones."

An emotion softened the doctor's voice a fraction. What was it? Sympathy? Pity?

Mel's lower lip trembled and she bit the inside of her

cheek to stop herself crying. The hard-faced doctor didn't seem the type to appreciate waterworks.

"That's right, Archer," Milliner said, nodding. "No use for tears. Won't do you any good in this place."

Mel nodded and wished she hadn't when the pounding headache increased in force.

She'd heard the rumours and had seen the predatory look in CM Thatcher's eyes the few times their paths had crossed. So far, and probably more by luck than judgement, she'd managed to avoid his close attention, but it could only be a matter of time before the prison's main predator engineered one of his "meetings". According to the rumour mill, Thatcher's "special interviews" usually took place in a private office, outside the range of the surveillance cameras.

"And you're okay with that?" Mel asked, surprised at the accusation and firmness in her voice.

"Okay with what?"

"With Mr Thatcher's … behaviour?"

Milliner shrugged. "No idea what you're talking about, Archer. Nothing to do with me. I can't act on rumours and speculation. No one's ever made an official complaint against the man, at least none that have stood up to scrutiny. Who am I to create waves. Besides"—she checked the time on her cheap, stainless-steel watch—"I'm here to patch up the inmates and the officers. It's not up to me to police the institution."

"But—"

"Lunchtime," she said, tapping the watch. "Nurse Stephens will be here soon. She'll organise you some food, if you can eat with that missing tooth."

"I-I think so."

"Maybe some jelly and custard to begin with. Easier on

your stomach. Don't want you vomiting and dirtying the bedding."

Milliner turned away, shoes clip-clopping on the tiles. She locked the door behind her, leaving Mel to fester.

With her one good eye, she took in the prison's impressively named *Health Care Centre*, which seemed nothing more than a poorly maintained room equipped with three rusted beds that looked like NHS rejects from the 1950s. Mel occupied the bed in the furthest corner from the exit door and across from the door marked "Staff Office". The other two beds were empty.

Chipped walls painted off-white long ago, grey-tiled floors, and high-level windows complete with wire-enforced, frosted glass on two of the four walls. With the TV switched off and no books to read—not that her migraine made reading possible—time dragged with infinite sluggishness.

She tried to get comfortable, but the firm pillows dug into the back of her head, and a deep cramp formed along her neck and shoulders. Nevertheless, apart from the impending face-to-face with CM Thatcher, she felt much better than when she'd first woken from the beating.

Tired though. So darned tired.

Her eyelid grew heavy. Couldn't keep it open.

Mel sucked in a yawn, but opening her mouth wide caused pain to shoot through her jaw. She reached her good hand up to touch the side of her face. The right cheek was swollen and tender. A bruise darkened her left forearm where she'd used it to try to protect her ribs. Within a few days, it would transform the arm into a beautiful display of colours—purples, blues, greens, and yellows. Nothing new to her.

Nothing new at all.

Mel closed her eye, shrugged herself lower in the bed,

and allowed her mind to drift. She travelled to her safe place, her quiet place. She transported herself to a place and time she was happy. A place and time that never happened.

One she could only imagine.

Chapter Three

Monday 12th April - Melanie Archer

Health Care Centre, HMP Falston Manor, Derbyshire, England

Keys rattled in a lock. A door squealed open.

Mel woke with a start, heart racing, blood pumping, temperature rising, breathing rate increasing.

Panic.

What now?

She snapped open her eye and eased her head towards the sound. The headache hadn't gone, not entirely. It still thumped and seared in the background.

A tall, well-built man in a smartly pressed uniform stood in the open doorway. A cynical smile split a beguilingly handsome face.

Custodial Manager Marcus Thatcher.

"Afternoon, Archer," he said, stepping into the ward. "Glad to see you're awake. We need to talk, you and I."

The Home Counties accent gave him the educated delivery of an old-time BBC newsreader, but his pale blue eyes were dead, emotionless. The lifeless, cloudy eyes of a fish served up on a silver platter.

He stood straight and stiff, carrying a clipboard in one hand and a pen in the other. From head to toe, Thatcher stood tall and immaculate. Leather shoes so highly polished they gleamed under the ward's fluorescent, strip lights. Black trousers with scalpel-sharp creases, and a shiny, leather, utility belt holding them up. Clipped to the belt, he wore the usual equipment of a prison officer—radio, hand-cuffs, a telescopic baton, and a canister of pepper spray.

According to Wendy, Mel's cellmate, the body camera fixed to the pocket of Thatcher's shirt had a nasty habit of powering itself off at the most inopportune moments.

Thatcher wore no jacket, the early-spring day was too warm for that. A peaked cap covered his hair, which had been trimmed to within an inch of its blond life. Nothing marred the uniform's perfection, especially not his honed and chiselled torso or his powerful arms.

The starched, white shirt of his prison uniform stretched so tight across his muscular frame, Mel wondered how the buttons stayed attached to the cloth. At any moment, she expected to have to protect herself from flying plastic shrapnel.

As Thatcher approached, a second officer, an athletic-looking woman almost as tall as the CM, entered in his shadow.

PO Saran Priestly, the most respected screw in the place, wore exactly the same uniform as Thatcher, but with the single piped line of a prison officer stitched to her epaulettes, rather than Thatcher's triple piping.

Mel forced the air slowly from her lungs and relaxed as much as the pain in her side, wrist, and head would allow—which wasn't a great deal.

With Priestly around, Thatcher would have to behave correctly.

Thank you, God.

The vile man approached to within four strides of her bed, keeping a respectable distance between them. Priestly stood at his right-hand side and slightly behind, showing the correct hierarchy. Thatcher was in charge, and he wanted Mel to know it.

Priestly took in Mel's condition and had the good grace to wince, especially when she studied Mel's face.

What must she look like?

A gargoyle?

Thatcher didn't bat either of his blue eyes.

Self-pitying tears watered Mel's restricted vision. She tried wiping them away, but they wouldn't stop falling. Why cry now? Crying never helped. Neither did the crushing headache.

"Now then, Archer," Thatcher said, checking the time and adding a note to the page attached to his clipboard, "exactly what happened in the shower this morning?"

She started to shake her head, but the stabbing migraine cut the action short.

"C-Can't remember exactly, sir."

Every inmate was required to call the screws either "sir" or "ma'am", no exceptions. A matter of showing and generating respect, they said. They told every new inmate on their first day inside. Restrictive rules were nothing new to

Mel. She'd been following similar instructions all her adult life.

The spiteful commands ran in a litany through her head.

"Don't smile."

"Don't look anyone directly in the eye."

"Don't answer back."

"Don't start any conversations."

"Don't make friends."

"Don't look at me like that, bitch!"

His rules were never-ending, and she knew them all. Followed them, too. Mostly.

Thatcher smiled. If he thought it made him look friendly and approachable, he'd be wrong. Dead wrong. The officer's flat-eyed smirk only served to tense Mel's stomach. She closed her good eye, squeezed out more tears, and forced it open again.

Stop crying, woman!

"Tell us what you *do* remember, Archer," Thatcher prompted, sliding half a step closer. Priestly slid him a sideways glance. A frown creased her otherwise-smooth forehead, but she said nothing.

"I can't have inmates fighting in my prison. That won't do at all. It's not conducive to the smooth running of the institution."

Mel took a breath, keeping it shallow.

"N-Not a fight, an attack."

"How so?" he asked, pen poised over paper.

"I-I was alone in the shower … at least, I-I thought I was alone. Then, I felt someone behind me. They grabbed my hair and slammed my face into the wall. Started punching. Kicking. That's really all—"

"'They'," Priestly interrupted. "You said, 'They'. There was more than one attacker?"

Mel nodded, grimacing at the movement. Stifling a groan, she reached for the cup and sipped only enough to wet her lips. Before long, she'd need a bedpan, but the nurse still hadn't arrived, so she had to hold her water.

"I-I think so," she answered. "There had to be more than one. One held me down by my hair while the other kicked the … stuffing out of me. They spoke, too."

She paused for another sip.

"What did they say?" Thatcher demanded.

"Can't remember the exact words. Everything's a blur."

Thatcher tightened his already firm stomach, popped his biceps, and bounced his pecs. His moobs were almost as large as Mel's breasts. How many hours would it take sweating in the gym to develop and maintain such a physique?

Overly buffed men like Thatcher were nothing but peacocks. So vain, the creature probably shaved his chest, not that Mel ever wanted to find out first hand. The overall effect might have impressed some women. Some naïve, empty-headed creatures, but it didn't impress Mel. Not one bit.

She couldn't decide whether to laugh or gag. She did neither.

"Can you give me any descriptions?" Thatcher asked offhandedly, clearly not expecting a detailed answer.

He gave the distinct impression of a disinterested man doing nothing more than following procedure.

"Sorry. I-I lost consciousness almost immediately. Thank God."

"That's a real shame," he said, again without emotion.

"Unless we have a description, there's not a whole lot we can do, I'm afraid."

"Weren't there any surveillance cameras?"

Thatcher snorted and broke out another of his stomach-churning grins.

"Cameras in a female shower block? Yes, indeed. The Howard League would really go for that one. They'd have a fit."

"Sorry, sir. I-I meant the ones in the corridor outside the block. There's only one entrance to the shower facilities. Can't you tell who else was there at the time?"

Thatcher dropped the smile.

"Don't presume to tell me how to do my job, Archer."

Mel hunched and tucked in her chin, bracing for a blow. "S-Sorry, sir."

"So you should be." He coughed and added another note to his form.

Priestly glanced at Thatcher before leaning forwards.

"Including you," she said, her voice quiet but firm, "there were seven inmates in the shower block. We've interviewed each one. None admits to seeing or hearing anything."

"Are you surprised, ma'am?"

"Not really, but …" Priestly shrugged. "We sometimes hear a whisper or two. Unfortunately, this time … nothing."

Thatcher stepped forwards another half-pace. His heavily spiced cologne did nothing to improve the smell of the bleach-saturated ward.

"Who've you been upsetting, Archer?"

"Excuse me, sir?"

"For someone to have done all this"—he waved a hand over her bed to encompass all her injuries—"you must have seriously upset a big player. Who was it?"

"Mr Thatcher, sir," Mel said, trying to hold back more tears, "I've barely spoken to anyone. I try to keep myself to myself."

She knew all about keeping quiet and toeing an invisible line. *He* had made her an expert at blending into the background. It had become her most valuable survival tactic. How strange it was to give *him* credit for anything, when *he'd* given her nothing but a life of misery.

"Maybe that's your problem," Thatcher said, adding another note and underlining it, twice.

"Excuse me, sir?"

"You need to join in, Archer. Make friends. This place works better when you have people on your side—protecting your back."

A good idea. She had Wendy, of course. But, given her cellmate's medical condition, probably not for long. Terminal cancer didn't make for long-term friendships.

Mel placed a hand over her damaged ribcage and shuffled a little higher up the bed.

"I won't be here long enough to make friends, sir," she said, trying to make herself sound more confident than she actually felt.

Again, the smile formed on the square-jawed face with the high cheekbones and the pale blue eyes. This one was wider, predatory. It exposed his teeth which were shiny, white, and perfect. Unlike Mel's. She tried not to think about the exposed and broken implant, but her tongue kept finding the gap.

Mel always took great care of her teeth, but sometimes, circumstances—

No, girl. Don't go there. No more crying.

"Archer, from what I hear, the case against you is pretty

strong," Thatcher said, leaning even closer. "Wouldn't get your hopes up if I were you."

"But … I-I'm innocent!"

"Yes, yes. Of course you are," he said, smooth and oily. "Archer, I hate to repeat the old cliché, but haven't you heard? Prisons are full of innocent men and women. The courts and juries just keep getting verdicts wrong." He sneered and added, "No. You're guilty as sin. A celebrity. A murderer. You're going down for it. You'll be here for years and years. I'd get used to it if I were you."

"I didn't kill him," she sobbed. "I didn't!"

Priestly moved alongside Thatcher. "Sir, I'm not sure you should be—"

"Don't presume to tell me how to talk to an inmate!" Thatcher snapped.

He turned from Mel and faced his colleague. Surprisingly, Priestly didn't back down. They stood for a moment, locked in a silent battle, the tension a solid mass between them, until the radio attached to Priestly's belt squawked. It forced her to blink first.

"You'd better take that," Thatcher said, turning to face Mel once more. "Might be important."

Priestly tugged the radio from its clip, turned her back on them, and walked away to answer the call. She spoke quietly.

Thatcher waited until Priestly reached the far end of the ward before making his move. He closed on Mel's bed and, using his body to hide the action, rested his right hand on her knee. His thumb caressed the inside of her upper thigh through the thin blanket and sheet.

Mel squirmed. Whimpered.

He bent at the waist, drawing even closer. She tried not to react but felt her upper lip curl, despite herself.

"I meant what I said about how you need to make friends," he whispered, inching his hand higher up her thigh.

Mel wanted to clamp her knees tight together, but the conditioning took over and the paralysis kicked in. *His* work would never leave her.

"But that doesn't mean you should just keep to the inmates," Thatcher continued, shooting a quick glance at Priestly, who still spoke quietly, her back turned to them. "The more friends you have in here, the easier your life will be. Understand?"

She shook her head and, again, the migraine flared.

"Yes, you understand. Beautiful women like you know how the world works. Those bruises and the swelling will soon fade. You and I are going to get along really well."

Looking at Priestly again, Thatcher lifted his hand from Mel's leg and cupped her breast. He squeezed—hard.

This time, Mel didn't whimper. A reaction—any reaction—would only encourage him. She'd learned the lesson long ago.

Don't move. Don't cry.

Do … not … cry!

"Nice tits," he whispered, his breath hot on her cheek. "Firm and little more than a handful. Never had any babies chomping on them. Have you? Lovely. Bet you've got dark nipples, too. Oh yes, you and I are going to become really good friends."

Although she fought against it, Mel's lower lip trembled, but at least the tears had stopped falling. She'd been trained well. Moulded. Subdued.

"Mr Thatcher?" Priestly called.

The vile animal straightened and turned towards his

subordinate, but not before winking at Mel. He had the power and the control, and he wanted her to know it.

"Yes, Officer Priestly?" he said, his back to Mel. "Problems?"

Priestly glanced at Mel before answering. Something in her expression told Mel she knew what Thatcher had done, but clearly, the PO couldn't be sure.

"Is everything okay here, Archer?" she asked, looking directly at Mel and ignoring Thatcher's question.

Tell her. Why don't you tell her?

No, no, she couldn't talk. That way led to more pain, more trouble. Thatcher would deny everything. A man's word against hers. She'd never win.

Thatcher had probably bruised her breast, left his finger marks all over her, but what were a few more bruises after the morning's beating? Who'd say the bruises were from him? Not Dr Milliner. No. Not her. Bloody woman.

Thatcher turned his head to glower at Mel. "Well, Archer? Answer the officer. Is everything okay here?"

His upper lip curled into another sneer, hidden from Priestly. His flinty eyes widened, making a direct challenge, but confident of the outcome. She could say nothing. It would be Thatcher's word against hers.

"You are nothing, woman. You don't count."

His words. *His* conditioning. No way out.

"Y-Yes," she said, "everything's okay, but … I-I have … a migraine. Dr Milliner said something about painkillers, but …."

Thatcher's triumphant expression said it all. With her answer, she'd sealed her fate.

Coward. Useless coward.

She'd always been a weakling. Always been a failure. Deserved nothing else but humiliation at the hands of men.

"So, what's up?" Thatcher asked Priestly, dismissing Mel with a sniff and showing her his broad and powerful back once again.

Priestly paused for a moment, her gaze lingering on Mel's crumpled top. She knew. She really did.

Ask me again. Go on. Please, ask me again.

If Priestly pushed harder, Mel would relent, tell her everything and hang the consequences. But no. It didn't happen. No one ever asked twice. No one ever cared enough to make things better.

"A disturbance in the canteen, Mr Thatcher. Nothing major, but SO Larkins wondered if you might like to have a word with the ringleaders."

Thatcher squared his shoulders. "Indeed I do, Ms Priestly. Indeed, I do. Can't have inmates quarrelling, now can we." He half-turned to look at Mel, who lowered her eyes. "You're in good hands here, Archer. As you'll discover, medical care in this institution is first class. One of the best in the prison service. I'm sure you'll recover from your injuries very quickly. Meanwhile, if you think of anything else regarding the attack, be sure to let me know. Okay?"

Mel dipped her chin.

"Yes, sir," she mumbled. "Thank you, sir."

"Very good. I'm sure I'll see you again very soon."

He winked and marched from the ward without a backwards glance, leaving Priestly behind.

The PO looked Mel over, head to toe and back up again.

"Are you sure you don't have anything to tell me?"

Too late. Much too late.

Was it? Was it really?

Before Mel could open her mouth, a bulbous black woman bustled through the door. Somehow, she'd managed to squeeze into a set of hospital scrubs at least one size too small, but a friendly smile graced her cheery face. The first real smile Mel had seen since entering the prison system.

Her resolve fled and the tears started flowing. No reason this time, but a simple, warm smile could do it.

"Afternoon, Saran," the newcomer said, addressing Priestly.

"Hi, Athena. You okay?"

"Yeah, I'm good. Can't wait for this shift to end. Marty's takin' me to the cinema. Meal first, though."

Priestly's genuine smile matched that of the nurse, and stood her apart from her boss.

"That husband of yours is a keeper."

"He surely is. I've kept him for thirty-two years and I ain't letting him go any time soon. Now, what have we here?" She turned and caught sight of Mel for the first time. "Oh dear me"—her hand flew up to a bosom the size of two pillows—"look at you!"

She hurried forwards, side-stepped around Priestly, and stopped beside Mel.

"What have they done to you, you poor thing?"

"Melanie Archer," Priestly said, by way of introduction. "Took a beating in the shower block this morning. I'll let you get to work. Archer"—she dipped her head to Mel and fixed her with a forceful stare—"you're in good hands here. You can trust Nurse Stephens."

"That you can, honey," the large nurse agreed, adding a chuckle. "Everyone around here knows I'm good people."

"That's true enough," Priestly said, "and Nurse Stephens will vouch for me, right?"

"Indeed I will. You're the best PO I've ever had the pleasure to work alongside."

"Thank you. Remember that, Archer. If you have

anything to tell me, you can send it through Athena. Anything at all."

"Thank you, ma'am," Mel muttered, unable to manage anything more.

The extra-large nurse's encouraging smile remained fixed in place until Priestly left the ward.

"So," the nurse said, turning serious while she studied Mel's injuries, "let's see what they've done to you, shall we? And, when the doc's not around, you can call me Athena. Okay?"

Athena wobbled to the foot of the bed, unhooked the clipboard, and started reading. Her wide forehead crinkled in concentration. After a short while, she looked up, her expression thoughtful.

"Damnation, loosing that tooth's gotta hurt, big time."

"Not really. It's an implant. The crown just broke off. Feels like the abutment's still in place, though. No movement on it. A decent orthodontist should be able to replace it easily enough."

Athena barked out a laugh, loud and hard. It took Mel off-guard. Not many people had cause to laugh inside prison.

"A decent orthodontist? Where you gonna find one of them around here, honey?"

Mel closed her mouth.

Good question.

"I'm not going to be in here for long," she said, although her words sounded hollow.

"Innocent, huh?"

"That's right. I didn't kill my husband. Why won't anyone believe me?"

Athena dipped her head. "If I was you, honey, I'd keep that 'innocent' part quiet. Some of the girls around here will be impressed by a sister who killed her abusive hubby. Some won't be, but they're in the minority, lucky for you."

"Lucky? How?"

"Aw, honey, who do you think pulled the alarm in the showers this morning? If not for someone being on your side, the POs would have been sliding you into a body bag this morning. You certainly wouldn't be sitting up in bed, wearing those pretty, pink pyjamas."

Mel tugged out the front of her pyjama top. Originally blue, they'd turned grey with age, and were baggy and totally ugly. How anyone could call them pretty was beyond her.

"Pink? Are you colour blind?"

Another guffaw exploded from Athena's wide mouth. This time, Mel couldn't help smiling along with her, much as it hurt her to do so.

"Sure I'm colour blind, honey! Can't you tell?"

Athena held up her hands and flapped them in the air.

"Darn it, girl. You're a real mess. Better get on with my job. I need to take your readings. Don't go nowhere, now. Y'hear?"

The good-natured nurse waddled over to a cabinet bolted to the wall opposite, tapped a combination into the keypad, and removed a medical bag. For the subsequent twenty minutes, Athena conducted a medical examination almost as thorough as the one Mel had undergone for the joint insurance assessment *he* forced her into—the one in a private clinic in Harley Street.

She even removed the bandage around Mel's head, to inspect the damage, and took great care doing so. Athena's touch was gentle and sure.

At the end of the session, Athena read aloud from her notes. "Blood pressure and heart rate are a little high, but that's not a surprise given what you've been through. Various bumps and bruises, which will heal in time. Not so sure about the cut over your eye, though. Needs better stitching. I'll ask Dr Milliner to call in Briana."

"Briana?"

"Briana Loughlin, one of the inmates. The best seamstress in the prison system. Now, don't look so worried, child. On the outside, Briana was a cosmetic surgeon. Had a thriving practice before developing a keen interest in the contents of her drugs cabinet."

She paused and leaned close to study the cut over Mel's right eye once more. This time, she used a magnifying glass.

"Hold still, now."

Humming tunelessly, she prodded and poked with a thin, plastic spatula. Surprisingly, none of it hurt.

"Yes, as I thought. Right down to the bone."

She pulled away, dropped the spatula into a sharps bin, and nodded. "Trust me, Archer. With that laceration and a face like yours, you don't want Hattie's stitches in there for long. No way." She paused for a breath. "Hell, girl, like as not, you'll end up looking like that monster, Frankenstein, sewed together. Don't want that, do you?"

She certainly didn't, but what did that matter if she was going to spend the next twenty-five years in prison?

Tears welled up again. She was such a wreck.

"Okay," Athena said. She peeled off her blue, surgical gloves, threw them in the bin, and packed the rest of her equipment back into the bag. "I'm just going to rebandage that head wound loosely and let you get some rest while I organise a hall pass for Briana."

"Thank you," Mel said and added, "Athena, can I ask you a question?"

"Sure you can."

"Do you have a mirror?"

For the first time since she entered the ward, Athena's smile faded and her expression stiffened. "Sorry, honey. That's probably not a good idea. Not until after Briana's paid her visit. Understand?"

Oh God!

Mel's chin trembled. She couldn't make it stop.

"Is it that bad? Am I ugly?"

Athena rested a hand on her shoulder, about the only place it didn't hurt.

"Looks worse than it is, honey. But, it's best you don't see it until the swelling's gone down a little. Okay?"

Mel swallowed hard, trying not to throw up over her not-pink, pyjama jacket.

Chapter Four

Tuesday 13th April - Melanie Archer

Health Care Centre, HMP Falston Manor,
Derbyshire, England

Deep in the middle of Mel's first night on the ward, the door flew open, shattering her peace, but not her sleep. Even before prison, she rarely slept through the night.

Mel's cellmate, Wendy Phillips, was rushed into the ward in a wheelchair by two prison officers, her condition having flared up overnight.

Mel watched in dismay while the night nurse hooked her friend up to machinery and inserted a drip. They didn't bother rolling out the confidentiality screen, and Mel saw everything. Throughout the process, Wendy didn't move. At one stage, Mel was certain her friend had died, but the cardiac monitor showed the fluctuating beats of life.

Finally, Mel tore her gaze from the dismal sight, rolled onto her back, and closed her eyes, desperate to find sleep that wouldn't come. Minutes ticked into hours. Gradually, daylight arrived, like a thief to steal the darkness and the quiet.

The blackness behind the ward's frosted windows slowly turned to grey, and then to white. The prison woke to its usual, boisterous cacophony. Eventually, Mel found the courage to turn towards her cellmate.

Plastic tubes pumped oxygen-rich air into Wendy's nose, and the bag suspended on a metal stand dripped clear fluids into her arm. If the liquid contained chemotherapy, the treatment didn't seem to be working particularly well. The poor woman's grey skin hung from her bones like a badly fitted bodysuit. On the rare occasions Wendy did manage to peel back her lids, her eyes were glazed, and she seemed oblivious to her surroundings.

Three times during the endless night, Wendy's ragged breathing had stopped, seemingly for minutes on end. Each time, Mel feared her cellmate had finally slipped away but, each time, the breathing started again. Why she clung so stubbornly to life was beyond Mel.

Wendy believed in God, believed in a heaven. Wendy believed she'd be going to a better place. A better place wouldn't be hard to find. Most places would be an improvement on prison.

Why didn't she let go? Why couldn't she set herself free?

In Wendy's situation, Mel would have given up. Wouldn't she?

At seven forty-three, according to the clock ticking away on the wall, Athena bounced into the ward, wearing her trademark smile and carrying Mel's breakfast on a faceted tray. As usual, it consisted of a small box of cereal, a carton of warm, long-life milk, a sachet of sugar, and a takeaway cup of what would, without doubt, turn out to be lukewarm and vile-tasting tea. She placed the tray on Mel's over-bed table and stepped back.

"How you feeling today, Melanie?"

"Better, thanks. How's Wendy doing?"

Athena fired a glance towards the middle bed, where the skeletal Wendy lay, still struggling for breath, still slipping in and out of consciousness.

"Let's take a look, shall we?"

The large nurse made use of the stethoscope and blood pressure cuff, and jotted notes onto the middle bed's clipboard. She treated Wendy with respect and dignity, speaking to her the whole time, offering soothing words of encouragement. Her eventual report to Mel didn't contain much in the way of optimism.

Mel settled back to resume her study of the cracked and mottled ceiling.

DR MILLINER DIDN'T MAKE her first appearance of the day until mid-morning, when she stood in the open doorway and chided Athena for the filthy state of the ward. During the harangue, Athena stood still, hands clasped in front, head slightly bowed, taking the insults in her stride. After her rant, the doctor, seemingly satisfied, turned about face and left the ward through the main exit, no doubt heading for another of her inevitable smoke breaks. She paid no attention to either of her patients.

"Is she like that all the time?" Mel asked quietly, once the doctor's clacking footsteps had faded into the distance.

"Pretty much," Athena answered, shrugging it off. "First time she did it was pretty scary. I was worried they'd let me go, but that was before I learned the truth."

"Which is?"

"Hell, girl. You think there's a queue of qualified nurses lined up begging to work in a prison? This here job vacancy was unfilled for seven months before I applied. Up 'til then, the governor had to pay through the nose for agency nursing. Crippled the medical budget, apparently. If Hattie ever succeeded in forcing me out, she'd end up having to do some of the menial work herself. And that certainly ain't going to happen. To be honest with you, it beats me how she fills her time. It ain't like she has to pay no house calls."

"How many inmates are there?"

"Around three hundred, including you remand prisoners."

"Not much of a patient list for a full-time doctor."

The nurse sucked in a deep breath, one that put even more stress on the buttons holding her uniform together.

"That's as may be," Athena answered eventually, "but a prison population ain't normal. Full of the sick and the needy, both physical and psychological. Hattie's full time alright, but the three of us nurse practitioners do the real work. You feel me, honey?"

Mel nodded and, for the first time since the beating, the headache had lessened enough for it not to hurt too much. A sure sign of improvement.

Darn it.

How long would it be before Dr Milliner sent her back to her grim, eight-by-four cell?

"Time for your next set of obs," Athena said, heading for the locked cupboard. "Mustn't be late or Hattie might burst a blood vessel. Honestly, if she wasn't already post-menopausal, I'd have thought the woman's curse lasted the whole month."

She returned to Mel's bed, holding up an electronic thermometer. She said her usual, "Open wide, as the bishop said to the actress," but stuck the probe into Mel's ear and carried on to collect the standard readings—core temperature, blood pressure, heart rate.

Once Athena had completed the tests, on both Mel and Wendy, she said her goodbyes and left for her rounds, pushing the metal meds trolley with the locked cover ahead of her.

A few minutes after she left, Mel witnessed her first ever medical miracle. Slowly, painfully, Wendy groaned and propped herself up on one elbow. Then she turned towards Mel. A grim smile of recognition spread across her withered face.

"Hi," she croaked, her breathing still laboured but not as much as it had been overnight, "how's my … roomie?"

Heart pounding, Mel's mouth fell open, but she couldn't speak.

"Yeah, I know," the grey-skinned woman said, with slightly more strength and a slightly less grim smile. "Bet you … thought … I was a … goner, huh?"

Wendy had to fight for every breath. Mel found herself breathing along with her, psychologically trying to help.

"I-I …"

"Nah. You was … all wrong. Still … plenty of … life left in old … Wendy Phillips."

Mel snapped her mouth closed and swallowed hard. Relief swept through her. She'd never been so happy to see anyone do anything as simple as sit up in bed.

"Wendy, you scared me half to death."

"Sorry, dearie. What … can I say?"

"How are you feeling?"

The moment the words left her mouth, Mel knew how ridiculous they sounded, but she didn't care. Wendy was alive and there with her. Life was looking up. Not by much, but she'd take any improvement on offer.

Wendy's eyes pulled into focus, drilling into Mel's. "Stupid question … girl. How … do you … think I feel. Like death …"

"…warmed up?"

"No, girlie. Just … like … death."

She flopped back onto the pillow. Slowly, her eyes drooped and then closed. Her ragged breathing slowed either in sleep or a coma.

Mel couldn't tell the difference.

Chapter Five

Tuesday 13th April - Melanie Archer

Health Care Centre, HMP Falston Manor, Derbyshire, England

Two hours after Wendy's brief revival and subsequent flop onto her pillow, the minor medical miracle repeated itself, this time on a more extended basis. Wendy had recovered enough to be sitting up in bed, reading.

As it turned out, Athena had witnessed similar miraculous recoveries in Wendy, and took the stunning event in her stride. She'd returned from her rounds armed with a pile of celeb mags and the most recent tabloid newspaper she could find—all of two months old. Wendy was currently devouring those very same rags, lips moving as she read silently.

For her part, Mel found the whole revival process remarkable. Evidently, whatever Dr Milliner injected into the plastic bag hanging from the metal stand worked the same miracle on a bi-monthly basis.

———

BY LATE AFTERNOON, with Athena out of the ward on a break and Dr Milliner absent, relative silence descended, the only sounds coming from outside the medical centre.

In prison, as Mel discovered on her first night "banged up", silence happened to be the rarest of all commodities. Even in the middle of the night, the prison thrummed and clunked with noise. Doors banged open and slammed closed, and prisoners cried, shouted, sang, and screamed obscenities through the night. The screws patrolled the metal walkways, their heavy boots clumping loud and their key chains fastened to utility belts, the keys rattling like ghosts out a-haunting.

The continuing headache and her general aches and pains didn't allow Mel to read, but she let her mind wander wherever it wanted to go.

Rio. Always to Rio.

How could she have got it so wrong?

Stop torturing yourself, woman.

She stared at the ceiling, willing herself to keep calm.

Wendy lowered the latest magazine she'd been absorbing and slowly turned her head towards Mel.

"There's something … I've been meaning to … ask you for ages. Do you mind?" Her voice was stronger, her breathing slightly easier. Even her skin colour had improved up the scale to a darker, slightly less unhealthy shade of grey.

"Ask away."

"How come you're ... in here, honey?"

Mel felt herself frowning beneath the bandages.

"You know why I'm here. We've already discussed it."

At length.

Wendy twisted at the waist to face her, grunting with the effort.

"I know what you're ... charged with. What I meant was, how come your high-priced lawyer didn't get you bail?" She gasped and rested before continuing. "Mega-rich woman like you ... ought to be swanning around under ... house arrest ... wearing one of them ... ankle bracelets. Monitors, you know?"

Again, Mel shook her head and, again, it no longer hurt. Her vision had also returned to its normal, perfect clarity—at least it had through the eye not covered by the crepe dressing.

"What makes you think I'm rich?"

"Hell, girl, I've been ... following your case since it ... hit the papers. Seen all them pictures of that ... fancy house of yours. A mansion. You're rich, alright."

Here we go.

"No," she said. "I'm not rich. I don't have a penny to my name."

Not officially.

So what if she lied? Wendy wouldn't be the first one she'd lied to. Probably wouldn't be the last, either. What was the term the spin doctors used? Being economical with the truth? Yes, that was it. She was most definitely being economical with the truth.

Wendy peeled back her upper lip. "Don't ... don't give me none of that ... bullshit. You're old man was ... a multi-millionaire."

Mel sighed. How many times would she have to go through the same, old stuff?

"Yes, you're right. James had money, but he kept me close to penniless."

At least towards the end.

"The idiot representing me is a duty solicitor, appointed by the courts. Useless, bloody woman. Little more than a child recently out of school."

Wendy's expression showed disbelief. "You're … broke?"

"James …" Mel took as deep a breath as she could manage while still minimising movement to her ribs. "James gave me only enough for the weekly shopping."

The monster didn't ask for receipts, though.

Although Mel told her cellmate some of the truth, she held the important information back. She'd watched enough crime shows on TV to know that conversations with fellow prisoners weren't always strictly confidential.

"What about all them … posh parties you used to go to?" Wendy managed, her tone taking on that of an inquisition. "Yeah, I seen all the … magazine photos. All them … sparklies. Diamond necklaces, bracelets, the rings, and shit. Hell, girl, you looked like a … fairy-tale princess. You telling me they … wasn't real?"

Wendy was growing more agitated, breathing faster, shallower. Maybe it was excitement more than agitation. Wendy had been sent away for theft and, once a thief … always a thief.

"Yes, the baubles were real enough." Mel sighed. "But they weren't mine. They were the Archer family jewels. James forced me to wear them at functions. It made him feel important. I was nothing more than window dressing. The moment we were home and out of sight of the paparazzi, he snatched the jewels from me. Locked them in the house safe."

A deep frown added to the wrinkles on Wendy's parchment forehead. "Still, you lived in that ... nice, big house, though. Right?"

"Yes, right," Mel said, unable to see the point in trying to explain the living arrangements *he* forced her to endure.

No one outside the household would understand why she'd put up with the restrictions, the torture *he'd* put her through for so long. And even if she did try to explain, it would only serve as motive. The police already had enough to charge her with. No point voluntarily adding fuel to their flames.

Poor Brendan.

Mel's vision blurred, although this time, it had nothing to do with concussion.

Wendy's head fell back against her pillows. She stared at the ceiling, mouth open, until her tortured breathing quietened. "Sorry for ... badgering you, love," she said. "Guess I dragged up some ... painful stuff, yeah?"

Mel tore a couple of squares of stiff paper from a toilet roll Athena had placed on her bedside table and dabbed her eye.

"Not just painful. Traumatic."

"Yeah. Suppose it ... must have been."

Mel blew her nose on the rough tissue, rolled it into a tight ball, and dropped it into the bin on the floor next to her bed.

"So," Wendy continued, "what you ... planning to do?"

"No idea. I definitely can't afford a better solicitor."

"You pleading not guilty?"

Mel sniffed and straightened her shoulders. Her ribs

protested at the movement, but she ignored it as best she could. She'd suffered far worse in her time.

"Of course I am. I didn't kill my husband."

Even though I wanted to.

"Can you prove it?" Wendy asked, still on her back.

"I don't know. Don't think so."

"You got an alibi for the time he croaked?"

"Again, I don't know. The police wouldn't tell me exactly when he died. They just kept asking me the same questions, over and over. Hour after hour. Later on, I was so exhausted and confused, I don't know what I said. Just needed to sleep."

"Jesus, honey. You didn't … confess, did you?"

Wendy bent at the waist, head raised, knees up. She started coughing. Horrible, wet, wracking coughs followed by desperate, sucking breaths. Mel wanted to help but couldn't drag herself from her bed. The poor woman continued coughing. On and on.

No one came to help. Not even Athena. Mel didn't expect Dr Milliner to bother.

Slowly, the coughing subsided. Wendy spat into a tissue she'd grabbed from the bedside table. Blood stained the paper red. She slumped back against the pillow, breathing hard but more easily.

"That's better," she said.

"Really?"

The terminally ill woman nodded. "Don't normally have the strength to cough so hard. Clears my … useless fucking lungs." She turned to Mel again and fixed her with shining, brown eyes. "Don't you ever start smoking. Hear me?"

"I've never smoked before, and I don't plan on starting any time soon."

Wendy jerked up her head in a nod. "Good, so … what were we talking about? … Oh yeah, the police. Didn't confess … did you?"

"No, of course not. Why would I confess to a crime I didn't commit?"

"It's been known, girl. You'd be … surprised how often … that's happened. Ain't you never heard of the … Birmingham Four and the Guildford Six… from back in the seventies?"

"You mean the Birmingham Six and the Guildford Four, don't you?"

"Yeah, that's right. Sometimes, I get my … miscarriages of justice mixed up. So many of the … chuffing things. There was a … 'seven' around the same time. Wasn't there?"

Mel dragged up the memory. "The Maguire Seven. Back in '74. They were falsely accused of handling the explosives used in the Guildford bombing."

"Yeah, sounds … about right. Hey, how come you … know this stuff? You could only have … been a kid at the time."

Mel tried to smile, but the cuts inside her mouth and her swollen lip made it too painful. She also found it difficult to talk, and the missing tooth made her speak with so much of a lisp, Mel was shocked that Wendy could understand a word she said.

"My father was a policeman," Mel mumbled, surprised at how the mere mention of her dad could still bring so much raw emotion to the surface.

"A cop?" Wendy said, her eyes wide. "Bet he's … pissed at how things turned out. Huh?"

Mel gulped. "Dad died years ago."

"Oh, sorry. Perhaps it's … for the best, though. Given where you are, ay?"

Mel chose to ignore the comment and continued talking, as much to herself as to her cellmate.

"Dad was a detective. I grew up with police investigations as my bedtime stories. Even when I was a little girl, Dad would share all the details of his goriest cases with me and my big brother, Brendan."

Some of the pictures Dad showed them gave her such nightmares that Brendan had to comfort her, hold her tight, sooth her back to sleep. Always her protector. Just as, in the end, she'd protected him. Not that he'd known anything about it. And now it was too late. Now, he'd never know the truth.

Thank God he couldn't see what had become of her. Keeping *his* abuse from Brendan had been the only positive thing she'd managed to achieve in her whole, sorry, married life. If Brendan had known, he'd have tried to save her, but that would have ended in disaster. He wouldn't have stood a chance. Mel knew it. *He* knew it.

Brendan didn't.

And now, he never would.

"One time, Dad told us about a body he found. Woman died of carbon monoxide poisoning. He laughed and said how the poison gave the woman rosy cheeks and cherry-red lips. Said it made her look like a doll."

Wendy coughed again, but this time, only once. "What a shitty thing … to tell a little girl. Your father … should have known better. These days, they'd call it … child abuse."

"Apart from Brendan, Dad was the best man I've ever known."

Until his breakdown.

But again, no one needed to know all the details of her

childhood, and certainly not Wendy. They didn't need to know what had caused Mel to make so many mistakes. Life choices that had eventually led her to prison—maybe for the rest of her life.

"And where was your mother when all this was going on?"

Damn, and there it is. The crux.

"Mother's dead. Don't want to talk about her."

Don't want to think about her, either. Not now, not ever.

"Excuse a … dying woman for saying this, but … but it sounds like you have family issues."

Really? You think?

When Mel didn't respond, Wendy eventually broke the silence. "Your brother … sounds like a decent bloke. Will he be visiting sometime?"

Mel squeezed her eyes closed, fighting yet another bout of tears.

"No," she whispered. "He … passed away last year."

"Hell, girlie. You're … all alone? Makes the two of us."

"No, Wendy. We have each other, right?"

Mel's cellmate gave her a sad smile. "Not for long, girlie."

Keys jangled, a lock turned, and a screw Mel didn't recognise pushed open the main door. He stood to one side and a woman entered, pushing a trolley. The newcomer had spiky, brown hair, dark eyes, and wore the yellow armband of a trusty. The trolley's rubber wheels squealed under the weight of well-thumbed books and magazines, haphazardly piled.

"Hey, Shirl. What you … got for us today?" Wendy asked.

"Same old, same old," Shirl answered, her thick, Brummie accent and drawn-out delivery making her sound glum and a little slow-witted. "A few new hand-me-downs from the screws might interest you, though."

The screw waited in the doorway. He leaned against the jamb, reading a folded newspaper, ignoring them.

Taking her time, Shirl pushed the trolley further into the room, eventually pulling it to a halt at the foot of Wendy's bed. She studied Mel for a moment, suspicious, guarded.

"You want anything to read? I got a couple of soppy love stories. Might help you pass the time."

Mel caught Wendy's warning glance and took the hint.

Shortly after Wendy had recovered some of her strength, she'd encouraged Mel to exaggerate her symptoms whenever possible. After all, why not do all she could to stay in the nice, warm hospital bed, since it was a darned sight more comfortable than the bunks in their shared cell? Safer, too.

She squinted at Shirl and added a grimace.

"Sorry, Shirl. Got the devil of a headache and can't see too well," Mel said. "Maybe tomorrow?"

Shirl sniffed. "Won't be back for a couple of days. By then, you'll prob'ly be sent back to gen-pop. Better take something for when you're feeling better. Here, this book might be of interest." She bent at the knees and took a battered and creased book from the bottom shelf.

"Darn it, Shirl," Wendy said, flicking her free hand in the trusty's direction. "You ain't … planning to give her that old book, are you?"

"What's wrong with *The Count of Monte Cristo*? It's a classic."

"It's about the … prison break, love. That joke's as … stale as the canteen's bread."

"Well, there you go ruining my fun again, babe. It's either Monte Cristo or Colditz. Pity I can't get hold of a copy of Fifty Shades, but the governor keeps cancelling all the orders I place."

"No, thanks," Mel said, doing her best to screw her lips into a smirk. "I already ploughed through Fifty Shades. It told me nothing I didn't already know."

For the first time since entering the room, Shirl became animated. She looked from Mel to Wendy and back again before bursting into an infectious, snorting laughter.

Shirl picked up a different book, stepped forwards, and dropped a long-fingered hand on Mel's knee.

"You're alright, girl. Here's a gentle romance. Now then"—she removed her hand and turned to face Wendy in the other bed—"how you doing, babe?"

"Hunky dory, love. Can't you tell?"

"I know." Shirl's sad eyes glazed over. "I got something real special in here for you."

"PO Scarsdale been generous again?"

"Yep."

"Scarsdale?" Mel asked.

"That's … right," Wendy answered, holding out her hand to Shirl and beckoning with her claw-like fingers. "When she's in a … good mood, Scarsdale's been known … to donate a used copy of *Cosmo*. Shirl has … first go and, for a price, holds onto it for me. Don't you, Shirl?"

"Ain't telling her what the price is, though. Are we, Wendy?" Shirl said, beaming at the cancer patient.

Most definitely, they were more than just friends.

The librarian trusty lifted her sweatshirt and pulled out a slightly furled magazine.

"Here you go, honey," she said, passing it to Wendy as though it was a precious gift. "Enjoy it, now."

Wendy hugged the creased magazine to her sunken chest. "Thank you, angel. Helps the … days fly by."

"She just loves following the latest fashions and all the celeb gossip," Shirl said to Mel. "Always has. Mad for it, she is."

Shirl shot a quick glance towards the doorway before stepping even closer to Wendy's bed. The screw had half-turned his back, head bowed, fully engrossed in his paper. Shirl rested her hand on Wendy's shoulder, leaned over, and kissed her gently on the lips.

"God I hate seeing you in here again," she whispered. "Get better soon. You hear me?"

Wendy dropped her hand over Shirl's and shook her head. "We both know that's … not happening, angel. Me? I ain't seeing another … Christmas."

"Stop it, please." Shirl's voice broke and Wendy tugged her into a gentle hug.

"What's all this then?" a man shouted from the doorway.

Thatcher.

The other screw snapped to attention.

Shirl jumped away from Wendy's bed and dried her eyes with the tips of her fingers.

"S-Sorry, Mr Thatcher," she said, hurrying to the trolley. "I-It's just … I hate to see her so … so—"

Thatcher grunted and sniffed simultaneously. It made him look and sound like a pig rooting around for truffles.

"She's getting the best medical care available. Run along now, Binder. Nothing more you can do here."

He stood to one side of the doorway, hands clasped behind his back, and waited for Shirl and her escort to leave before striding further into the ward.

"And how are we today, Archer?" he asked, studiously ignoring Wendy.

Once again, his dead-eyed smile churned Mel's stomach.

"Leave her alone, Thatcher," Wendy snapped. Her upper lip peeled back into a snarl so aggressive and contemptuous, it stunned Mel and almost made her shudder. "She don't need none o' your special care and attention."

Mel gasped.

How did she expect to get away with such insolence?

Thatcher spun to face Wendy, his creepy smile turning into an scowl. "Don't address me like that, Phillips. Show some respect for your betters."

"You ain't no better … than no one!" She coughed again. Pink spittle formed at the edges of her mouth. "You don't deserve … no respect."

Thatcher made a move closer to Wendy's bed, but a shadow in the doorway caught his attention and made him stop. Shirl poked her head around the jamb and stayed there, looking at Thatcher, her face expressionless, but her eyes flinty.

The senior screw hesitated a moment before leaning back and resuming his earlier, hands-behind-his-back pose. He bounced up and down on the balls of his feet three times, lifting his heels high off the floor each time.

"This sort of disrespect will not be tolerated," he said quietly, staring at Mel. "Do you understand?"

Mel dipped her head. "Y-yes, sir."

"As for you, Phillips," he said, turning towards Wendy. "Don't think that drip sticking into your arm earns you any special privileges. You're skating on thin ice, let me tell you!"

"How you gonna make me … suffer any more than I already am, Thatcher?" Wendy demanded, her delivery more a growl than actual speech. "Push off back … to your hole. You ain't needed around here!"

The door to the staff office opened and Dr Milliner entered the ward.

"Hello, Mr Thatcher," Milliner said. "Wasn't expecting you this morning. Can I help you with anything?"

Thatcher's shoulders relaxed, and his sickening smile returned.

"No thanks, Dr Milliner. Just doing my rounds. Making sure everything's running smoothly."

The doctor dipped her head. "Very good. Well, now you're here, perhaps this would be a good time to discuss my quarterly report. As you know, I'm working on a proposal to increase the clinic's budget. Your input would be gratefully appreciated. Do you have a couple of free hours?"

"Ah, yes. I see," Thatcher said, nodding and cupping his strong chin with a hand. "Unfortunately, I'm on my way to a meeting with the governor. Perhaps we can schedule a time for later in the month?"

"Very well," Milliner said, flaring her nostrils and sighing deeply. "As you're so busy, I suppose that will have to do."

If she was trying to look disappointed, it didn't work.

Thatcher dipped his head in a curt nod, shot a look at Mel that said he wasn't finished with her yet, and turned towards Wendy. "I do hope your condition improves soon, Phillips. Don't like to see any of the inmates in such discomfort. Still, I'm sure we'll see you back on the wing again really soon."

He tipped his cap to Dr Milliner and headed through the door.

"Along you go now, Binder," he said as he passed Shirl

and her escort in the corridor. "Mustn't keep your customers waiting."

His rubber-soled shoes squeaked all the way along the outer hallway until they stopped and a metal door slammed shut.

"I knew asking him to discuss my budget would work," Milliner said, wringing her hands as though trying to rub away some dirt. "CM Thatcher knows he's not supposed to come in here without my permission, or without a female officer present. Ah well, he's gone now. And how are you feeling, Archer? Any improvement in that migraine?"

Mel made a point to grimace.

"Still hurts, doctor. And my vision still won't clear," she said, avoiding eye contact with Wendy.

The doctor pursed her lips and pointed to the book in Mel's hand.

"Better not do any reading until that headache clears. Painkillers not helping?"

"Not much, doctor. My chest hurts, too. And is there any chance of my seeing a dentist? I keep cutting my tongue and lip on the exposed implant."

"I'll see what I can arrange, but I can't promise to give you back your smile anytime soon. The prison budget doesn't stretch to ceramic crowns."

"My husband paid for private dental insurance. Would that still be valid, do you think?"

"It might be—assuming he kept up the payments. We'd have to arrange for an outpatient visit. Not sure whether the governor would sign off on that, mind you. Let me look into it."

"Thank you, doctor."

Milliner approached Wendy's bed. "Now then, Wendy, how are you faring today?"

Wendy leaned more heavily into her pillows. "To tell you … the truth, Dr Milliner, I've … been better. You know I don't … like to complain, but … everything hurts. Don't suppose … you have any morphine … lying around?"

"Very funny, Phillips. Now, while I'm here, let's take a quick look at that catheter."

The doctor dragged the privacy curtain around Wendy's bed and Mel did her best to tune out the ensuing conversation. Trying to ignore the pain pulsing through her broken wrist and cracked ribs, she lay back against the pillows and closed her eyes.

Chapter Six

HMP Falston Manor, Derbyshire, England

Irritating voices cut into Mel's sunlit world of sand and sea and love. Peace and quiet. A place she'd only ever visited in her mind, never for real. A place she'd promised to take Rio … one day.

She twitched, groaned, and covered a yawn with the back of her hand.

"Evening, sleepyhead," Wendy said, a strength in her voice that had been absent earlier.

Mel winked open her eye. The headache was back, but this one had more to do with the awkward way she'd slept than being beaten close to death by a couple of prison thugs. The crick in her neck felt as though someone was stabbing her with a blunt knife. A coppery taste in her mouth resulted from the aftermath of a fresh cut on the inside of her upper lip. She'd abraded it against the implant again.

She straightened her head and struggled to find a more comfortable position, but everything hurt. Everything. Legs, hips, back, neck, face, and head. Each injury fought for prime place in her attention.

She tried meditation. To isolate the pain, send it away.

Didn't work.

"I said, 'Evening, sleepyhead'," Wendy said. "Don't make me … repeat myself, honey. I'm too … tired."

"Sorry." Mel hissed the reply, working hard to make herself understood, and to avoid cutting another slice out of her lip and tongue. "How do you feel?"

"Been better, thanks. This … dying of cancer thing really sucks."

Mel opened her eye and closed it against the harsh sunlight slicing through the west-facing windows. Somehow, she'd been asleep for hours. Missed lunch, such as it was. No wonder her stomach rumbled and her mouth tasted like the bottom of a budgie's cage, or at least the way she imagined one would taste. Dry, gritty, metallic. In short, horrible. To become human again, she not only needed to clean her teeth, but also needed her hairbrush and a mirror, but the nurses still refused to provide any of those things.

Mel reached up. The bandage still covered her right eye. She pressed harder with her fingertips, digging, prodding. Uncomfortable rather than unbearable.

Why did she always have to be someone's punching bag?

Mel took as deep a breath as possible and relaxed. She opened her eye again, this time, better prepared for the brightness. Wendy was still propped up in bed. The bag of fluids suspended from the metal stand was nearly empty. Wendy's skin looked pinker than it had earlier. Her smile had strengthened, and her cheeks appeared slightly more plump. The whites of her eyes were less yellow.

Despite the improvement, Wendy still looked close to death. Time for what the frightful nuns in convent school used to call a "little white lie".

"You look good," Mel said, hoping for a positive vibe.

"Liar. I look like … shit, and I will do until they … take me away in a cheap, pine box."

She turned away from Mel and threw up into a sick bag.

"Sorry 'bout that," Wendy said after crumpling up the end of the bag and wiping her mouth with a paper towel.

"No need to apologise. You can't help it."

Wendy sighed and a weak smile made it to her washed-out face. "Chemo's a bitch. Each treatment's worse than … the last."

"If it's that bad, have you thought of stopping treatment?"

Wendy looked at Mel as though she'd said something totally ludicrous.

"And give up three days every fortnight in the infirmary in this comfortable bed and one hour of colour telly every night?" She pointed to the silent TV bolted to a shelf on the opposite wall below the sunlit window. "Are you mad?"

"Sorry, I forgot."

"I know, honey. 'Sides," Wendy said, after taking another stuttering breath and turning the page on her magazine, "I don't want to give the … screws the satisfaction of dying early. They have to … keep checking on me and the more work I give them, the better it makes me feel."

Mel grinned, unsure of how seriously to take Wendy's

words. She'd shown a grudging respect for some of the prison officers, Thatcher excluded, and her words were probably the bravado of a woman who'd sinned and was now scared to meet her maker.

Wendy turned the magazine towards Mel, showing her a picture of an ageing Hollywood A-lister and a woman at least thirty-five years his junior.

"Damn it," she said, "Bugger's showing his age. It's obvious what she's … doing with him. Bloody gold-digger."

"Good for her. There's nothing wrong with marrying for money *and* love."

Liar.

Originally, Mel had fallen head-over-heels in love with the once-handsome and dashing James Archer—*him*—and that hadn't turned out too well for her.

"You ever … read women's magazines?"

Mel shrugged. "Not much into gossip, me. I'm more of an *FT* girl. Need to keep up with the latest market trends. Balance my investment portfolio."

"Thought you was broke," Wendy said, levering herself slightly higher in her bed.

"I am. Don't have a penny to my name. Doesn't mean I can't dream. Does it?"

Which was absolutely true. She didn't have a penny in her married name but Wendy didn't need to know the truth. If the police ever found out about her "Escape Fund", it would be yet another nail in her legal coffin. More motive.

The door to the staff office opened and Athena arrived to run the obs, make her notes, and perform her bed baths. After dealing with Wendy from behind the privacy curtains, she turned to Mel and, as usual, was surprisingly gentle about it. By the time the bubbly nurse finished her ministrations, Mel felt much better. Fresher, cleaner, almost human.

Still in the dark as to how she looked, but she could live with that. Her looks had never helped her in the past.

When Athena left, Mel rested her eye and allowed her mind to drift while Wendy kept turning the pages of PO Scarsdale's donated magazine.

Although the ward was peaceful and quiet, the noises of a working prison filtered through the solid walls. The intermittent slamming of metal doors against wooden jambs was the worst. For some reason, none of the screws had learned the art of closing the doors quietly. Maybe it was down to the age of the doors, making them impossible to close without slamming. More likely, the metallic crashing formed part of the punishment. Psychological warfare.

Wendy turned another page and sighed as she shook out the creases. This month's *Cosmo* must have been riveting, since she'd already read it from cover to cover. And, judging by the time it took her to turn the pages, she either took in every word or she read really slowly. Maybe both.

"Shoot, there it is again. How much … d'you reckon it costs to advertise in here?" Wendy asked.

"No idea. Thousands, probably. Why? Are you thinking of trying to sell your autobiography?"

Wendy's smile returned, and this one had more strength than the earlier ones.

"Honey, if I ever got around to … writing my life story, it would blow everybody's socks off. Be such a sure-fire … bestseller, I wouldn't have to advertise it nowhere. No, I just wondered, 'cause this ad's in here again. Same one for the last … seven months. First time I saw it, I thought it must be some kind of con, y'know?"

"No, Wendy. I don't have a clue. What's it advertising?"

"But I'm guessing if they're … paying all that cash to advertise, it must be legit, right?" She continued talking as if she hadn't heard Mel's question. Perhaps the drugs were damaging her hearing as well as upsetting her stomach. Hearing loss was a known side-effect of some chemotherapy. She'd run an online search when the doctors started treating *him* for one of *his* cancers—testicular.

Oh how she'd laughed in private at that particular diagnosis. Served the pig right for everything *he'd* done in *his* miserable, worthless life.

Stop it, Mel.

If she didn't stop letting *him* invade her mind, *he'd* win. Even in death, *he'd* win. She couldn't let that happen. Somehow, she had to keep *him* out. Keep herself sane.

"Some people … have all the luck. Well, not exactly, but … you know what I mean."

"No, I don't," Mel said, speaking a little louder.

Wendy jerked her head up from the magazine's glossy pages and stared at her in confusion. "Huh? What'd you say?"

"Wendy, I have no idea what the heck you're talking about."

Wendy's tired, bloodshot eyes narrowed momentarily, before understanding dawned. "Oh right. Sorry. Get so … wrapped up in these stories, I forget other people aren't so interested. Remember the plane … that crashed in the North Sea last year? The one where that soldier arsehole … blew up all them poor souls on their way to Holland? Flight BE1555?"

A burning spear drove through Mel's heart. Her mouth dried and her stomach roiled. She couldn't prevent a shudder running through her whole body. Cold sweat formed under the bandages and on her exposed skin.

Did she remember Flight BE1555?

Did she remember the day she lost Brendan, the brother

she'd tried to protect from *his* jealous anger? The wonderful brother who'd done nothing in his life but try to help people. Try to save lives.

Yes, she remembered. She bloody remembered.

She'd never forget the day she learned of Brendan's death, or the braying laugh that spewed from *his* blistered lips—a side effect of the latest experimental chemo treatment. Even in *his* weakened state, the evil swine could still torture her with nothing but words.

"Yes," she said, quietly to Wendy, "I remember Flight BE1555, and the terrorist who shot it down. Ryan Liam Kaine, the most evil man on the planet."

At least he was now that *his* rotting corpse was feeding the worms.

"Why?" she added, trying not to appear too keen.

Chapter Seven

Tuesday 13th April - Early Morning

Blu Skandia Hotel, Valdemsgade, Aarhus, Denmark

The low sun shot a knife-edge of light through the sliver of a gap between the curtains. It woke Ryan Kaine from another burgeoning nightmare of airliners exploding in clear, evening skies and of burned corpses floating in the turbulent and inky-black North Sea.

He turned over in bed and punched the pillows into submission.

Shit!

The questions and guilt returned afresh. How could he have been such a bloody idiot?

Could he have done anything to prevent the atrocity?

Yes, with hindsight, of course he could. But he'd been blind-sided by Gravel, his long-time friend and former CO.

Gravel had set up the whole putrid operation. Kaine had let Gravel handle all the details. He'd been too damned trusting. Too bloody naïve. Should have double-checked everything for himself.

Damn it to hell and back.

Kaine hadn't even broken down the rocket launcher to confirm its function. Hadn't searched the trawler, *Herring Gull*, for explosives, either.

What a bloody, God-awful mess.

Never again. Bloody hell no.

He didn't suffer the visions often, but when they bit deep into his sleep, the effects could be debilitating. Luckily, this time, the stiletto-blade of sunlight woke him before the nightmare had the chance, and he'd yet to reach the sweating, screaming-himself-awake stage.

Kaine balled his hands into fists and knuckled the sleep —and the hellish images—from his eyes. He read the time from his watch.

Reveille.

At his side, Lara still slept the deep, restful sleep of the innocent and the pure of heart. Her naked shoulder peeked out over the edge of the duvet in all its tanned and smooth perfection. Gently, he rolled over in the bed and kissed her skin.

She twitched, whimpered.

"Morning," she mumbled, her voice thick with sleep.

"Morning, love," he whispered. "Sorry to wake you, but it's time for you to make a move. Mustn't keep the tutors waiting. We don't have any apples to give them."

She groaned and pushed him away.

"Fancy a cuppa before room service arrives with breakfast?"

"Can't be that time already. I'm exhausted."

Kaine laughed quietly. "You've had more than enough sleep, soldier."

"What time is it?" she asked, still on her side, facing away.

"A shade after six."

She rolled onto her back and, disappointingly, pulled the covers up to her chin.

"Really?" she said, smiling and watching where his eyes strayed. "A full seven hours' sleep and I'm still jaded. Must be getting old."

"Not from where I'm lying, lass," he said, adding a grin and deliberately adjusting his head to make it appear as though he was trying to get a better look.

"Thanks. You say the sweetest things."

"I try, and it's all true." He leaned forwards and kissed her again. This time, on the lips.

She responded enthusiastically. He forced himself to pull away before things became too heated.

"No time for ... anything?" Lara asked, sitting up in bed and letting the duvet slip a little.

"I'd really, really love to," he said, meaning each word, "but you're spoken for this morning. I don't want the star student flunking the course for tardiness."

Kaine rolled out of the comfortable hotel bed. He stood, looked down at her, and sighed.

She sat up and lobbed one of his pillows at him. He let it hit him full in the face and fall to the carpet.

"Spoilsport," she said, making no effort to recover herself.

Her temptress act was working. It wouldn't take much more for him to weaken.

"Litter lout," he countered, letting his gaze fall from her sultry grin. "You're picking up that pillow, not me."

"Spoilsport," she repeated.

"You already said that."

"I know, but the repetition doesn't make it any less true."

"I'll make that tea."

Lara huffed and flopped back onto the pillows. "Okay, fine. Give me a few minutes to psych myself up for a riveting morning of lectures."

"What's on the agenda today?" he asked as though he hadn't already memorised the full course itinerary, session by detailed session.

"Battlefield dressings and pharmacology this morning," she said, almost sighing. "Defensive tactics and fieldcraft this afternoon."

"Yep," he said, nodding. "Sounds riveting enough."

After another kiss—this one only a peck—Kaine left the playful torturer in bed. He grabbed his dressing gown and headed for the galley kitchen.

The Blu Skandia Hotel's luxury suite provided a decent hospitality tray, one they'd augmented with teabags from the UK aisle in the local Bilka shopping centre. As he'd learned very early in their relationship, Lara craved tea first thing.

———

FIFTY-FIVE MINUTES LATER, they'd showered, dressed, and devoured a continental breakfast. Lara, in military fatigues, had transformed into Dr Grace Sloane, trainee trauma medic. Kaine wore casual civvies—polo shirt, black jeans, and trainers—in readiness for a day monitoring everything from the university's surveillance feeds and the hotel room's balcony. No way was he going to allow her out of his sight, not even during a training course.

Never again.

The bedside phone chirruped. Kaine jumped up to answer.

"Hello?"

"*God morgen*, Mr O'Keefe. This is Birgit from reception."

"Morning, Birgit," Kaine answered.

"The taxi has arrived for Dr Sloane, sir."

"Thank you. She'll be right down."

He dropped the handset into its cradle and returned to the suite's dining area.

"That's you up, Dr Sloane."

Lara was already standing and shaking her head.

Kaine closed the gap between them and they hugged.

"Be safe out there, girl."

She kissed his bearded cheek.

"I'm on a training course in the middle of Denmark. What's to be scared of?"

Kaine frowned.

"That South African fool's getting a bit mouthy."

"Krüger, you mean?"

"Yep. If he doesn't start minding his manners, I'll be paying the ignorant prick a quiet social call one night. You should hear the way he talks about the women on the course when you're out of earshot. The idiot's a real throwback."

She laughed. "You don't have to worry about Krüger. He's nothing but a loud-mouthed bully. All hot air and nothing to back it up with. I've faced plenty of Neanderthals like Roelf "Pik" Krüger in my time. You'd be surprised at how many farmers still think women should keep their veterinary practices to toy poodles, cats, and hamsters."

"No, love. I wouldn't."

They kissed again. He accompanied her to the lift and waited for the doors to slide together before hurrying back to their room. He already had his first job of the day lined up.

Kaine settled in front of his monitors, donned his head-phones, and entered a short, alpha-numeric string on the keyboard. Within seconds, Corky's chubby and smiling face appeared on the main screen.

"Whatcha, Mr K. How you diddling?"

"Hi, Corky. I'm fine, thanks. How's it going with the extended background sweep on Krüger?"

"Pretty good, Mr K. Corky's snaffled a nice package of dirt on 'im. Corky were just waiting for our morning chat to send it. You should have it by now."

Kaine nodded his thanks, navigated to the secure server where Corky sent all his special "packages", and smiled. "You are a genius, my friend. There's a lot here. It'll take me a little while to work through it, though."

"Corky's added a management summary," the IT genius said, and a file opened up on Kaine's computer. "So while you get started, Corky's going to splice back into the univer-sity security feed so we're all hunky dory for when the doc arrives. Back in a tic."

Before Kaine could thank him again, Corky's face melted from the screen to be replaced by a view of the hotel's reception area as shown by the in-house, CCTV feed. Through it, he watched a rather attractive, dark-haired woman marching towards the entrance doors.

Chapter Eight

Tuesday 13th April - Melanie Archer

Health Care Centre, HMP Falston Manor, Derbyshire, England

Mel focused her one good eye on Wendy, who stared at her as though she was an out-of-touch dimwit.

"You really don't have a … clue, do you?"

"Wendy," Mel said through a sigh, "as far as I'm concerned, you're talking in riddles."

Wendy held up her precious *Cosmo*. "First time anyone inside here saw this advert—"

"What advert?"

"This one," she said, still not letting Mel see the page.

Typical of Wendy, she seemed keen to drag out the

suspense. Inside prison, inmates took their little pleasures wherever and whenever they could.

"Wendy, please!"

"Like I said, the … first time anyone in here saw this advert, the story … spread through this place faster than … faster than the outbreak of … listeria a couple of years back. A real scandal. The old governor—money-grubbing bastard—outsourced the catering to a company that operated on the cheap. Pre-packed sandwiches, chilled meals … to be reheated, you know the type of crap, yeah?"

"Wendy," Mel said, exasperation taking over, "you're waffling."

"Anyhow," Wendy continued, her strength improving as the excitement of her story took hold, "two inmates died and a remand prisoner lost the baby she was carrying. Terrible it was. Some of the POs took sick, too. The place was like a … war zone. Inmates on full shutdown.

"Heads rolled on account of it, too. They brought in a new governor and CM Thatcher. Shut down the food company. You probably didn't … hear about it 'cause the government hushed it up. But like I said, a proper scandal, it was."

Mel clenched her good fist. She wanted to scream. Wanted to beg Wendy to get to the point, but she sat back and waited. When on a roll, nothing would deflect Wendy from her course. Mel had learned the hard way after the first day sharing a cell with the woman.

"Sorry, honey," Wendy said, the strength almost visibly draining away from her. "I get carried away … with myself. … Kind of helps take my mind off of … stuff, you know?"

"No, no. I get it. You said something about the plane crash and getting lucky?"

"Yeah," Wendy said, grimacing as another wave of

nausea must have struck. "Turns out some … kind souls have set up a … a charity to help the families of … the people who died on the plane. They … called it The 83 Trust."

"Never heard of it. Is it official?"

Wendy swallowed and twitched up a shoulder. The most she could do by way of a shrug.

"Seems legit, enough."

"What are they selling?"

"Apparently, if you're … one of the relatives of the victims, there's money in the pot for you … if you need it. Of course, they don't say how much … you're entitled to, or if it's means tested, like benefits, but …"

Carefully, Mel rolled onto her side and stretched out her hand. "Can I read it?"

Wendy pulled the pages further away from Mel's grasping fingers.

"Don't be stupid. What happens if Hattie or one of the screws sees you reading? They'll send you straight back to your cell. Want me to read it out for you?"

"Yes, please."

This'll be interesting.

"Don't you look at me like that, child. Maybe I didn't go to … university like some, but I *can* read. Don't just buy the … magazine to look at the pretty pictures."

"I wasn't looking at you funny," Mel lied, trying to appear hurt while doing so.

Wendy shuffled the magazine once more and folded it back on itself. "So, where was I? Here it is. Ahem …"

She adjusted herself in the bed and continued.

"It says here, 'Did you have a relative aboard Flight BE1555? Are you struggling to cope? If so, we can help.'" She paused for breath before carrying on. "'The 83 Trust was set up to offer support for the families of the eighty-three passengers and crew who died in that terrible incident—"

"'Incident'?" Mel cut in. "It wasn't a bloody 'incident'. It was an act of terror. Ryan Kaine murdered my—all those innocent people. Plain and simple."

Wendy dipped her head and gave Mel "the eye".

"I'm struggling to … breathe here, girl. Want me to carry on?"

"Yes, please. Sorry."

She'd been completely wrong. Wendy read confidently and well, with plenty of intonation and without hesitation. Mel should have known better than to succumb to prejudice. She'd faced enough of it in her time. Guilt spread through her in a hot wave.

Wendy raised the magazine once more.

"Right. Where was I? Oh, yeah. 'Thanks to the generosity of our many benefactors … generous corporate and private donors, The 83 Trust has … access to emergency funds … for those facing financial hardship and to support the … families of the victims. Furthermore, we can provide the contact details … of counsellors who may be able to help reduce emotional stress.'"

Close to exhaustion, Wendy paused to clear her throat and take a sip of water before continuing.

"'We have sent … registered letters to as many of the heads of the … eighty-three families as we can identify, explaining the help available. If you have not yet received … your letter, please visit our website, the-83.com, where you will be able to … apply for support as and when necessary.'"

Chest heaving, Wendy stopped reading. After a few moments' recuperation, she glanced at Mel.

"I know what you're going to ask next. Yes, the website does exist. Me and a few of the girls have actually visited it, on the QT, you understand. One or two have even hit the button and begged for help."

"Button? What button?"

"There's a ... big, red, 'call to action' button in the middle of the ... page. Says something like ... 'If you need urgent help, click here'."

Mel's heartrate climbed. She tried to swallow past the dryness in her mouth.

"What happened when you hit the button?"

Wendy gave her an old-fashioned look. "No family member ... of mine died on that plane. What makes you ... think I pressed the button?"

"Because it's what I'd have done. Don't try telling me you weren't curious. So, what happened?"

Wendy's quiet, "I didn't," came as a bit of a surprise.

"Really?"

Her ensuing quiet chuckle bubbled into another series of hacking coughs. She wiped her mouth before speaking again. "Inmates ain't allowed ... access to social media, and we can't interact with anyone online ... at least, not if we want to ... keep our library privileges."

"But you found a way around that issue, didn't you?"

"'Course I did, girlie. You already ... know me too well."

"Shirl gave you access?"

Wendy swallowed. "Nothing gets past you."

"So, what happened when you did it?"

"Nothing much. I ... I half-expected flashing lights ... and 'jackpot' signs, but it didn't go nothing like that. The screen flipped into ... a drop-down questionnaire. You know the kind of thing. Multiple choice answers and ... boxes for comments. Promises of confidentiality, and … and the usual bullshit."

"And?"

"And what?"

"What happened when you completed the questionnaire and hit 'send'?"

"You're so sure I … I tried to con a charity out of money? That's hurtful."

Yeah, right.

"Well, did you?"

Wendy's thin lips twisted into a weak smile. "Damned right I did. Gave them the … full spiel. Claimed my … sister had been on the plane. Laid it on real thick … with plenty of hardship, mental distress, PTSD. The lot. Gave them my … sister's email address in Sheffield, but …"

She seemed to run out of energy. Her eyelids drooped.

"But?" Mel pressed.

Wendy took another series of shallow breaths. "Couple of … days later, my sister received an email—one of them … automated message type things."

Mel held her breath, not daring to hope.

"What did it say?"

"It gave her a … bit of a bollocking for trying to … defraud a registered charity out of … scarce funds. My sister was … really pissed. We're … hardly on the best of terms after all my time being … in here, but she called it the last straw. Hasn't … spoken to me since. Even cancelled last month's visit."

"That's awful."

Wendy up-nodded and winced. "She'll get over it. Eventually. I was only trying to … put money into my family's bank account. Is that such a … bad thing?"

"It is when you do it fraudulently," Mel said, unable to hold it in.

The wince turned in to a sneer. "Hark at you, little Miss ... Holier Than Thou."

"Sorry."

Mel took a settling breath. The next part needed to go perfectly. She'd try the unofficial way first. If that didn't work, she'd end up going through official channels, but to do that, she'd probably have to approach CM Thatcher, which was the last thing she wanted. Using official channels would take longer, too.

"Wendy," she said, "I need your help."

"Yeah, thought you might."

"You did?"

"Ain't much ... gets past me either, girlie. I could see how ... hot and bothered you got when I ... when I started talking 'bout that plane crash. C'mon, girl. Tell your ... Aunt Wendy all about it."

Mel closed her eye, unable to face rejection, should it come.

"Do you think Shirl will help me access the internet?"

"Might do, if I ... asked her nicely."

Mel tried to tamp down the excitement flooding through her system. So many false dawns. Could she—dare she—hold out any hope?

"Will you, please?"

Wendy pressed the flat of her hand into her chest and took a slow, rattling breath. "Why would I ... want to do that? What's in it for me?"

"I-I don't know. My thanks and my eternal gratitude."

Wendy snorted and grunted as she turned onto her side. Sweat shone on her brow.

"My family can't … serve up none of your gratitude on a dinner plate, girlie."

Mel bit back a snappy retort. Allowing anger to take over wouldn't help.

"If this Trust thing isn't a con, if it really does have the funding, and they send me some money, I'd see your family right."

"One of your relatives were on that plane?"

Mel swallowed the bile produced by the memory of the news and the way *he* delivered it. The anger. The loss. The helplessness.

She couldn't afford to let the same madness take control again. She held back the kneejerk response and calmed herself.

Eventually, Mel dragged up the strength to answer, each word more painful than the last. She started slowly, quietly. "My … brother, Brendan. He was heading to Amsterdam for a firefighter conference. When he died, I lost the only thing in the world I ever truly loved."

Wendy tilted her head to one side as if to improve her hearing. "This true? No bullshit?"

"Honest to God. I swear it," Mel answered, crossing a finger over her heart.

"You lucky thing. … Well, I'm … I'm sorry for the … loss of your brother of course, but you … might just have won the lottery, girlie."

Mel tried to hold back the hope still fluttering in her breast.

"You're serious?"

"Sure am, honey. There ain't … as many rich people in prison as poor ones, and it ain't because them … bastards is any more honest than us … paupers. It's on account of them being … able to afford better … barristers. You know it as well as I do."

Once again, tears formed behind Mel's closed eyes, tears of hope laced with incredulity. After all that had happened to her over the past month, all the fear and shock, was her luck finally about to turn?

Hold it together, Mel.

She couldn't let herself get carried away.

"Still doesn't answer my … question, though," Wendy said. "What do I get … out of helping you?"

"What do you want?"

"Nothing much."

"I'll give you anything I can."

"Yeah, you say that now, but … what happens if you do get out of here? You're likely to … forget all about your bestie."

Mel propped herself up on her elbow, causing her damaged ribcage and the broken wrist to scream in protest. She tried not to show it for fear of Wendy thinking she was lying.

"Wendy, you have my word. I won't forget you, nor will I break a solemn promise. What do you want from me?"

"For me, it's way too late. I don't want … nothing for me personally, but I … I got a daughter. They put her in … care when they locked me up. She were … only a baby at the time."

"If I get out, you want me to find her and convince her to visit?"

"Hell no, girlie. The lass is … better off without me. What good will it do … for her to find out her mother's an … old thief dying of cancer? All I want … is to know she's okay. Will you find her and let me know how she's doing?"

Mel dipped her head and stared at Wendy through her one good eye.

"I will. I promise, but everything depends on whether these Trust people are for real. The whole thing could be a con."

"Yeah, I know, and there is one more thing."

"Okay, fire away."

This better not be too difficult.

"In five months … Shirl is due for release. When she gets out of here, she doesn't … have no place to go. Will you look after her?"

"If I can. Assuming I can look after myself."

"Honey, you was … married to a millionaire, yeah? From what I know of the law, if you're found … not guilty, you'll end up back in that fancy mansion of yours … living the high life. There'll be … plenty of room for Shirl to play the house guest."

Mel only hesitated for a moment before placing a hand on her heart.

"Wendy, you have my word."

"Okay, girlie. Guess it won't … hurt to trust you."

Mel swore the solemn oath, even though she still found it hard to believe one word of the advert. Good things never happened to her.

Not ever.

Chapter Nine

Wednesday 14th April - Evening

Heading North, M1, Bedfordshire, England

With Luton Airport and a cramped flight on a budget airline safely behind them, Kaine, behind the wheel of an expensive hire car, filtered into the middle lane of the M1. The minute they reached the speed limit, he engaged cruise control and turned to Lara in the front passenger seat beside him.

She rested her forehead on the window, the right side of her face exposed, showing the angry, red welt.

"Lara," he whispered, "are you awake?"

She stirred and turned to face him.

"I am now," she said and gave up a tired smile.

"How's your cheek?"

"Lord above, how many times?" Her smile slid into a frown. "My cheek's fine. Krüger barely touched me. Will you please stop fretting. I'm more worried about the state of your hand."

Kaine's left forearm still throbbed from where his first uncontrolled punch landed awkwardly, but he wasn't going to tell Lara. At least the tingling in his fingers had eased since leaving Aarhus. The pain had lessened, too. He'd aggravated the injury he received during their Walthamstow mission, but it would heal fully. Eventually.

Maintaining his attention on the traffic, Kaine held up the hand in question and waggled his fingers, smiling through the slight discomfort.

"Look," he said, "good as new."

"Liar. I saw the way you led with your right during the first fight. You're not normally a southpaw."

He shrugged. "I'm adaptable."

Rain hit the windscreen in a sudden torrent. Sensors activated the automatic wipers, which attacked the downpour with sweeping efficiency.

"Tell you what," he said, "let's make a deal. I won't pester you about your cheek if you don't ask about my wrist."

"Okay, but I'm your doctor. If that injury's not healing properly, I need to know about it."

"It is, I promise," Kaine answered, feigning frustration, but in fact pleased to have someone who cared enough to be concerned for his health. "There's some minor discomfort, but it's already on the mend. Be right as ninepence in a day or two. Try to get some more shuteye. Won't take us long to reach the farm."

They eased into a comfortable silence. The miles rolled under their wheels, the tyres producing an intermittent and discordant bumping-thump with each crease and broken surface they encountered.

———

THEY'D LEFT the well-lit motorway behind and were rumbling along the unlit A5, a familiar, two-lane black top in the middle of the Northamptonshire countryside. Kaine eased up on the accelerator in preparation for an upcoming turn.

Lara stirred, covered a yawn with the back of her hand, and stretched her arms towards the windscreen. She stared through the rain-streaked glass at the cone of headlights piercing the blackness.

"Where are we?"

"Long Buckby Wharf. We're about to turn off the A5."

"How long have I been asleep?"

"Your snoring's been deafening me for the past half hour." Kaine grinned in anticipation of her response.

"Ryan Liam Kaine, I do not snore!"

"No, Doc. Of course you don't. No way. That burble-burble-popping noise must have come from the engine."

She shot out an arm and punched his shoulder.

"Ouch," he winced and rubbed his arm as though it hurt. "You've turned into a right thug. I should have let you vent your anger on Krüger."

Kaine made the turn on to the tree-and-hedge-lined Three Bridge Road and reduced their speed even further, cautious of the undulating and cracked surface.

"Your phone buzzed while you were in dreamland. Sounded like a text."

Lara searched through her handbag for the mobile and

tapped the device awake. Its screen lit her face in a gentle light.

"It's from Corky. He's just double confirmed the identity. Melanie Anne Archer *is* a legitimate member of The 83. Currently on remand at Falston Manor, accused of murdering her husband."

"If we didn't already know that, we'd be in Nice right now starting our holiday on the French Riviera. We wouldn't be driving through the rain-drenched Northants countryside about to disturb Mike's peace and quiet."

"Mike loves you like a father. He'll be delighted to see you, and you know it."

They approached a slow-moving truck and, with no room to overtake on the winding road, Kaine had to match its speed—a little over forty mph.

"Nonsense," Kaine said, still smiling, "Royal Navy CPOs have hearts of granite. It's an essential requirement. Part of their job description. If he's happy to see anyone, it'll be you. You bought his affection with your shared love of thoroughbred nags."

She brushed away his mildly insulting comment and continued reading. "Corky's also confirmed Melanie's story about being beaten nearly to death in the showers. So far, everything she claimed on the SOS form is legit. He's added some detail to her profile on the server and has downloaded police files on the case against her."

"Good, old Corky. Don't know where we'd be without him."

"I'll tell him you said that during the next video call."

The truck ahead slowed even further, indicated left, and turned into a petrol station, leaving the road into Long Buckby clear. Kaine added a little pressure to the accelerator.

Seven miles later, after negotiating the quiet streets of the ancient market town, Kaine found his way onto the winding lane running into Mike's farm. Easy to miss in the dark.

Kaine pulled up at the farm's gated entrance and jumped out to unlock the five-bar gate before Lara had the chance. He had to dodge puddles along the way and returned to the driver's seat dripping wet. Once through, he reversed the procedure, keeping Lara warm and dry.

He drove around to the back of the stone-built farmhouse, and parked in the rear courtyard as close as he could to the back door.

Mike—a grizzled, seventy-four-year-old widower with a full, white beard and a ramrod-straight back—met them at the door and ushered them into the boot room.

"Lass, you must be exhausted," Mike said, taking Lara's coat and bundling her into the warm kitchen, barely giving Kaine much more than a welcoming nod in the process.

Mike's two dogs, more pets than working farm animals, skittered around their feet in yelping, slavering, tail-wagging excitement. Lara dropped to her haunches and greeted them like the old friends they were.

"A little, Mike," she said, standing and facing the old man. "I managed to get some sleep on the plane and during the drive, but—".

"Good Lord, lass. What the hell happened to your face?" He reached out to touch her bruised cheek with his gnarled fingers.

She pulled away and shook her head.

"It's nothing, Mike. Really. You should see the other guy."

Mike spun around and scowled at Kaine.

"Ryan! What the hell?"

Kaine threw him a pained expression. "A little trouble in Denmark. We'll tell you about it later."

"Honestly, Mike," Lara said, "it looks far worse than it is. I can barely feel it."

Mike shot Kaine another accusatory scowl and shook his head. His expression made it clear that he hadn't finished with the matter, but he'd park the detailed interrogation until later.

Lara made her way to the lounge, taking the dogs with her. Mike followed, leaving Kaine in the boot room to peel off his own coat and dry his long hair on a clean towel specifically provided for the purpose.

"Bet you could do with something decent to eat, eh?" Mike asked Lara, keeping his angry back to Kaine.

In the lounge, Lara held her hands out to the glowing fire. "Yes, please. Anything hot would be lovely."

"I've some beef stew warming on the range."

Lara smiled tiredly and lowered herself onto the sofa beside the fireplace, soaking up the heat. The dogs settled at her feet, eyeing Lara and Kaine in turn.

"Close the door, Captain," Mike said, his eyes flinty. "There's a draft."

AFTER SUPPER, which included a detailed explanation of the events in Denmark and yet more passive-aggression from Mike, Lara made her excuses and turned in early.

The moment he heard Lara's footsteps on the stairs, the barriers fell and Mike launched into a furious attack on Kaine's inability to keep her safe.

"For pity's sake, man. What were you thinking, letting her stroll into danger like that?"

"Mike, you know Lara. I tried my best to convince her not to sign up for that course, but once she's set her mind to something—"

"Yes, but the danger—"

"I did everything I could to protect her. Kept my eye on her the whole bloody time. You know I …" His voice broke. "You know what she means to me."

He'd almost used the L word but didn't want Mike to witness such an overt show of weakness. The old sailor wouldn't have appreciated it.

Yeah, right.

Kaine coughed and turned to stare at the fading embers of the fire.

Mike lowered his eyes, drained his large tot of rum in one go, and stretched forwards to place the empty glass on the coffee table.

"I know, son," he said quietly. "Sorry to go off on you, but if anything happened to that lass, I—"

"I understand, Chief. I do my utmost to keep her safe. You know that, right?"

"Aye, that I do."

"But, man, you should have seen the way she defended herself. Krüger was twice her size and didn't know what hit him." Kaine smiled at the memory of Lara landing a series of lightning blows to the big, blond bastard. "She was magnificent."

"But without your intervention …" Mike didn't need to complete the statement.

Kaine shuddered, both at the idea of what might have happened if he hadn't reached Lara in time, and at how he'd lost control and nearly torn out Krüger's throat in front of her. During his retelling of the fight, Kaine left out the part where his loss of control led to the mistimed punch that aggravated the injury to his forearm. Some information was best left hidden.

"So," Mike said, drawing an end to the subject, "what now?"

"Now, Mike," Kaine answered, "if you don't mind, I'd like to discuss our options regarding Melanie Archer. Fancy a trip to the comms room?"

Mike rubbed his hands together. "Thought you'd never ask. I fired up the systems before you arrived. We'll probably still need our coats, though. It can get pretty chilly up there this time of year." He jumped to his feet. "C'mon lad, what's keeping you?"

———

THEY SPENT four straight hours locked inside the airconditioned room over the barn that contained a state-of-the-art comms system—equipment that would have been the envy of many of the UK's county police forces, had any of them known of its existence.

For most of the session, Corky joined them on a video link from … wherever he lived in the world.

As usual, Corky had delivered an in-depth masterpiece of intel-gathering and fact-checking—and had done it in rapid-quick time. The information armed Kaine with all the ammunition he needed to devise a number of potential plans of action.

Kaine ended the video call by tasking Corky with producing the required legend and supporting documentation for Plan B—just in case. Kaine stood, intending to catch up on some lost sleep, but Mike was having none of it.

"Complete bloody madness," he said. "Didn't want to say anything in front of Corky, but … for God's sake, son, you've spent the past eight months trying to keep yourself *out* of prison."

Kaine opened his hands in a shrug. "Like I said, Mike, it's only the backup plan. I'm keeping my options open, that's all. If Corky finds nothing to back up Melanie Archer's claims, we run with Plan A and call it quits."

"But if she's *not* delusional and someone *is* trying to kill her?"

"We resort to Plan B."

"Like I said. Pure bloody madness. Why take the risk?"

Kaine sighed. "She swears she didn't kill her husband. I need to look into her eyes when she tells me that. I need to be certain."

"Damn it, Ryan. How many prisoners claim they're innocent?"

"She's one of The 83," Kaine said as though it were explanation enough.

"Doesn't mean she's innocent. And it doesn't mean she's worth risking your freedom for."

"Yes, Mike," Kaine said with finality, "it does."

Mike shook his head again, this time sadly. "And what are you going to do if Melanie Archer *does* convince you she is innocent and in real danger?"

"No idea. We'll cross that bridge …" Kaine let the rest of the thought trail into silence.

Mike sighed and seemed to concede the point. He stood, grunted from the effort, and rested a hand on Kaine's shoulder. "Good luck, son."

"Thanks, but with Corky's documentation, it'll be a breeze."

Mike pursed his lips and sucked air between his teeth. "No, I meant good luck in the morning. Don't fancy your chances of convincing Lara that you know what you're doing."

Kaine winced.

"Ah, yes. About that. Thought I'd leave the little matter of prepping Lara to you," Kaine said, double-hitching his eyebrows. "Perhaps you can mention it during your morning ride? I'm sure I'll be able to find other ways to occupy my time until Corky gets back in touch."

"Dear God," Mike said, making a big show of shrinking in horror. "Fat chance, son. That's one conversation I want no part of." He turned and made his way to the door. "Tell you one thing though."

"What's that?"

"Never thought I'd live long enough to see Captain Ryan Kaine running scared of such a wee slip of a thing. The world's just tilted on its axis."

They locked the comms room, descended the creaky stairs to the floor of the barn, and returned to the house. The whole time, Kaine had to endure Mike's quiet clucking noises and his chicken-wing arm flapping.

He couldn't argue, though. In that particular instance, CPO Mike Procter happened to be absolutely spot on.

Chapter Ten

Thursday 15th April - Early Morning

Mike's Farm, Long Buckby, Northants, England

The following morning, after six straight hours of revitalising rest, Kaine left Lara asleep in bed and slipped out of the house for a five-mile run followed by thirty minutes of stretching and strengthening exercises, going easy on his weakened arm. He ended with a refreshing shower and entered the house to find Mike already in his favourite, comfy chair in front of the fire, his gnarled hands wrapped around a huge mug of black coffee.

"Morning, Mike. How's tricks?"

Mike looked up from studying the black stuff. Despite his age, the early hour, and his lack of a full night's sleep, his brown eyes were alive and sparkling. He raised the mug, which might well have stood in for a fire bucket, and used it to point Kaine towards the kitchen, where a stove large enough to cook a medieval banquet stood.

"Morning, Captain. Fresh coffee in the pot and teabags in the caddy. Help yourself. I'll start breakfast in a little while. I'm guessing Lara will be starving. She hardly ate a thing last night."

Kaine nodded his thanks and set to work, preparing a pot of tea for Lara and a far less viscous coffee for himself. He left her tea to mash and took a tentative sip—white, no sugar—to kickstart his day.

"Any messages?" he asked, stepping back into the lounge and walking closer to Mike so he didn't have to strain his neck.

Although lean and fit for a septuagenarian, Kaine had noticed a stiffness in Mike when he tried to turn quickly, not that he'd ever embarrass the old salt by asking after his health. Men of Mike's vintage were self-contained, hard-working, and tended to dial their upper-lip stiffness all the way up to eleven.

"Nothing yet," Mike answered after slurping his drink. "Give Corky time. He's got an awful lot to do. Some might say you've asked for the near impossible."

Kaine shook his head emphatically.

"You'd be surprised what Corky can manage, and how fast he can manage it."

Mike sniffed. "Didn't seem too pleased to hear from you. Surly little chap, if you ask me."

"That's just Corky's way. He comes across as self-important and cheeky, but he loves his work and has never let us down."

"Not so far." Mike sniffed again. "Never did trust a man

with a shaggy beard and long hair—present company excepted."

In the eight months since his old life had ended so dramatically and permanently, Kaine had let his cropped, military haircut grow out, and he currently sported a full, "shaggy" beard. Although he hated the new look, Lara approved, and it had become an important component of his ongoing life as a fugitive.

"As I said, Corky's a little eccentric, but he is solid. We wouldn't be able to operate half as effectively without his peculiar skillset."

"What about your other tech genius, the French lass?"

"Sabrina?"

"Yes, her. She seems to have dropped off the face of the earth recently."

"Last I heard, she was in the States, investigating one of her grandfather's subsidiaries."

"She's been off grid an awful long time. Any thoughts of finding out how she is?"

"I plan to contact her *Grand-père* Mo-Mo, soon as I have a spare moment."

"Her granddad's called Mo-Mo?"

"Her pet name for Maurice LeMaître. You may have heard of him," Kaine said, waiting for the penny to clatter to the flagstone floor.

"LeMaître?" Mike asked, tilting his head as though trying to force out a memory. "Maurice LeMaître, as in … the Chairman of ESAPP?"

Kaine tapped the side of his nose with an index finger. "Spot on, Mike. Sabrina is the future owner of European Small Arms and Personal Protection, A/S, the largest private arms manufacturer in France."

"Bloody hell. Why didn't you tell me that before?"

"You didn't ask before."

"*Touché.*"

"*Cède, mon ami.* Yield, my friend."

"Ruddy hell," Mike said, "she taught you French, and you're barely able to speak English. The lass must be really impressive."

Creaking on the staircase announced Lara's impending arrival.

"She is indeed," Kaine agreed, walking to the kitchen to pour the tea and returning to the lounge, cup in hand. "Highly impressive."

The door from the inner hallway opened and Lara entered, dressed for spending a day outdoors and smiling wide enough to brighten anyone's life.

"Who's highly impressive?" she asked, heading straight for Mike and kissing his bearded cheek before he could stand. "Do I have some competition?"

Kaine handed her cuppa across and said in all seriousness, "Not on this planet, Doc."

Mike said, "Oh dear," half under his breath, "she's broken Captain Ryan Kaine. Never thought I'd live to see the day."

"Pack it in, Mike," Kaine said and turned to Lara to add, "we were talking about Sabrina. She's been silent far too long."

After taking a delicate sip of her tea and nodding her thanks to Mike for its quality and to Kaine for its preparation, she said, "Yes, I'm getting worried about her. Maybe we should contact *Grand-père* Mo-Mo and find out—"

"Which is exactly what I was telling Mike before your appearance. When we've dealt with the Melanie Archer situation, fancy taking a detour through Paris on our way home? It would be nice to meet *Grand-père* Mo-Mo in the flesh. Paris in the late spring is supposed to be well worth a visit."

"Mike, did you hear that?" Lara asked.

"I did indeed. I'll be your witness, lass."

"Excellent," she said, "there's no backing out now, Captain Kaine."

"As if I'd do that. Man of honour, me. Famed for it the world over." Kaine drained his mug and raised it towards their host. "Mike?"

"No, thanks," he said, grunting as he levered himself out of his chair and onto his feet. "If I'm not mistaken, the prettiest woman this farm's seen since Ellie passed away didn't get up this early, or dress like that, just for a cup of top-class tea and a bowl of porridge. Am I right?"

Kaine had noticed Lara's gear, too. Warm sweater, tight jeans that could stand in for jodhpurs, and walking boots. Near perfect for an early morning ride on her—and Mike's —favourite horse, Dynamite.

"Sorry, but I'm not sure the ride's going to happen this morning, lass," Mike said, his bearded cheeks bulging from an apologetic smile. "I'll go check on the animals. Give you both time for breakfast and a … chat."

He winked at Kaine.

"Mike!" Kaine said, unable to disguise the warning in his voice.

Their host raised his hands in surrender. "Over to you, lad. I'm heading for cover."

He hurried past Lara, pausing only long enough to pat her arm and say, "Try talking some sense into him, lass." He nodded his support to Kaine and headed through the kitchen door and into the boot room.

"Ryan?" Lara said, approaching him with a frown. "What was that all about?"

Kaine grimaced and pointed to Lara's cup. "Better drink up. We have a lot to discuss."

"Ryan, you'd better tell me everything this time."

She sounded strangely calm.

Kaine led her to the kitchen and pulled out a dining chair for her. "Please, love. Take a seat."

Lara set her cup down on a coaster and lowered herself into the chair.

Chapter Eleven

Thursday 15th April – Lara Orchard

Mike's Farm, Long Buckby, Northants, England

Ordinarily, Ryan's overly serious, "Please, love. Take a seat," would have sent a tremor up and down Lara's spine, but she'd been waiting for it, and she'd arrived at the party forewarned and ready to dance.

Even so, her nerves jangled and her mouth dried.

Okay, Here goes.

"Before you launch into an explanation and a defence of your ridiculous Plan B," she announced, "let me tell you it's an, 'Oh no you bloody don't!' from me."

Ryan's confused frown was as adorable as it was anticipated.

"Sorry?" he asked, lowering his mug to the table next to her cup and sitting beside her.

Steady, Lara. You can do this.

"You are not, I repeat, not, blagging your way into Falston Manor posing as Melanie Archer's expensive, new solicitor. At least, not alone."

"You know?" He gasped.

"Of course I know. I called Corky and wheedled it out of him while you were out on your run."

"You did what!" He straightened in his chair and clenched his fists on the table.

She'd rarely seen Ryan angry at her, but this time he wasn't doing a good job of hiding it.

"You heard," she said, stiffening her resolve.

"Bloody hell, Lara," he said, finally locating his voice. "What have you done? And what do you mean by, 'At least not alone'?"

"If you're going into Falston Manor, I'm going in with you."

Ryan jumped to his feet, sending his chair crashing to the flagstone floor. "No, you bloody aren't!"

He leaned forwards and planted his palms on the table, breathing heavily through his nose, grinding his teeth. Anyone looking at the scene from a distance might have interpreted his posture as threatening. The same people might have feared for her safety.

Lara didn't. Ryan would give his life to protect her, as he would each member of The 83.

She paused for a moment before placing a hand on one of his, hoping to calm him. "Ryan, please. Listen to me for a minute, will you?"

"No, damn it! If I go—and it's still a bloody big 'if'—there's no way you're coming with me. And that's final."

"Please, Ryan." She spoke quietly, staring into his eyes. "Sit."

Ryan took a deep breath and nodded as though he'd reached a decision. He broke eye contact, but only long enough to right his chair, pull it towards the table, and drop onto the seat. He leaned forwards again. This time, he rested his forearms on the table, cupping his mug in both hands.

"Well?" he demanded.

"If Plan B proves necessary, your intention is to stroll right into prison and pretend to be her new solicitor, correct?"

Ryan's jaw tightened again. He hesitated before answering.

"Correct. Corky's setting up the full legend. He's also going to provide the paperwork and all the necessary identification."

"As usual."

Ryan nodded. "As usual." He lifted his mug, but thought better of drinking and lowered it to the table again. "But this is by no means a given. We still need to wait for his updated report."

"Let's make the assumption you're heading for prison, okay?"

"If you insist," he said through clenched teeth.

"I do."

"Okay," he said, meeting her gaze and holding it steady.

"You haven't thought this through."

He folded his arms and drilled his usually warm, brown eyes into hers. "Not fully, but I'm working on it. At the moment, it's only a backup strategy."

"What do we actually know about Melanie Archer? Have you considered her emotional state?"

"You know I try to consider everything," he snapped, then tilted his head a little as if in doubt. "What do you mean?"

"You read the statement she made when the police finally charged her?"

"I did. Of course I—"

"Including the part where she claims to have suffered decades of spousal abuse?"

"Yes, I read it. And your point?"

"If it is true and she *was* the victim of coercive control, how do you think those years of abuse might colour her reaction to a strange man turning up, claiming to be her saviour?"

Ryan's frown deepened, but he didn't respond.

Lara took her chance to drive the message home.

"If I'm there, alongside you … as your associate, don't you think it'll help ease her mind?"

"But she called the Trust. She begged for our help."

"I know that, but after all she's been through over the years, not to mention being charged with her abusive husband's murder … and the recent attack. She's currently being treated in the medical ward, remember. There's no telling what sort of state she's in, mentally or physically."

"No, Lara. You're not going. It's too dangerous."

Got you.

She tried not to allow any sort of reaction to show on her face.

"It's too dangerous for me, but not for you? Is that right?"

He reached his hand up to scrub his forehead, then raked his fingers through his mop of wavy hair. Ryan could see the strength of her argument. That much was obvious. Didn't mean he liked it, though.

"God's sake, Lara. Of course it's dangerous, but I can handle myself."

He was weakening. She had him.

"So can I, Ryan. Remember what happened in Walthamstow? I can take care of myself."

She hid a shudder.

Although essential, killing someone, even a man as evil as Byron "Barcode" Codell, went against everything she stood for as a medic. The memory of clubbing a man to death gave her constant nightmares. Nightmares she couldn't discuss with Ryan for fear of causing him more pain. If he knew how the guilt affected her, Ryan would do anything to make it right, including sending her away for her own safety. And she wasn't about to let that happen. Not a chance.

At some stage, she'd come to terms with her actions, but for the time being she'd have to live with the guilt.

"No, you can't, not fully. London was a bloody disaster, and you know it." Ryan reached up and touched her bruised cheek. "And look at what happened yesterday. If we do this, we'll both be walking into the high possibility of life behind bars. I can't take that risk."

Lara put her hand over his, still on her cheek, and leaned in. "In that case, neither of us should go. Let's just hire real solicitors. Let them do their jobs."

"But, if Melanie really is in danger—"

"Official channels will take too long. Yes, I know. A bail hearing would take weeks to arrange, and there's no guarantee it'll succeed. In the meantime Melanie might be …" She let the thought hang in the air for a moment before moving on to the second phase of her prepped argument. "There's another thing. Melanie's brother died on Flight BE1555, which is the reason we're here, right?"

Ryan pulled his hand away from hers and dipped his head, and Lara winced at his obvious pain but carried on.

"As far as Melanie's concerned, you murdered her brother in cold blood. She might recognise you."

"But I'll be in disguise. It's not the first time I've appeared in public."

"Ryan, your mugshot will be burned into Melanie's psyche. A beard and coloured contact lenses might not be good enough this time. What happens if she *does* recognise you? You'll be *in prison* for God's sake. You'll have walked yourself right into a set of handcuffs—or worse."

She paused, waiting for her point to hit its target.

"So? What's the alternative?"

"Let me go in with you. Act as your assistant. Let me be the first one she sees. I'll be able to get close, gain her trust. It'll also give me a chance to assess her injuries. No telling what sort of medical treatment she's receiving inside prison."

She waited for the explosion. It didn't arrive.

He stared at her—no, through her—for what felt like minutes. "We need to think this through," he said.

"Yes, we do," she said, trying to keep the triumph from her voice.

"If we have to go down this route," he added, quietly and almost as though talking to himself, thinking aloud, "we'll have to give Corky enough time to research the prison population, both the guards and the inmates."

"Yes." She nodded, although Ryan was lost in his thoughts and not looking at her.

"Hell, I've just bloody realised …" His eyes came into focus and he stared hard at her. "Loads of military personnel end up in jail when they leave the service—either as inmates or prison officers. There's no telling who I might have bumped into in the past. Can't take the risk of anyone else recognising me."

"If Corky turns up anyone in Falston Manor with links to you, we scrub the operation. Agreed?"

"Yes. Agreed." He nodded and paused for another moment's thought. "And if we do have to set foot inside Falston Manor, you do exactly as I say without hesitation. Agreed?"

She raised her head. "Agreed. One hundred percent."

Ryan took hold of her hand and held it tight. "And if I am exposed and taken, you have to disown me. As far as you're concerned, we're work colleagues who've only known each other a few weeks. You have no knowledge of my true identity. Understand?"

"Yes, Ryan. Okay. But you must agree to something else, too."

"Go on."

"If you're arrested, we release the proof of your innocence immediately. We make sure Corky floods all the news outlets and social media platforms with the video of your torture and Sir Malcolm Sampson's confession. Even if it means you have to hand back most of the Trust's money. Deal?"

He squeezed her hand and breathed deeply. "Deal."

"No going back on it?"

"Nope. In any event, if Corky's current research comes up blank, this whole conversation is moot."

"Exactly."

Ryan released his grip and stood, this time more slowly. This time, his chair scraped on the flagstone, but remained upright. She stood and moved alongside him.

"Where are you going?"

Ryan turned towards the back door. "The comms room.

I need to contact Corky and give him the news. He needs to start building you into the new legend."

Lara smiled and dragged Ryan into a hug.

"Not necessary," she said, speaking into the side of his neck, "he already is."

Ryan pushed her away and held her at arm's length.

"He's what?"

"When I spoke to Corky this morning I asked him to factor me into your ridiculous Plan B. Right now, he's hard at it, legend-building the only way he knows how. By the way, you're going to be a condescending snob who speaks down to everybody, which will come naturally to you, obviously."

He relaxed his grip and she slid in close again.

"That's a bit harsh."

"Just kidding, darling. Laurence Pratt is nothing like you."

"Laurence Pratt? Corky's making me a Pratt?"

"Fitting, don't you think?"

Ryan sighed heavily. "And who'll you be?"

She smiled.

"Me? Oh, I'm Ms Emma Braithwaite, your plucky and hard-working associate."

He shook his head slowly. "You've just played me, haven't you. Wrapped me around your little finger."

"Pleased to make your acquaintance, Mr Pratt," she said, and kissed him on the cheek.

"Don't try soft-soaping me, Lara. Our arrangement still stands. If the crap hits the fan during the operation, I'm in charge. I make the decisions."

"Yes, Mr Pratt." She kissed his cheek again. "Certainly, Mr Pratt." She kissed his other cheek. "Anything you say, Mr Pratt."

Finally, she kissed him full on the mouth. He responded appropriately and wonderfully, and she moulded herself into his firm body. After an age, he broke their hold and eased her away again.

"That's more than enough smooching for one day, Ms Braithwaite. Run along now, there's filing to be done. Letters to type. Teas to make."

Although he smiled through the light-hearted delivery, his eyes betrayed deep concern.

"Ryan," she said, cupping his cheek in her hand, "we'll be fine. Hopefully, Corky won't find anything to worry about, and we won't be going anywhere near Falston Manor."

"Yes, and I'll be the one to make that decision, not you."

The steel in his brown eyes confirmed he wasn't best pleased to have lost that round, and it certainly wasn't the time for round two. She dropped her hand and followed him to the comms room.

To reduce all risk to a minimum, a great deal of work lay ahead. Absorbing new legends and new identities would take time and effort. They couldn't leave anything to chance. Ryan's freedom—his life—depended upon it.

In that moment, the idea of stepping behind the high, stone walls of Falston Manor became ever so real and ever so scary.

Lara hoped to God she wouldn't let him down.

Chapter Twelve

Thursday 15th April - Afternoon

Mike's Farm, Long Buckby, Northants, England

"Okay, okay. Hold on. I'm coming!"

Kaine opened the front door to stop the hammering from echoing through the house and waking the world. A tall, well-built man, with piercing blue eyes and wavy, blond hair in need of a heavy shearing, smiled wide.

"Afternoon, Captain," he said, before leaning to one side and looking past Kaine and into the gloom of the hallway. "I expected Mike. Which is why I knocked so loud. His hearing isn't what it used to be, y'know?"

"Easy, Danny. He'd have your hide for that."

Danny grinned. "Kidding, boss. The chief's a diamond."

Kaine stood aside to allow Danny room to enter.

The youngster picked up the heavy backpack he'd dropped at his feet and stepped over the threshold. Kaine closed the door behind him, blocking out the howling gale that had blown up since Lara and Mike had left for their ride.

He led the way through to the kitchen, where he'd set up the makings for coffee. Danny took his with milk, and rarely refused a biscuit of any description, although he preferred them coated in thick, dark chocolate.

They faced each other for a moment, before Kaine nodded and pushed out his right hand. Danny grabbed it, added a forearm brace, and they shook.

"That's a nasty shiner," Kaine said, taking in the bruise to Danny's left cheek, which closely matched the one on Lara's right. "It didn't show up on our last video call."

Danny shrugged.

"Draycott got a lucky punch in," he said, embarrassment colouring his face and his words. "But only the one. What about you, Captain? Fully recovered from your argument with that car?"

"Pretty much" Kaine answered, automatically flexing and rotating his left wrist, which still ached, but not too badly.

Danny nodded. "Good, good."

"How's the shoulder?"

"Where you shot me, you mean?" Danny asked, grimacing in apparent distress when he rolled the offending joint.

Kaine growled and flicked his hand in front of Danny's face. "Bloody hell, Danny. How many times do I have to apologise for saving your worthless hide!"

Danny's answering grin lifted Kaine's mood. "Kidding,

Captain. I'm as right as rain, see?" He thumped the top of his left shoulder and rotated his arm in the action of a fast bowler delivering a bouncer. He let the arm fall back to his side and, after receiving permission, helped himself to a coffee.

He took a delicate sip and smacked his lips. "That hits the spot. Mike always did stock a decent blend."

Kaine poured himself a fresh mug. "Thanks for dropping everything."

Again, Danny shrugged. "You called, I came."

"I'd have asked Cough or Stefan to stand in, but …" Kaine tilted his head and winced, "they don't have your skillset."

"Really, boss?"

"We'll get on to that later."

"Can't wait, boss."

"How's Angela?"

"Much better. She's throwing herself into the new project. It's doing her the world of good to be taking the cash we 'liberated' from Campese and redistributing it to his ripped-off clients. She says it's making her feel really alive and useful."

"Excellent," he said. "And Bobbie?"

"Bobbie's … great, boss," Danny answered, his face reddening ever so slightly. He lowered his head to take another sip, this one longer and with more of a slurp.

"We'll have to discuss Angela and Bobbie's ongoing security coverage at some stage," Kaine said. "Since we left the area, Corky's been monitoring the situation on the south coast. Things are looking … promising."

Kaine lowered his eyes and nodded to his drink.

Danny had been with Kaine when he'd killed Pony Tedesco, the animal who'd assaulted Angela Shafer as a prelude to killing her—on the instructions of his elder brother, Teddy.

Neither man would hurt anyone ever again.

Since he'd become a fugitive, Kaine had discovered one significant and positive side-effect. He could act outside the law with relative impunity. When he'd killed Pony Tedesco, he'd purged the world of a monster and saved the UK taxpayer the cost of a long and expensive trial. The same turned out to be true of Teddy Tedesco. Although Kaine hadn't ended Teddy's life personally, handing him over to a long-time enemy had produced the same result. In the eyes of the law, Kaine may have been guilty of arranging Teddy Tedesco's murder, but he'd been morally justified, and no one he respected would think differently. In that single respect, his conscience was crystal clear.

"Yes, boss," Danny said. "Looks like the Tedesco mob's a done deal."

"But the Shafer situation can wait until we've dealt with the current mission. Cough and Stefan are happy to cover for you in the meantime."

"Yes, boss, and thanks. I wouldn't want to remove their protection without warning and without easing them into it first. Angela won't mind Cough looking after her, though. They get on well."

"They do?"

"Yes, boss. Really well. And Stefan's much easier to cope with since Cough's domesticated him," Danny said, adding a cheery smile. "Changing the subject, boss. Is the doc about? Haven't seen her since Southampton."

"She's with Mike. They're out there somewhere"—he pointed to the rolling landscape visible through the kitchen window—"riding a couple of Mike's nags through all those muddy fields. No idea what they get out of it. They swear blind it's a fun thing to do."

"I hear you, boss. Give me a motorbike over a horse any day of the week." Danny shook his head. "But I wouldn't let the doc or Mike hear you call his pedigree horseflesh 'nags'. And if you do, give me plenty of warning first."

"To give you time to leave the room?" Kaine asked. He pulled a chair out from under the kitchen table and eased himself onto it.

"No, Captain," Danny answered, taking the chair opposite and resting his elbows on the table top, coffee mug clamped between his big mitts. "To give me time to grab my phone and open the camera app. That conversation should be recorded for posterity. I mean, the world is convinced that Ryan Kaine is one tough son-of-a ... well, you know. If they saw how hen-pecked you were they'd—"

"Hen-pecked? *Moi?*"

Kaine smiled. He'd missed Danny, whose positive attitude and quick wit rarely failed to improve his mood. The fact that Danny "call me Pinkie and die" Pinkerton was one of the toughest and most skilful marines he'd ever commanded was a significant bonus. Also, Danny was as good with radio comms and military ordnance as he was with his fists. A real asset to a man in Kaine's current line of work.

"Yes, boss," Danny said, grinning. "You, boss." He took another deep sip.

"I'm going to let your rank insubordination pass for the moment, Sergeant," Kaine said, "but only because you're a volunteer. Don't let it happen again."

They sat for a few moments, enjoying their coffees and listening to the wind bludgeoning the farmhouse's stone walls.

Eventually, Danny broke the extended silence.

"So, Captain," he said after finishing his drink and pushing the empty mug forwards to accept a refill. "Why am I here? Another contact via the website?"

"That's right. Have you been following the Melanie Archer case?"

"Melanie Archer?" Danny rolled his eyes up to the left and scratched the side of his neck. "Melanie Archer. Sounds familiar. Oh yes. She's the woman arrested for killing her invalid husband."

"Correct," Kaine said, refilling Danny's drink and topping up his own.

Danny retrieved his mug, but held it on the table, rolling it between his hands as if to warm his fingers. "Claims she didn't kill him, but doesn't have a decent alibi. Does she qualify for our help? I mean, she's definitely a member of The 83?" He sniffed and curled his upper lip as though he'd just inhaled a bad smell.

Kaine nodded. "Her brother, Brendan Bowman, was a passenger on the plane. Melanie Archer's his only living relative."

Danny's face creased into a grim smile. "That's ironic."

"What is?"

"Well, for a Bowman to marry an Archer. Think of hyphenating that to Melanie Bowman-Archer. They'd have to call their son Fletcher."

"Be serious, Danny. This isn't funny."

"I know it isn't, boss," Danny snapped. "The woman killed her crippled husband, for Christ's sake. Although she claimed the man had been abusive, she couldn't show anyone any proof. What was that phrase her solicitor bandied about? Oh yeah, 'coercive control'. I mean, I ask you … 'coercive control', for fuck's sake. How many murderers are going to climb on that bandwagon? From what I read, Archer claimed her old man had abused her for years. Used to beat her until the illness made him too weak. The bloody woman stayed with him for nearly twenty-five years, though. If he was that bad, why didn't she bugger off? Why not leave?"

Kaine tried to keep the surprise from showing on his face. He'd never seen Danny so ... dismissive and uncompromising. Melanie Archer's case had definitely hit a nerve.

"Isn't that what they say of all spouses who've suffered abuse?" he asked.

Danny blew out his cheeks and took a long drink before answering. "Yes, you're right. I'm sorry. Afraid I'm a little ... biased when it comes to claims of domestic abuse."

"Really? You could have fooled me."

Kaine didn't often resort to sarcasm, but in this instance it seemed justified.

"Sorry, Captain," Danny repeated and downed another slug of coffee.

"Care to tell me about it?"

Danny nodded, but took another sip before opening up.

"During an acrimonious divorce, my Aunt Trina accused my Uncle Howard of physical abuse. Took him to the cleaners as a result. The conniving bitch lied through her teeth. Uncle Howard was one of the nicest, sweetest men you could ever meet. A real gentleman, you know? The episode broke him. He ended up swallowing a bottle of sleeping pills."

"He died?"

Danny shook his head. "Survived, but suffered a major stroke. Sometimes, I think it would have been better if he'd ..." He coughed and straightened in his chair. "Sorry,

Captain. Still a little raw, you know? I visit Uncle Howard as often as I can. Sometimes, I even think he recognises me."

"Anything we can do for him?"

Danny coughed again and rubbed his eyes. "Not a thing, Captain. Not a single thing. I'm covering all his expenses. Anyway, back to Mrs Archer. Does she really deserve our help?"

"Not sure yet," Kaine said, truthfully. "Waiting to hear back from Corky."

Kaine didn't want to elaborate. One serious review of the validity of his decision-making process was quite enough for one day.

Danny raised his mug again. Before taking a drink, he asked, "What's she after? Money for a more expensive defence team?"

Kaine shook his head. "She's not asking for money."

"What then?"

Kaine pulled his mobile from his pocket and found the original call-to-action message.

"Here, read this."

He handed the phone to Danny, who picked it up and scrolled through an email that Kaine had read often enough to commit to memory.

My name is Melanie Archer. Brendan Bowman was my brother. I'm innocent. I did not murder my husband, James Archer. I swear to Almighty God. I'm currently in prison, Falston Manor. Someone is trying to kill me. Please, please help.

Danny scrolled to the top of the message and reread it.

"Interesting," he said, his response noncommittal.

"That's what I thought. Any initial reaction?"

"Doesn't tell us much. Gives rise to a couple of questions, though."

"Such as?"

"How are we going to confirm her story, and what can we do about it anyway? I imagine you're considering a trip to Falston Manor?"

Kaine stiffened. Did someone else know more about his plans than they should?

"You've spoken to Lara and Mike?"

Danny shook his head. "Nope. Just making an assumption. I know what you're like, boss."

"It's only an option at the moment. Corky's working on a legend to give me and the doc access."

"For fuck's—you're not serious?"

"About what?"

"Taking the doc with you."

"I don't want to, but … she had some very good operational input."

"You *are* serious."

Kaine nodded. "Deadly."

"What do you hope to achieve?"

"I simply want to ask her a few questions … and see the look in her eyes while she answers."

"And you can't do that via video link, I suppose?"

"No, Danny," Kaine answered, shaking his head. "I can't."

Danny took a deep breath and released it in a sigh.

"So," he said, "we're all going to jail?"

Kaine pulled his lips into a tight wince. "Depending on what Corky comes up with, yes. Probably."

"Oh dear, oh Lord," Danny said quietly. His shoulders slumped and he looked as serious as Kaine had ever seen him.

"You don't have to be a part of it, Danny. This is a purely voluntary operation. They all are."

Danny didn't hesitate to say, "I know that, boss, and of course I'm in. You know you can count on me."

"Thanks, Sergeant."

Kaine's relief was genuine. Danny had a special role in Plan C. A plan that neither Lara nor Mike knew anything about. At least, not yet.

"But I've just thought of a third question," Danny said. "One you're not going to like."

"Fire away."

"Assuming you and the doc do interview Mrs Archer and you do get away with it, what happens if you believe her? What the hell do we do then?"

He gave Danny the same response he'd given Mike overnight. "We'll cross that bridge—"

"Bloody hell, Captain. You're not planning a prison break?"

And there he had it. Danny had the innate knack of finding and asking the relevant questions, which was precisely the reason Kaine had called on him instead of the much more sanguine Rollo. The only questions Rollo probably would have asked were, "When are we going and what equipment do we need?"

Kaine paused before replying. Could he really imagine throwing a grappling hook over a prison wall and scaling a knotted rope? And if he did free Melanie Archer, she'd spend the rest of her life looking over her shoulder, waiting for the tug.

Knowing what the life of a fugitive entailed, could he force that upon someone else?

"Danny," Kaine said, "to be completely honest, I have absolutely no idea."

Chapter Thirteen

Thursday 15th April - Afternoon

Mike's Farm, Long Buckby, Northants, England

Slow hoofbeats announced the return of the intrepid riders. At the same time, Kaine's mobile vibrated on the table where Danny had left it. He glanced at the screen—a text message.

Danny jumped to his feet, but Kaine took the time to read the four-word text.

Call me. One hour.

He deleted the message and followed Danny through the back door, out into the courtyard, and on towards the fenced paddock.

"Danny!" Lara called, showing her delight with a bright and welcoming smile. She sat astride the huge, black, heavily muscled Dynamite, a thoroughbred creature who'd won a number of serious steeplechases before being put out to grass under Mike's loving care.

The animal radiated power and speed, and steamed gently from its morning exertions. Kaine could have done without the earthy smell emanating from the creatures, but chose not to mention it. No point upsetting the horse lovers for no valid reason. Once, after she'd returned from an extended ride, he made the mistake of asking Lara for directions to the nearest glue factory. His heartless joke fell on angry and upset ears. He would never make the same blunder again.

The colour in Lara's cheeks added to her healthy tan, masking the bruising, and the sparkle in her eyes came from the pure joy she found in riding. The Good Lord may have known why riding horses delighted her, but Kaine certainly didn't.

At her side, Mike rode a chestnut mare only a fraction smaller than Dynamite. Whereas Lara slid from her saddle with a litheness and grace Kaine could only watch with admiration, Mike took his time. He climbed down from the saddle as though every joint in his body ached which, given his age, they probably did. Kaine had no difficulty remembering how much discomfort his first and, so far, only riding lesson had generated. He gave Mike his full sympathy.

While Kaine and Danny—a young man with the same affection for, and knowledge of, horses as Kaine—kept their distance from the powerful beasts, Lara tethered Dynamite and hurried towards them. She gave Danny an extended hug, which he returned.

"Bloody hell, Doc," Danny said, looking at the bruise decorating Lara's cheek. "What happened to your face?"

"The same thing that happened to yours, I imagine. Someone hit me," she said, after breaking her hold on Danny and stepping alongside Kaine.

Danny caught Kaine's eye.

"The South African?" he asked.

"The South African," Kaine said. He frowned and shook his head—gestures that told Danny, "We'll discuss it later."

"Draycott?" Lara suggested.

"He got lucky," Danny answered. "But only the once."

Kaine tutted at Danny's repeated joke. He'd clearly practiced the line and didn't mind the way it sounded.

"How's Bobbie?" Lara asked, skipping on.

"Totally awesome, thanks. Sends you both her love."

Lara removed her leather riding gloves and took Kaine's hand in hers. Her hand was warm from the exercise, much warmer than his.

"And Angela? How is she?"

She squeezed Kaine's hand tighter, probably trying to offer comfort for opening old wounds. Kaine still felt guilt over Angela Shafer's ordeal. If they'd reached Angela's cottage thirty minutes earlier, they'd have prevented the assault. The fact they'd arrived in time to save her life alleviated some of his sense of culpability, but not all.

"Angela's in fine form," Danny answered, glancing at Kaine before concentrating on Lara. "In fact, she's started dating again, which Bobbie and I are delighted about. Shows a good recovery, right?"

Lara dipped her head in agreement.

"Dating?" Kaine said. "You didn't tell me she and Cough were dating."

"Didn't I?" Danny asked, eyes wide in innocence.

"I'll phone her as soon as I have a free moment," Lara said, squeezing Kaine's hand again.

"You knew?" Kaine asked her.

"Only that she liked him," she said. "Not that they'd actually gone out together."

"Last weekend," Danny piped up, nodding, "before the attack on Bobbie's friend. They seemed to enjoy themselves, too. And Angela didn't seem at all put out when I told her Cough was taking over minding duties from me for a while."

"I'm happy for her. Cough's a lovely man."

"You and Angela keep in touch?" Kaine asked.

"Of course. I'm not just her medic. We're friends. Mike?" she called to their host, who was walking the horses from the paddock to the stables. "Can I help?"

"No need, lass. But thank you."

Lara glanced at Kaine and spoke quietly. "Even if he doesn't want my help, he's going to get it. I don't spend enough time with horses these days. Grooming them is half the joy, you know?"

He didn't, but nodded anyway.

"And Mike needs all the help he can get, right?" Kaine asked, fully appreciating Lara's thoughtfulness.

"Did you hear from Corky yet?"

"Yep. He texted as you arrived. Wants me to video call him in a while, but I can hold off until you're finished brushing the nags."

She punched his arm, playfully.

"Don't you dare call Dynamite a nag. He's better looking than you are. Not nearly as many scars."

"Ouch, that'll bruise," Kaine said, rubbing the area. "Grounds for divorce, I call that. And I've got witnesses."

He pointed to Danny, who stared into the swelling clouds.

"Don't bring me into this. I saw nothing."

Lara tipped her head back and crossed her arms. "You can't demand a divorce. We're not married!"

Kaine smiled. "Take a look at the names on our latest passports, Mrs Cowdrey. As far as the UK Border Force is concerned, you and I have been hitched for fourteen years."

"Call Dynamite and Clancy's Girl nags once more and this wife will be searching for directions to the nearest funeral parlour."

Kaine tugged his forelock. "Sorry, Mrs Cowdrey. It'll never happen again. How long are you likely to be?"

"Can you give me forty minutes?"

"It takes that long to brush down a horse?"

"I'll need a shower and a change of clothes as well," she called over her shoulder while heading for the stable.

"I'll expect you in thirty."

"Expect away, Mr Cowdrey," she said and ducked through the stable half-door.

Danny finished investigating the cloud formations and glanced at Kaine. "You two get along really well, boss. If you don't mind me saying."

"No, Sergeant. I don't mind you saying that at all."

"Planning any wedding bells in the foreseeable future?"

Kaine and Danny locked eyes for a moment before he answered. "Danny, I'd love nothing more than to ask her, but ..."

"Under different circumstances?"

"Something like that. Did you bring any other bags with you besides the backpack?"

"No, boss. I'm traveling light. I imagine you and Mike

have the equipment we'll need for whatever your planning?"

"Probably. C'mon, let's get you billeted before we chat to the helpful, little, internet gnome. Mike's given you Rollo's old room."

Kaine led the way through the kitchen to the foot of the staircase, giving Danny time to collect his pack.

"Any news from the quartermaster, boss? Will he be joining us?"

"Hope not. We'll only need him in a real emergency. You've not spoken to him for a while?"

Danny heaved the heavy backpack onto his shoulder and shook his head. "Only once since he returned from his honeymoon. The newlyweds seem to have enjoyed their time in New Caledonia," he said, ending with a double-hitch to his eyebrows.

"A sub-tropical island in the southwest Pacific? What's not to enjoy? And wipe that smirk from your face, Sergeant. Rollo deserves all the happiness he can find."

"Right you are, boss. Won't find any argument from me on that score."

Danny all but saluted, but since neither were in uniform or in official military service, it would have been inappropriate.

"Top floor, third door on the left," Kaine said, pointing Danny up the staircase. "Unpack and get yourself settled. Meet us in the comms room over the barn in thirty."

Kaine headed back to the kitchen. Lara and Mike would probably appreciate a fresh brew after their workout, and he'd almost never pass up the opportunity for refreshments ahead of any operation.

———

"HULLO THERE, Mr K. How you diddling? Who's that with you in the background. Ah, Danny-boy, and ... hey, Doc. How's tricks?"

Corky's expression crossed the spectrum between a cheeky grin and a smirk. Although the man's talents as a hacker could justifiably be described as world class, his social and grammatical skills most certainly could not. At least he'd recently changed his style from gaudy, Hawaiian monstrosities and this time sported a modest, dark blue T-shirt. He'd even trimmed his beard and combed his hair during the night.

"Really good, thanks, Corky," Lara said. "I have to say, you're looking rather dapper. Another date?"

Corky coughed and lowered his head, but not in time to hide the crimson blush that darkened his plump cheeks.

"Er ... well, yeah. As a matter of fact—"

"Nice one, Corky, but what did you learn?" Kaine asked, to cover the younger man's discomfort as much as to move things along. "Does Mrs Archer need our help?"

Immediately Corky brightened up at the chance to show off his genius, as Kaine knew he would. Kaine and Lara's ongoing freedom and security owed a great deal to Corky's skills and support, and if it took a little flattery on Kaine's part, it wasn't too arduous a task.

"Yeah, Mr K," Corky said, shifting his gaze from Lara to Kaine. "'Fraid she might. There's something not quite right going on at Falston Manor. Something off."

Kaine sat up a little straighter.

"Care to explain yourself?"

"Ain't nothing obvious, but suspicious just the same. It seems that before they sent Mrs A down on remand, there weren't one single report of serious violence amongst the inmates for the previous twelve months. At least none that led to an inmate's 'ospitalisation. Not a one. Then, two weeks after she arrives, Mrs A is beaten near to death in a shower block. That seemed fishy to ol' Corky, so he decided to do some checking."

"And what did you come up with?" Danny asked, speaking for the first time since Corky opened the connection.

"Whatcha, Danny-boy. How's it hanging with you and Bobbie?"

"Let's keep on point," Kaine said before they disappeared down another rabbit warren. "You and Danny can catch up later."

Corky's bushy eyebrows meshed together, forming a frown beneath the floppy hairline, but he returned his focus to Kaine.

"Yeah, you is right, Mr K. Now, judging from their records, HMP Falston Manor is about the safest prison in the UK. On average, it reports sixty-eight percent fewer violent incidents than any other Category A prison in the country. Seventy-seven percent fewer if you factor in incidents from women's prisons alone."

"And what do you read into that?" Lara asked.

Corky leaned away from the camera and smiled. "Couple of things, Doc. First up, it seems strange that Mrs A were the only prisoner hospitalised as a result of a beating this year, especially strange since she's a first-timer."

"Why strange?" Lara asked when Corky paused in apparent need of a prompt.

She'd talked to the little man often enough to learn how he operated, and could be a savant when it came to reading non-verbal cues.

"That's simple, Doc. If Mrs A were a repeat offender, she could easily have made enemies on the inside, but she's squeaky clean. In fact, since she were banged up for murdering her old man, she should've generated some sort of hero worship with the other inmates. There's a pecking order in the nick, you know?"

Danny nodded. "Yes, I've seen the documentaries. Prison populations operate a hierarchical structure, with sex offenders and dirty cops at the bottom of the pile and murderers at the top. Mrs Archer should have generated respect, if not real fear."

"That weren't the case for Mrs Archer," Corky added.

"Why not?" Danny asked.

"Good question," Kaine said.

"Obvious answer," Lara added. "She's been deliberately targeted. Exactly when was Melanie attacked?"

"Early Tuesday morning."

"And she's still in the prison hospital?" Lara asked, a mixture of surprise and concern in her expression.

"Far as Corky can tell," he said, curling his upper lip.

"No chance of giving the doc a gander at the medical records, I suppose?" Kaine asked.

The upper lip curled even more and turned into a full-blown sneer.

"Not a chance, Mr K. Corky's good, but he ain't your actual miracle worker. Looks like Falston Manor don't have their medical records online yet. Far as Corky knows, they're still using paper and pen. Bloody prehistoric, you ask ol' Corky."

"So," Kaine said, after a quick glance at Lara, "if we want to find out how Mrs Archer really is, we'll have to go and ask her in person, right?"

"Corky's way ahead of you, Mr K."

"Good," Kaine said, "I rather thought you might be."

He slid another glance at Lara and accepted her acknowledgment. She'd already worked out the ramifications of Corky's investigations and, judging by Danny's reaction, he'd done the same.

Plan B had just transformed into Plan A.

Chapter Fourteen

Monday 19th April - Melanie Archer

**Health Care Centre, HMP Falston Manor,
Derbyshire, England**

Five days.

Five whole days and nothing.

No one from the Trust had contacted her through Wendy or Shirl, not even to tell her to, "Sod off, The 83 Trust doesn't waste its limited resources on suspected murderers!"

Nothing.

Why was she surprised?

As expected, the whole Trust thing was either a nasty joke invented by a sick mind to drive the victims' families over the edge, or a con to dupe the bank details out of some poor, unsuspecting, and grieving marks. Neither of which should have upset or surprised Mel. Her whole adult life had been one nasty con perpetrated on her by a man with the sickest of minds and supported by a world that didn't give a hoot.

Well, it wouldn't work on her. If life with *him* had taught her anything, it was self-reliance. The only person she could believe in and rely on was Melanie Archer. No one else. Not since Brendan …

No, she wouldn't give up her hidden bank details to anyone, not the so-called 83 Trust and most definitely not the police. She'd keep that piece of information hidden. Mel had grown highly skilled at keeping secrets. Secrets from *him* and secrets from the world. Without her ability to suppress information, she'd have lost her mind long, long ago.

Mel wouldn't let the con artists drive her any closer to the edge of insanity. *He* had driven her close enough to that particular precipice many times, but she hadn't succumbed.

No way, thank you very much.

She'd surprised herself by falling for the ruse in the first place. The 83 Trust! Bloody thing probably didn't even exist. Why had she bothered? Seemed like a good idea at the time. And she didn't exactly have a whole lot to lose.

Despite her initial reservations, she'd accepted Wendy's deal and things had progressed much more quickly than she'd expected.

From her sickbed, Wendy begged the willing Athena to sanction a special needs visit from her "bestie". Shirl had arrived within a couple of hours, armed with a delivery of magazines and a paper and pen for Mel to write a note for the Trust. Without having too much thinking time, she'd scribbled something short and to the point, and Shirl had promised to send it right away.

The following day, Dr Milliner removed Wendy's chemo drip, checked her vitals, and returned her to D Wing.

Since then, nothing.

Relative silence.

Mel lay in her bed, utterly alone in the solitude and silence of an empty ward. Relief of sorts, but the quiet allowed her thoughts to roam free. Fear returned. The terror of knowing, really knowing, she had nothing and no one to rely on for support. No one in the world.

The prospect of endless years of incarceration stretched out before her. Haunted her waking hours and filled her sleep with night terrors.

Everyone considered her a murderer.

Everyone.

Maybe she *should* have killed the monster years ago, when the abuse first started. But no, she hadn't learned the full truth about *him* until it was too late and she'd already been cowed by the mental and physical torture. A wasted life, where she'd learned to believe *his* lies. Eventually, after years of the constant drip-drip of *his* vile poison, she actually started to believe that everything was her fault. If she'd been a better wife, *he* wouldn't have had to punish her. If she'd given *him* children, their marriage would have been complete. Somehow, she even believed *him* when *he* said she was responsible for losing little Bella, even though *his* blows to her tummy had caused the miscarriage. At least little Bella was safe. She'd never have to suffer *his* abuse.

The main door burst open and Athena bustled in, full of energy, face cracked into a brighter-than-usual smile.

"Morning, Melanie," she said, breathing hard. "How are you this fine day?"

"Not too … good," she said, remembering Wendy's advice. She'd only just managed to change her initial response from, "Not too bad, thanks."

"Still fighting that headache?" Athena asked, her smile changing into an empathetic frown.

Mel winced when she nodded, putting on a show, but not overdoing it. In truth, her migraine had fully faded by the end of the second day, along with her blurred vision. By Friday morning, she'd been able to see perfectly well again through her one good eye, not that she had anything worth looking at. Not that she'd admitted it to anyone, either. She'd even kept it from Wendy. Didn't feel guilty about that, though. No telling who was on her side. In short, she couldn't trust anyone. Not Wendy, not Shirl, not The 83 Trust.

Paranoia.

Another legacy of her life with *him*. The evil swine.

Athena pushed a trolley close to Mel's bed and took an optician's light from the locked drawer. She shone the white beam in Mel's eye and made her follow it without moving her head.

"Looks normal to me," she announced, her breath smelling of peppermints. "Good vascularisation. I mean, no problem with the blood vessels. Time to remove that bandage. You ready?"

She placed the optician's scope on the tray.

"I thought Dr Milliner was going to be here for that?"

In the middle of snapping on a pair of surgical gloves, Athena let loose her bellow of a laugh. "Lord above. Hattie doesn't come in on Mondays. Not unless it's an emergency. Likes her long weekends, does our Hattie. Now, let's see what it's like under there, shall we?"

As the jolly nurse unwound the wrapping, the butterflies

—which had been churning around pretty much continually since her arrest—started kicking up a storm in Mel's tummy. What sort of Frankenstein's monster did she look like beneath all the wadding? As *he* kept drumming into her, without her looks, she had nothing. And, as *he* never ceased to remind her, looks faded over time.

Damn his *rotting, black heart.*

As she removed the bandages, Athena chatted away, and Mel's head grew lighter and cooler. The eternal darkness behind her right eyelid brightened. Not blind. She wasn't blind! She'd be able to see! But what horrors would she discover in the mirror.

Athena unwound another turn of crepe, keeping her expression neutral. "Keep still now while I take off this last, little strip. The eye pad will be sticking to the wound. I'll need to soak it in sterilised water. If I tug it off dry, it'll likely tear out those neat stitches." She took Mel's good hand and gently pressed the fingertips against the eyepatch. "Hold that for a moment."

Athena stood back and tilted her head to one side, taking a good look. Again, her expression gave nothing away.

"Heavy bruising and a little more swelling than I expected, but I've seen a lot worse. You'll mend and that cut won't leave too much of a scar. No apparent nerve damage, either. A little makeup and you'll be good as new."

Mel tried to believe her, but had little success. She released a stuttering sigh. Tears blurred her good eye and squeezed between the closed lids of the damaged one.

"Hang tough, girl. It really ain't that bad. Trust me on this."

Athena handed her a tissue from a box on the trolley, and Mel blew her nose gently.

Even without the restrictive bandage, the right side of her face felt heavy and swollen. The pulse throbbed through the wound and the area surrounding it tingled so much she desperately wanted to scratch the devil out of it.

Athena set to work dabbing the eyepatch with the sodden swab. It took six cotton-wool balls and a great deal of gentle tugging to free the eyepatch completely.

"Keep your eye closed while I reduce the light in here. Don't want to damage your retina, or worsen that ... headache of yours." Athena all but placed air quotes around the word "headache" and probably would have done if her hands had been empty.

At the window, Athena tugged on a string to close the blinds and returned to the bed.

"Okay, open up. Let's take a look."

Light and shade.

She *could* see!

Mel endured more peppermint breath and followed the slices of light from the scope once again. Eventually, Athena stood back.

"Looks pretty good to me. Clear and healthy," she said, returned the instrument to its drawer, and keyed the lock. "The prison has a contract with the local eye clinic. I'll ask Dr Milliner to book you an appointment, just to make sure. Don't get too excited, though. You won't be getting a day out. The optician pays house calls. I wouldn't hold your breath, either. The medical budget's tight and the doc isn't that keen on spending it. Not on remand patients who might be getting out soon."

Getting out soon?

Like that was going to happen any time within the next twenty years.

Mel burst into tears and let it all go. She didn't even try

to hold back the flood. Athena appeared by her side and draped a soft and heavy arm around her shoulders.

"Let it out, honey," she soothed, rubbing Mel's back. "Ain't no shame in crying. Although I'm surprised you didn't wait until *after* I gave you a mirror."

Mel stopped bawling, twisted at the waist, fighting the pain that radiated from her cracked ribs, and stared at the fleshy nurse through liquid eyes.

"What?"

Athena greeted her with another puffy-cheeked smile and a cartoon wink. "Just kidding, honey. There ain't no chance of me giving you a mirror. Might smash it and use the shards to slash your wrists, and I ain't risking another seven years' bad luck. Had more than my fair share of bad luck in my time."

Surprisingly, the words made Mel feel better, which was probably Athena's intention. Mel had considered ending her suffering many times, since well before her arrest, but suicide was a mortal sin, perhaps the worst sin of all. No, she could never take the coward's way out.

Anyway, if she could survive life with *him*, she could probably survive just about anything. Thermonuclear war might end her, but little else. At least that's what she kept telling herself.

Athena patted her back one more time and levered herself up from the bed. The springs squeaked with relief and Mel rose five centimetres into the air.

"That's me done here," the nurse said. "You need anything before I set off on my rounds?"

Mel sniffed away the remaining tears. "Water and a tissue would be nice, thanks. And thank you for being so kind."

"It's what I do, honey."

Athena handed her a fresh box of prison-issue, scratchy tissues, and refilled her water jug. "I'll be back to check on you after rounds. Meanwhile, you try getting some rest. Sleep's the best medicine."

Within moments of Athena bustling from the ward, the door opened again to admit Mel's worse nightmare—Marcus Thatcher.

Oh God. Now what?

It was almost as though the creep had been waiting for her to leave. Thatcher's handsome face broke into a cheery smile, but again, it didn't reach his lifeless eyes and made him look like a hunter focusing on its prey.

"Hello again, Archer," he said, stepping into the ward and closing the door firmly behind him. "Feeling better, I hope? At least the bandages are off now. Doesn't look too bad from here. Loughlin did a good job with those stitches. Good with her hands, she is. Very nimble."

All the while he spoke, Thatcher drew closer to her. The only thing giving her any hope was the fact he hadn't locked the door behind him.

He stopped alongside her bed, standing far too close, his hand within millimetres of her foot.

"Have you given any thought to my … offer?" Thatcher asked. His dark gaze studied her face in detail before lowering to take in her breasts. It lingered there far too long before dropping down and then returning to her face.

His proximity made her squirm. She wanted to hurl, but swallowed hard, trying to hold back the bile sliding up her throat.

She shook her head, unable to speak for fear of bursting into tears again. Showing any form of weakness in front of a predator like Thatcher would do nothing but encourage him.

"That's a shame."

He reached out his left hand to touch her toes through the bedding. It took every gram of willpower in her not to jerk her foot from his grasp.

Don't fight him. Don't encourage him. Don't do anything.

"A real shame." He released his grip and patted the covers. "Still, never mind. It's entirely up to you. I can wait, for a while. No one's ever accused Marcus Thatcher of impatience." He took a step closer to the head of the bed. "On the other hand, I don't mind a little coercion myself."

She gasped and threw a hand to her mouth. The swelling to her lip had gone down and the split had scabbed over, but the implant still tore the skin inside and her tongue kept worrying away at the razor-sharp thread.

How anyone, even Thatcher, could find her attractive in her current state was beyond her. She wasn't attractive, she was ugly and in pain. The pig wanted to demonstrate his power over her, nothing more. Same treatment *he* had given her.

Maybe she should let Thatcher have his way. Make things easier on herself. Perhaps she didn't care anymore. So long as he got it over with quickly, she could put up with the humiliation and the torment. She'd done it often enough before.

Still, something deep within her railed against the idea of giving in. That way led to destruction. What did she have left to fight for but her soul?

Thatcher's hand moved again, this time it came to rest on her hip and ran down the outside of her thigh. Mel stared at his fingers as they traced a line down to her knee and then slid to the inside of her leg and moved upwards, stroking, caressing. Bile leaped into her throat once again. She didn't draw her gaze from his hand. If she looked into his dead eyes, she'd have started crying, started pleading, which was exactly what the pig wanted.

Please, God. Please make him stop.

After a sharp rap, the door squeaked open and Prison Officer Priestly appeared in the opening. Thatcher snatched his hand away and spun to face the new arrival.

"Mr Thatcher?" Priestly asked, staying in the doorway, but taking in the situation.

Mel couldn't tell what the officer was thinking. Priestly controlled her expression too well for that, but her scrutiny took in Mel's face and nothing else before she locked eyes with Thatcher.

"Yes, Officer Priestly," Thatcher said. "How can I help you?"

Priestly took half a step into the room and stayed there, holding tight to the door handle. Mel had the sense she was waiting for Thatcher to come to her, rather than the other way around. She looked at Mel again. Something in the prison officer's expression told Mel she knew what Thatcher had been doing, but she said nothing.

"Well?" Thatcher said when Priestly still hadn't answered after a count of five.

"I have a message for you, sir."

Thatcher turned to face Priestly, full on. He stood, feet apart, hands clasped behind his back.

"Come in here and tell me then."

Officer Priestly stood at attention, but stayed in the doorway.

"What are you waiting for!" Thatcher shouted.

The veins on his neck ballooned and his face turned red. Mel looked on in fascination.

Blinking hard, Priestly lowered her eyes, apparently unable to stare Thatcher down.

"PSIs state that …" Priestly mumbled so much, it was difficult to make out exactly what she said.

"What was that?" Thatcher shouted over her. "Speak up, damn it!"

Priestly coughed and lifted her head. Although her lower lip trembled under Thatcher's intimidatory glare, the younger officer seemed to find a reserve of strength from somewhere. She braced her shoulders.

"Sorry, sir. I said, PSIs state that, except for emergencies, male officers shouldn't be alone with female inmates, sir." She spoke up, her voice firmer.

Thatcher's heels left the floor as he bounced up and down twice before marching towards the young woman. He stopped two paces in front of her, practically skidding to a halt. Priestly seemed to wilt under the barrage, blinking rapidly.

"What did you just say?"

"Sorry, sir. It's just that—"

Again, both heels left the floor. "Don't you *dare* quote prison regulations to me, Priestly. I practically wrote the damned PSIs!" Behind his back, Thatcher's right hand balled into a fist, and his knuckles cracked under the strain.

"Yes, sir. I know, but—"

"*I'm* in charge here, Priestly!" Thatcher yelled. "And don't you ever forget it"

The man's spittle flew. Some hit Priestly in the face. She jerked back her head as though reacting to a blow.

"Mr Thatcher," Priestly said, keeping her voice low, "w-we shouldn't … not here." She shot a glance at Mel, which suggested a prisoner shouldn't be allowed to see an altercation between prison officers. In doing so, she also indicated that Mel would make a good witness to Thatcher's intimidation.

Mel stared into Priestly's eyes and nodded.

You only have to ask.

Thatcher seemed to shrink inside his shirt. The soles of his shoes squeaked as he half-turned to look at Mel. He cleared his throat with a wet cough and paused for breath. Moments later, his fist opened and he flexed his fingers, the crisis, if not averted, then at least delayed.

"Why *are* you here, *Officer* Priestly?" Thatcher said, with unconcealed fury.

The prison officer swallowed hard and relaxed her shoulders before answering. "I came to tell you that Mrs Archer has visitors."

"She has what?"

"Visitors, sir," Priestly repeated, her voice firm. "Her solicitor and his assistant."

Mel's heart started racing and the pulse pounded in her ears.

Visitors? She had visitors?

Her court-appointed solicitor had made it clear she'd be too busy to visit Mel until they'd received a date for the trial which was unlikely to happen before autumn. Six months at the earliest.

What on earth was going on?

Chapter Fifteen

Monday 19th April - Early Afternoon

Heading North, M1, Leicestershire, England

Even though he tried to put on a relaxed front for Lara's benefit, for the first time in as long as he could remember, Kaine's nerves bounced and jumped. He and Lara barely exchanged a word during the first part of the ninety-minute journey from Mike's farm to Falston Manor. At first, he'd tried to make a joke about wandering voluntarily into the lion's den but her expression, angst mixed with concentration, ended that particular conversation in really short order.

Instead, she spent the drive with her nose buried in Corky's detailed legend—the one they'd taken the best part of three days to memorise.

Keeping well below the maximum speed limit was as likely to draw as much unwanted police attention as edging slightly above it, and Kaine matched the speed of their fellow travellers on the dual carriageway, blending in with the rest of the speedsters. If a radar-happy traffic cop did pull them over, they'd find nothing to quibble over. Corky had provided perfect documentation and the machines in Mike's comms room—miraculously sourced by the team's quartermaster—rivalled those of the most secure printing facilities in the country. One of which could even produce top-notch holograms for the certified IDs.

Officially, Kaine and Lara were precisely who their documents claimed them to be. With aging makeup to support the idea, Kaine played the fifty-seven-year-old Laurence Pratt, a senior partner in the legal entity, Corcoran, Whitney, and Verger LLP, solicitors with offices in Nottingham. Lara's identity confirmed her as the much younger, Ms Emma Braithwaite, Pratt's paralegal, gofer, and general dogsbody.

Corky had spent the weekend modifying the online footprint of Corcoran, Whitney, and Verger LLP, adding two new bios to the partner and associate register. Anyone who'd visited the updated site for the previous three days would have been able to read a comprehensive overview of the legal careers of both Pratt and Braithwaite—and they'd be able to do so only for the duration of Kaine and Lara's visit.

"What happens if anyone asks us a legal question?" Kaine asked to take his mind off the danger they were travelling towards at a shade over seventy-five miles per hour.

"We'll have to wing it."

"Wing it on A Wing?" he said, adding a forced laugh. "I love it."

"We're actually visiting the medical centre, which is on C Wing."

"No need to be so pedantic."

"Yes, there is. We can't mess this up."

"I know," he said, dropping the smile. Time to be serious. "We're heading into prison. Any mistake could prove disastrous."

"Someone might recognise you," she suggested unhelpfully.

"What, in this rig?"

Kaine waved a hand over his expensive suit and highly polished, Italian loafers, and ended by smoothing his neatly trimmed beard. Before they'd left Mike's farm that morning, Lara had even tidied the mop that passed for his hair and added more grey. Cosmetic contact lenses, tinted blue, and uncorrected horn-rimmed glasses completed the disguise.

"I doubt anyone from my military days would recognise me like this. Damn it, I hardly recognise myself with all this bloody fluff. Before growing this shaggy crop, I had no idea my hair was curly."

"Soft waves," Lara said, running her fingers through his hair, "not curls. There is a difference."

"I'll take your word for it, Vidal." He loved the way she ruffled his hair. It almost made growing it long worth the discomfort. "Besides," he added, returning to the point and trying to concentrate, "Corky ran the records of all the prisoners. None had spent time in the military. Same for the guards on duty today. As far as he can tell, I've never come into direct contact with anyone in Falston Manor."

"What about people on cover for annual leave or sickness?" she asked, doing nothing to ease the tension, which increased the closer they drew to the place of incarceration.

"You heard what Corky said, love. He's expanding his

search to incorporate the whole of Falston Manor's employment roster, including the civilian admin staff. Don't know how he manages to do so much so quickly. There's only so many hours in his day. Besides, it's not too late."

"Not too late for what?"

"I can always drop you off before we get there. You could call a cab to take you back to the farm."

"Not a chance, matey. They're expecting two of us. It might raise suspicions if I don't turn up. Besides, we've already been through the arguments. We're in this together and that's final."

She inhaled deeply through her nose and exhaled slowly through her mouth—a relaxation technique he'd taught her during their regular training sessions. Lara happened to be one of the best students he'd ever taught, a fast learner who punched way above her weight—in all aspects of the phrase. However, although he was proud of her progress to date, she still had so much to learn.

The green road sign showed two miles to their turning. Kaine lifted his foot off the throttle and eased the car into the nearside lane.

"Not long now," he said. "Last chance to change your mind."

She smiled, but said nothing.

"Okay, let's do this, Ms Braithwaite."

"Right you are, Mr Pratt."

Kaine shook his head. "Hate that bloody name. What's wrong with Mason?"

"As in Perry Mason?"

"Yep," he said, flicking the indicator stalk and taking the slip road. "That would be a hell of a way to blend in."

They slowed to negotiate a left turn onto the quiet, two-lane Uttoxeter Drive and bounced and slalomed over its pothole-encrusted tarmac. Half a mile later, they made a right turn onto Woodland Spur and caught their first sight of the imposing, not to mention terrifying, Falston Manor.

Originally a hunting lodge owned by a wealthy family who'd fallen on hard times and sold the building to the county, the Manor must once have been a hugely impressive home-away-from-home. Dark granite walls stretched up three storeys to scrape at a slate-grey sky. A stainless-steel, double-skinned chain-link fence, topped with double hoops of razor wire, surrounded a five-acre site that was dominated by the Manor, the prison wings, and the surrounding outhouses.

Woodland Spur took them directly to the entrance. Two huge blast gates stood open, rolled back into their metal casements. In the ten-metre gap behind them, metal barriers on either side of a guardhouse blocked their way into the grounds. Kaine pulled to a stop and rolled down his window.

During the drive north-east, the weather had closed in. Clouds had gathered and descended, threatening an imminent downpour. It matched Kaine's sombre mood.

The uniformed officer at the gate studied their IDs closely. He paid particular attention to Lara's photo, taking a while to compare it with her face—what red-blooded male wouldn't—and confirm the details with the information on his clipboard. He strolled one lap of their car, although he failed to use a mirror to search for a bomb—which Kaine would have expected—before handing each of them a visitor's pass.

"Attach them to your jackets and keep them on display at all times," he said. "Wouldn't want you being unable to leave now, would we, Ms Braithwaite?" He spoke directly to Lara, ignoring Kaine.

"If you allowed that to happen, Officer Haldane," Kaine said, reading the nameplate on the guard's uniform jacket, "I'd probably have your job."

He gave Haldane a cold stare and the officer dropped his friendly smile in an instant. He did, though, give Lara a pitying glance, at which she smiled in apparently nervous gratitude.

"Park over there, Mr *Pratt*," Haldane said, overemphasising the surname, "and stay in the car. I'll get someone to escort you inside the moment I have a chance. As you can see, *sir*, I'm a little occupied at the moment." He jerked his head towards the single car waiting behind theirs at the barrier.

Kaine gritted his teeth and allowed his anger to show in his reddened face and bulging eyes. "I'm not used to being kept waiting, Officer Haldane. I'm a busy man. Ms Braithwaite," he said and turned to Lara, "make a note of this officer's name and his attitude. I refuse to put up with such disrespect."

Lara searched her briefcase, picking through a heap of legal papers.

"What are you waiting for?"

"Sorry, Mr Pratt. I know my notebook is in here somewhere. I packed it this morning."

"Useless, bloody woman," Kaine said, slipping their Mercedes-AMG A 35 into drive and heading to the distant visitor's parking spaces as indicated by Haldane.

"Nicely done, Ryan. Just the right amount of obnoxious," she said, hiding her smile from Haldane with the offending notebook.

"Thought I might have been going a little over the top. Didn't really want to draw so much attention to myself."

"Nope, you hit the perfect note with a junior rank, but I

imagine Pratt would tone it down a little if he came across the governor or a custodial manager."

He reverse-parked their Mercedes into the nearest available spot to the main gates, pointing the nose at the guardhouse, ready for a quick getaway. If one were required, they'd need any advantage on offer.

"That's exactly the way I intended to play it. Anyway, given the way Officer Haldane couldn't take his eyes off you, I doubt he'd be able to pull me out of a police line-up if his life depended on it."

"Which is why I decided to 'glam up' rather than play it mousy as usual. I imagine an arrogant piece of work like Pratt would choose his assistants based on looks as much as brains."

Kaine released his seatbelt, turning at the waist to do so. He used the opportunity as a different reason to study "glammed up" Lara. She wore a long, blonde, real-hair wig, glasses with tinted lenses, and a dark blue power suit, the skirt long enough to be professional, but short enough to show the right amount of leg to draw admiring glances. A silk blouse in cream and leather shoes with two-inch heels completed the business-like ensemble. God, she was stunning. He didn't tell her often enough, and this was certainly not the time to do so.

"I really wish you didn't have to be here. It's too bloody dangerous," he whispered, barely moving his lips in case they were being watched.

Paranoia wasn't always a bad thing.

"Ryan," she said, equally as quiet, "let's not go there again."

"Lara, I—"

Movement from the main building a hundred metres away drew their attention and interrupted Kaine's response.

A wicket gate in the lower quadrant of the huge front door opened. Two people exited and headed straight for them. Kaine recognised the man from Corky's information package—Supervising Officer Larkins. He couldn't identify the woman, but as she drew closer, her name badge read "PO Priestly".

Larkins led the way with a swagger.

Above-average height but carrying at least twenty kilos of excess weight mainly around his middle, Larkins wore a baggy uniform in desperate need of a press. He aimed a thin smile at Kaine, and then turned his eyes to Lara. The smile became more welcoming.

Larkins headed to Kaine's side of their hired Merc and stood far enough away for Kaine to open the door without crushing the man's kneecaps.

"Mr Pratt?" the SO asked, dipping his head slightly and keeping well clear of Kaine's personal space.

"Yes, and you are?"

"Supervising Officer Larkins, sir. Pleased to meet you. And you must be Ms Braithwaite," Larkins said, checking something on his clipboard. As he turned to face Lara, who exited the car and rushed to Kaine's side, his smile grew more animated and his eyes sparkled.

"Yes," Kaine said, answering for her, "my assistant." He dismissed Lara with a backhanded wave.

Larkins took a pace closer to Lara. "Pleased to meet you, Ms Braithwaite."

"Will this take long, Mr Larkins?" Kaine interrupted, stepping between the senior officer and Lara. He had to cant his head upwards slightly to take in the taller man's face. "We've been waiting long enough. Would you mind taking me to my client … please?"

Larkins stiffened and looked Kaine up and down with barely concealed contempt.

"Well now. Wouldn't want to keep these important people waiting, would we, PO Priestly?" he said, glancing at his sidekick.

"No, sir," Priestly answered, "we wouldn't."

Larkins turned about-face sharply, said, "Follow me. Keep up," and marched away at pace.

Priestly shot Lara an apologetic glance and they hurried to match pace with the fast-moving Larkins.

"Too much?" Kaine asked Lara from the corner of his mouth, without turning his head to look at her.

"A little. Don't hold your breath for a dinner invitation," she said, falling into step beside him.

Larkins and Priestly led them through the wicket gate. Priestly held back and slammed it behind them. The noise shuddered through Kaine's soul.

The point of no return.

He swallowed hard but tried to maintain an outward appearance of bored impatience. Lara gave him a look that seemed to ask, "What the hell are we doing here?"

Keeping in character, he frowned deeply at her, but tugged on his left earlobe at the same time—an encouraging signal and part of the non-verbal code they'd developed overnight.

They passed through a series of locked doors, which took them deep into the bowels of the scruffy prison, and ended up in an oppressive, windowless room lit by a single string of fluorescent strips.

Larkins turned to Kaine, his face an expressionless mask. "Before we allow you in any further, we need to take your keys, wallets, and mobile phones, please."

Kaine tutted and sighed all the while he and Lara

placed the requested items in the envelopes provided. None of which were originals or irreplaceable, and nothing could lead the authorities back to them or Mike's farm if anything went wrong.

"Do you have any of these articles in your possession?" Larkins asked and presented them with a card containing a list of forbidden goods, including spare mobile phones, weapons, and drugs.

"Oh for goodness' sake, of course we don't," Kaine said. "This isn't the first time I've visited a client in one of Her Majesty's Custodial Institutions, Larkins. Can we hurry this along, please? After this meeting, I have an important appointment in town. One I'd rather not be late for."

Larkins looked down his nose at Kaine, an act made easy by the difference in their height. "We have our procedures, Mr Pratt. The sooner we conclude them, the sooner you can have access to Mrs Archer. You can either answer our questions and sign the form, undergo a strip search, or leave. It's entirely up to you."

"This is completely ridiculous!" Kaine huffed. "I can hereby categorically confirm that neither I, nor my assistant, have any of these contraband materials on our persons." He grabbed Larkins' proffered clipboard, took an expensive pen from the inner pocket of his jacket, and made a great show of signing both his and Lara's forms. "Is that acceptable?"

"Perfectly, Mr Pratt," Larkins said, "but I need Ms Braithwaite to make the declaration independently."

Kaine sighed and passed Lara the clipboard.

Lara dutifully signed her form and returned the clipboard to Priestly, who had finished searching Lara's handbag and briefcase.

Larkins took Kaine's aluminium attaché case and placed

it on a table that had been bolted to the wall. "Would you mind opening this briefcase, please, sir?"

Chuntering to himself, Kaine dialled the code into each lock, slid the catches to release the clips, and snapped them open. He spun the case around so the open side faced Larkins and stood with folded arms, tapping his foot, while Larkins took forever to rifle through the innards. Finally, after coming up empty, Larkins spun the attaché case back to Kaine.

"Thank you, Mr Pratt. That all seems to be in order," Larkins said, his expression making it perfectly clear that he wished he'd found something incriminating in the arrogant solicitor's case—something like a baggie of coke.

"As I told you," Kaine said and added a grunt of impatience. He shot back his jacket sleeve to read the time from his watch, but made no further comment.

Larkins nodded towards his subordinate. "PO Priestly will escort you to the prisoner. She's in the medical centre on C Wing."

"Excuse me," Lara said, defying the wrath of her "boss". "Did you say the medical centre?"

"Yes, Ms Braithwaite," Larkins answered, dropping his aggressive stance a little. "Weren't you informed?"

"For goodness' sakes, man," Kaine said, snapping closed the locks on his attaché case and seething with apparent rage. "If we'd been informed our client was in the hospital wing, my assistant wouldn't have asked the question. She's not an idiot! Why is Mrs …" He shot an angry look at Lara and rolled his right hand forward.

"Melanie Archer, sir," she answered. "On remand for murdering her husband."

Again, Kaine dismissed her with an airy wave. "Yes, yes, I know what she's been charged with. So," he said, returning his attention to Larkins and fixing the man with his most ferocious scowl, "why is my client in hospital?"

Larkins exchanged an uncomfortable glance with Priestly before returning Kaine's dark look with a steady stare. "Mrs Archer was involved in an … incident last week. In the showers. It seems she was set upon by at least one other prisoner."

"Oh no," Lara gasped, pressing a hand to her mouth. "What happened? Is she seriously hurt?"

Before Larkins had the chance to answer, Kaine butted in with a question. "Why wasn't her legal team notified of this … *incident*?"

Larkins, on the back foot, shook his head. "As far as I'm aware, the investigating officer sent the incident report to the governor's office, along with a detailed medical assessment and prognosis, sir. Protocol states that the prisoner's solicitors are informed as soon as reasonably possible."

"Precisely when did this attack occur?" Kaine asked, leaning closer to the senior officer, trying to intimidate, but not really putting his heart into it.

"Last Monday morning, Mr Pratt," Priestly answered for Larkins, her expression showing discomfort.

"Last *Monday*?" Kaine practically shouted the question. "For pity's sake, that's a week ago, and we still haven't been informed! What sort of a place are you running here, Larkins? This inefficiency is totally unacceptable."

"I can only assume the paperwork is on its way to you, sir," Larkins said, squaring his shoulders and standing his ground. "Perhaps Mrs Archer's original solicitor is in the process of forwarding the report to your practice."

"Oh yes," Kaine said, nodding slowly, "blame someone else. I'd expect nothing less. What's the name of the officer?"

"Which officer?" Larkins asked, a frown deepening the creases on his forehead.

"The one who's supposedly investigating this attack? What's his name? I'll want to interview him after I've met with my client."

Larkins shot another glance at Priestly, who lowered her eyes.

"That would be CM Thatcher, sir," Larkins said. "As it happens, the custodial manager is on duty today. If you like, I'll find out if he's free to see you."

Kaine sneered at the senior officer, who seemed to have shrunk a few centimetres.

"Thank you, Mr Larkins," he said, his voice loaded with sarcasm, "that would be absolutely marvellous."

"Excuse me, Mr Larkins," Lara said, after clearing her throat gently.

"Yes, Ms Braithwaite?"

"Mrs Archer's been in hospital for a week. Exactly how badly injured is she?"

"I, er … I'm not really sure, ma'am." Larkins turned to his side. "Officer Priestly?"

The blonde prison officer shook her head and lifted both eyebrows.

"You'll have to ask at C Wing, Ms Braithwaite," Larkins said through an apologetic and tentative smile.

Kaine hefted his ridiculously over-the-top attaché case. "I will be wanting a full medical report from Doctor …?" He lowered one eyebrow in question at the backtracking senior officer.

"Our chief medical officer is Dr Milliner, Mr Pratt, but I'm afraid she's not on duty today."

"In which case, I'll talk to her assistant." He raised his

attaché as though to demand the way to the C Wing. "Are we done here, Mr Larkins?"

Larkins dipped his head in apparent deference. "PO Priestly will take you to C Wing, while I locate CM Thatcher and see if he's available to see you."

"Thank you, Mr Larkins," Kaine said, letting the case fall and slap against his leg. "I appreciate your assistance in this matter. Please impress upon this *CM Thatcher* that I shall be most upset if he is unable to make himself available to me this afternoon. Most upset, indeed. In fact I shall be so upset, I might have a quiet word with my very dear friend, the Right Honourable Roland Bartholomew QC MP. I assume you recognise the name?"

The blank expression Larkins put on gave Kaine his answer. He sighed and shook his head in disbelief.

"Given that Roland is the Lord Chancellor and Secretary of State for Justice—and your ultimate boss—you should know his name, Larkins. You really should. Now, am I going to see my client before I really start to lose my patience?"

Larkins' cheeks reddened. "PO Priestly, please show Mr Pratt and Ms Braithwaite to the infirmary."

Priestly smiled awkwardly. "Follow me, please. It's not far."

"Thank you, Officer Priestly," Lara said.

Kaine gave Larkins his most disdainful look, but said nothing further.

Chapter Sixteen

Monday 19th April - Early Afternoon

Health Care Centre, HMP Falston Manor,
Derbyshire, England

The slender prison officer led them along a gloomy corridor, through three heavy, locked doors, and into a central concourse from which the two-storey wings radiated outwards, like the spokes on a wheel. The wings were named alphabetically, A to E.

PO Priestly crossed the concourse and headed directly to C Wing. They ran the gauntlet of a few dozen inquisitive eyes, mostly female, but a few of them male officers wearing the same uniform as Priestly—white, short-sleeved, dress shirt, black trousers, black boots with rubber soles that squeaked on the polished-concrete floors.

The hairs on the nape of Kaine's neck prickled and his tongue stuck to the roof of a chalk-dry mouth. As unlikely as it seemed, given his disguise, any one of these people might recognise him from his mugshot, which would probably mean the end of freedom both for him and Lara. In quiet moments he would sometimes ask himself how hard he would fight to maintain his liberty—and hers. The same answer always remained. He'd fight hard, but would never risk serious injury to innocent people in an escape bid.

For the whole trip through the prison, he'd been checking the potential routes for an enforced exit. Given that they were deep in the heart of a maximum-security facility, the prospects of escape didn't seem at all promising.

Individually, or in small groups, the guards themselves wouldn't prove much of an obstacle. Armed with nothing more than telescopic truncheons and pepper spray—against which Kaine had developed a certain degree of tolerance following long sessions of aversion therapy—he'd be able to take the officers down easily enough. The real challenge would be to incapacitate them without imparting serious damage, and doing it quickly enough to make a clean escape before the prison authorities activated their automatic lockdown protocols.

Lara's presence added an extra layer of complication. After all the time they'd jointly spent on her self-defence and fieldcraft training, Lara could handle herself better than any female civilian Kaine had ever met, and most military-trained females, too. However, although she'd shown her mettle and resourcefulness time and time again, her lack of actual field experience would count against her. On top of everything else, her very presence would impact on his total concentration during any attempted escape.

Rather than try to fight his way out from the centre of a

prison and risk injuring innocents, it would probably be better in the longer term if he allowed himself to be taken. With his skills in escape and evasion, he'd likely be able to work an escape during a transfer from Falston Manor to the nearest high-security male prison. But that would leave Lara deep in the excrement.

Kaine stopped his train of thought. He was double guessing too many factors. At this point, they could only play things through to their conclusion. He and Lara had made it past the first few hurdles and there was no reason to fear the worst.

That's it, Kaine. Look on the bright side.

Priestly used her set of keys—which hung from her belt by a retractable leash—to gain access to C Wing and let them into another long corridor. Unlike the dull grey of the rest of the prison, this wing had cream-painted walls and floors with non-slip tiles. The left wall allowed natural sunlight through obscured-glass windows that cut into the top quarter of the brickwork. The inner wall contained three internal doors, each sporting a sign. "Dr Milliner—Chief Medical Officer", "Staff Office", and finally, "Ward A".

Kaine couldn't locate a Ward B.

Priestly stopped, turned, and held up a hand.

"Wait here while I check on the ward," she said, in little more than a whisper, pointing to a row of three metal chairs.

Too tense to sit, Kaine grunted and checked his wristwatch, an original Hublot Big Bang—leased by the week. Priestly ignored his obvious attempt to hurry her along. She slid a sympathetic glance at Lara as though to say, "I feel your pain, sister." She turned sharply on one heel, marched ten metres along the corridor, and rapped quietly on the door to the ward.

Without waiting for a response, she pushed the door open.

"Mr Thatcher?" she said, staying in the doorway.

A man responded, his tone aggressive, his accent smooth and well-modulated. "Yes, Officer Priestly. How can I help you?"

Priestly glanced at Kaine and Lara, her expression tense, before stepping part way into the room. She kept within sight of Kaine and Lara, who exchanged glances. Kaine raised his hand to tell Lara to stay put, while he worked his way closer to the open door. Eavesdropping wasn't always a bad thing.

Priestly gripped the door handle so tight, her knuckles turned white.

"Well?" Thatcher asked, his tone changing from general annoyance to definite anger.

"I have a message for you, sir."

From his position, five metres away, Kaine could only see Priestly's arm and back, but could still make out the obvious tension in her shoulders.

"Come in here and tell me then."

Officer Priestly snapped to a smart attention, but stayed in the doorway.

"What are you waiting for!"

"PSIs state that …" Priestly began, but seemed unable to continue.

"What was that?" Thatcher shouted. "Speak up, damn it!"

Priestly coughed and squared her shoulders.

"Sorry, sir. I said, PSIs state that, except for emergencies, male officers shouldn't be alone with female inmates, sir."

What the hell's going on here?

Kaine glanced at Lara, who approached him and stood close at his side.

Squeaking footsteps from inside the ward grew closer.

"What did you just say?" Thatcher demanded.

Kaine ground his teeth. Bullies were amongst the lowest forms of life. In any other situation, he'd have jumped to Priestly's defence, but he'd been playing an aggressive tyrant since the heavy gates of Falston Manor slammed shut behind them, and he needed to stay in character. At his side, Lara stiffened, ready to act, but Kaine rested a hand on her forearm and shook his head.

The time to act might not be far off, but this wasn't it.

Priestly apologised again and the bully's aggressive bluster continued until Thatcher eventually bellowed, "Why *are* you here, *Officer* Priestly?"

Tension in the young woman's shoulders eased. "I came to tell you that Mrs Archer has visitors."

"She has what?"

"Visitors, sir. Her solicitor and his assistant."

"Where are they?" Thatcher asked.

"Just outside, along the corridor, Mr Thatcher. I hope, they didn't hear our … discussion," Priestly said, lowering her voice to a stage whisper and shooting another sideways glance along the corridor at them.

Kaine smiled. Priestly had engineered the confrontation to show Thatcher in all his arrogant viciousness. He grabbed Lara's arm and they hurried back to the far end of the corridor before Thatcher could spot them.

"I like her," Lara whispered when they'd made their ground.

"Me too," Kaine replied.

From their new position at the distant end of the corridor, and with Priestly and Thatcher talking quietly, Kaine failed to catch the rest of the officers' conversation, but an SO Grant's name was mentioned a couple of times, and Thatcher's voice turned into a deep-throated growl.

Priestly backed into the corridor, and Thatcher followed closely. Tall and blond with the powerful build of a man who spent many years pumping iron, Thatcher spotted Kaine and Lara at what his relieved expression suggested was a safe distance. His voice softened. "Why wasn't I informed of this at the morning briefing?"

Priestly shook her head. "Afraid I don't know, sir. Perhaps you should ask SO Grant?"

"Oh, I will do that very thing." He jutted out his chin and Priestly pulled further away. "Well?"

"Sorry, sir?"

Thatcher threw out his chest in a bombastic reproduction of every parade ground sergeant Kaine had ever seen in full flow.

"Don't just stand there, Priestly," he said, his attitude cordial, his expression welcoming. "Mustn't keep our guests waiting. Show them in, show them in."

He turned to face Kaine and Lara, and broke out the great, big, friendly smile of a hail-fellow-well-met. Kaine wanted to slap the insincere grin from the arsehole's face.

Priestly turned towards Kaine and Lara, and beckoned them with a brief nod. When they'd reached the doorway, she made the introductions.

"CM Thatcher, this is Mr Pratt, Mrs Archer's solicitor, and this is his associate, Ms Braithwaite."

To maintain character, Kaine flared his nostrils at her use of the term "associate" rather than "assistant", but decided not to take it further. No need to overegg the soufflé.

Thatcher showed Kaine an obsequious smile and practically leered at Lara.

"Good morning, Mr Platt," Thatcher said, although his eyes never left Lara.

"Good day, Mr Thatcher," Kaine said, looking sideways at the much taller man. "Are you finally going to allow me to see my client? And my name is Pratt, not Platt."

Thatcher's sharp, blue eyes finally found focus on Kaine. They looked him up and down, head to toe and back again, and didn't seem overly impressed with what they told him. His smile faded slightly.

"We have certain procedures to follow, Mr Pratt. I'm sure you understand." His tone cooled a few degrees from its initial warmth.

"I do understand, Mr Thatcher, but criminal law gives me the right to consult with my client with all due haste. Now, where is Mrs Archer?"

Thatcher made a half-turn. "Follow me, *sir*."

He entered the ward and stopped in the middle of the room, barring Kaine and Lara's further approach. Lara's gasp seemed natural. Kaine made sure his shock appeared forced.

Lara stared at Thatcher, her anger obvious. "What on earth—"

Thatcher let out an embarrassed cough. "As you know, there was an … incident. The inmate was involved in an altercation with a number of other—"

"An altercation!" Lara shouted, sidestepping the human blockade and rushing towards the only patient in the three-bed ward. "Good Lord, this is terrible."

She stopped close to the bed and bent forwards to

examine Melanie Archer's injuries, which were obvious and serious. The right side of her face was a swollen mass of multi-coloured bruises. A livid, nine-centimetre cut, held together with a dozen fine stitches, ran in an arc over her left eye, following the line of the eyebrow. A deep split on her upper lip completed the grim spectacle.

Kaine had seen—and even received—many facial injuries in his time, but rarely on such an inherently attractive and innocent-looking face.

The moment Lara showed such concern, Melanie broke down and started crying, hiding her face with her left hand, movement of the right being restricted by a white, plaster cast and a sling. Battered face, broken wrist, probably internal damage, too. A real mess.

Kaine stepped alongside Thatcher, who looked at the show of emotion with aloof disinterest. Still standing close to the door, Priestly's expression exhibited the same concern Kaine would have expected in any human being with normal emotions—her lips thinned and her eyes showed deep compassion. The same could not be said for Thatcher.

"I need to speak to my client right away," Kaine said, addressing his words to Thatcher, but keeping his eyes on the scene playing out on the hospital bed. "Leave us."

Thatcher remained where he was, stiff and immobile. Kaine stared hard at the muscular officer. "I take it there are no cameras or recording devices in this room?"

"Of course not," Thatcher said, as though it was the most ridiculous thing he'd ever heard. "This is a hospital ward, not an interview room."

Kaine shot a glance at Priestly, who nodded in confirmation of Thatcher's claim. "Might I remind you that my presence here, together with that of my assistant, falls under the rules of legal confidentiality. Even though we aren't in a designated interview space, no one can be privy to the discussions between my client and her legal team. Is that clear?"

"Perfectly," Thatcher answered, curtly. "PO Priestly and I will be outside until you finish. You have one hour."

Kaine pulled in a deep breath. "I'll have as long as I deem necessary, *Mister* Thatcher. My client and I have a great deal to discuss, and we will not be interrupted. Do I make myself clear!"

"Now listen here—"

"No, you listen to me," Kaine said with forced calmness, "and listen closely. Until now, my client has had inferior representation. She has a spotless reputation and has never had so much as a speeding ticket. Had I been her solicitor from the outset, I would have made sure she was bailed. Of that, there is no doubt, such is the pitiful state of the prosecution's case. And within two weeks of her incarceration, this happens!" He waved his hand in Melanie's general direction. "This is an utter disgrace. What sort of an institution are you running here, man?"

When it became clear Thatcher didn't have an answer, Kaine waved him away.

"I'll knock on the door to let you know when we're finished. Now, leave us, if you please."

Priestly reacted first. She turned through one-eighty degrees, yanked open the door, and held it ajar for Thatcher. For his part, the custodial manager bounced on his heels a couple of times before fixing his eyes on his prisoner and holding the glare for a few moments. When the patient refused to pull her hand from her face, Thatcher broke his pose.

"Very well, very well," he said, barely moving his lips.

"Please be as quick as you can. PO Priestly will be outside when you're done. I have a prison to run here."

Kaine shot another glance at Priestly before stepping far enough to one side so Thatcher's broad shoulders blocked her view of his face.

"We won't be that long, CM Thatcher," Kaine said, keeping his voice low enough for Priestly not to hear. "If you're still here when I'm finished, I might have something of mutual interest to discuss. Understand?"

The crow's feet around Thatcher's blue eyes deepened in suspicion. Out of sight of Priestly, Kaine rubbed his thumb against the tips of his fingers in the universal sign for money. Understanding dawned and interest shone in Thatcher's eyes—their first sign of any emotion other than aggression and contempt.

"I'll see what I can do," he said, matching Kaine's conspiratorial tone and volume.

"Excellent. Thank you," Kaine said loudly and spun to face the bed.

Behind him, the squeaking of Thatcher's receding boot-steps, followed by the slam of a door, told Kaine they were finally alone with the Trust's new client. He had no doubt that his enigmatic parting shot would play on the custodial manager's mind powerfully enough for him to stay outside the door and be ready for whatever Kaine decided to throw at him—be it threat or bribe. Either way, given the injuries visible on Melanie's face, there was no way they could leave her in prison unprotected.

Even if she did kill her husband, as a member of The 83, the least she deserved was his undivided attention for the next few minutes.

Whether she could convince him to do anything but

provide the finances for a real defence team was a different matter entirely.

Chapter Seventeen

Monday 19th April - Lara Orchard

**Health Care Centre, HMP Falston Manor,
Derbyshire, England**

After a snap, initial look at Melanie, her new patient, Lara's new medical training kicked in, along with her protective instincts. The slightly built woman had taken a terrible beating.

Ignoring Thatcher, she darted to the side of the bed and threw an arm gently across Melanie's heaving shoulders.

"Sorry for my reaction," she said quietly. "I didn't mean to shock you. I just wasn't prepared for the ... extent of your injuries. Please forgive me."

Melanie lowered the hand from her head. "They haven't given me a mirror. Am I hideous?"

Lara rubbed the distraught woman's back. "Not at all. It's a mess, certainly, but nothing that won't heal, given enough time."

"But the cut … the stitches. I-I can't …"

Again, she broke down. Tears rolled down the side of her nose and dripped onto a pyjama jacket that had greyed with age.

"Don't worry. It's not as serious as you might fear. It follows the curve of the supraorbital ridge."

"What?"

"Sorry. I mean the upper curve of the eye. When it fully heals, it'll hardly be noticeable. A little foundation and some eyeshadow and nobody will see it."

Melanie sniffed, but winced at the same time. "Are you sure?"

Lara nodded.

She wasn't going to mention the need for a consultation with a top-class cosmetic surgeon so early in their discussion. Lara's latest patient was hardly in an emotional state to take on such news.

The brave, tear-streaked smile on the battered face was enough to melt Lara's heart.

"You said something about a ridge. A-Are you a doctor?"

"I have some medical training," Lara said, sidestepping the question. "It's often helpful in my line of work." She glanced towards the closed door, leaned closer, and lowered her voice. "The 83 Trust sent us."

Melanie turned her head sharply, winced again, and looked up. Her eyes widened in shock. "They did?"

Lara raised a finger to her lips.

"Oh my God," Melanie whispered. "I-I'd given up hope."

Melanie's tentative smile revealed a missing, upper right incisor, and the metallic glint showed the exposed head of a dental implant. Why would someone of Melanie's age—forty-seven—and in otherwise good health require a dental implant? It suggested trauma rather than decay, especially since the rest of her teeth seemed in excellent condition. Perhaps her claim to have suffered long-term spousal abuse held water.

"We're sorry to have taken so long," Ryan said, stepping alongside Lara but keeping a respectful distance from the medical bed. "But I'm sure you understand, there's quite a bit of call on our time."

"They told me you were my new legal team," Melanie said, the missing tooth giving her a gentle lisp.

"Part of it," Ryan said. He, too, raised his finger to his lips and moved it across to tap his ear.

Melanie frowned in confusion, but relaxed when Lara nodded and gave her good hand a reassuring squeeze.

"Would you have any objection to my assistant reading your medical notes?" Ryan asked, moving away from Melanie and Lara, and closer to the middle bed. "She has experience with medical issues, and I imagine she's rather keen to know the exact nature of your injuries."

He placed his heavy attaché case on the stained covers of the middle bed and unlocked the clasps. He flipped open the lid and took out a large but innocuous-looking pocket calculator.

Ryan nodded to Lara, who took the hint and lifted the clipboard from the foot of Melanie's bed. She held it up to Melanie and arched a questioning eyebrow.

"Do you mind?"

"N-No. Not at all. Please do," Melanie said, nodding.

Ryan unrolled a set of earphones, plugged the jack into

a socket on the calculator, and hit the power button. The device lit up with a row of green LEDs and took on the appearance of a miniature games console.

Melanie followed his performance in silence.

"What do the notes say, Ms Braithwaite?" Ryan asked loudly.

Lara cleared her throat and started reading, but a little louder than was strictly necessary. "Concussion from an indeterminate number of blows to the head. Severe migraine which has only recently diminished. Fractured right ulnar. Three cracked ribs …"

While Lara read through the harrowing list of injuries and the ongoing treatment protocols, Ryan fitted the earphones and set to work, quartering the room quickly, raising and lowering the "calculator" as he went.

Before Lara finished reading the notes, Ryan had removed and re-furled the earphones and returned the "calculator" to his attaché case.

"All clear," he announced quietly, closing the lid and clipping the locks in place. "We can talk freely, but let's keep the volume down. I wouldn't put it past that big, blond buffoon to stand on the other side of the door with his ears pressed against an inverted, glass tumbler."

He pointed to a pair of visitors' chairs on the far side of the ward. "May we sit?"

"Please," Melanie said, waving her good hand. "Looking up hurts my head."

Ryan grabbed the chairs and dragged them next to the bed. They sat on Melanie's left side, to make it easier for her to see through the uninjured eye.

"First, the introductions. My name is Laurence Pratt, and this is Emma Braithwaite. We're here representing Corcoran, Whitney, and Verger LLP, Nottinghamshire's leading legal partnership." Ryan lowered his voice further but maintained a professional demeanour.

On the drive from Mike's farm, she and Ryan had discussed the best way to approach the initial interview. They jointly decided to stay in character, at least to begin with. It seemed safer that way.

"I-I don't have any money," Melanie said, fighting back more tears.

"If necessary," Ryan said, using his most clipped manner, "the Trust *may* be prepared to cover all the legal costs."

"Really? That could be tens of thousands of pounds."

"Mrs Archer, as a litigator, I am one of the best in the UK. My firm's fees will run to significantly more than you might imagine. However, we mustn't get ahead of ourselves. My partnership's continued representation depends entirely upon the outcome of this interview," he said, looking away.

Ryan slumped against the back of the chair and crossed one leg over the other, feigning disinterest.

Lara gave Melanie's uninjured hand another reassuring squeeze and released it. "Should we accept your case, the Trust has the funds to cover any and all of your legal expenses. May I ask you some questions?"

"Yes. Of course."

Lara leaned closer. "Your missing tooth. Can I see the tip of an implant?"

Melanie nodded.

"The exposed thread must be uncomfortable."

She covered her partially healed, split lip with her fingers. "I'd call it 'excruciating' if I could say the word without sounding like a two year old."

Still playing his part, Ryan snorted, apparently unimpressed by his client's response.

Lara took a legal pad and pen from her briefcase and sat poised, ready to take notes. "For our records," she said, "do you mind telling me how you lost the tooth?"

Melanie glanced from Lara to Ryan and lowered her head.

"And please don't try to convince us you walked into an open door," Ryan said, looking for dirt under his fingernails.

She jerked up her head. "You've seen my medical notes?"

"Your former solicitor sent them, along with what she had by way of case notes—such as they were," he said, lying and doing it ever so convincingly.

Ryan glanced at Lara and nodded, encouraging her to take over.

"In spousal abuse cases," she said, "you'll be surprised at how many times the victim uses that same reason for their injuries."

The poor woman took in a long, fractured breath, wincing. Her injured ribs must have been causing discomfort.

"It's what James, my husband, forced me to say." Once again, tears filled her eyes and threatened to spill down her bruised and puffy cheeks.

Ryan's expression betrayed none of the sympathy Lara knew he felt. He said nothing, leaving Lara to create the bond of trust.

"If we are to take on your case and mount a robust defence," Lara began, "you have to trust us, Mrs Archer. We need the truth, the whole truth, and ... well, you know the rest." She smiled encouragingly. "So, what exactly happened?"

Melanie closed her eyes and the tears did fall. She swiped them away with her fingertips, taking care to go gently around the most heavily bruised and swollen areas.

"He ... slammed my face into a wall," she said, her voice catching on the words.

She fell silent for a moment, but the instant relief on her face suggested it was probably the first time she'd admitted the truth aloud to anyone.

Ryan's jaw muscles clenched, rippling beneath his distinguished beard. Lara knew what he thought of men hitting women—indeed, what he thought of bullies in general—but he was trying hard to hide his disgust and maintain a cool, professional demeanour.

"Are you able to give us any details?" Lara asked.

Melanie swallowed hard before taking another stuttering breath and releasing it slowly. She closed her eyes and kept them shut.

"We were in the dining room. I-I spilled some wine on the tablecloth. H-He went berserk."

"What happened immediately after he hurt you?" Lara asked, speaking through clenched teeth. "Was he apologetic? Effusive about it?"

"Not in the slightest," she said, shaking her head gently and keeping her eyes closed. "He blamed me for making him angry. Ordered me to lie to the doctor."

"I know this must be difficult for you and forgive us for asking, but why didn't you make an official police complaint or leave your husband?"

She looked at Lara and the tears gushed again. Lara handed her a tissue and patted her leg through the bed covers.

"Y-You would never understand. I-It's not easy to explain ..."

"Please try," Lara said, quietly urging, encouraging. "It could prove crucial to your case."

After another deep breath, she spoke slowly. "All our

married life, James bullied and belittled me. It reached the stage where I started believing his insults. James was controlling, did I say?"

Lara nodded. "In what way?"

"At home, he forced me to dress in dowdy clothes and wouldn't allow me to wear any makeup. Once, he caught me wearing lipstick and called me a whore, displaying myself to the tradesmen."

Once she'd started, the words flooded out in a cathartic stream.

"When we went to parties," she continued, breathlessly, "James would choose my clothes, the amount of makeup I wore, my jewellery, everything. I wasn't allowed to mingle. He said I represented him and his family, and I had to look and act accordingly. He told me what to say, what to do, and how to behave. When visitors came to the house ..."

She continued for quite a few minutes, detailing incident after shocking incident and finished with, "In the end, he controlled every move I made ... until I ... until, in the end, I-I lost my identity." Her shoulders sagged and more tears fell. "Sounds pathetic, I know." She glanced at Ryan and then turned her limpid, teary eyes on Lara.

"Not at all, Mrs Archer," Lara said, leaning forwards in her chair.

During the revelation, Ryan said nothing and barely moved. He just stared at Melanie, absorbing her every move, her every word.

"When you lost the tooth," Lara said, keeping her voice calm but sympathetic, "was it the first time your husband had been physically violent?"

Melanie blinked more tears away. "He'd pushed me a few times and grabbed my arms hard enough to leave bruises, but he'd never actually hit me before."

"But his behaviour deteriorated. Around what stage of your relationship was this?"

"A couple of years into the marriage. He'd been getting worse, more hostile, even more illogical. And he was drinking too much. He'd always been a heavy drinker, but in the months leading up to his first major stroke, he became the worst form of alcoholic. Abusive, irrational, aggressive. It was … awful. Awful. That's when … when I tried leaving him."

Lara and Ryan shared a glance.

"You'd finally had enough?" Lara asked.

"Y-Yes. Things had become so bad, I was worried he might even kill me. I took Brutus and left in the middle of the night."

"Brutus?"

"My puppy. A stray who turned up in our back garden one day," Melanie said, a faraway look in her blue eyes.

"Did your husband come after you?"

Melanie's head dipped and her eyes closed. "No … no he didn't. After two days I went back home, tail between my legs. Once I left the house, I was lost. I-I had no money. No ID. No car. No friends. Nothing."

"What about your brother, Brendan. Didn't you go to him?"

"No," Melanie answered, speaking in barely more than a whisper.

"Why ever not?" Lara asked.

Melanie hesitated, lowered her gaze from Lara to the hands in her lap. The silence extended. Lara and Ryan said nothing, giving her all the time she needed.

"After he broke my tooth," she began at length, "James threatened to send Terrance to hurt Brendan if I ever told him about it. Terrance would have done it, too. Evil pig of a man."

"Terrance Elphick, the old, family retainer?" Ryan scoffed, playing his part to the full. "Are you serious?"

For the first time since their arrival, Melanie became angry. She scowled at Ryan, but addressed her reply to Lara.

"Terrance might be pushing sixty, but he's a total thug. Used to be a professional boxer, and quite a successful one. He still works out every day. He'd do anything for James. Once, I overheard James telling Terrance to teach someone a lesson. The next day, I learned that the person concerned had been mugged in the street. Beaten half to death, poor man."

"You knew the victim," Ryan said.

Melanie dipped her head again. "He was the … the builder James contracted to make some internal changes to the house after his first stroke."

"Why did they target the builder?" Lara asked, although she already had her suspicions.

"I used to make him and his team cups of tea, and he smiled at me once. Innocently, and just to thank me for the drinks. James saw it through his bedroom door. Went ballistic." She paused and took a breath before continuing. "Terrance killed Brutus, too. Under James' instructions."

"He killed your dog?" Ryan asked. "Are you certain? Did you see him do it?"

"No," Melanie answered, "but Brutus disappeared and Terrance told me what he'd done."

Oh Lord. The poor, little dog.

Lara closed her eyes for a moment. As a vet, she'd looked after plenty of animals that had been mistreated by their owners, and she still couldn't understand how anyone could be so evil.

"After his stroke, you say your husband was incapacitated, yes?" Ryan asked, his face expressionless.

She nodded. "That's right, he lost the use of both legs and suffered permanent weakness down his right side. Could barely move his right arm."

"But he still mistreated you?"

Melanie swallowed.

"Not … physically. He didn't have the strength anymore, especially when they discovered the tumour. Testicular cancer." A thin smile stretched across her battered face as she said the words almost gleefully. "Poetic justice, if you ask me. It served the bas—served him right. But despite his infirmity, he was just as nasty. Wouldn't let me leave the house without Terrance, and then only to run errands for him. We did most of our grocery shopping online, to be delivered. The house became a prison." She pulled her eyes from Lara and took in the room. "Almost as bad as this place."

Melanie seemed to run out of steam. She dropped her hands to her sides and rested her head on the pillow.

Ryan touched Lara's shoulder. She shot him a glance and he lifted an eyebrow. He'd made up his mind about something, but she had no idea what. She only knew that she needed to go along with it.

He stood and leaned closer to the bed—intimidating and making it obvious. Lara winced as Melanie looked up and jerked her whole body away from him, leaning as far back as the bed would allow.

"So, Mrs Archer," Ryan said, keeping his manner cool and detached, "would it be fair to say that you don't lament the premature demise of your husband?"

Melanie raised her head and fixed him with her watery, blue eyes. "What?"

"Mrs Archer, please answer my question. Are you sad your husband is dead?"

"Mr Pratt!" Lara said, not knowing where Ryan was heading, but feeling the need to play her part as his down-trodden assistant.

Ryan raised his open hand to silence her and continued to stare at Melanie, awaiting her response.

"Well?" he asked, even more firmly.

"No," Melanie cried. "No, I'm not sad at all. In fact, I'm delighted the evil swine is dead. But that doesn't mean I killed him. I didn't. I swear it!"

"Try and keep calm, Mrs Archer. Your histrionics do not impress me." He flapped his hand between him and Lara. "Ms Braithwaite and I have read the statement you made to the police. Is there anything you would like to change about it?" Rather than wait for her reply, he pressed on. "And before you answer, consider this. From what you've told me today, I have absolutely no doubt that I can make an excellent case for the defence. We can claim coercive control since your husband's stroke, combined with a history of physical abuse before his … incapacitation."

Ryan paused for a moment to let the statement sink in.

What's he doing?

"As I said earlier, Mrs Archer," he continued. "I am very good at my job. There is a high probability of a jury of your peers finding you not guilty. In short, I can almost guarantee that you'll walk free." Again he paused to emphasise his point before adding, "Now, is there anything you would like to change with regard to your police statement?"

Lara had no idea what Ryan was up to, or how could be

so confident in his prediction. She wanted to intervene but had no option other than to let him run with it.

"No, nothing," Melanie said quietly, the tears once again rolling down her cheeks.

"Did you kill your husband?" Ryan asked quietly.

"No, I didn't. I didn't! I swear it!" she answered, her voice growing louder, almost screaming. "I wanted to. Hundreds of times, I dreamed of it but, so help me, I didn't touch him. I did not kill him!"

Lara wanted to stop the interrogation, but Ryan wouldn't have been so aggressive if he didn't need to be.

"Really? This man who beat you, controlled you, humiliated you for more than twenty years? This man who had your puppy killed and threatened your brother's life? The man who was so weak he needed constant care and couldn't defend himself? You still claim not to have held his head under the water?"

"Yes, yes. That's right."

Ryan jutted his head forwards.

"Yes? You did kill him?" Ryan said, leaning further over the bed and almost shouting the question.

"No," she said, "I mean … yes, I'm still saying I didn't kill him. Oh God, why doesn't anybody believe me?"

Ryan pulled away and retook his seat. "If you didn't drown your husband, why does Terrance Elphick say you did?"

Melanie stopped crying long enough to ask, "He does?"

"You didn't know?"

She shook her head. "No, the … the police didn't tell me."

"Is there any reason for Terrance to lie?"

"No, I … Not that I know of."

"Hmmm," Ryan said, tugging his left earlobe again. "That is interesting."

The signal. He'd learned something. Lara focussed harder, trying to work it out for herself.

"What is?" Melaine asked.

"Well, I expected you to give the obvious answer."

Melanie took another tissue from the box Lara had brought with her and wiped her eyes carefully. "What obvious answer?"

"Well," he said, glancing at Lara, "I expected you to accuse Terrance of killing James himself. For the money."

"Money? What money?"

"Terrance stands to inherit a significant portion of the Archer estate. Didn't you know?"

Corky had discovered James Archer's last will and testament, and had uploaded it to the Trust's server along with detailed information on each of the beneficiaries.

"No," Melanie answered. "James never talked to me about financial matters. Called me an air-head. Stupid. But it doesn't surprise me, and it doesn't make a difference. Terrance would never have killed James."

"Really?" Ryan pulled away. "What makes you so certain of that? Blaming him would be another reasonable defence strategy we might bring into play."

"Because ..." She blinked rapidly and stared at Ryan. "... because James and Terrance were lovers. They had been for years." She swallowed and continued. "They kept it secret, but you should have seen the way Terrance cried when James had his first stroke. I had no idea the pig had any real emotions, but he bawled for days. If he'd known anything about medicine, I'm certain he'd have looked after James instead of hiring all the agency nurses he kept sending away."

"Who kept sending them away? Your husband or Terrance Elphick?"

"Either, both. One or the other. I don't know. Towards the end, I kept as far away from them as I could. Staying invisible was my best defence. The only way I could survive. I-I couldn't turn to anyone for help in case I dragged them into danger, too."

Something in Melanie's eyes told Lara she'd been telling the truth, but only partially. She couldn't avoid feeling that Melanie was holding something back, but what it could be, Lara had no idea.

"Okay," Ryan said after they'd been silent for a few moments. He smiled and nodded to Lara. "I'm convinced. Thank you."

"Convinced? Convinced of what?" Melanie asked, taken aback by Ryan's abrupt change in attitude.

"I'm convinced you didn't kill your husband," he said, confidence flowed through his calm delivery.

"What?"

Ryan's smile broadened.

"Although you had plenty of motive and ample opportunity," he said, "you did not kill your husband."

Their client frowned in obvious confusion. "Why? Why do you believe me?"

Lara needed an answer to the same question, but didn't want to interrupt Ryan's flow.

"It's simple," he said. "I've just given you plenty of opportunity to wheedle your way out of this mess. When I said we could use coercive control as a sure-fire defence strategy and offered you the chance to change your police statement, you didn't take me up on it. You even refused to point the finger at Terrance when I gave you the opportunity. All this suggests to me that you are innocent. Please forgive me for being so hard on you, but I needed to be sure."

Melanie stared at Ryan, wide-eyed. "Y-You believe me? You really do?"

"Yes. That is what I've just said, isn't it?"

"And, for what it's worth," Lara said, "so do I."

Melanie froze. She looked from Ryan to Lara and back again before slumping back into her pillows. Her relieved and heartfelt, "Thank you," spoke volumes. She took another tissue and quietly blew her nose.

"Thank you so much," she repeated, chin trembling and tears flowing afresh. "You have no idea what that means to me."

Ryan nodded and returned to his chair. He gave Melanie time to recover from his overly aggressive interrogation, but he only allowed her a minute.

"Now that's done and dusted," he said, rubbing his hands together to emphasise the point, "would you mind telling Ms Braithwaite all you can about Andrew Braemar?"

Melanie's face creased in confusion.

"Andrew?" she said. "James' cousin?"

Ryan nodded. "That's the man."

"Erm, yes. I suppose so. Why?"

"Just to fill in some blanks for us. Nothing to worry about. It's just that he's another beneficiary mentioned in your husband's will."

"He is?"

"You didn't know that either?"

Melanie's stunned expression answered for her.

"I told you. I have no idea what James' will contained. Nobody would tell me."

Ryan nodded.

"Okay, that's all for now."

"It is?"

Ryan smiled, slapped his hands to his knees, and used them to push himself to his feet. He even grunted with the effort, playing the tired, older man for all his worth.

"Where are you going, sir?" Lara asked.

"Won't be long. I just need a quick word with CM Thatcher. Let's see if we can't persuade him to protect our client a little better than he has been doing, shall we?"

"No, please don't—" Melanie threw a hand to her mouth.

"Sorry?" Ryan said.

Melanie snapped her mouth closed.

"Is there something you'd like to tell me?" Ryan asked.

She looked away. "No, no. … There isn't."

"Has CM Thatcher said or done anything … inappropriate?" Lara asked, picking up on Ryan's implication.

"I-I … No, no. He hasn't."

"Mrs Archer," Ryan said, leaning to one side, trying to catch her eye, "I am aware of certain unsavoury rumours associated with CM Thatcher. Are you sure there isn't something I, or Ms Braithwaite, should be made aware of?"

Melanie swallowed hard, lowered her eyes, and shook her head again. "Nothing. Really. There's been nothing. Nothing at all."

It's true, damn it.

Thatcher *was* using his authority to pressure the inmates. It confirmed Lara's interpretation of the snippets of angry conversation Priestly had engineered with Thatcher when they reached the ward.

Lara studied Ryan's reaction—grinding teeth, flared nostrils, clenched fists. He was struggling to maintain his control. Thatcher would pay for his crimes. Of that, Lara was in no doubt. Only two questions remained—when and how.

"Okay," he said, glancing from Melanie to Lara and back again, jaw tense. "I'll be right back."

He offered Melanie his hand. She took a timid grip and he held it loosely.

"Mrs Archer, Melanie," he said, quietly, "please try to remain positive. Remember, Ms Braithwaite and I are absolutely, one hundred percent on your side. We will do everything in our power to help and protect you. If there is anything you need, do not hesitate to call us, night or day. Ms Braithwaite will give you our contact details."

Melanie shook her head. "The rules only allow me one phone call per week."

Ryan released her hand, straightened, and showed her a confident smile. "Oh, I'm sure there are things we can do to circumvent the usual protocols. You are on remand here, and the standard prison rules don't necessarily apply. Besides, it's only a matter of asking the right people and using the right, shall we say, incentives. Leave it with me, Mrs Archer."

Ryan heaved the silver attaché case from the next bed and marched towards the door. He twisted the handle—found it locked—and rapped hard on its upper panel.

"Mr Thatcher?" he called. "Might I have a word, please?"

Lara smiled at a worried-looking Melanie Archer.

"Don't worry," she whispered, "Mr Pratt knows what he's doing."

Ryan Kaine knew what he was doing, too.

Lara wished they hadn't decided to forgo their comms units before entering the prison. She would have loved to hear how Ryan dealt with CM Thatcher, the evil bastard.

Chapter Eighteen

Monday 19th April - Afternoon

**Health Care Centre, HMP Falston Manor,
Derbyshire, England**

Forcing his rage to simmer below the surface, Kaine offered
Melanie his hand. She took a light, trembling grip and he
held it gently.

"Mrs Archer," he said, quietly, "please try to remain
positive. Remember, Ms Braithwaite and I are absolutely,
one hundred percent on your side. We will do everything in
our power to help and protect you. If there is anything you
need, do not hesitate to call us, night or day. Ms Braithwaite
will give you our contact details."

Melanie shook her head.

"The rules only allow me one phone call per week." As

she spoke, her lower lip trembled and her eyes filled with more tears.

Kaine released her hand and responded as best he could, trying to reassure, but knowing Lara would make a much better fist of it than he could. He ended with, "Leave it with me, Mrs Archer," and turned away, nodding to Lara. She'd take over and, no doubt, learn much more than he ever would.

With the heavy attaché slapping against his leg, he hurried to the door. The bloody thing was locked. Of course it was bloody locked. What did he expect in a prison? He knocked on the door, finding it even more difficult to keep his temper in check.

"Mr Thatcher?" he called. "Might I have a word, please?"

For some strange reason, since arriving at Falston Manor, Kaine had developed an aversion to locked doors. He couldn't be certain, but it might have had something to do with the battalion of men in heavy boots marching over his future grave.

When nothing happened after a rapid count of ten, Kaine pounded on the door with the side of his fist.

"Thatcher? Priestly? Is anyone there?"

He turned to face Lara, who'd lowered her legal pad and half-risen, concern written clear on her lovely face.

"Okay, okay," Thatcher called from the other side of the door. "We haven't forgotten you."

The clunk of a key turning in the lock turned into a symphony for Kaine's ears. He swallowed in relief and stood back as the heavy, metal door opened inwards to reveal the blond-haired custodial manager, who brushed past Kaine and blustered into the middle of the ward. His demeanour hadn't improved much since Kaine's earlier dismissal.

PO Priestly stood in the corridor behind Thatcher, apparently unwilling to enter the room.

"You locked the door, damn it!" Kaine said, blurting it out as a fierce accusation.

"This is a prison, Mr *Pratt*," Thatcher answered, turning to face him square on. He held his arms stiff at his sides, and jutted out his jaw in an act of barely disguised aggression. "Of course we lock the doors. Did you expect anything else?"

"My client is in a hospital bed with broken ribs, a fractured wrist, and serious concussion. She's going nowhere of her own volition. Did you think I was going to try and spirit her away in my attaché case, man?" He lifted the heavy object to underline the point.

If Thatcher was intimidated by Kaine's bellicose outburst, he managed to hide it well.

"Rules are rules, Mr Pratt. Are you finished with the prisoner?" he asked, peering over Kaine's shoulder at Lara and Melanie.

"For the moment."

"Good," Thatcher said, sniffing the air and adding a derisive sneer. "Perhaps you'd allow me to get back to my work now?"

"There are still one or two things we need to discuss, Mr Thatcher," Kaine said, adding a little oil to his voice. "I'd like a quick word in private, if you wouldn't mind." He glanced at PO Priestly who remained in the outer hall.

Thatcher pursed his lips in consideration. After a moment's pause, he said, "If you insist, Mr Pratt."

Kaine's earlier suggestion of them sharing a "mutual

interest" had clearly worked its way into Thatcher's head, acting like an earworm.

"Oh, I do, Mr Thatcher. I do indeed." Kaine gave Thatcher a thin smile.

Without further comment and without a backwards glance at Lara or the ward's only patient, Thatcher turned swiftly and marched from the room. Kaine depressed the end cap of the ballpoint pen clipped to the breast pocket of his jacket and followed a few paces behind.

The custodial manager took a right at the door, rudely brushed past Priestly, and indicated she should stay put. Thatcher headed along the corridor until it ended in a painted-brick wall, where he made a smart about-face and stood at military ease, waiting for a slow-moving Kaine to catch up.

Face to face, two paces apart, they stared each other down, Thatcher imperiously, Kaine with equal arrogance and no little anger.

"And how exactly might I be able to help you, Mr *Pratt*?" Again his mocking emphasis of Kaine's temporary surname was calculated to annoy, which it did—in spades.

Kaine pulled back his shoulders and locked eyes with the snarky custodial manager.

"Firstly, Mr Thatcher, I'm fully aware of the amusement my surname invokes in some *weak-minded* individuals. Please remember who you are talking to and show me the respect due a man in my position."

"Oh yes? And what position might that be?"

From Thatcher's overbearing posture, Kaine imagined the creep wanted to add "little man" as a rider to the question. The fact he managed to hold back the insult didn't improve Kaine's opinion of the ignorant, muscle-bound arsehole.

"Me, Mr Thatcher?" Kaine asked, keeping his voice soft to make sure PO Priestly couldn't hear. "I happen to be the man with the power to have Her Majesty's Inspectorate of Prisons descend upon this place by the end of this very day and have them run a fine-toothed comb through your operational procedures. How would an unannounced inspection affect your various … activities, *Mister* Thatcher?"

Thatcher pulled in his square jaw and blinked before asking, "What do you mean, my 'activities'?"

Kaine arched an eyebrow and allowed the question to hang in the air for a moment. Long enough to emphasise the point.

"I meant the normal, day-to-day activities of an institution such as this. Why?" Kaine leaned closer and fixed his steadiest glare on the taller man. "What did you think I meant?"

Thatcher spluttered for a while, apparently unable to find an answer.

"Falston Manor received a higher-than-average rating in our most recent annual review," he said eventually. He even managed to give a fairly decent impression of a man proud of his achievements.

"And so it did," Kaine said, nodding and pursing his lips, "but I wonder what a snap inspection would discover today."

"I run a tight—"

"Yes, I'm sure you do, Mr Thatcher," Kaine said, "but …" He paused again, aiming to draw out the tension.

"But?"

"But lots of things can affect an assessment of this nature."

"Life inside prison is fluid, Mr Pratt," Thatcher said,

this time using a more neutral intonation for Kaine's adopted surname.

"I am fully aware of that, Mr Thatcher. However, before I broach the real point of this discussion, will you answer one question?"

Thatcher hesitated and turned his head to one side.

"If I can," he said, more defensive in his demeanour.

"According to this institution's recent reports to the Ministry of Justice, all signed by both you and by the governor, Falston Manor has the lowest incidence of violence of all the high-security institutions in England and Wales. Is that correct?"

Thatcher's expression of surprise gave Kaine the response he expected and hoped for.

"You've been checking up on us, and me in particular?"

Kaine nodded and mirrored Thatcher's expression. "Of course I have, Mr Thatcher. As part of my firm's due diligence, don't you know. Would you expect anything else?" Again Kaine paused, awaiting an answer.

"Well ... no. I wouldn't."

"Exactly," Kaine said, adding a cold smile. "Tell me, is your incident report in any way ... accurate?"

The custodial manager's surprise changed to anger and his whole body tightened so much, it almost thrummed like the strings of a bass guitar.

"Of course it's accurate! How dare you accuse—"

"Calm down, Mr Thatcher. I'm not accusing you of anything," Kaine said, flapping his free hand in the air between them. "Nevertheless, how can you explain the fact that within two weeks of what I fully anticipate to be her *temporary* incarceration, my client was beaten half to death?"

Thatcher threw out an open-handed shrug. "There is no

explanation. From time to time, these events happen, no matter how well-run the establishment is."

"I totally understand," Kaine said, lowering his voice still further,. "That being the case"—he leaned even closer —"I have to say, strictly between you and me, that I've had it up to here with whingeing prisoners who don't know how well-off they really are. Bloody people. I consider most inmates are the lowest of the low."

Kaine winked conspiratorially and hesitated long enough for Thatcher to absorb the implications of his revelation.

"Really?" Thatcher asked, his body tense, defensive.

"Yes, Mr Thatcher. Do you doubt me?"

"No, but …" The custodial manager's shoulders relaxed, but only fractionally.

"On the other hand," Kaine continued, "I happen to be paid a great deal of money to do the absolute best for my clients. To that end, I might have a *mutually beneficial* proposition for you. The one I suggested earlier, if you remember."

"A proposition, you say?"

"Hmm," Kaine answered, nodding.

"What sort of … proposition?"

Thatcher's broad shoulders dropped a little more. He was definitely intrigued by the current direction of the conversation.

Time to turn the screw—so to speak.

"I'll get to that in a moment," Kaine said, glancing towards PO Priestly, who stared at them, curiosity written all over her face. "First, do you mind telling me what plans you have to ensure my client's safety?"

Kaine leaned away from Thatcher, whose body lotion emitted a sickly sweet fragrance that was overpowering in the close confines of the airless corridor.

Thatcher's eyes lost focus for a moment as he tried to find an answer. "I … well …"

"Have you conducted a thorough risk assessment?" Kaine asked, forcing the issue and adding to Thatcher's discomfort.

Keeping the interrogated off balance was key in situations such as this and Kaine could tell his technique was working.

"Not yet."

"Really? In the week since the attack you've done nothing to ensure my client's safety?"

"As I've said, not yet. My resources are stretched to—"

"Have you considered placing her in protective custody? I take it you have such a facility in this place, in this … institution?"

"No, not really. The best we could offer is solitary confinement, but that's not the sort of place we'd normally keep remand prisoners. It's rather severe. We prefer to house all the inmates in the open areas as part of the general population. It's … better for morale and makes the facility easier to manage on an operational basis, day-to-day."

"It's cheaper, you mean?"

"Well … I suppose it is slightly easier on resources, yes," Thatcher admitted, dipping his head in a nod.

Although he was probably aiming for confident, his delivery came across as belligerent and defensive.

"Is that all you have to say?"

"For the moment, yes."

"In that case, let me put this in a way that even a simpleton such as yourself can understand." Kaine shook his head and raised an index finger to forestall the expected, angry response to his insult. "If anything else happens to my client while she's under your care, I shall hold you personally responsible."

"You will?" Thatcher asked, speaking through a sneer.

It took all of Kaine's willpower not to pummel the arrogant smirk from the man's chiselled face, but as pleasant as that might have been, it wouldn't further Melanie Archer's cause.

"Yes, Mr Thatcher. I will make it my life's work to ruin you. And, to be honest, it won't take that much effort. Compared to me, you are an insignificant slug."

Thatcher ground his teeth.

"You arrogant little—"

"Listen to me, Thatcher," Kaine barked, raising both hands in preparation. He'd been pushing pretty hard and Thatcher might just have had enough. "And listen carefully. If Mrs Archer suffers anything worse than a hangnail, I'll come after you with everything I have." Kaine took a deep breath before continuing. "And believe me, Thatcher, I have a great deal of ammunition at my disposal. Do I make myself clear?"

"I don't take kindly to threats, Mr Pratt," Thatcher said, full of arrogant bluster. He'd already clenched his fists, but fortunately, had yet to throw a punch—fortunately for Thatcher.

"That wasn't a threat, Mr Thatcher. I don't make threats, I make calculated promises. And I never, ever, break my promises."

Thatcher blinked and, even in the coolness of the corridor, sweat gleamed on his upper lip as the confidence deserted him. "What sort of ammunition?"

Kaine smirked. "I wondered when you were going to pick up on that, Thatcher. Maybe you're not quite as dense as I assumed. In fact, my ammunition comes in the stick and carrot variety."

The creases on Thatcher's forehead deepened.

"Go on," he said, uncertainly.

Kaine grinned. He'd gained the man's attention with the idea of a carrot. In Corky's delve into Thatcher's background, he'd yet to come across any obvious indication of financial malpractice but, so far, he'd only had time to scratch at the surface of Thatcher's life. From Kaine's face-to-face perspective, the interest sparkling in Thatcher's eyes suggested greed, and Kaine planned to use it.

"First," Kaine said, making the upturned index finger into a counter, "the stick. As it happens, one of my colleagues, who is based in London, has a client in Holloway Prison."

Thatcher stiffened at the mention of his previous place of work.

"Ah," Kaine said, reinforcing it with a knowing head dip, "I can see we are beginning to understand each other."

"I have no idea what—"

"Oh come on, Thatcher. Do I need to spell it out? You have a position of authority over the inmates and you like to exert that power ... especially over the physically attractive ones. Now, this particular Holloway prisoner has made a number of unsavoury allegations against a former member of staff. I shall offer no prizes for guessing the name of that former member of staff." Kaine stared hard at the custodial manager.

Thatcher's face lost a dozen shades of colour. He seemed to shrink a couple of clothes sizes, too.

"As to the name of the prisoner, let's just call her Inmate A for the moment, shall we? After all, I wouldn't want an 'accident' to befall her before she can make a formal state-ment regarding her accusation."

"What? I-I would never—"

"Shut your mouth, Thatcher. I'm not interested in your spluttering," Kaine snapped, lowering his voice to a whisper once again. "To be perfectly honest, I don't give a damn what happens to Inmate A, but my client is off limits. Do you hear me? Should anything … unfortunate happen to Mrs Archer, it would upset my plans, and I can't have that. And while she remains healthy, my London colleague will ensure Inmate A is disinclined to make any official complaints against you. Do we understand each other now?"

When Thatcher still hadn't replied after a longer wait than Kaine deemed necessary, he leaned close again, eyeballing the custodial manager and braving the spicy body scrub.

"I asked you a question, Mr Thatcher. Do we under-stand each other?"

Thatcher tilted his head sideways and narrowed his eyes, which made his expression one of pure cunning. "Yes, Mr Pratt. We understand each other perfectly. I'll do all I can to keep Mrs Archer safe. As I do to all the prisoners under my care." He paused for a moment before adding, "So, I've heard the stick part. You mentioned a … carrot?"

Kaine made his grin as sly as Thatcher's.

"Yes. Indeed. I rather thought you'd be interested in the idea of a carrot." He extended his middle finger and placed it alongside the index. "In fact, we can call keeping Inmate A quiet one half of the carrot. As for the other half, you might be interested to learn that my partners and I main-tain a … well, let's just call it a contingency fund, shall we?"

Thatcher's demeanour oozed calculation. "You can call it whatever you like, but what's this fund used for?"

"From time to time, my company incurs certain expenditures that fall outside the fiscal norm. Expenditures we like to keep out of the public domain, if you see my meaning."

Thatcher's smug grin returned. "Yes, I'm following. You're making yourself perfectly clear."

"Good, good." Kaine straightened his face and became more serious. "As it happens, I can see a reason to access those funds in this particular situation. Can you?"

"I have no idea what you mean," Thatcher answered. Every twitch and mannerism betrayed his attentiveness, but he evidently didn't want to be drawn too far along the route without learning more. "What exactly are you suggesting?"

Kaine had baited the hook and the fish had bitten. Time to strike and reel in the catch.

"As I said, I'm simply interested in the welfare of my client. In no way am I asking you to do anything untoward or unethical. Oh dear me, no. What I *am* asking is for Mrs Archer's total safety while she's under your 'protection'."

Thatcher nodded. "If you're asking for special treatment … I'm not sure that's poss—"

"Not special treatment as such. In fact, I'm only asking for you to extend my client the protection that is guaranteed by the Ministry of Justice. If you can make this happen, my partners and I will show you our heartfelt appreciation."

"In what way?" Thatcher asked, lowering his voice to match Kaine's. He even leaned closer, increasing Kaine's exposure to the eye-watering pungency of the overpowering body lotion.

"Okay," Kaine said, "how does two thousand pounds a week sound? Tax free, and paid into any account of your choice. If you like, we could call it a retainer."

After a sharp intake of breath, Thatcher said, "Sounds pretty good to me." The smile in his eyes matched the one on his lips. "What exactly would I have to do in order to earn this … retainer?"

Gotcha!

Kaine scrunched up his face. "Nothing much. But let me make this crystal clear. For every week my client is on remand, you will receive your retainer, just as long as she remains in perfect health. If I hear of any more 'incidents' such as the one that led to her current condition, not only will I cut you off, but my partner will expedite the legal proceedings involving Inmate A. Do you understand what I'm saying?"

Although Kaine had his catch landed and floundering on the riverbank, Thatcher didn't know it yet. He still needed the final convincer.

"What makes Archer so special?" Thatcher asked.

Kaine eyed the custodial manager closely and delayed his response long enough to make the man think he was having trouble deciding how much was prudent to reveal, whereas Kaine was, in fact, playing things entirely off the cuff. However, he did have one thing firmly in his favour. He was absolutely certain he'd read his prey correctly.

"It's all a matter of economics, my good man. Risk and reward," Kaine said, rubbing his thumb and fingertips together as he had earlier. "As you know, my client stands accused of killing her *multi-millionaire* husband. When I clear her name, she will inherit a significant portion of the estate. And when that happens, she has promised to move all her legal and accounting business to my partnership. It doesn't take a genius to work out that this will result in a huge boost to my firm's bottom line and my ongoing, personal, end-of-year bonuses. None of this will happen if the poor woman fails to reach court because she dies in prison. It's worth two thousand pounds per week to my partnership to facilitate her ongoing good health. After all, one does have to speculate to accumulate."

Thatcher's smile grew wide enough to expose a set of teeth so bright they must have cost a fortune to whiten. The damned things blazed through his salon tan.

"Yes, Mr Pratt. You're making things perfectly clear," Thatcher said, rubbing his hands together. "Actually, your interesting problem has set me to thinking."

Double gotcha.

"And where do those thoughts lead you, Mr Thatcher? Somewhere productive, I hope."

"Given the prisoner's notoriety for killing her husband for the inheritance—allegedly—I'm sure it won't be too difficult to make a case for special treatment." He accentuated his statement with pursed lips and slow nods. "Yes, yes. Okay, I can certainly sell that to the governor."

"And what form will that special treatment take?"

"Nothing too drastic. I can arrange to keep Archer in protective custody for the foreseeable future. At least until we know the verdict. Can I assume that if she's found guilty, our arrangement will cease to function?"

"You can, CM Thatcher. You most certainly can. However, since the police's case is punctured by so many holes it cannot possibly hold water, I am absolutely certain our investment will prove … fruitful."

Kaine couldn't believe Thatcher would fall for such bullshit, but the jerky excitement of the custodial manager's mannerisms confirmed he'd been reeled in, and the hidden recording would ensure his continuing compliance.

"By the way," Kaine said, "there is one more thing I need."

Thatcher stiffened. "There is?"

"No need to worry. It isn't onerous."

"What do you want?"

"From time to time, I may need to speak with my client, or she may need to contact me. Would that be possible?"

Thatcher shrugged. "Don't see why not. The solitary suite has a landline at the officer's station. I can make it clear that Mrs Archer should be allowed to make calls, but only to your firm."

"Good," Kaine said. "And the calls must not be monitored. The discussions with my client must remain completely confidential."

"They will be. I can assure you."

Kaine nodded. "Excellent, excellent."

"So, what happens next?" Thatcher asked, all but holding out his hand for the first instalment.

"Next," Kaine said through a forced smile, "my assistant and I will take our leave of our client, and exit this"—he looked around and sniffed—"delightful establishment."

"And our arrangement? The ... retainer?"

"Don't worry, Mr Thatcher. I haven't forgotten. Sometime this evening, after you leave work, one of my associates will contact you to collect your bank account details. It wouldn't be prudent to discuss such things here, would it?"

"No, it wouldn't. Of course not. Okay, let's get you on your way so I can arrange protective accommodation for Mrs Archer for when she leaves the clinic."

Again, Thatcher's arrogant grin made Kaine want to bludgeon it from his lips, but he simply turned and walked alongside the custodial manager, smiling warmly as though they were the world's greatest bosom buddies.

Chapter Nineteen

Monday 19th April - Afternoon

Health Care Centre, HMP Falston Manor, Derbyshire, England

"Everything okay here?" Kaine asked Lara as soon as Thatcher opened the door to the ward and allowed him through.

"Yes, thank you, sir," she said, jumping to her feet and patting Melanie Archer on the shoulder. "I have a list of everything Mrs Archer needs. Will she be able to receive a fresh set of clothing and some toiletries?" She addressed her question to PO Priestly, who'd entered the room along with the men.

"All care packages will be subject to restrictions and

searches, Ms Braithwaite. You'll find a list of acceptable and controlled items on our website, isn't that right, Mr Thatcher?"

"Quite right, PO Priestly." Thatcher nodded effusively. "Quite right. You may go about your duties now. I shall escort Mr Pratt and Ms Braithwaite from the premises."

Priestly looked from Thatcher to Lara and Melanie before resting her gaze on Kaine, who nodded curtly. "Thank you for all your help, PO Priestly. It is most appreciated."

After she left, Kaine signalled for Thatcher to stay in the doorway and approached Melanie, who seemed more relaxed. Her tears had dried and her eyes seemed a little less puffy.

He leaned close and spoke softly. "You'll have no more problems with CM Thatcher, Mrs Archer. I can assure you of that. In fact, he's just agreed to be your absolute guardian angel."

Melanie shot a furtive glance towards Thatcher.

"A-Are you certain?" she asked, her voice faltering and timid.

Kaine explained how she'd be moved into the prison's secure unit and kept away from the general population, and it would happen as soon as Dr Milliner decided she was fit enough to leave the medical centre.

"Really?" she asked, her eyes brimming again. Her emotions had plainly been put through the wringer recently, as well as for the past two decades.

"How did you manage that?" she asked, reaching for yet another tissue.

"We have our methods, Mrs Archer," he said, deciding it was wiser not to elaborate. "We'll be leaving now but please rest assured, my colleagues and I will be doing our very best on your behalf."

Kaine and Lara left their client to her recovery and trailed behind Thatcher through the labyrinthine corridors of Falston Manor. Apart from the position of the sunlight blazing through the frosted glass in the high windows and the length of the shadows it cast, little had changed since the start of their visit to the medical wing. The inmates still watched them as closely as the prison officers, and the rubber soles of Thatcher's boots still squeaked annoyingly on the hard floors.

Halfway along a particularly extended hallway, Kaine sidled closer to Lara. "Learn anything interesting about Andrew Braemar?" he asked through the side of his mouth.

"Interesting enough to recommend a closer look at his business finances."

"I thought that might be the case. We'll talk about it in the car. I've a feeling Danny and I will be busy over the next week or so. I've always fancied playing private detective."

Thatcher took them along a changed route than earlier, leading them in the opposite direction to the administration block where their bags had been searched and their stuff had been confiscated on the way in.

Kaine's senses jangled.

"Why are we going a different way?" he asked, pulling alongside the custodial manager, who glanced sideways at him.

"This is the quickest route to the visitors' car park, sir. We're headed towards the employee's wing."

"But you have our phones and keys," Lara called out from behind.

Thatcher paused at yet another locked door, this one bearing a sign that read, "Official Use Only", and glanced at her from over his shoulder. "That's alright, Miss," he said, as condescending as he was before he and Kaine had come to their understanding. "I instructed PO Priestly to call ahead and have your things sent to the secondary entrance. You can pick them up on your way out. Your belongings are perfectly safe, I can assure you."

He pressed a button on the wall and a bell rang behind the door. He looked up at a mesh grill above the door and said, "Say cheese."

The red light on the surveillance camera behind the grill flashed once, the electronic lock fizz-clicked, and Thatcher pulled open the door. They followed him into an empty room that smelled of stale coffee and last night's takeaway.

"Excuse the whiff," Thatcher said, beckoning them past a row of chairs with mismatched and stained upholstery that faced a small TV. "We're right next to the kitchens and the ventilation system keeps breaking down. No money in the budget to replace it, so everything stinks of burger and chips. Stay in here long enough, and you get used to it." He sighed and grinned at Lara, still trying it on. "One can get used to anything after a while, I imagine."

Thatcher led them through the long, narrow staff room to a brick wall painted the same dull grey as the rest of the prison. The wall housed two more locked doors. He keyed the door on the right. Again, the heavy lock clunked. Thatcher yanked the door open and stood aside to allow Kaine and Lara into the anteroom ahead of them.

Kaine's senses flashed to full alert. Something felt wrong.

The open door led into a six-by-four-metre cage, with one door in and another out, nothing else.

"I'll be leaving you here," Thatcher said. "Not enough room in there for three, unless we're the closest of friends.

When I close this door, you'll be able to open the other one after ten seconds. A bit of a pain, but security … you know. Your possessions will be on the desk in the outer office."

A mantrap—one door wouldn't open unless the other was firmly closed.

Shit.

Kaine didn't like it. Not one little bit.

He blustered in ahead of Lara, something he'd never have done were he not playing such an odious and self-important prick. On the way through the door, he stumbled and bunted heavily into Thatcher, knocking him to the floor. In a flash, he took hold of the uniformed man's arm and helped him to his feet.

"My dear fellow," Kaine said, brushing creases from the front of Thatcher's shirt and straightening his utility belt, "I'm most terribly sorry. Bloody attaché case is forever getting in the way. I should buy one of those wheeled bags with an extendable handle."

"It's quite all right, Mr Pratt. Think nothing of it," Thatcher said, raising his arms to ward off Kaine's effusive ministrations. "Accidents will happen."

Thatcher smiled thinly at Kaine, ogled Lara once more, stepped back, and pushed the door closed. The second the door slammed shut, Kaine started counting. His mouth dried.

One … two …

As a general rule, Kaine was no more claustrophobic than any other highly trained, special forces operative—which was not in the slightest—but the mantrap's walls seemed to close around them.

… four … five …

At his side, Lara shivered. "Bloody man gives me the—"

Kaine raised a finger to his lips and she stopped talking.

He reached for the handle of the exit door and gripped it tight.

... seven ...

He tried pushing the handle, but the door held firm. How long did ten seconds actually take?

... nine ... ten.

Click!

The door pulled open as though of its own volition and took Kaine by surprise. On the other side, a squat, uniformed man—with the double lines of a Supervising Officer sewn into his epaulettes—stared at them in surprise.

"Sorry, sir, madam," he said, looking from Kaine to Lara and back again, "the green light was showing and I wasn't expecting anyone to—" He frowned and pointed a stubby, brown-nailed finger at Kaine. "Hang on, do I know you?"

Kaine recognised the man instantly as a sergeant he met in Fallujah—a member of the Royal Engineers, a Sapper. He'd been one of the team inspecting the integrity of a road bridge Kaine and his men had defended from an insurgent attack. While taking cover during a renewed assault, they'd struck up an intense, but friendly conversation. Kaine rarely forgot the face of a man he'd met in battle, and evidently, Sergeant Gilligan "Gill" Faulkner was of a similar disposition.

"My God, Ryan Kai—"

Kaine shot an underhand, straight-fingered jab into a point directly below Faulkner's sternum. The tips of his fingers dug into the upper bundle of the man's solar plexus. Kaine pulled the blow slightly, using minimum force, wanting only to incapacitate for a short while, not impart serious damage.

Faulkner coughed once and folded around Kaine's

extended fist. Kaine took the man's full weight, held him up with the hand in his midriff, and patted him on the back with the other.

"Sorry, Gill," he whispered into the former Sapper's ear, "no time to explain. Just try to breathe normally. You'll be okay in a few minutes, I promise."

Kaine lowered him to the floor, making sure his legs dangled outside the mantrap to keep the exit door ajar.

"Watch your step, man," Kaine grumbled, smoothing the creases from his jacket and playing to the inevitable, overhead camera and the prison officer who would be watching on a monitor somewhere. "What do you think you're doing? Too much to drink last night?"

Lara moved closer to Kaine and the fallen man.

"What's—" she started, but broke off when Kaine shook his head and rolled his eyes upwards. Lara clearly understood the implication.

"He'll be okay in a minute. Let's go."

Kaine left Faulkner where he lay, half in and half out of the cage. The exit door rested against his legs. It wouldn't be long before the open door would trigger an alarm—perhaps in as little as ten seconds.

He wanted to take Lara's hand, but that wouldn't look right.

"Follow me. Move fast, but don't run."

A banging on the inner door of the cage told Kaine that Thatcher had seen Faulkner's collapse, if not the reason for it, but the open door prevented him gaining entrance to the mantrap. They were nearly out of time.

"Hello? Is anyone there?" Kaine called, breathing hard and trying to keep his racing heart from exploding through his chest wall.

At his side, Lara appeared calm on the outside, but her rapid breathing told a different story.

A short passageway led to another room, furnished like a military guardhouse, with a counter looking into the room, and a glass screen and hatch looking out over the visitor's car park. Thatcher had been true to his word. He'd taken them on a more direct route through the prison, avoiding most of the locked security doors.

A grey-haired woman with a large chest leaned over the counter, craning her neck to see what the fuss was all about. "Yes, sir?"

Behind her, a single desk monitor scrolled through a number of different camera angles, staying on each shot for about four seconds before snapping onto the next. It currently showed the mantrap, with Faulkner's legs sticking out through the part-open door.

Any moment now, the alarm will—

"I'm Mr Pratt, and this is Ms Braithwaite," he said, forcing his words through a parched mouth. "Mr Thatcher let us through the officers' mess."

"Yes," she said, nodding enough for the glasses dangling on the chain around her neck to jiggle wildly, "he informed me." She turned to reach for something under the counter. At the same moment, the picture on the monitor changed to show an overhead shot of the car park—including their shiny, black, hire car.

Bloody hell. So close.

The woman's hand came up, clutching the manila envelopes containing their phones, computer tablets, wallets —and, more importantly, the car keys. She pushed them across the counter and spun a clipboard with a receipt form towards him. Kaine snatched the envelopes from her, handed one to Lara, and scribbled his false name at the foot of the form.

"Aren't you going to examine the contents?" she asked, holding her glasses out to check his scribbled entry.

Despite the need for haste and the fact that her place in the elevated booth put her in a position of ascendancy, Kaine looked down his nose at her.

"Madam," he said in as haughty a manner as he could manage, given the acid roiling in his gut, "I have spent more than enough time in this ... establishment. Please allow us to leave."

He waved his hand at the heavily barred exit door.

"It's unlocked, sir," the woman said stiffly, making it clear she wanted rid of him as much as he wanted to go.

Kaine pulled on the stainless-steel handle and the door swung open, working against the spring of an automatic closer.

"The only one unlocked in this whole place, I imagine," he said, his manner as arrogant as ever.

On the monitor behind the security guard, the image rotated back to the mantrap. Faulkner's foot twitched, and his leg moved.

Good timing.

Kaine forced himself not to dart through the opening, which led directly into the car park. A mere one hundred metres and the pair of open blast gates stood between them and freedom. He allowed Lara through the door first, pointed the key fob at their Mercedes, and hit the button. The hazards flashed.

Almost there.

He turned to face the woman behind the security desk.

"Oh, thought you should know, there's been some sort of incident in that security box thing. One of your officers has had a slight fall. I think the fellow might need some medical attention."

He smiled and headed out into the overcast day, desperate to run, but not quite free yet.

"What did you say?" the woman asked.

By the time the wailing alarm started echoing around the car park, Kaine had dived behind the wheel of the Mercedes, fired up the beast of an engine, and threw it into drive. He paused long enough for Lara to slam her door closed, then stamped on the accelerator.

Traction control bit, keeping all four wheels firmly attached to the concrete—he'd left the car in Race Start mode for exactly such an eventuality.

They roared from the parking spot, wheels spinning, tyres smoking, engine screaming, as the huge, metallic gates started to close. The gap between the two gates narrowed stupidly fast.

"Ryan, we won't make it!"

"Seatbelt on," he yelled. "This'll be tight."

Buildings flashed by in a blur. Uniformed officers burst out of doors, arms raised, hands waving, mouths open, their voices drowned out by the wailing sirens and the Mercedes' screaming engine.

Eighty-five metres from the rolling gates, and still gathering speed, the Mercedes' tyres hit the stingers—retractable metal spikes protruding from the concrete. Designed to puncture the tyres of a fleeing vehicle slowly, immobilising but without catastrophic rupture, Kaine retained control. The car's run-flat tyres would give him a little more time.

With twenty metres to go, the gap between the gates stood at a little over six metres—and closing rapidly.

Ten metres away, a four metre gap.

Calculations flashed through Kaine's head.

How wide is the Mercedes? Two metres? More? Less?

Five metres distant. The engine roared. Alarms howled. People shouted, one of them Lara.

When they struck the gap with a juddering screech of metal on metal, the Merc's speedometer showed ninety-three miles per hour.

Orange sparks flew.

Chapter Twenty

Monday 19th April - Afternoon

Blast Gates, HMP Falston Manor, Derbyshire, England

The Mercedes shrieked in metallic agony.

The three-metre-tall gates stretched up and around them, their rollers, anchored into deep grooves buried in reinforced concrete, continued to close. Pneumatic pistons, inexorably powering them along the tracks, rammed both halves of the barrier together.

Grinding, screaming, buckling. More flying sparks.

The speedo fell to eighty miles per hour, seventy-five, sixty. Kaine mashed the throttle pedal into the carpet, as though it would make a blind bit of difference.

"Ryan!"

He whipped the steering wheel left, then right.

In one convulsive jerk, they tore free, exploding from the pincer grip of the gates as fast as the shell from a mortar. The mighty car careened along the tarmac on slowly deflating tyres.

"You okay?" he called, wrestling with the wheel and fighting the wild thrashing of the seriously wounded Merc, unwilling to risk a sideways glance.

"Yes," she answered, tension flattening her delivery. "Did you say something about a tight squeeze?"

"We made it, but might have scraped the paintwork a little."

"You think?"

He hit the brakes and threw the car into a four-wheel slide, making a hard left turn, taking them off Woodland Spur and onto the single track of Coplow Lane, heading in the opposite direction from when they'd arrived. They flapped through the tiny village of Falston. At less than a mile from the Manor, they weren't anywhere close to being out of danger.

"Where are they?" Lara asked, her voice raised, but more natural than before.

"Who?"

"The chasing cars."

"Wouldn't expect them for a while. They're going to take some time to figure out what happened. And the blast gates will be damaged. Might hold them up a little."

"The tyres. How far can we get?"

"Not far. Couple of miles maybe."

He stopped talking to concentrate on his driving. Keeping the damaged machine on the road with partially deflated tyres and broken suspension was proving a tad challenging, oversteering into one corner, understeering out of the next. Kaine felt as much in control of the big, German car as he had during the one and only time he'd allowed Lara to talk him into sitting on the back of a horse.

Although Coplow Lane maintained a reasonably straight line between the cultivated fields, heavy, overgrown hedges encroached on either side, restricting his view ahead. The low branches of ivy-shrouded oaks reached out to claw at the crippled vehicle. Under different circumstances, he might have enjoyed the challenge of keeping the car on the tarmac, but having Lara alongside added a pressure he could have done without.

Despite trying to play it down to Lara, at any moment, the police might send up a helicopter, and before that, patrol cars would likely flood the area. They didn't have as much time as he wanted, or maybe needed.

On a slow left-hander, the rear end of the Mercedes lost traction and jagged right. The offside, rear wheel hit the outer verge, sideswiped the bramble hedgerow, and bounced back onto the lane. Lara squeaked, either in fear or excitement, but Kaine wasn't about to ask which.

He eased the pressure from the throttle and reduced the speed of their headlong dash from fifty to thirty-five miles per hour. The pace seemed massively pedestrian by comparison, but the Mercedes became slightly easier to control.

"What happened back there?" she asked.

"Sorry, love," he said, relaxing his clenched jaw muscles enough to allow him to speak, "but the rear tyres are a little worse for wear. Damned stinger punched a load of holes in the rubber."

"I didn't mean that nasty, little shunt," she said.

He risked a lightning-quick glance. The red glow to her

cheeks, the glint in her eyes, and the stern frown gave him the answer to his earlier, unasked question.

A sign flashing by on their left warned of a T-junction one hundred metres ahead. Kaine removed his foot from the throttle and added it to the brake, pressing gently for fear of losing control entirely. The flapping of rubber on road and the bottoming out onto the rims when the car hit yet another pothole had increased during the previous quarter mile. The rubber wouldn't hold together much longer.

Still, they didn't have much further to go.

They reached the junction, at a pedestrian crawl, made a right, ignored the immediate left onto Mill Lane, and picked up speed to a breathtaking twenty-five miles per hour. The new road, unnamed by the dashboard's GPS, turned out to be little more than a farm track with two heavily pitted ruts running on either side of a central grass strip, which ground against the car's underside.

Lara, who'd stayed quiet while he negotiated the triple junction, spoke again when the curves in the track straightened out. "I meant back in the mantrap. That prison officer, he recognised you."

Kaine nodded.

"A guy I met in Fallujah. A Sapper. Sergeant Gill Faulkner. Nice bloke. Didn't want to hit him, but …" He shrugged. "Couldn't risk him holding us up too long."

"You didn't hurt him, though?"

"'Course not. He'll find breathing deeply a little painful for a couple of days, but there won't be any permanent damage. I don't hurt good people, you know that."

"Not even to save me?"

He winced before answering. Already, she knew him so well. Truth was, had he been alone, he'd probably have tried talking it through with Faulkner, but with Lara's freedom at stake, he wasn't about to take any risks. Yet here they were, flashing through the countryside on wheelrims.

He'd probably screwed up big time.

Occasionally, the Merc's exhaust caught on larger, central tufts of grass but, in an impressive demonstration of the manufacturer's build quality, the exhaust system held together.

"Okay, here we go," Kaine said, over the slapping of flayed rubber on gravelled road.

"I assume you know where we're going?" Lara said, finally asking the question he'd expected since their sudden departure from the Manor.

"Not far now," he said, knowing she'd take the hint and give him time to concentrate on his fight with the steering wheel.

The lane took a gentle, uphill arc to the right, past a thin gauntlet of hawthorn bushes and sweet chestnut trees on either side of the tracks. At the crest, it levelled out and carried on straight for another half mile, where it ended at a staggered crossroads with Crowfoot, Hay, and Woodhouse Lanes.

Farm buildings on the apex of the hill marked the end of their mad dash. Kaine couldn't risk travelling any further and, mercifully, had no need to do so.

They reached two oak trees guarding the entrance to a field, the gate to which stood invitingly open. Kaine pulled the fatally wounded Mercedes onto the rutted track and parked sideways, blocking the gap between the hedgerows.

Twenty metres away, on a rut running around the field, stood a pair of powerful, all-terrain motorcycles and a smiling Danny Pinkerton. He wore black leathers and carried a matt-black crash helmet.

Chapter Twenty-One

Monday 19th April - Afternoon

Farm Field, Crowfoot Lane, Derbyshire, England

"Hi there," Danny shouted as Kaine and Lara jumped out of their valiant, but doomed chariot. "What took you so long? The sirens started howling ages ago. I thought you'd been nabbed."

Danny marched a rapid circuit of the car and sucked air between his teeth as he took in the damage. "Still haven't learned to drive, I see, Captain. We really must enrol you in that beginner's driving course. Terrible way to treat such a beautiful piece of machinery."

Kaine scowled at Danny as he rolled the cramp from his neck and shoulders. The strain of holding the injured beast on the tarmac had taken its toll. He pulled in a deep breath of the fresh country air and released it slowly.

"Don't just stand there flapping your gums, Sergeant. Close the bloody gate before the police arrive and take us all away."

Danny grinned and jumped into action.

"Bike gear, Lara. Now. It and your helmet's in the top box of the Honda." Kaine pointed to the red, white, and blue Africa Twin, sitting beside Danny's garish, orange Triumph Tiger, and stripped off his expensive suit. He'd packed his comfortable and well-used bike jacket and leggings in the Merc that morning while Lara was still asleep.

"You've brought me motorcycle leathers?"

"I asked Mike to pick you up a set. Don't want you riding pillion without proper protection. He had to guess your size. For the helmet, too. You'll find an earpiece in the jacket pocket. Be quick, love. We've already been here way too long."

She picked her way through the green sprouts of early wheat to the bikes, yanked off the blonde wig, and started stripping out of her clothes. Danny climbed astride his Tiger and, to spare Lara's blushes, turned his back to pull on his helmet. The tinted visor hid his face, which would probably prove handy later. Although there were no CCTV cameras this far away from the prison, they'd eventually be riding through villages and towns, and would all need to keep a low profile.

"Lara, throw your clothes into the back of the Merc. We can't leave any trace of you for the forensics boys. C'mon, Danny. Chop, chop."

Danny lowered the zip on his jacket and pulled out a small, black object the size of a packet of cigarettes. He gently lobbed it to Kaine, who caught it left-handed, slipped the device into his open jacket, and waited for Lara to finish dressing. The black-leather bike gear fitted her like a second skin, and she looked stunning in it. The ankle-length boots, however, looked a couple of sizes too large, but they'd suffice for one ride, no matter how extended it might be.

She retraced her steps through the knee-high crop and tossed her skirt suit and wig into the back of the doomed car. Kaine, now dressed in his bike gear, took one circuit of the Mercedes, sliding his boots through the mud to obscure their footprints while he ran a final check before the off.

"Okay," he shouted, "we're good to go."

Danny fired up the Tiger, which purred like the big cat after which it was named. He twisted the throttle a couple of times and the bike roared.

"The GPS is loaded and the waypoints look sound, boss," Danny shouted and kicked into first, spinning the rear wheel in a mud-splattering, slide turn. "Follow me when you're ready. The route doesn't look too tricky."

He took off, running the Tiger around the outside of the field, following close to the hedgerow to minimise crop damage. The gate at the opposite side of the field stood open, and Danny would be ready to close it after Ryan and Lara caught up.

Kaine took Lara's hand and led her to the Honda. He pulled on his skid lid and watched her draw her helmet over her short hair and struggle to fasten the strap. For the first time, it dawned on him.

"Bloody hell," he said, lifting his visor so she could hear him clearly, "you've never ridden pillion?"

Lara shook her head and shot him a hopeful smile. "Just like riding a horse, right?"

"Sort of," he said, fastening her chinstrap and checking the helmet fit—not perfect, but acceptable for a single ride and he had no plans to crash. "Basically, get on behind me and hold tight." He paused long enough to make eye contact and ensure she was paying attention. "Keep your shoulders in line with mine through the corners. Trust me and we'll be fine."

He threw his leg over the saddle, leaned down to lower the pillion foot pegs, and took the bike's full weight when he kicked up the side stand. He patted the pillion seat and said, "Okay. On you get."

Nimbly, Lara climbed aboard and barely made a difference to the balance on the bike as she did so. He hit the starter and the Honda's beautifully tuned, 1000cc engine caught and growled louder than the Tiger, but not loud enough to drown out the change in pitch of the sirens coming from the direction of Falston Manor.

"Can you hear that, Charlie One? Over," Kaine said, knowing his earpiece would transmit his words to Danny. Despite the restriction of the helmets, the system had worked well enough during the previous night's testing session.

"*Loud and clear, boss. Cops are on their way. No time to hang around. Over.*" Danny's voice sounded crystal clear over the noise of the motorcycle engines.

"Foxtrot One, are you receiving me? Over."

"Yes, Alpha One. I hear you. Over.

"Hold tight. Over."

Lara's arms wrapped firmly around his waist.

Kaine knocked the Africa Twin into first and pulled away much more slowly than if he'd been riding solo.

Lara moulded herself into his back, and their crash helmets tapped together in the lightest of kisses. He smiled.

Under different circumstances the upcoming ride would prove interesting on so many levels.

He gunned the Africa Twin's engine a little more until they reached the Mercedes, and slowed long enough to tug the device Danny had given him from its nest inside his jacket. He hit the "activate" button, lobbed it through the open rear door, and roared away, following Danny's route around the field.

Lara squealed and hugged even tighter.

"You okay? Over?"

"*Wow! This is great. Loving it. Over.*"

"Hoped you would," he said, opening the throttle a little more and picking up speed. Danny stood alongside the open gate, waving them through. "If you feel up to it, take a look behind you and tell me what you see. Over."

Although they bounced and bucked over the uneven terrain, Lara loosened her grip and he felt her twist at the waist.

"*Blue lights in the distance, from the Manor, heading closer. And … wow, the Mercedes just blew up.*"

Although muffled by the padding inside his helmet, the ragged crump of the explosion reached Kaine at the same time Lara described it.

"*It's on fire now. Over.*"

"Danny's incendiary bomb worked a treat. Over."

"*Wondered what you threw in the back and why you parked the Mercedes in the opening. To block the police cars, right? Over.*"

"Yep. That's exactly it. Over."

"*That's so cool. Foxtrot One, out.*"

Kaine ran the big Honda through the open gate. Danny closed it behind them, dived back onto his Tiger, and led them southwest and slightly downhill. They bounced and leaped along a deeply rutted track, heading for a dark opening in dense woods that spread out across the floor of the valley.

Danny had spent much of the time Kaine and Lara were in the Manor planning an optimal route out of the area and out of sight of any aerial surveillance. Kaine trusted his young friend's navigational skills enough to follow without question, even though they seemed to be heading towards the main road—a dual carriageway which would be the obvious first place for the police to throw up any road blocks.

Pushing forty-five miles per hour on a track only suitable for slow-moving farm vehicles, they entered the dark tunnel of trees. The dappled sunlight glinting on Kaine's visor restricted visibility. He kept his eye on the Tiger's rear reflector, which kept flashing, illuminated by the Honda's dipped headlight.

The previous evening, while Lara and Mike were bedding down the horses—or whatever people did to horses overnight—Kaine and Danny had discussed the idea of disabling the bikes' headlights. They'd decided against the option, working on the principle that motor-bikes not showing lights would probably draw more attention.

Ahead, Danny slowed, indicated right, and entered a denser thicket of trees. The track they rode over was more overgrown drainage ditch than actual pathway. After five minutes of crashing through vegetation and brambles, they burst into full sunlight once more. It took Kaine a moment to realise that Danny had taken them into the middle of a working farmyard, and he just managed to avoid a mud-covered tractor towing a muck spreader.

"*I'm glad Farmer Giles doesn't have that thing switched on and flinging sewage. Over,*" Lara said, the amusement and relief in her voice audible over the grey-bearded farmer's bellowed cussing.

He followed the Tiger's taillight right at the end of the muddy yard, then left onto another gravelled farm track, before jagging left onto a green lane, this one far more suitable for a high-speed, two-wheeled escape.

"Charlie One," Kaine shouted, "where are we heading? Over."

"*Don't know about you, boss,*" he said, his laughter obvious even through the distortion of the electronics, "*but I fancied a round of golf. There's a par three course up ahead. Over.*"

"Don't you go chewing up any putting greens. Over."

"*As if I'd do anything so heinous. You cut me, boss. You cut me deeply. Over.*"

"We're running really close to the dual carriageway," he said, worried they might be seen by a patrol car. "Over."

"*No alternative, boss,*" Danny said, sounding more serious. "*We'll be turning north after the golf course and heading for Derby. After that, it's pretty much green lanes and minor roads all the way from there to the M1. The terrain's none too hairy from what I can tell on the GPS. Over.*"

"Thanks, Charlie One. Let's take it easy from here. We're far enough away from the Manor. No need to draw any more attention to ourselves. Over."

"*Right you are, boss. Using these lanes, it'll take us about ninety minutes to pick up the motorway, but we're in no hurry. Over.*"

"Fair enough. We'll stop for a break at the first services southbound." He paused a moment before tapping Lara on the thigh. "You pick up all that, Foxtrot One? Over."

"*Yes, thanks. Over.*"

"Everything okay back there? Over."

"*Of course. This is great. Why haven't you taken me pillion before? Over.*"

"Didn't think you'd fancy it. Besides, when do we ever have time for fun? Over."

"*That's true. Maybe when were done with this … mission? Over.*"

"No can do. After this, we'll be heading to Paris. Over," he said, squeezing Lara's knee.

The Tiger made a sharp, right-hand turn and braked hard as another tractor blocked their way. Danny rode up the grass verge and allowed the tractor to pass, but the expression Farmer Giles' younger and beard-free brother shot him might have curdled the milk in the trailer he was towing. Kaine followed Danny onto the verge and around the obstruction.

"*Next right along here will put us on another green lane. Couple of miles. Should be traffic free. Over,*" Danny said.

"Excellent. The further we are from the Manor and that dual carriageway, the happier I'll be. Over."

They made the turn and, as Danny predicted, the green lane proved empty of traffic. The terrain was also as smooth and easy to negotiate as any they'd travelled on so far, and wide enough for Kaine to pull alongside Danny and ride two abreast. They increased the pace, taking the speed to the maximum safe envelope of forty-five miles per hour.

Before long, the sun burst through a bubbling bank of cloud and made the ride the joy it promised to be. They'd seen no hint of blue lights or of a police helicopter since torching the Mercedes, and the mad-dash getaway turned into a gentle, afternoon ride out.

Twenty minutes and two more green lanes later, Danny broke them out onto a minor road which was in good enough condition for them to roar up to the national maximum speed of sixty. They took an easy and circuitous route, taking their time wending through the picturesque villages of Radbourne and Kirk Langley, and turned south-east onto Ashbourne Road, heading for Derby.

They skirted the main roads north of Derby, weaving in and out of the growing traffic in the way of all motorcy-clists, and eventually picked up the M1 at Junction 25.

All told, the whole meandering route took them the better part of two hours, twice as long as it would have done, had they not been evading what turned out to be a slow and poorly organised police chase. Still, it had given Kaine time to reflect on all he'd learned during their visit to one of Her Majesty's places of incarceration. Foremost of which being, he'd rather not visit one again any time soon, and certainly not as an inmate.

Chapter Twenty-Two

Monday 19th April - Lara Orchard

Donington Park Services, M1, Leicestershire, England

Ten miles of riding a little over the speed limit on the M1 heading south—if she stretched her neck enough, Lara could see over Ryan's shoulder to read the motorbike's speedo—took them to the Donington Park Services and a much-needed rest break.

Ryan overtook Danny on the approach to the slip road, signalled left, and they parked within sight of the main entrance. He had to help her off the bike and out of her helmet. They tapped the earpieces inactive.

"You okay, love?"

She shook out her recently shortened hair and ran her fingers through it to work out the tangles.

"You were right about it being different from riding horses. My legs and backside are as stiff as anything."

"Muscle specificity," he said. "We'll take a recovery break here for a little while. See where we are. We need to refuel both us and the bikes."

"It was fun, though." She smiled and arched the stiffness out of her lower back. "Apart from all that being-chased-by-the-police part."

"We were being chased? When was that?" He gave her one of his warm and reassuring grins, which rarely failed to improve her mood.

Lara stretched out as best she could in her close-fitting leathers, paying particular attention to her legs, working loose the stiffness in her knees, calves, and ankles. She'd work on her glutes in the nearest restroom rather than provoke the stares of the goggle-eyed men who seemed more intent on ogling her than watching where they were going. One middle-aged man with a combover almost walked into a lamppost.

"Don't know what Mike was thinking when he bought this gear," she said, starting to pull down the zip on her jacket before thinking better of the idea.

When they'd abandoned the Mercedes, she'd struggled to squeeze into the leathers and had to remove her blouse along with her skirt and jacket. Under her leathers, she wore nothing but underwear, and the Lord knew how see-through the bra would be after all the sweating she'd done while holding herself on the saddle.

"It is a little ... snug," Ryan said, scowling at another passer-by who couldn't draw his eyes away, before smiling apologetically at her. "But ... wow!"

She had no trouble accepting Ryan's appreciative gaze, though. None whatsoever.

Behind Ryan, Danny couldn't hide his discomfort. "Sorry, Doc," he said. "Can't let Mike take the blame for that one. My fault, I'm afraid. He asked me your size and I thought you were similar to Bobbie. I took her on a motorcycle track day last month and that was her size." He pointed at the leathers, smiling in apology.

"For heaven's sake, Danny," Lara said, "Bobbie's at least one dress size smaller than me, except for her obvious … assets."

Lara couldn't prevent herself from laughing when Danny's jaw dropped and he blushed bright red. In battle, he was as lethal as Ryan, Rollo, and every other member of Ryan's team, but off-mission he could still be as shy around women as a sixth former.

On the other hand, she loved him like a younger brother and couldn't have been more delighted he'd found a soulmate in Bobbie Shafer.

WITH A HALF-FINISHED MUG of coffee in hand and an empty plate which had once held a chicken panini on the table before her, Lara cast her mind back to the first time she been in a motorway services café with Ryan and Danny. On that occasion, Rollo had been with them and they'd narrowly missed being blown to pieces alongside Ryan's former friend and boss, "Gravel", and his wife. How naïve she'd been back then, and how much she'd learned since.

During that long-ago pit stop, the only thing on her mind had been how soon she'd be able to return to her life as a country vet. Her interesting, safe, but ultimately unfulfilling life. Not anymore. Not on this occasion. Although they hadn't said it in so many words, in the months since that terrifying and lethal dash for freedom, she and Ryan had committed themselves to each other. For the rest of their time on the planet, however short that might be, they would live and, eventually, die together. But not today.

No, not today.

Danny drained the last of his diet cola, set the glass bottle on the table in front of him, and rotated it between finger and thumb. "Why the smile, Doc?"

She shook her head. "Just remembering something."

"Last time we were in a place like this?"

This time, she nodded. "That's right. Lot of water under the bridge since then."

"Certainly has been. Any regrets?"

"Not many," she said and opened her hands to show him the transparent strips that masked her fingerprints. "Didn't need to wear a disguise back then, but"—she started picking the pads free of the thin film—"I'm getting used to it."

"Depending on the motivation, you'll be surprised at what you can—"

"Lara," Ryan said, interrupting what was probably going to be a deep and meaningful conversation, "I imagine you have a few questions?"

"You could say that."

"Ask away. We have time, and I'm sure Danny's interested in what happened back at the Manor."

Danny nodded his agreement and leaned closer so Lara didn't have to raise her voice. Although they'd taken a corner table, as far away as possible from prying eyes and open ears, the café was jumping and plenty of patrons sat within a craned earshot. The overhead surveillance cameras weren't an issue as they sat directly beneath one, whose lens pointed at the entrance forecourt and couldn't depress deeply enough to pick them up. As usual, Ryan and Danny sat with their backs to the wall, with good views of the exits and entrances, while she sat opposite, feeling confident and well protected. They all wore baseball caps to obscure their faces. Ryan left little to chance.

"Okay, first question," she started. "Back in the prison when we were collecting our phones and the car key, what took Thatcher so long to raise the alarm?"

"Oh, that."

"Yes, that." Lara waited for Ryan to say something, but he just stared at her, wearing an annoyingly knowing smile. Lara grunted. "The security guard with the dangling glasses took an absolute age to let us out. I expected the alarms to sound long before they did."

"Thatcher was a little … what should I call it? Confused and distracted?"

"Thatcher?" Danny interrupted. "You're talking about the custodial manager, right?"

"Yep," Ryan said, "that's the fellow."

"Why would he have been 'confused and distracted'?" Lara asked, her frustration building. She hated when Ryan hid things from her. Being kept in the dark about having to escape on motorbikes was bad enough, but being trapped in that room, moments away from becoming a permanent fixture, and without any knowledge of his plan, had frightened her more than she cared to admit.

"On account of the bribe he accepted during our private conversation while you were talking with Melanie Archer." Ryan's annoying smile grew as he gave them a brief overview of his private conversation with Thatcher.

"You offered him two grand a week to protect Mrs

Archer?" Danny asked, his eyebrows lifting a fraction—as much a show of surprise as Danny would ever give.

"What made you think he wouldn't cry foul and arrest us both for trying to bribe an official?" Lara added, her anger rising at Ryan's surprising lack of caution. Surprising for him, at least.

Ryan shrugged, his gaze still taking in the café and the customers milling around. "Something about him screamed 'bent'. Not just his record, but the way he behaved when PO Priestly barged in on him and Melanie in the hospital ward. And, I didn't like the way she overre-acted when I told her I wanted a chat with Thatcher. I was playing a hunch."

"So," Danny said, turning to face Ryan and momen-tarily dropping his surveillance, "you have a verbal agree-ment with a greedy prison officer, and that was enough for him to delay raising the alarm?"

Ryan tilted his head to one side as a sort of nod. "That and the fact that I disabled his radio when I bumped into him on the way into the mantrap."

Lara nodded, the image clearing. "I wondered what was happening there. Not like you to be so clumsy. Thought you were overacting again. Playing the doddery, old man."

Ryan rolled his hand like a magician revealing a trick.

"Wait a minute," she said. "How did you manage to damage his radio so quickly? That stumble only took a second or two."

"A pin in the radio's headphone jack?" Danny asked.

"That's right. An old trick, but it still works."

"You took a pin into prison with you?" she couldn't help asking.

"Yep. Stuck into the seam of my lapel. Another schoolboy trick that still seems to work pretty well."

"But why?" she asked. "Things were going well. Did you suspect something was wrong?"

"Not really. Just hedging my bets. The idea of stepping into a mantrap gave me the willies. You were right about things going so well up to that point, but the closer we were to the exit, the more antsy I got. Felt the need to do something proactive."

"So," Lara said, not wanting to let go of the subject, "just because he couldn't use his radio, why couldn't he use another method to raise the alarm?"

Again, Ryan worked his knowing smile. "Didn't you notice the lack of panic buttons in the officers' rec room? After seeing poor Sergeant Faulkner take a tumble and being unable to open the door on his side, I'm guessing Thatcher wasted a few seconds trying to raise the control room with his radio. After that, he'd have had to return to the main part of the prison to hit the alarm. That all takes time and, if you remember, I also distracted the security guard from looking at her monitor."

"In short," Danny said, returning to studying the café's patrons, "you got lucky."

"Dead right," Ryan said through a brief laugh. "In short, we got lucky."

"Your forethought created the luck, Ryan," she said, unwilling to let him dismiss his actions so readily.

"Possibly," he said, "but it might have been something else entirely. Thatcher might not have realised what was going on with Faulkner or he might have been worried about losing a tax-free two grand a week. Either that, or he could have thought I'd drop him in the mire if we were captured."

"Shame we've lost our hold over him, though," Lara said. "Even though Marcus Thatcher is a bona fide, first-class creep, he would have worked hard for his money. Now no one's going to protect Melanie. I'm absolutely certain she's in real danger. The poor thing wouldn't say boo to a goose. She's the least likely person I've ever met to upset anyone."

"Don't be too sure of not having a hold over the oily custodial manager," Ryan said. His lovely smile grew as he lowered the zip on his bike jacket and reached his hand into the inner pocket. When he pulled it out again, it was clutching a silver ballpoint pen. Slightly larger than normal, but just the thing a ridiculously over-priced solicitor would choose to carry.

"You're kidding?" Danny sighed. "He didn't fall for that old chestnut, did he?"

"What old chestnut?" Lara asked, starting to grow really tired of the double act sitting across the sticky table from her.

"This, dear Lara," Ryan said, holding up the pen and twiddling it between index finger and thumb, "is pure James Bond."

"What do you mean by 'pure James Bond'?"

"As well as being a rather effective writing implement, this little darling is a highly sensitive voice recorder. You can buy cheap versions from online spy gizmo shops. Apparently, they start at less than sixty quid."

"You have a recording of him accepting a bribe?" she asked, finally getting the message.

"Hope so. I haven't had the chance to hear it yet. I wanted to pop into the loo to check the sound quality while we were still inside. Wanted to play it for Thatcher to make sure he didn't play silly buggers on the way out, but things rather got away from us. Still, let's see what we have, eh?"

He held up the pen and clicked the end cap once. Nothing happened.

Hugely disappointed, Lara opened her mouth to say something, but Ryan held up his hand in a "wait for it" gesture.

"Give it a chance. I switched it on while Thatcher and I were walking along the corridor outside the ward, and it took a while before either of us spoke."

As the seconds ticked by, Lara found herself leaning closer and closer to the pen. At the same time, she held her breath.

The pen's silence was broken by squeaks and rustles, and then came the words, "And how exactly might I be able to help you, Mr Pratt?"

Although slightly muffled due to it having been in Ryan's pocket, Thatcher's unmistakeably cultured voice sprouted from the pen loud and perfectly understandable. Lara released her pent up breath. Ryan allowed the recording to continue for a few more seconds before clicking the pen once more to end the replay.

"That's a relief," Ryan said, the twinkle in his eye showing he'd had every faith in the device's effectiveness. "Was worried it mightn't work or I'd screwed up somehow."

"Online spy shop, my arse," Danny scoffed, wagging his finger at the ballpoint. "Don't let him fool you, Doc. Those cheap, spy shop devices aren't much chop. More like toys. That there is a military grade spy-pen. Not only can it record for up to twelve hours continuously, it transmits the data via microwave to anywhere within a five-mile radius, once you're out in the open. There ought to be a copy of the recording on a receiver in the top box of the Africa Twin. Right?"

Ryan nodded. "And from there, it's been automatically

transmitted to our server and backed up a dozen times. No way that recording's going missing. It's too valuable and might end up playing a part in saving Melanie's life."

"I don't know how, but you think of everything," Lara said, nodding at the pen.

"I didn't predict Faulkner's arrival, but whenever I'm dealing with a greedy man, I always think it best to work on the principal that I'll need some leverage to keep him 'on side'."

"I'm surprised Corky didn't let us know about Faulkner," Danny said. Lara followed his gaze and found him concentrating on an overweight security guard. She was patrolling the area near a row of ATM machines and staring hard at a couple of suspicious-looking youths in hoodies.

"Corky can't do everything," Ryan said. "Besides, I asked him to concentrate his research on Andrew Braemar and Terrance Elphick."

"And he's been helping Angela with another project, don't forget," Danny said.

"Redistributing Max Campese's ill-gotten gains, you mean?" Lara asked.

"I do indeed."

"You did a good thing there, Danny," Lara said.

"Thanks, Doc."

Danny smiled and slid his scrutiny from the security guard to the view through the windows. They'd left the bikes in clear sight of the entrance, and the two mud-spattered machines kept receiving the same admiring glances Lara received in her clingy leathers.

Men and their daydreams.

Ryan slid the spy-pen back into his jacket pocket and pulled up the zip.

"So, what's our next move?" Lara asked, already antici-pating Ryan's reply and preparing her response to it.

"*My* next move is to poodle up to Nottingham where I'll wait outside Marcus Thatcher's home until he returns from what I imagine is going to be a long, long day at the coal-face. When I'm certain he's alone and ready to listen, I'll play him this recording." He patted his bike jacket over the area of the ballpoint. "Thatcher probably thinks he's well out of it after our daring escape, but I'm going to make sure he keeps Melanie safe until she has her day in court. No way am I going to let the Trust fork out two thousand a month to force that crook to do his job. That money's for The 83, not greedy arseholes like Marcus-bloody-Thatcher."

"And what about Danny and me?" Lara asked, letting her argument fall before wasting her time and energy trying to change the mind of a man who thought he knew best—and usually did.

"*Your* next move," Ryan said, his knowing smile suggesting he could read her mind, "is to head back to Mike's place with Danny and hire a real firm of solicitors for Melanie. The best the Trust can afford. I'd like to find out if a professional and fully funded defence team can arrange a bail hearing."

"Okay," Lara said, nodding and leaving her objections unspoken. At least Ryan had a plan that made some sense, which was a damn sight more than she had. "It's worth a try. Melanie's never been in trouble with the police before and she told me her court-appointed brief didn't even make a bail application. The useless idiot claimed it wasn't worth the effort since the charge was so serious and the police were bound to oppose any application. At the time, Melanie was too disorientated to argue the point."

"And, at the time," Ryan added, "the only place she could go to was the family home, which happened to be the crime scene. So, the police didn't have a location to bail her to. With the Trust's funding, we can house her in a hotel until the end of the trial. I doubt she'll object to wearing a tracker. If it's at all possible to arrange a bail hearing, we have to try it. And the sooner the better."

Lara couldn't argue the logic and settled back in her chair, making the most of the time she had left in comfort. Not that she'd admit it to Ryan, but her backside still ached from the mad dash through the green lanes of Derbyshire and she didn't particularly relish the idea of riding pillion again so soon. Riding behind Danny might be an issue, too. He didn't seem to have the same smooth, bike-handling skills as Ryan. Danny had bounced and slid the Triumph around the lanes like a beginner. Lack of experience might have had something to do with it. Or perhaps typical, male bravado.

"Can you explain something that's been annoying me since we abandoned the Mercedes?" she asked.

"Shoot," Ryan and Danny said together.

"How did you manage to get two bikes in that field on your own?" She fired the question at Danny, who smiled and turned his blue eyes on her for a moment before continuing to watch the food court. While he took the left quarter, Ryan covered the right. She'd rarely felt as well protected.

"Wondered when you were going to ask that," Danny said. "As you can imagine, I couldn't do it alone."

"Of course not."

"It was easy, really. Mike and I put the bikes on his low-loader soon after you left this morning. Then we searched for a place far enough from Falston Manor to be safe, but close enough to reach easily if you got into trouble." He smiled. "Which, of course, you did."

"And I suppose you had Corky hack into the Mercedes with GPS co-ordinates so it could lead us directly to the bikes?" This question, she aimed at Ryan.

"Got it in one." He grinned. "Everything's so much simpler when you have a Corky on your side."

"Isn't it just," Lara said, once again marvelling at the planning of the man who'd devoted his existence to protecting the people whose lives he'd inadvertently damaged. People including her.

"Damn it," Ryan said, looking past Lara's shoulder. "Lara, we've got company. Keep your head down. Danny, keep her safe."

Before Danny could respond, Ryan climbed to his feet, touched her shoulder, and headed towards the entrance concourse.

Keeping her head lowered, Lara risked a glance behind her.

Her heart fluttered.

Outside, in the pale, early-evening sunlight, a young, red-headed man wearing the uniform and reflective, yellow vest of a motorway cop stood over their bikes, taking a particularly close interest in Ryan's Africa Twin.

Chapter Twenty-Three

Monday 19th April – Melanie Archer

Health Care Centre, HMP Falston Manor, Derbyshire, England

Even in the relative quiet of her sickbed, Mel had heard the strident alarms. Couldn't have missed them even if she'd tried. However, until the prison officers arrived, she had no idea what caused the emergency—fire, riot, jailbreak—and half-expected to be evacuated from the infirmary at any moment.

Two female prison officers she'd never seen before burst in while the sirens still screamed. They strip-searched her, and did it none too gently. She cried the whole time, mostly in shock, but also in pain as they kept jogging her broken arm and ribs, which fired bolts of agony through her whole body. At one stage, the younger officer inadvertently rested an elbow against Mel's ribs and she yelped.

The two women ignored her screams and, for some reason, kept asking her about Ryan Kaine, for Heaven's sake.

What the heck?

She asked why, but that only made them ask louder.

The older of the two, a supervising officer, led the interrogation. A grey-haired woman in her fifties, she had three chins, a protruding belly, and rough, calloused hands with nails chomped down to the quick.

The senior officer repeated her question, almost shouting.

"W-Who?" Mel answered, barely able to speak through the sobs and the pain.

The younger one took pity and helped lean her back against the disrupted pillows. Mel eased over to one side, trying to lessen the discomfort in her grating ribs. Her right hand throbbed and her eyes watered.

"Ryan Kaine," Supervising Officer Fatso snapped. "He was here for hours. What did he want?"

"What? What did you say?"

"You heard me. What did Ryan Kaine want?"

"Ryan Kaine? What? I have no—"

"Cut the crap, Archer!"

Mel shook her head and the pounding migraine returned with so much force it was like the flaming thing had never gone away.

Still firing questions to which she had no answers, they allowed her to dress. With only one workable hand, it wasn't easy. The younger officer helped her with the buttons of the pyjama jacket.

SO Fatso stood back from the bed and fixed Mel with a pair of angry, brown eyes. "What did Kaine want?"

"S-Sorry, but you're making no sense. I have no idea what you're talking about."

"The man you spoke to today, the man calling himself Laurence Pratt, what did he want?"

Mel tried to shake her head again but it hurt so much, it made her wince. "Oh no, Mr Pratt was my solicitor, and he told me not to tell anyone what we talked about. Privileged … information, he called it."

SO Fatso glowered at her. "Laurence Pratt was Ryan Kaine."

"What? That's insane! Why would …"

Kaine? Pratt was Kaine?

He couldn't be. No way.

Mel closed her eyes in abject denial. "Don't be stup— silly. You were the ones who let him in, for goodness' sake. Surely you checked his … credentials? Mr Pratt looked nothing like Ryan Kaine."

"Why was he here? What did he want?"

"It's just like I said. He was my solicitor. We talked about my case. That's all."

"You really expect me to believe that?"

Mel ground her teeth together, and breathed as slowly and deeply as she could. Nothing made any sense. "Believe whatever you like. It's the truth."

"What about the woman, Braithwaite? What did she do or say?"

Mel hugged her throbbing arm against her chest. The plaster cast was cold and hard, unforgiving. "She did nothing but take notes and examine my injuries."

"Is that all you're going to say?"

Mel found herself frowning, stretching the stitches over her eye. "That's all there *is* to say."

"I've read your file," SO Fatso said.

"Have you?"

She was surprised the tubby brute could read.

"Kaine killed your brother, but you're still prepared to protect him. Why is that?"

"I'm not, and he wasn't Kaine. I'd know Ryan Kaine anywhere. His picture is printed on my brain." She tapped her temple with a finger. "Why on earth would I have anything to do with the monster responsible for Brendan's death?"

"Were you planning an escape?"

"What? Don't be ridiculous. If I were a man, I might have tried to find Kaine and kill him, but collude with him in an escape attempt? Are you insane?"

SO Fatso's upper lip curled into another sneer. She was certain. Absolutely convinced. She was wrong. Had to be. But …

Dear Lord, what if they were right?

They were.

They *were* right. Their eyes confirmed it.

Mel had been in the same room as Ryan Kaine! She'd spoken to him. Shaken his hand. Touched him.

Mel's stomach heaved, forcing bile into her throat. She threw her hand to her mouth.

"Sick," she said. "I'm going to be—"

She retched again. The younger officer leaped forwards, grabbed a cardboard tray from a nearby trolley, and stuck it under Mel's chin at the same moment the vomit spewed from her throat and nose.

While she wiped her mouth with a paper towel, the main

door crashed open. Dr Milliner burst into the room, closely followed by CM Thatcher who was so pumped up with testosterone-fuelled anger he looked as though he might explode. Behind Thatcher, another person trailed in, another stranger.

Mel had to take a second and then a third look to determine whether the unknown person was male or female before settling on the latter. Dressed in a dark blue, tailored suit, she was slim-hipped, and wore her dark hair in a severe, almost military cut. Her unlined face was makeup free, and her horn-rimmed glasses were at least two sizes larger than necessary, as though an attempt to hide her extraordinarily piercing, blue eyes. Haunting eyes.

SO Fatso and the other officer stepped aside to allow Dr Milliner access to the bed, while Thatcher and the other one stood back, talking in hushed tones. Thatcher appeared deferential to the slim woman in the dapper suit, deferential to the point of obsequious, which made Mel even more uneasy. Her stomach railed again, but this time she managed to swallow down the nausea.

Dr Milliner prodded and poked and asked a few medical questions, which Mel answered truthfully, but they elicited no respite.

Yes, she was in pain. Her arm throbbed, her heart raced, her ribs ached, and sweat leached out of every pore. But worst of all, the thumping headache and blurred vision had returned to torment her.

Milliner nodded noncommittally to every answer and jotted a couple of notes onto the form on the clipboard she'd plucked from the foot of the bed. She stuck an electronic thermometer in Mel's ear and held up her finger for silence. Thatcher and the strange-looking woman stopped talking, probably to make sure Mel couldn't hear what they were saying. They stood still, staring at Mel with undisguised distaste.

Why? What had she done wrong? It wasn't fair. Nothing was fair. The whole world stood against her and the first moment she saw any light in the darkness, it had been cruelly extinguished. Pratt and Braithwaite had offered comfort, hope, but even that had turned out to be nothing more than mental torture. So cruel.

Did Kaine really break into prison and risk capture just to torture her with the possibility of salvation? Could anybody be that nasty? That brutal.

Damn it, Mel. You are so naïve.

Kaine murdered Brendan and all those others. Of course he could be that bloody brutal!

The thermometer bleeped, Milliner removed it from Mel's ear, glanced at the reading, and nodded.

"Normal," she said and turned to Thatcher. "She's okay to be interviewed."

"What? A-Are you certain?" Mel asked.

She was panting. So bathed in sweat that the bed was saturated, yet Milliner claimed her temperature was normal and she was fit to be interrogated? What kind of a doctor was she? A rubbish one, that was for sure.

Thatcher and the woman approached the bed, while Milliner and SO Fatso left the room. The young PO stood by the door, notebook and pencil at the ready like a cop witnessing an interrogation.

The strange woman spoke first.

"I'm Alan Bancroft," he said with a voice as deep as any man Mel had ever heard. "Governor of Falston Manor."

Alan? A man? Really?

Once again, Mel's deductive skills had proven as flawed as everything else in her life. She'd failed to recognise the governor as a man, as she'd failed to recognise the man who killed her brother. What the Devil was wrong with her?

At least it explained what the young PO was doing standing by the door. She was acting as Mel's chaperone and had nothing to do with note-taking.

The governor continued. "You've caused me and my officers a great deal of effort, Mrs Archer. A facility of this type is a powder keg waiting to explode around our ears. We are stretched to the limit daily, and for an inmate such as you to be involved in an incident such as this—"

"But I'm *not* involved. I'm not! I had no idea—"

"Don't you dare interrupt the governor, Archer!" Thatcher snarled.

Bancroft's cold, sideways glance at Thatcher suggested he didn't need the custodial manager to fight his battles, but he didn't give voice to his opinions.

"Sorry, sir," Mel mumbled to her bedding, unable to look either man in the eye, "but I didn't have anything to do with Mr Pratt's … or rather, Ryan Kaine's visit. I mean, I had no idea Mr Pratt *was* Ryan Kaine, and I still find it hard to believe. Are you certain it was him?"

Bancroft nodded definitively. "It was Kaine, all right." His deep voice resonated through the ward like the bass line of an R&B track. The rumble coming from such a slightly built man was truly unusual, almost as though it was forced. "One of my officers recognised him and was seriously injured for his troubles. We've had to rush him to hospital for treatment and observation."

Thatcher pursed his lips and nodded in support of Bancroft's words, but the glance they exchanged made Mel wonder whether the governor was telling her the entire truth. However, considering everything that had happened, Mel was so thoroughly confused and distrusting of her ability to interpret even the most obvious signals, she chose not to believe her own suspicions.

Keep quiet. Don't give anything away.

"Again," Mel said, "I'm sorry, but I had no idea."

"What did Kaine want?" Thatcher asked, lifting his heels from the floor to loom over both the bed and tower over the diminutive Bancroft.

To defend against the expected pain, Mel squeezed her eyelids together and shook her head gently. "Like I told Supervising Officer Fat—sorry, the supervising officer, we just discussed my case and the direction our defence should take."

Bancroft shuffled half a step away from the muscular brute and asked, "Which was?"

Mel lowered her head and looked down at her hands. "Isn't that privileged information?"

"Damn it, Archer!" Thatcher snapped. "Kaine isn't a bloody solicitor, *privilege does not apply here!*"

"CM Thatcher, modulate your tone, if you please."

Although the governor didn't raise his voice, the words cut through the room with a finality that couldn't be ignored. Thatcher's heels dropped to the floor and he almost wilted under Bancroft's ice-cold stare.

If Mel's face hadn't been so bruised and swollen, and if she hadn't been so thoroughly confused, she might have been able to raise a smile at Thatcher's discomfort.

"Yes, Governor. My apologies," the horrid man said.

"I don't need your apology, CM Thatcher," Bancroft said, turning to face the custodial manager full on, "but I'm certain Mrs Archer would appreciate it."

Thatcher's double-take was a picture and his subsequent, "My apologies, Mrs Archer," could not have been delivered with less grace or enthusiasm. Pulling wisdom teeth without anaesthesia might have proved less painful to the man. Again, Mel was hard put not to laugh.

Bancroft turned to face Mel again. "Now, I repeat. What did you and Kaine discuss?"

"As I said, we only talked about the case. Kaine"—she shuddered at the use of his name—"asked me some questions, which I seemed to answer to his liking, and that was pretty much it. In fact, CM Thatcher spent more time with the vile creature than I did. Why don't you ask him about it?"

Mel had thrown down the gauntlet and waited for the musclebound bully to bend down and scoop it up. He did nothing more than scowl, and the imagined gauntlet lay on the floor where she'd thrown it.

"Is this true?" Bancroft asked when it became clear that Thatcher wasn't going to answer.

"Not in the slightest," Thatcher answered, lying through his perfect, white teeth.

Mel snapped up her head, and once again, the pulse pounded through her temples. "You did too!"

Bancroft held up his hand for silence. The hand was much larger than expected, the nails glossy and beautifully manicured. Their clear lacquer shone under the harsh lighting.

"Are you saying you did not talk privately with Kaine," he asked, addressing the question to Thatcher.

"No," Thatcher said, his tone adamant, "I'm not saying that at all. It's just that I don't like the implication Archer is making. I did, however, talk in private to the man I *thought* was her solicitor."

"And what did you find to say to each other?"

Thatcher raised his broad shoulders in a shrug and

pinched his lips together. "Might we discuss this in private, sir?"

Bancroft shook his head. "Here is good enough, CM Thatcher. Please continue."

Thatcher puffed out his chest and tightened his tummy muscles.

"Well, sir," he said, speaking through a clenched jaw, "we didn't say much. As I said, no one had any reason to think Mr Pratt was anything other than what he claimed to be. Basically, he tried to convince me that Mrs Archer's life was at risk. He wanted me to place her into protective custody."

"And what did you tell him?"

Thatcher scoffed. "I told him to mind his own darned business. Although, I did tell him very politely, sir. I mean, we can't have any Tom, Dick, or ..." He wilted under Bancroft's frosty glare.

"Harry?" Mel suggested, unwilling to let the bully slide out from under the governor's scrutiny.

"Thank you, Mrs Archer," Bancroft said. "Is there any reason to think you are in immediate danger?"

Is he serious?

Mel allowed her mouth to drop open until her jaw muscles pulled at the skin on her swollen cheek and stretched the cut over her eye.

She waved her good hand over her plaster cast and in front of her face. "Are you seriously asking me that, sir?"

Bancroft sniffed and, for the first time, his unlined face became animated, although Mel still found it difficult to read the man's expression. Amusement, maybe? Annoyance? Shock?

"How is the investigation going, CM Thatcher?" he asked.

"Investigation, sir?"

Bancroft's eyes narrowed. "Have you identified the culprits who attacked Mrs Archer?"

Thatcher let out a breath that, at first, sounded suspiciously like a sigh but changed into a throat-clearing exercise. "Unfortunately not, sir," he said. "As usual, nobody saw or heard anything. And Mrs Archer has been unable or unwilling to help. I'm afraid it's probably one of those inmate arguments that got out of hand. You know how it is, sir."

"It wasn't an argument," Mel said, trying not to allow Thatcher's glower to intimidate her. "I was taking a shower and … the attack was unprovoked."

"Really?" Thatcher said, his manner both defensive and somehow threatening. "This is your first time inside, Archer. You have no idea how prisons work. Sometimes even the most apparently insignificant, unguarded comment or sideways glance can cause offence. Are you sure you didn't annoy anyone? Even unknowingly?"

A spike of anger scorched Mel's belly and she retorted, "If I did something 'unknowingly', how could I be expected to answer that sort of question?"

Bancroft cut his hand through the air. "This is getting us nowhere." He faced Mel again. "Are you sure there's nothing you can tell us about either the attack or the reason for Kaine's visit? And before you answer that question, remember this. If you help us in this matter, we will be able to put in a good word for you at your trial. If you are found guilty of the charges against you, the support of a prison governor will stand you in good stead in the longer term."

Mel paused to think on what the governor was saying. "You mean, if I'm found guilty of murdering my husband, a nod from you might earn me a day or two off my life sentence?"

"Unlikely," Bancroft said, noncommittally, "but we might be able to provide you with special treatment when you arrive in our care. A single cell, perhaps."

Care? Yes, right. Of course you will.

Mel allowed her tongue to run over the gap where her dental crown used to be.

"I'm sorry, Governor Bancroft," she said, sadly. "If I knew anything that could help you, I'd tell you. Truly, I would. But I have no idea who attacked me or why, and I really don't know what Ryan Kaine wanted. I'd tell you if I did. Honestly. I have no reason to protect that man."

At least the second part of that statement was true. She did have an idea who might have been behind the attempt on her life. Unfortunately, the only person she'd told was Emma Braithwaite, who worked for Kaine, a man she wanted to kill with her bare hands. What was the evil monster up to?

Chapter Twenty-Four

Monday 19th April - Early Evening

Donington Park Services, M1, Leicestershire, England

With his helmet hanging from its strap around his wrist—ready to use as a weapon, but only if absolutely necessary—Kaine sauntered through the automatic doors and out into the cool of the early evening.

The idea that the police could have identified their bikes as the getaway vehicles so quickly seemed unlikely, but in an age of instant communications, satellite imaging, and blanket surveillance, anything was possible.

From the moment he left Lara in Danny's more-than-capable hands, he'd been regretting his decision to stop at the services. They should have pushed through and made it to Mike's in one run. The added forty-five-mile journey would have taken less than forty minutes, but the way Lara had started to fidget on the pillion seat enforced the rest break. Even though the Africa Twin had undergone a massive redesign before its relaunch, the bike's rear seat was notoriously uncomfortable and must have taken its toll on Lara during her first pillion ride. The fact she didn't once complain showed her endurance and her inner strength. A wonderful woman in every way, he struggled to forgive himself for ripping her from her safe, happy existence and forcing her into the life of a fugitive. An outlaw.

Once again, Kaine berated himself for not working out a way to return her to her former life of safety. Truth was, he hadn't even tried. Shame on him for his weakness. One day soon, he'd find a method to send her home, even though it would be painful. Without Lara, his life would be empty, but he couldn't allow his weakness to lead her into even more danger. The escapade in Falston Manor, and the trouble in Denmark, showed how reckless he'd become. Against his better judgement, he'd allowed her to talk him into entering the dragon's lair, and that should never have happened. Irrespective of the logic of her argument, he should have overridden her insistence. Recently, Lara had become directly involved in more and more of his activities and it simply had to stop.

One day, sooner or later, their luck would run out and … the result didn't bear thinking about.

Falston Manor would be the last time he'd let her walk into danger. Absolutely the last time.

He approached the young police officer, but avoided eye contact—an innocent biker on his way home, minding his own business.

"Is this your bike, sir?" the lone constable said, calm and

friendly, giving no sign of being on his guard. The lad—PC Lucci according to the badge attached to his hi-vis tabard—took in Kaine's mud-encased Honda, his eyes full of appreciation rather than suspicion.

Kaine stopped short as though noticing the cop for the first time.

"Oh, hi there, Officer," he said, the tension ebbing away from his shoulders and gut. "Yeah, the big beastie's all mine."

"Nice," PC Lucci said, smiling and barely able to tear his eyes from the machine, which suited Kaine well enough. "Really nice."

The youngster was a keen biker, as his manner made perfectly clear.

Instantly relaxed, Kaine gave up on the idea of using the crash helmet as a weapon and pulled it over his head instead. Far better to use it the way it was originally designed—and to hide his face at the same time—instead of a blunt object to bludgeon an innocent officer of the law.

He fastened the strap under his chin and, rather than raise Lucci's suspicions, he lifted the visor, to leave only his eyes and cheeks exposed. His coloured contacts would hide any possible resemblance to the outlaw, Ryan Kaine.

Kaine stood back and watched the cop make a slow circuit of the red, white, and blue liveried machine.

"My dad had one back when I was a kid," the impossibly youthful-looking officer said, totally unaware of the irony of his words. "I remember it as a huge monster of a thing," he continued, "built to ride clear of the dunes during the Paris-Dakar Rally, back in the late '80s."

"Sure was," Kaine agreed. "Honda won the race with it from '86 to '89. Beautiful machine. Rugged, you know? Bulletproof."

Lucci nodded along with Kaine's bull. No motorbike ever built could survive a bullet, and neither could its rider. But it sounded good.

"My dad's close to six foot tall and he could barely reach the ground with his toes. The bloody thing kept toppling over at low speed, especially with a full tank. How do you manage ... I mean what's the new one like to handle?"

He had the good grace to look embarrassed by his innocent mistake.

"For a short-arse like me, you mean?" Kaine asked, laughing as he did so and giving Danny the divers' "okay" signal behind his back.

Danny would take his lead from Kaine and make sure he and Lara came out already wearing their skid lids.

"No offence meant, sir," the officer said, his cheeks flushed.

"None taken, Officer," Kaine said, shaking his head. "None at all. I couldn't handle the original version, but the revamp has lowered the saddle height by a few centimetres. I've also fitted the new, compact seat. Works a treat now, but it's still uncomfortable for the pillion rider. Overall though, it has beautiful balance and a similar ground clearance as the original. More beef in the engine, too. Runs as smooth as you like."

The officer turned to watch Danny and Lara's approach.

"I see you've taken them off-road today?" Lucci asked, returning to his topic of primary interest and checking out the fresh mud.

"No point having bikes like this and only using them for the daily commute," Danny said, striding up to the Triumph and throwing his leg over the saddle. He straightened the bike, kicked up the stand, and waited for Lara to climb aboard before keying the ignition.

"Sorry to rush you, Constable Lucci," Kaine said, "but we need to get these to the pressure washer before this mud cakes on too hard."

"I fully understand, sir," Lucci said, smiling.

He took a couple of steps back to admire their departure, unaware of how close he'd been to an arrest that would have made his career—and given him hero status in the national media. Either that, or the humiliation of being yet another police officer to suffer the embarrassment of being defeated by an apparently scrawny, little man who couldn't ride the original Africa Twin, and who couldn't possibly be the vicious terrorist, Ryan Kaine.

Danny revved the Tiger while Kaine mounted the object of Lucci's desire and they rolled away, heading for the petrol station.

"*Bloody hell,*" Danny said over the radio, "*that was close. Trust us to spark the interest of the UK's version of CHiPs. Over.*"

"Not to worry. Officer Lucci's a tad height-ist, but anyone who wants an Africa Twin for Christmas can't be all bad. Foxtrot One, you okay? Over."

"*Okay, thanks. This saddle's much better than yours. More padding. Over.*"

"Everyone's a critic. Don't tell our new friend, Constable Lucci. He'll be mortified. Over."

They remained silent while filling both tanks with premium unleaded, and rode in parallel for a while before separating at the roundabout leading onto the M1. Kaine aimed north, heading to Nottingham, while Danny and Lara turned south, aiming for Long Buckby and the safety of Mike's farm.

Kaine waved farewell.

"See you later, Foxtrot One. I should make it back to Mike's overnight. Charlie One, take care. You're carrying precious cargo. Over."

"You can trust me, Captain. Charlie One, out."

As Kaine ended the chat, an ominous sense of dread overtook him. For the first time in years, he wanted to scrub his mission and reverse direction, but he'd made a promise and could not renege on it.

Melanie Archer, one of The 83, needed his help and he'd provide it, at least for as long as he believed her innocent of murder. However, if he learned anything to cast serious doubt on that belief, he'd withdraw all but the Trust's financial support.

On the slip road to the motorway, Kaine opened the throttle and the Honda's powerful engine shot him and the bike into the heavy, northbound traffic. He filtered through the lanes and roared ahead. Marcus Thatcher needed a visit and Kaine didn't want to let the avaricious bastard down.

After twenty minutes' defensive, motorway riding, the GPS took him off the M1 at Junction 25, onto the slightly more picturesque A52, a dual carriageway that seemed to be the home of aggressive drivers hell-bent on ruining the lives of motorcyclists who dared to infest their lanes. A left turn onto the tree-lined, and far less busy, Thoresby Road enabled him to slow and breathe more normally. Bramcote Way turned out to be an equally easy ride in the gloom of an early dusk.

By the time he reached Wollaton and turned into Lambourne Way, the streetlights shone and the worst of the rush-hour traffic had faded into a dark memory.

Marcus Thatcher's bachelor pad—a nondescript, seventies-built bungalow—turned out to be as good a home as any for a middle-grade public servant with an annual income of around forty thousand pounds. With walls of red brick, a grey-tiled roof, and a pebbled front garden, it looked like a dozen of its neighbours. Unlike its fellows, the place was dark and currently unoccupied. Kaine could find no sign of Thatcher's eight-year-old Porsche Boxster or its cherished plates—T222 MBT—on the drive, which would be where a braggart like Thatcher would park it. The bugger would see no point in having a fancy-looking car unless he could show it off to the neighbours.

According to Corky's research, Thatcher had bought the bungalow outright with the equity from the sale of his London apartment, but how he could afford to buy digs in London in the first place needed a deeper dive.

Kaine rode past the target house as slowly as possible without drawing attention to himself, taking in the area in one extended sweep.

A left turn off Lambourne Way led to a likely spot— Harborough's Plantation, a miniature nature reserve only slightly larger than a picnic blanket. Although small, it did have the benefit of off-road parking for the Honda, accessed via a footpath which was defended by one-metre-tall, wooden stakes. Thankfully, the stakes had been planted wide enough apart for Kaine to squeeze the Africa Twin through and hide it in the middle of a growth of bushes, propped against a mature ash tree.

From the pathway, the bike was hidden, but mainly because all but one of the nearby streetlights had blown, leaving the area as dark as such a spot in suburbia would ever get. Whether the Honda would be there on his return was anyone's guess. If some opportunistic scrote stole it, Kaine could always ask to borrow Thatcher's Porsche. Thatcher wouldn't be in a position to refuse such a reasonable request.

After an extended phone call to confirm that Lara and Danny had reached the farm safely, he strolled gentle laps of the woods, taking slightly longer each time and soaking in the tranquillity—decompressing.

When he'd judged the time optimal—with Corky's assistance—he sauntered away from Wollaton's diminutive version of nature and retraced his route to Thatcher's place, mentally prepping himself ahead of the expected action to come.

Chapter Twenty-Five

Monday 19th April - Marcus Thatcher

Lambourne Way, Wollaton, Nottingham, England

Marcus Thatcher indicated left and pulled the roaring Boxster into its usual spot on the driveway, aware of the twitching curtains of his jealous, Ford Mondeo-owning neighbours.

Yeah, gawp away, peons.

He killed the three-point-four litre, flat-six engine, but waited for the current track—complete with its booming, bass rhythm—to end before turning off the ignition and powering down the CD player. Another curtain twitch confirmed he'd made his arrival known to more of the dullards.

Thanks to Ryan-fucking-Kaine's escape, and the subsequent investigation and debrief, he'd struggled through a long, hard day. He'd even missed his session at the gym for the first time in months. Marcus could find no reason why the neighbours shouldn't suffer a little, too.

Marcus pushed open the driver's door, wincing as the hinges squealed in protest. Fuck it, the mechanic swore he'd greased the bloody things during its last service. The next time he had a spare moment, he'd take his baby back to the garage and play merry hell with the scrawny grease monkey. No one fucked with Marcus Thatcher and lived long enough to laugh about it down the pub.

No one.

He marched around the front of his beautiful machine, pausing long enough to polish a speck of dust from the bonnet with the sleeve of his civilian jacket, and headed for the sanctity of his new home and the comfort of his nice, warm bed. Next time he had a full weekend off, he might finally get around to unpacking the last of the boxes in the spare room. He'd lived too long as though he was just passing through, but after the day he'd endured, he felt the need to plant some roots.

Kaine! Ryan-bloody-Kaine!

So bloody close, but who the fuck could have known?

However inadvertently, when Gill Faulkner recognised Laurence Pratt as Ryan Kaine, he'd probably saved Marcus' career. Maybe even his life.

Fuck's sake, he'd actually been close to jumping into bed with a bloody terrorist!

Sure, two grand a week would have helped boost his growing bank balance, but working for a monster like Kaine would have been a step too far, even for Marcus. Not that he minded stretching the rules a little if it felt good and padded the bank account, but Ryan-fucking-Kaine?

No way, José. No bloody way.

Yep, Gill had saved his bacon all right. So much so, he'd pick up a bottle of whisky for the knackered, old soldier. He'd helped Marcus dodge the bullet and no one could ever accuse Marcus Thatcher of ingratitude. But he wouldn't stump up for Gill's favourite tipple, Glenfiddich. Not a chance. He'd pick up a cheaper alternative, maybe a half-bottle of Wild Turkey.

Marcus wasn't all that grateful.

He jabbed his front door key into the lock and turned the handle. The door opened into a dark and chilly hallway. Frigging heating hadn't come on again. Bloody timer. He could never figure out how the damn thing worked. He hit the light switch. Nothing. Clicked it on and off again as though that would make a difference.

No electricity.

Couldn't be a fucking power cut. Lights were blazing away in the rest of the street so brightly it could have been bonfire night. He growled in annoyance, threw his keys on the phone table in the hall, and pulled out his mobile. Its built-in light shot out a brilliant, white glow to illuminate the hallway.

Where the hell did they hide the electricity meter and the circuit breakers in this place?

Ah yes, airing cupboard. Kitchen.

With the mobile's stark torchlight leading the way, Marcus—grumbling the whole time about "shoddy builders in the sticks"—reached the kitchen and found the cupboard. Two banks of trip switches all showed green, but the main breaker showed red. He pressed the button and held it in for the three seconds needed to lock it in place.

The kitchen's fluorescent strip lights flickered into life

and then held. Marcus closed the cupboard door. Movement behind him and to his side made him freeze.

"You should consider upgrading your lighting, CM Thatcher. Fluorescent tubes are an ecological nightmare, didn't you know?"

Heart racing, Marcus spun.

"What the fuck?"

A shortish, slim man in motorcycle gear stood in the middle of the kitchen. Smiling.

Curly hair, beard.

Kaine!

Fucking hell. Ryan Kaine!

In Marcus' fucking kitchen stood the mass murderer, Ryan-fucking-Kaine!

He nearly wet himself.

Oh fuck, I'm dead.

No.

Wait.

Jesus, no. Not dead. Not yet.

Marcus raised his fists and backed away until stopped by the cooker. Rounded knobs dug into his buttocks. He glanced at the killer's hands, expecting to see a gun or a knife, a club maybe, but they were empty. No weapon in sight. The arrogant arsehole hadn't even raided the drawers for a kitchen knife.

What the fuck?

Unarmed.

Marcus had a chance.

Ryan Kaine, the UK's most dangerous and wanted man, was in his kitchen and unarmed. The short-arse fucking git had the nerve to—

Marcus stiffened in preparation.

"How dare you break into my home!"

The killer's smile distorted into a jeer. He clapped his hands in sarcastic, mocking applause.

How the fuck dare he!

"So brave, CM Thatcher. Nice—"

The mobile in Marcus' pocket buzzed.

"Don't check that, Thatcher. Whoever it is will have to wait."

Marcus levered himself away from the cooker. It moved under the load and floor tiles screeched. He screamed, threw a clubbing left at the killer's jaw, then a straight right to his belly. Both punches found empty air as Kaine slid to his right, gliding over the floor like an ice-skater, silent and fast.

What the shit?

Marcus stumbled forwards, pushed against the kitchen counter to right himself, and spun to face Kaine once again. The killer nodded in appreciation.

"Not bad. Quite mobile for such a big man," Kaine said, taunting.

He held up his open hands, but in defence, not surrender, right ahead of left. A southpaw stance.

Awkward fucker.

Kaine continued. "Next time, gain your balance before throwing the first punch. You'll generate more power and accuracy that way."

"You fucking—"

Kaine's open right hand moved so fast, Marcus didn't have time to react before it reached his cheek in a humiliating slap that rang loud in his ears and reverberated throughout the kitchen.

The blow stung. Flames set his skin alight.

Marcus roared, more in embarrassment than in pain, and raised his fists again.

"Don't bother, son," Kaine said, mocking and derisive, but quiet and almost conversational. "I could do this all night, and you really aren't very good."

"You supercilious fucking dwarf," Marcus screamed. He prowled forwards, arms wide and rounded, reducing the distance between him and Kaine, cutting the little bastard's room for manoeuvre, aiming to pin him into the corner between the units.

Two more steps and he'd have the tiny shit trapped. A bear hug would slow down the fuckwit's fancy dance moves.

The words of Marcus' boxing coach flooded back. "A good big 'un will always beat a good little 'un." Ryan-fuck-ing-Kaine was about to find out how good a big 'un Marcus could be.

Kaine twisted, bobbed down and to his right so fast, Marcus hardly saw the movement.

A second blur.

Knifing pain exploded through Marcus' left kidney. He grunted, buckled, pulled his arms tight into his ribs in protection against another blow.

Kaine ducked past Marcus' failed attempt to trap him in the corner and stepped into the middle of the room. Another slicing, driving kidney shot put Marcus on his knees, gasping for breath, forehead braced against a cold, hard drawer front.

A hand grasped his shoulder, pulled Marcus around, and pushed him on his arse. Looming over him, a killer. A smiling killer. Marcus was dead.

Oh God. No. Please no!

"What's the matter, Marcus?" Kaine taunted, the smile morphing into a teeth-revealing snarl. "Not so big now, are you? I'm not one of your female inmates. I'm not someone you can bully and force into anything, you pitiful coward."

"I-I ... Please, don't hurt me. Don't kill me."

The murderer shot him a quizzical look and shook his head slowly. "Kill you? What makes you think I'm here to kill you?"

What?

Marcus swallowed hard. He tried to straighten, but the pulsing furnace that was his kidney burned fire. He groaned at the effort and slumped back against the creaking kitchen unit.

Kaine squatted in front of Marcus and held his right hand up to Marcus' face. The straight fingers formed a sharp blade. "Your kidney. Hurt much?"

Marcus nodded, too scared to speak in case he burst into humiliating tears. Despite the cold of the kitchen, sweat poured out of him. His heart raced and he struggled to breathe properly. Each time he sucked in a breath, the pain in his lower back flared anew.

How'd the fucker manage it? So fast ... so damned fast. Lightning.

"Not to worry, son," the killer said. Without breaking the sightline, he half-turned, pulled a stool from beneath the breakfast bar, dragged it across the floor, and plonked it in front of Marcus. "I didn't follow through on my shots. Doubt there's much damage done. You'll probably be able to pee by morning. If it flows red, head for your nearest hospital. I shouldn't imagine the damage is permanent, but dialysis will keep you alive, and I hear it isn't too uncomfortable these days."

What? Kidney damage? Oh Jesus ...

Kaine laughed. He actually laughed.

"Just kidding, Thatcher, old sport," he said, derision in his voice and on his face. "My friends—and I have many friends—tell me I have a wicked sense of humour. Now, pop up here, please. You and I need to chat."

He slapped the seat of the stool, the noise it made so loud it hurt Marcus' eardrums.

"Come on, up you get. I don't have all night, and I'm certainly not giving you a helping hand."

Kaine took two backwards steps and leaned against the cooker. Again it screeched. Kaine looked at the floor, tutted, and returned the unit back into its original spot, in line with the floor tiles.

"That's better," he said. "Hate seeing things out of alignment, me. My tidy nature, don't you know. Some might think I'm a little OCD."

Kaine flicked up his left hand, telling Marcus to hurry.

Grunting against the agony, Marcus struggled to his feet and slipped one arse cheek onto the stool, having to battle to hold back the nausea threatening to make him puke. He teetered on the edge of the seat, trying to keep his balance and breathe more freely.

"Good, good," Kaine said, smiling again. "This is much better, isn't it? Much more civilised."

Marcus took another breath, this one deeper, and summoned up the strength to speak. Dizziness washed over him. "W-What—"

"What am I doing here?"

Marcus nodded.

"That's a much better attitude. Don't you regret all that macho posturing? If you'd listened in the first place, you wouldn't be in so much discomfort right now. Fisticuffs is so unnecessary and, as I suggested a little earlier, you really aren't very good at it. Those muscles you flaunt in your overly tight shirts might impress the ladies and the uninitiated, but if you can't marry them with power and technique, they're pretty useless in a rumble."

He wrung his hands and examined Marcus carefully, apparently appraising his condition. Eventually, he nodded. "Now then, are you ready for a polite chat?"

Marcus lowered a hand and massaged his kidney. Breathing came easier, and the sharp pain dulled into a throbbing ache.

"Yes," he managed, the word forced out between tense lips. "What ... what do you want?"

"Actually, what I'd really like is a nice, strong cup of tea but, since this isn't one of those chats, I'll wait 'til later. As for what I'm doing here, have you forgotten already?"

"Forgotten? I ..."

What the fuck's he on about?

"Oh, come now. Don't tell me you've dismissed our little arrangement already?"

"What fuckin—"

Kaine leaned forwards and flicked the tip of Marcus' nose with his index finger. Marcus jerked back his head and snapped his mouth shut. Fresh pain knifed through his lower back. He tried not to cry out, but his nose stung and started running.

Bleeding?

God, what's happening?

"Watch your language, Marcus. Swearing is the last resort of the ignorant mind," he said, taunting again. "This conversation should be civilised. Are we in agreement here?"

Marcus sniffled and wiped his nose with the back of a sweaty, trembling hand. He blinked away some tears and glanced down at the smear. Clear, not blood. Jesus, a runny nose, like a snotty brat.

Pitiful, he was so pitiful.

What an unholy mess.

How could such a short-arse be so powerful and deadly? Kaine was a wanted killer, but no one would ever know it to look at him. No wonder the police hadn't caught him yet. He had Marcus on toast, despite his superior size and bulk. The only way to survive was to agree.

"Y-Yes. Civilised. I-I'm sorry."

That's it. Play along.

If he survived the night, maybe he could turn the tables somehow.

Think. Live. Survive.

"To jog your memory, when I visited your establishment this afternoon, you and I came to a certain understanding."

"What? You can't be serious!"

Kaine winced and shook his head. "Oh dear, let's cut the bad John McEnroe impressions, shall we?"

"John who?"

"You don't follow tennis?"

"What? Tennis. I … I'm sorry," Marcus said, shaking his head and wondering if the killer was totally out of his box, a nutter. "Yes, yes. McEnroe, I know who you mean. It's just that—"

"Not to worry, Thatcher," he said. "Thought it might be an age thing. How old are you? Thirty-seven, yes?"

Fucking hell.

"You know my age?"

Again, the small man with the brutal fighting skills tutted and added a deep nod. "Dear me, we know more about you than your age, Thatcher."

We? He has friends?

Of course he had friends. How else could the fucker have avoided capture for so many months. And there was the cute, blonde woman, too. What was her name? Braithwaite.

"For instance," Kaine continued, "mumps and measles before you started school. Left you with a lazy right eye and a severe squint. Corrective surgery at aged ten."

Kaine paused, looked Marcus directly in the eyes, and nodded appreciatively. "Yep, they did a good job. The squint is barely noticeable these days. So, where was I?" After another pause, and a tilt of the head, he continued, speaking as though reading from a shopping list. "At the tender age of fourteen, you broke your left tibia falling off your bike at Keithley Park. Had to wear that cast for four-teen weeks. All summer in a thigh-length, plaster cast. Must have been terribly uncomfortable for you, poor lad. And then your appendix burst when you were fifteen. Sickly, little kid, weren't you? Probably why you pump so much iron these days. Trying to compensate?"

Kaine stood again and flexed his fingers in front of his chest as though he'd damaged them when jabbing Marcus in the kidney, twice.

Good. Hope they hurt, you bastard.

"From there we reach exam time," Kaine droned on. "Oh dear, oh dear, your exams. Fancy allowing yourself to be caught cheating!"

He paused and slowly shook his head while Marcus' face warmed.

Christ, he knows everything.

How did he know that? The school were supposed to have deleted the records.

"How did you manage to survive the accusations? Well, Daddy's a wealthy man. What was it? Yes, he made a considerable donation to the school's new gymnasium, didn't he. Need I go on?"

Marcus shook his head and lowered his eyes.

"No," he said, sounding as defeated as he felt.

If Kaine knew that much, maybe he knew more. Maybe he knew it all.

"As I said this afternoon, someone would be in touch to discuss the payment details."

Marcus dared a look up, directly into the cold eyes of a killer. The eyes of a man who'd murdered all those people on that plane. If Kaine chose to, he could add Marcus to his list of victims and there wasn't a thing Marcus could do to stop it. Powerlessness was a terrible thing. A pitiful thing.

Jesus.

Something had changed about Kaine since the prison, and not just the clothes. His face was different. He'd removed the glasses and his eyes had changed colour from blue to brown. Subtle, but it made a hell of a difference. The blue lenses had made him look cold and aloof, an arrogant bastard, but the brown gave him an even harder edge. They gave him the lifeless, brown eyes of a stone-cold killer.

But this killer had broken into his home. Why?

"What?" Marcus managed to blurt out, despite a dry mouth and a pounding heart. "You can't seriously think I'm going to do anything for you. You must be out of your mind."

Kaine's mouth twitched and his head tilted to the other side. "Some people have levelled that accusation at me, and it's difficult to argue the case for the defence at times, but ..."

"But what?"

That's it, Marcus. Keep him talking.

"But, if I *am* insane," the mass murderer continued, calm and quiet, "it doesn't bode well for your chances of surviving into the morning. Does it, Marcus?"

Marcus opened his mouth, but the words wouldn't come.

Kaine smiled his stone-eyed smile and Marcus, once again, fought hard not to wet himself. In his job, he'd faced murderers of all descriptions. Serial killers, gang-bangers, men and women who'd lost control and killed in rage, and those who'd killed by accident. But at work, he had power and control. At work, he had backup. At work, with the full might of the state supporting him, he was pretty near invulnerable. Inside, he had protection, but now, outside, he was alone.

"So," Kaine continued, "now we have everything out in the open, do you have any questions?"

"What, me?"

Kaine cast his eyes about the kitchen, making a point, the arrogant bastard. "Can't see anyone else here but the two of us, old chap. Yes, you," he said and leaned menacingly closer. "I asked, 'Do … you … have … any … questions?' Aren't I making myself clear enough?"

Think, Marcus, think.

Kaine must be mad to think he'd honour a deal with a wanted man. The minute Kaine left—assuming he did leave—Marcus would be on the phone to the cops.

Play along. Agree to anything.

"Ah, yes. I remember. You wanted my bank details, didn't you? To transfer the money?"

"That's what I said earlier," Kaine said, pursing his lips, "but that won't actually be necessary," he said, offhandedly. "I already have the details of all your bank accounts. Even the Overseas Territories account under the name Martin Thornton."

Jesus fucking Christ!

"What? … How?"

Marcus' emotions reached a new low. Acid boiled away at the lining of his stomach and bile scorched his throat. He swallowed it back, nearly gagging on the caustic fluid.

"We know everything about you, Marcus, dear man. Everything. Haven't I already demonstrated that? Oh, just a sec." Kaine said, and raised his hand and pressed the fingertips into his forehead like he was picking up a message from the atmosphere. "In case you think you can renege on our deal the moment I leave you alone, consider this." He spoke through a supercilious smirk. "Before my visit here tonight, one of my many associates deposited ten thousand pounds into your ordinary savings account. Yes, the one you *do* declare to the Tax Office."

Dear God. The bastard had Marcus on toast—buttered and with dollops of strawberry jam.

"I'll let you work out how to explain the funds to your tax man," Kaine continued. "Perhaps you can tell them you won it playing online poker."

He dipped a hand into the pocket of his motorcycle jacket and took a pace closer. Marcus recoiled so much he nearly fell from the stool.

"Don't worry, old chap. There won't be any more fisticuffs. I just wanted to give you this to pass to Mrs Archer."

When the hand came out of the pocket, it was holding a small mobile phone wrapped in its charger cable. He offered it to Marcus, who jerked backwards. He slipped from the stool and backed away until stopped by the wall.

"I-I … No, I can't do that. If I'm caught, it'll cost me my job."

Kaine set the mobile down on the seat of the stool.

"Better not get caught then, eh? It's a burner, untraceable to you. Much better than having her ask her guards to use a landline. Absolutely no chance for a trace, either."

Something was missing. No pain. His kidneys no longer throbbed. Marcus barely noticed it had gone in his desperation to please the killer and make him leave.

"If I'm protecting her, why does she need it? Are you planning a break—"

"Of course not," Kaine said, shaking his head and adding a deep frown. "That's not going to help Mrs Archer in the long term. My client is an innocent woman who deserves to clear her name in a court of law."

Client? What the fuck?

Christ. Did the man actually believe the rubbish he was spouting? Delusional as well as aggressive. Marcus needed to tread even more carefully. No telling what Kaine would do if upset.

Then again, the whole damned country knew exactly what the madman was capable of. The eighty-three victims aboard that plane were proof positive of the man's capacity for murder.

Kaine sniffed and the light of madness shone in the dark brown eyes. "If I broke her out of that sieve you call a prison," he said, manic laughter colouring his words, "she'd spend the rest of her life on the run. Looking over her shoulder. And that's not something I'd recommend."

Regret? Was he showing regret?

What the fuck's going on here?

"To put your mind at rest, dear Marcus, she's only going to use it to let me know what you're up to. If you slip up in any way. I'll get to know about it first hand and very quickly. Is that clear, Marcus, old chap?"

Kaine smiled, interlaced his fingers, and reversed his hands to crack his knuckles. He yawned wide and loud, covering his mouth as he did so. "Excuse me, Marcus. As you can imagine, it's been a long and tiring day. I'll be off now, toodle pip."

Going? He's going? Thank God.

Kaine moved towards the back door, passing close to Marcus, who shrank into the corner of the room, trying to make himself invisible.

The killer grasped the door handle, twisted, and pulled. The wooden door screeched as it caught on the frame and Kaine had to yank hard to open it fully. He turned to face Marcus again, the madman's eyes drilling deep into his very soul. "You need to get that fixed, old chap. And before I forget, when I leave, you might think of calling the police …"

"I-I won't. I sw—"

"Before you do that," Kaine interrupted, raising his free hand in a dismissive gesture, "check your phone. That notification you received earlier was a message from another of my friends. I've a feeling you'll find it rather illuminating. Cheerio."

He pointed at the pocket where Marcus kept his mobile. Marcus looked down. By the time he looked back up, Kaine had vanished like a ghost into the night.

Marcus breathed deeply, let the breath out slowly, and allowed his shoulders to drop. He moved the burner phone from the stool and dropped it on the kitchen counter. As he climbed back onto the stool, his eyes flicked to the clock on the cooker. 00:22.

He'd only been home twenty minutes.

Is that all?

It seemed more like hours.

Twenty minutes earlier, Marcus Thatcher had been a dead man, he'd known it, felt it. But now, he was alone in his defiled home, but he still breathed. If he'd been a religious man, Marcus would have fallen to his knees in prayer, but … bollocks to that.

What next?

The cops? Yeah, the cops.

If he told them about Kaine, and his attempts to force Marcus to break the law, they'd believe him. The killer had left evidence in the shape of the burner phone. Maybe the police could work out where Kaine bought it and trace the purchase back to him. As for the money in Marcus' bank account, it would add more fuel to his claims of being threatened, coerced.

Yeah, the cops would believe him. Of course they would. They had to.

Marcus pulled the mobile from his pocket and swiped the screen into life. One message. Unknown number. Marcus considered deleting it and hitting the emergency number, but Kaine's parting words still echoed in his ear. What would he find "illuminating" about a text message from a killer he'd already met face-to-face and survived to tell the tale?

He hit the screen to open the text message.

CM Thatcher, see attachment.

With a growing sense of dread, Marcus reluctantly followed the instruction and opened the attachment—a sound file. He swallowed hard and hit the forward arrow to play the recording.

Long before the sound file finished playing, Marcus knew, he just knew, his life had changed forever.

Chapter Twenty-Six

Tuesday 20th April - Lara Orchard

Mike's Farm, Long Buckby, Northants, England

The bedroom door sighed open, but not soundlessly enough for Lara to miss it. So attuned was she to the creaks and groans of Mike's old farmhouse, it would have woken her even if she had managed to fall asleep.

She sat bolt upright and hit the switch on the bedside lamp. The old-fashioned, forty-watt bulb was still bright enough to dazzle her sleep-deprived eyes as well as illuminate the small room. She blinked away the discomfort.

"What time do you call this?"

Ryan checked his watch. "Two thirty-seven. Sorry to wake you, love."

"Wasn't asleep. Rarely sleep when you're off galivanting."

She drew the bedclothes back for him and watched as he pulled the towel from around his waist and folded it neatly before draping it over the back of the spare chair. He removed his diver's watch and placed it on his bedside table. As a throwback to his military days, Ryan always kept his belongings neat and squared away. He always washed before turning in, too, even if he was away and the nearest water source was a freezing river. Lara didn't mind watching him pad around the room fully naked. Didn't mind one little bit and, judging by his gentle smile, Ryan didn't mind her looking, either.

He slid in beside her and she snuggled under his arm, relishing in his just-showered warmth and freshness.

"Successful evening?"

She had to ask, knowing he wouldn't volunteer the information otherwise.

The arm he'd placed around her shoulder squeezed a little tighter as he strained to kiss the top of her head. "I'm tired, love. Will the debrief wait 'til morning?"

She pulled away and propped herself up on one elbow.

"Ryan Liam Kaine," she said in a stage whisper, "I've been awake half the night, waiting for you to return safely. If you think I'm going to be able to—"

"Okay, okay," he said in the pained-but-patient way he had when she goaded him into doing something he didn't want to. He sat up and pulled her back into his arms. "Marcus Thatcher and I had a brief and informative discussion where I impressed upon him the importance of keeping to his promises ..."

He spoke for a few minutes, detailing his "discussion" with the creep of a custodial manager, leaving out any violence he'd used to subdue the much larger man, but that was more for brevity than to spare Lara's worries. If Ryan had suffered any injuries from a fight, he'd have asked her to treat him. Besides, she'd seen every inch of him before he'd climbed into bed, and he showed no obvious signs of recent trauma. If Ryan and Thatcher had fought, the prison officer had failed to land a single telling blow.

"So," she said after he'd finished, "are you sure he's going to do as you tell him?"

Ryan smiled. He looked so handsome when he did that. She wished he had more opportunity.

"Oh, he'll comply, right enough. I sent him a copy of the recording from the spy-pen. One false move from our friend, Thatcher, and that recording will find its way into the inboxes of the prison governor, the Minister of Justice, and the editors of half a dozen national newspapers. Marcus Thatcher is going to ensure Melanie reaches court safe and sound. And the Trust is going to make sure she receives the best legal help money can buy."

"So, that's it?" Lara asked, knowing what his answer would be. "We can leave Melanie in the safe hands of British jurisprudence?"

Ryan screwed up his face in that cute way he had of weighing up the information before saying no.

"Almost," he said, "but not quite."

"Thought so. What's left to do?"

"First, we'll need to wait until we receive a few calls from Melanie to let us know how well Thatcher's behaving himself …" Ryan trailed off, apparently deep in thought.

"And second?" Lara prompted after waiting a full five seconds.

"Second?" he said. "Second, I'd like to learn as much as I can about two more interested parties."

"These two interested parties wouldn't be called Terrance Elphick and Andrew Braemar, by any chance?"

"My darling Lara," he said, easing her into a firmer hug, "as usual, you are one hundred percent correct. Apparently, in criminal investigations, the detectives always follow the money."

"Yes, I'd heard that, too."

"And in this case, I think we need to follow who stands to *inherit* the money."

"Good idea," she said, smiling.

"Yes, I'm full of good ideas."

"Are you?"

"Usually."

"Prove it."

He snuggled closer and they kissed goodnight—for a lovely, long time.

Chapter Twenty-Seven

Tuesday 20th April - Melanie Archer

Health Care Centre, HMP Falston Manor, Derbyshire, England

Mel had finally managed to doze off after hours of mulling through the nightmare that was her life when the main door to the ward squealed open, snapping her into a drowsy wakefulness. The clock on the wall told her it was only mid-afternoon. She'd had less than thirty minutes' rest. Were these constant disturbances the best way for a patient to recover from her injuries?

She looked up to see the obese, foul-smelling, and mean-spirited DCI Harrison, accompanied by his quiet sidekick, DS Simpson.

Oh dear Lord! What now?

CM Thatcher and PO Priestly showed the detectives into the ward, and stood back to let them approach Mel's bed.

Something about Thatcher drew Mel's attention. He seemed different somehow, his shoulders appeared narrower, his usually straight back, slightly hunched. The strange expression he fired at her was totally disconcerting, but she couldn't interpret its meaning. A slight puffiness around his cheeks suggested he'd either been punched or crying, which seemed a ridiculous idea. Mel couldn't imagine the over-confident and aggressive custodial manager crying over anything—except perhaps if he dribbled coffee down his immaculate uniform shirt.

And as for Thatcher's shirt, today's didn't match its usual, crisp, and freshly ironed perfection. Yes, something had definitely happened to the man since she'd last seen him. Something unpleasant. A car crash, perhaps?

Good.

She'd waste no sympathy on the likes of CM Thatcher.

Wow, hadn't she become the hard-hearted bitch over the years? Mel had changed so much, she barely recognised herself from the naïve soul who'd married *him* so many years earlier.

She nodded to herself. Life could do that to a person.

As usual, Harrison took the lead. He waddled towards her bed. The mousy and drably clothed Simpson trailed in his wake, notepad and pen at the ready. On the way, the DCI grabbed one of the tubular-steel visitors' chairs, carried it to within a metre of her bed, and plonked himself down in it.

His enormous backside completely obscured the seat, the flabby cheeks dripping down either side like ice-cream melting over the edges of a cone. With his heavy jowls and the loose-fitting, grey suit draped over his fleshy body, the hideous policeman reminded her of the beached elephant seals she'd seen on wildlife TV shows.

She shuddered.

Simpson remained standing, keeping her distance from the gargantuan in the baggy suit. The stench of body odour and stale tobacco hung in the air between Harrison and Mel. If she hadn't already spent hours and hours cooped up in an interview room with the DCI and developed a partial tolerance to the stink as a result, she might have asked Simpson to pass her a sick bag.

"Now then, Archer," Harrison opened, showing his stained and misaligned teeth in a mocking smile, "what have you been up to?"

Mel lowered her eyes from the travesty of a human and kept her mouth shut. No way was she going to give the sorry excuse for a detective more rope with which he could hang her. She'd finally learned her lesson.

"Come now, Archer," Harrison said, leaning closer and pushing more of his foul murk towards her, "you can help yourself here. What did Kaine want? What did you two talk about?"

Mel raised her head and stared through the grimy windows. Clouds covered the sky and dulled the day. It matched her mood. She said nothing in answer to Harrison's continuing barrage of questions. He repeated the same ones over and over.

"What did Kaine want?"

"What did you two talk about?"

"Did he tell you where he was staying … what he wanted … why he shot down that plane? Who … what … where … why … when?"

The questions continued and expanded to take in Ms Braithwaite.

"Who was she?"

"Did she act like she was being threatened? Bullied?"

"Was she working with Kaine voluntarily?"

"What did she say? What did she do? Who … what … where … why … when?"

The minutes stretched on and Mel kept her mouth closed the whole time. She said not a single solitary word. Not even a, "No comment." She didn't want to. Didn't have to.

Twenty-seven minutes into the interrogation—she'd watched them tick by on the wall clock—Thatcher interrupted Harrison's one-sided interrogation.

"That's enough," he said, stepping further into the room. "It's clear Mrs Archer isn't going to say anything. It's time for you to leave."

Thatcher continued approaching until he'd reached DS Simpson, where he stopped, as though unwilling to get too close to the miasma surrounding the DCI. His nostrils wrinkled and he shook his head.

"Even though Governor Bancroft allowed it," Thatcher continued, "you shouldn't be interviewing the prisoner without her solicitor present, so I'm stopping this now."

Harrison struggled to twist enough in his seat to fix his eyes on Thatcher. Unable to complete the task, the DCI levered himself out of the chair and faced the slightly taller man. Breathing hard from the exertion of simply standing, Harrison planted his fists into his colossal hips and stared at Thatcher until he'd recovered his wind.

"Don't interrupt me, Thatcher. What sort of a prison are you running here, man? Letting a national fugitive wander around the—"

"As I said," Thatcher cut in so angrily, Harrison's jaw hung open in surprise, "that's enough. Mrs Archer is under my protection, and I won't allow her to be browbeaten like this. You know you're not supposed to question her without a solicitor being present. This may come back to shaft you, and no one wants that."

"What do you mean by that?" Harrison asked, recovering quickly from his shock.

"Questioning her like this could affect your case against her. She needs a solicitor present."

What's this?

Thatcher was coming to her defence, for goodness' sake! A miracle?

Mel stared hard at the custodial manager. This couldn't be right. What was happening? She glanced at PO Priestly, who hadn't moved from her place near the door. Her confused expression confirmed Mel's suspicions that Priestly didn't know what to make of Thatcher's change of attitude either.

Harrison dropped his hands and leaned closer to Thatcher, trying to intimidate the taller man. However, the effect was ruined when Harrison leaned so far, he nearly toppled over and had to push one foot ahead of the other to maintain his balance. When he spoke again, he was somewhat breathless.

The man was one packet of ciggies and one fish-and-chip supper away from the cardiac ward. For the briefest moments, Mel found herself considering the delicious irony of a police detective being treated for a heart attack in a prison hospital while being watched by a woman he was determined to put away for murder.

Take any pleasure where you can, girl.

"These current questions," Harrison wheezed, "have

nothing to do with the murder case, *Mister* Thatcher. I'm asking about Kaine's visit, nothing else. I haven't even mentioned the fact she murdered her invalid husband. Not one single time. There's no need, since the case against her is as watertight as any murder investigation I've ever worked on." His momentary glance at Mel carried a smirk of supreme confidence.

"Anyway," Harrison continued, breathing more easily and speaking with more control, "how can I question her with a solicitor present when she doesn't bloody well have one!"

"Nonetheless," Thatcher said, "we all need to follow the law. If the police wish to talk to Mrs Archer on *any* subject, a solicitor needs to be in attendance. How else can we guarantee her legal rights? Given the current circumstances, I'm sure a new defence team will be in place before long."

"You're sure, are you?"

Thatcher continued speaking as though ignoring the interruption. "Furthermore, in order to maintain transparency, the next time the police want to question Mrs Archer about Kaine's visit, I suggest you send someone who isn't directly involved in the case against her. Do I make myself clear?"

Harrison practically bounced on a pair of feet that looked too small to carry his enormous bulk. "Who the bloody hell do you think you are?"

Thatcher lifted one of his broad shoulders in a half-shrug, stood sideways to the overweight DCI, and pointed him towards the door.

"Now, sir," he said, "if you wouldn't mind. PO Priestly will escort you from the building while I complete a report on this breach of procedure, which Governor Bancroft will countersign in line with protocol and copy to your chief constable. I expect the governor will also copy it to the Ministry of Justice as a matter of some urgency."

Thatcher stood, right arm outstretched, waiting for the senior police officer to react.

"Covering your back, Thatcher?" Harrison said and, after a momentary pause where the custodial manager didn't move, added, "Trying to deflect attention away from your cockup?"

"My cockup?"

"Yes, your cockup. You gave a fugitive the run of this prison, and—"

"Never you fear, Mr Harrison. We'll find out what happened. In fact, we've asked the Counter Terrorism Unit for their help."

Harrison's face grew three shades darker and a blood vessel stood out fat on his temple. "The CTU? That bunch of numpties? This is a local issue. Nottinghamshire Police should be taking the lead."

Thatcher shook his head. "Ryan Kaine is a terrorist. One of the UK's most wanted men. And besides"—he paused and shot a look at Mel before continuing—"this is not a discussion we should be having in front of an inmate. Now, if you wouldn't mind?"

Mel reached a hand up to cover her smile. Somehow, she'd entered an alternative reality where life had been turned on its head. All she could think to do was lie in her bed and soak up the magic.

Thatcher and Priestly shepherded the detectives from the ward, the DCI complaining the whole way. For her part, Simpson hadn't uttered a single word during the entire visit.

Alone again, Mel lay back, reviewing the fight between Thatcher and Harrison in her head. Had it really happened? She'd been told of the animosity that sometimes bubbled between the prison service and the police, but she never expected to witness a confrontation of such ferocity. She'd viewed similar scenes unfolding in TV crime shows but, in real life, the drama was even more exciting. And Thatcher's part in it had been a revelation.

What had happened to the man? One day after he'd tried to coerce her into an illicit liaison, he was arguing with a senior police officer and acting in her defence. It simply didn't make sense.

The ward's main door opened quietly and, to Mel's horror, CM Thatcher quietly stepped into the room, alone. He closed the door gently behind him and hurried towards her bed.

Oh God, what now?

Was he coming to claim his reward for leaping to her defence? Mel tried to block out dreadful images of the powerful man, pinning her down, forcing himself upon her, but it didn't work. Her heart raced, tension knotted her stomach. She pulled in a huge breath, preparing to scream, but Thatcher stopped well short of her bed.

The man raised a finger to his lips. "Don't shout, Archer. I'm not staying. You're perfectly safe. Just needed to give you this."

Thatcher dipped a hand into his trouser pocket. It came out holding something small and black, wrapped in a charging lead. He closed on the bed, handed her the object —a small mobile phone—and stepped away again.

"That's from the man who called himself Pratt."

"Kaine!"

Mel dropped the phone as though it had belted her with an electric charge.

"Shush, woman," Thatcher hissed, throwing a furtive glance at the door. "Keep your bloody noise down."

"You've seen Ryan Kaine?" she asked, quietly.

The marks on Thatcher's face and his change in demeanour suddenly had an explanation—he and Kaine had met and exchanged blows. The revelation answered some of her questions, but not all. The one topmost in her mind screamed in her ear.

What the hell's Kaine up to?

Thatcher nodded, his frown deepening. "Yeah, bastard paid me a visit," he said, fingering the puffiness below his left eye.

"What did he want?"

Thatcher lowered his gaze as though unable to maintain eye contact with her.

"To ensure your safety," he answered, coldly.

"Why?"

Again, the man lifted a shoulder in a shrug. "No fucking idea, woman. All I know is he told me to give you that phone. Said something about always keeping his promises. Also said you'd know what he meant."

She picked up the small mobile. "He wants me to call him?"

"Apparently."

"Why should I?"

"Stop asking me questions I can't answer. You'll have to call him to find out. Only be careful when and where you use it. Make sure no one sees you or we'll both be in the shit."

"Why are you helping him ... and me?"

Slowly, Thatcher met her scrutiny. His blue eyes, which she'd initially considered dead, now contained humility, regret, and ... fear.

"Just be grateful that I am." A noise in the outside corridor made him jump. His head snapped towards the sound. "Shit, I can't be seen here alone." He started heading for the door. "I've got to go, but listen carefully. When Dr Milliner says you're fit for release, I'll be placing you into protective custody. You'll be in solitary on the wing with all the child molesters and sex offenders. Sorry, but it's the only way I can keep you safe."

"Why are you doing this?"

Thatcher stopped and turned to face her. "Let's just say Kaine impressed on me how important it was to keep you alive."

"Important for whom?"

"For me, of course," he snapped, reaching for the door handle. "I don't give a fuck about you, you murdering bitch."

With his true colours shining through once more, the world tilted back into alignment. Thatcher opened the door, slid around its edge, and disappeared.

He left Mel alone, staring at the mobile phone in her hand, wondering what on earth had just happened.

Chapter Twenty-Eight

Tuesday 20th April – Early Morning

Mike's Farm, Long Buckby, Northants, England

Kaine and Lara entered the warm kitchen to be greeted by a cheery Danny and the mouth-watering aroma of grilled bacon and toasted bread. Of Mike, there was no sign.

"Morning, Doc," Danny said from the table, holding up a slice of toast that carried a liberal dollop of marmalade. "Any adverse reaction to being bounced around on the pillion seat for the first time?"

Lara smiled. "Morning, Danny. My legs are a little stiff, but it's nothing an early-morning canter won't cure."

"Glad to hear it," Danny said around a mouthful of toast. "The way the captain was mishandling that Honda and hitting all the potholes in Derbyshire yesterday, it's a wonder you don't need traction."

"Easy does it, Sergeant," Kaine said, pouring Lara a cup of breakfast tea, "let's have a little respect for your elders and betters, eh?"

He let Lara add her own milk and poured himself a large mugful.

Danny's smirk didn't falter. "Elders certainly, Captain. You won't get any argument from me on that point, but betters?" He scoffed. "In some things, yes. Maybe even in most things, but I watched the way you handled that poor bike." He shook his head slowly. "Crunching gear changes, excessive use of the brakes. My heart went out to the doc. At least you had a decent, smooth ride the rest of the way from Donington. Showed you how a motorbike should be ridden." He finished with a mischievous, swollen-cheeked wink, which made Lara grin.

Kaine dropped two slices of bread into the warm toaster and slid into a chair beside Lara and across from the self-appointed critic of his bike-handling skills.

"You're rather chipper this morning, Danny," he said. "How is your sweet, young undergraduate?"

Danny's expression didn't falter. "Bobbie sends her love … to the doc. You, boss, she ignores."

The toast erupted from the toaster and Kaine grabbed them before Danny could lean across to snaffle them for himself. He applied a thin smear of butter, added a couple of rashers of bacon and a dollop of tomato sauce, made a sandwich, and started munching. Lara had already helped herself to her usual, healthy bowl of cereal—with no added sugar.

"Besides Bobbie Shafer, is there any other reason you're being so feisty today, Sergeant?" Kaine asked, pushing part of the half-chewed buttie to the side of his mouth.

Danny shook his head. "Just a little light-hearted banter, boss. Didn't think you'd mind." He paused before adding, "There is one thing, though."

"Which is?"

"Don't suppose you'd care to tell me what happened during your chat with Thatcher last night? I'm dying to know."

"All in good time, Danny. Breakfast comes first. We all need to fuel up."

Kaine swallowed, bit off another mouthful, and started munching—slowly.

"Mmm, this is lovely," he said, turning to Lara. "Can't beat a decent bit of granary loaf and back bacon. How's your muesli?"

Lara lowered her spoon to the near-empty bowl and sighed. "Will you stop winding each other up? I swear, it's like being back at school with you two sometimes."

"Okay, fair enough," Kaine said, popping the last of his bacon buttie into his mouth and chewing quickly. "You won't be surprised to learn that Thatcher wasn't expecting my visit, nor was he particularly happy about it …"

Kaine took a few moments to deliver the salient components of the previous night's escapade, leaving out all mention of Thatcher's ineffectual acts of aggression, but Danny wasn't falling for his glossed-over approach.

"I'd have loved to see you and the berk grapple," he said, buttering his third slice since their arrival. "Do much damage to his kitchen, boss?"

Kaine threw him a look encouraging him to shut up, but Danny wasn't wearing it.

"C'mon, Captain," he said, "the doc and I had a long

chat last night while you were playing the unwanted house-guest. She knows a man like Marcus Thatcher wouldn't sit still while someone broke into his home. Are you going to tell us what really happened?"

Kaine grunted, half-clearing his throat and half-issuing a guttural command for silence. He shook his head again. "Thatcher threw a couple of wild punches. Both missed, and then he fell over. And that's all I have to say on the matter, Sergeant Pinkerton."

Danny had single-handedly worked his way through most of a pot of marmalade and showed no signs of going easy with the helping on the current slice. Smiling as he spread the dark orange preserve over the toast, he said, "If you say so, boss," and bit into the offering.

Muesli finished, Lara pushed her bowl towards the middle of the table, and shook her head at the two jousters. "So, any idea what we should do next? We won't be able to use the Pratt and Braithwaite cover again."

"Absolutely not," Kaine agreed. "In fact, last night on the way home from Nottingham, I asked Corky to delete all internet references to Pratt and his delightful associate. This morning, Danny will shred and burn all the documentation we have on them. For all intents and purposes, by midday, I expect Laurence Pratt and Emma Braithwaite will never have existed."

Danny swallowed the final part of his breakfast before speaking.

"Yesterday's escapade will have embarrassed the hell out of the prison service," he said, "and the police are going to be royally pissed. I can just imagine the conversation between the prison governor and the guy running the Archer case. What was his name again?"

"DCI Harrison's the Senior Officer-in-Charge," Lara

answered, "but a DI Carlisle handled the initial investigation."

"Yeah, that's right," Danny responded, nodding and
smirking. "I can picture the conversation now." He wiped
his mouth with a paper towel, puffed out his chest, and
deepened his voice. "'You allowed a wanted terrorist to
interview my prisoner, and then you let him escape? What
sort of a prison are you running here, Governor Bancroft?'
That's a conversation I'd love to have ears on. Perhaps
Thatcher will give us a full report."

Kaine smiled. "By now, the Corcoran, Whitney, and
Verger LLP website will be back to the way it was last weekend. Pristine. The governor and Thatcher won't have
anything to show the police other than a series of emails,
some photocopied IDs, and a couple of missing hours of
CCTV footage, thanks to Corky doctoring the prison's
surveillance system. No idea how we'd survive without our
little hacker."

"Corky's brilliant. No doubt about it," Lara agreed.

"In the meantime," Danny said, "are we going to just sit
here and wait for Mrs Archer to phone us?"

"Assuming she'll want anything to do with me," Kaine
said, trying not to sound dispirited.

"Perhaps Thatcher will keep in touch?" Danny offered.

Kaine shook his head. "Don't know about you, lad, but
I'm not inclined to sit here twiddling my thumbs, waiting for
others to do their thing. I've been working on an alternative
plan of action." He paused and made sure he had their full
attention. "First things first, the Trust needs to hire a real
defence team. Lara, after breakfast, do you mind popping
across to the comms room and researching the best in the
business, please?"

"Is this your way of getting the 'little woman' out of the

way while the menfolk discuss the interesting and dangerous stuff?" she asked, her forehead wrinkling into an angry frown.

Kaine anticipated her reaction and remained unfazed. "Not in the slightest, Lara. It's simply a matter of efficient use of resources. You are the best equipped out of the four of us to run a detailed internet search."

"Don't you dare think you're leaving me out of the loop here, Ryan Liam Kaine. I'm as involved in this as anyone," she said, her cheeks flushed in anger. "The way I see it, Melanie Archer is innocent and is being victimised, and I want to help. And by the way, last night, while you were playing 'super vigilante', I spent my time identifying the best criminal defence team in the East Midlands, who happen to be Lawson and Luscombe, LLP. They're based in Leicester." She paused and cocked her head as though waiting for a response, which Kaine knew better than to offer. A compliment would have been seen as either patronising, or too little, too late. Anything else would have appeared churlish.

Danny studied his empty plate, apparently trying not to chortle.

With her challenge refused, Lara continued. "I contacted their out-of-hours hotline and arranged a conference call for"—she checked the time on her watch—"exactly forty-seven minutes' time." She stood. "So, if you don't mind, right now, I'm heading to set up the comms room. As best I can, I'm going to make it look like an office rather than the attic of a barn. I'm not leaving because you told me to, but because I've already decided upon the best course of action and will handle it myself, thank you very much."

Kaine couldn't avoid smiling at her performance and

wondered whether Danny believed she was really angry. Behind her back, the door creaked open, letting in a blast of chilled air. Mike appeared, dressed in cold-weather gear. Mike's dogs scampered past him and headed straight for Lara, who squatted and fussed over them. Their lolling tongues and frantically wagging tails confirmed their delight in her attention.

On a single command from Mike, the dogs dashed through the kitchen, paused momentarily to sniff Danny's ankles and eye Kaine with what he imagined might be suspicion, and then padded to their beds on the rug in front of the fire.

"Morning, Lara," Mike said, "Evening, Captain, Sergeant. Forgot to set the alarm again, I see."

Kaine shook his head. "Everyone's a comedian."

"Fancy a ride out, Lara?" Mike asked, but she shook her head.

"Sorry, Mike. Not just yet. The *boss* is doling out the work tasks. Better watch out or you'll be roped into transcribing hours of surveillance recordings."

She lifted her nose at Kaine and wafted through the doorway Mike had so recently closed.

The old farmer removed his gloves, dropped them on a kitchen surface, and headed straight to the range to warm his hands. "You've got a good one there, Captain," he said grinning through his Father Christmas beard.

"No need to tell me that, Mike," Kaine responded, gloomily. "She's the best. I only wish we'd never clapped eyes on each other."

Mike nodded. Both he and Danny knew how much Lara meant to Kaine and neither needed reminding of the circumstances under which they'd met.

"She doesn't regret meeting you for one second," Mike

said, looking Kaine in the eye. "We talked about it during our last ride. She hates it when you leave her to go off on one of your, what did she call them? Excursions."

Kaine opened his mouth, but Mike held up a hand to forestall his interruption. "We all understand why you exclude her from some tasks, but she's very capable, Captain. And by the way, she's also concerned you're trying to work out a way to ease her back into her old life. Very perceptive is our doc. Wants me to tell you she's with you for the long haul and will fight you rather than let you ship her out to safety."

He ended the speech—one of the longest Kaine had ever heard the tight-lipped, former CPO make—with a shrug and a lop-sided smile.

"To be honest," Mike added, a twinkle in his eye, "I have no idea what she sees in you."

Danny snorted, said, "No comment," placed Lara's bowl on top of his empty plate, and leaned against the back of his chair. Eyes lowered, he folded his arms and waited for Kaine's instructions, making it clear he was unwilling to be drawn into the discussion. Maybe he felt the same way about his new life partner. What would happen if Bobbie ever asked to join Danny on one of his "excursions"?

"Okay, Danny," Kaine said, drawing a line under Mike's revelations and facing his young friend, "how are your building skills?"

Confusion darkened Danny's eyes. "My building skills?"

"Could you pass muster on a construction site as a brickie or a plumber?"

"Not a chance," he said, shaking his head. He unfolded his arms and showed Kaine his palms. "Not enough callouses. But I've done a bit of sparky work in the past. Before I joined up, I used to help one of my father's mates who happened to be a commercial electrician. At least I know which end of a wire-stripper to hold. Why?"

"How do you fancy a trip to Burton-on-Trent?"

Danny's forehead creased even further. "Why on earth would I want to go there?"

"Why wouldn't you? A nice, old, industrial town in Staffordshire close to the river Trent. What's not to like?"

Understanding showed on Danny's face and his shoulders straightened. "A building site in Burton? Am I going undercover?"

Kaine smiled. "Just for the day, Sergeant. A nice spell out in the fresh air will do you the power of good, I imagine. I've noticed you've been growing a bit peaky of late."

"Fresh air in Burton?" Danny grinned. "Last time that happened was before the industrial revolution, but I'm game."

"Excellent. Knew I could count on you."

Danny pushed his chair away from the table. "And while I'm freezing my nuts off in Burton, mind telling me what you'll be up to?"

"Not in the least, Sergeant. While you're busy gathering vital intel, the doc and I will be going hunting in Nottingham."

"Er, you know she's a vet, right? I can't see her as part of the huntin' and fishin' crowd."

"She isn't. She doesn't know it yet, but we'll be reprising our roles as Mr and Mrs Griffin. Only, this time, we won't be house hunting, we'll be searching for information."

"Ah, I see," Danny said, adding a decisive nod. "Good idea, I think."

Mike, who'd been leaning against the sink and earwigging the conversation, coughed. "Mr and Mrs Griffin and house hunting? Care to explain?"

"Afraid there's no time for that right now, Chief," Kaine answered through an enforced scowl. "Maybe you can ask Lara to tell you all about it next time you're out on one of your interminable canters."

Mike's right eyebrow shot up towards his receding hairline. "Hit a sore spot, did I, Captain?"

Kaine stood and pushed his chair into the table. "Not at all, Mike. Now, if you'll excuse me, I need to go and smooth things over with my good lady wife."

Mike and Danny's quiet sniggering followed him all the way out of the kitchen, through the boot room, and into the cold, fresh air of the rear courtyard.

Chapter Twenty-Nine

Tuesday 20th April - Afternoon

Mike's Farm, Long Buckby, Northants, England

Sitting in Mike's comfortable chair in front of a warm fire, Kaine squeezed the tennis ball in his left hand and rotated the wrist clockwise and anticlockwise through its full range of motion. Although the bones had fully knitted from his most recent injury, the arm still hadn't recovered full mobility or strength. The tennis ball was doing its job, but the occasional twinge of pain he suffered wasn't encouraging. He usually threw off injuries much more quickly, but this one was taking longer to heal than normal for him. Part of the aging process Kaine assumed.

Lara, the most competent trauma medic he'd seen

outside of a war zone, kept telling him his powers of recovery were astonishing, but he knew better. Age had started to slow him down. Eventually, his life in the firing line, his multiple brushes with death, would catch up to him. One day, maybe not soon, but one day, he'd be too slow and too weak to protect himself and the people he cared for.

But not today.

Kaine compressed the tennis ball five more times before swapping hands to complete thirty reps with the right. To maintain comprehensive, whole-body fitness, balance was the key.

Happy voices in the boot room beyond the kitchen made Kaine jump to his feet. He dropped the tennis ball into the chair and met Lara and Mike at the kitchen table.

"Ride go okay?" he asked Lara, whose windblown hair, flushed complexion, and bright-eyed smile had already given him his answer.

"Wonderful, thanks. It's bracing out there."

The view through the window looking out over the paddock showed a sharp, spring sun and a stiff, westerly breeze forcing the trees to lean or break.

"Good, good."

"Any news from Danny?" Lara asked.

"Nothing yet, and I'm not expecting anything for a while." Kaine turned to Mike. "How 'bout you, Mike. Everything okay?"

Mike continued filling the kettle, prepping his post-ride coffee. "It's a beautiful, spring day, and I've had wonderful company on my ride. Why wouldn't it be okay?" His beard stretched into a smile and he held up the kettle. "You having one?"

Kaine shook his head. "No, thanks. I've tasted the battery acid you call coffee. I'm good."

"Heathen." Mike threw the switch on the kettle and proceeded to add four heaped teaspoons of coffee granules to his half-litre mug. "Lara?" he asked, pointing to her slightly more dainty cup.

"Yes, please. I'll be down in a minute."

Kaine checked his watch. "How long are you really going to be?" He winked.

She sighed. "Give me twenty minutes. I need a shower and a change of clothing if I'm to pass muster."

He allowed his eyes to feast on the way the skin-tight jeans and the figure-hugging sweater clung to her. As far as Kaine was concerned, dressed the same way, she'd pass muster anywhere.

Lara smiled and was about to make a further comment when Kaine's mobile buzzed in his pocket. The ring tone— set for Melanie Archer's burner—made them all sit up and pay attention.

"It's the prison," Lara said unnecessarily while Kaine yanked out the phone and rushed to hit the connect button.

"Hello?" he said, surprised at how nervous he felt.

Silence stretched out into eternity.

Lara, eyes wide in query, opened her hands and mouthed, "Well?"

Kaine hit the speaker button and repeated his opening. "Hello?"

"H-Hello," Melanie said, her voice weak and trembling. "Is that … Ryan Kaine?"

He swallowed hard. Speaking to the disembodied voice of a member of The 83 turned out far more difficult than he'd imagined. He hesitated for a moment, trying to decide whether he'd be incriminating himself by answering if anyone else was listening in on Melanie's side of the call but he dismissed his worries. He'd asked her to call and would never withdraw his offer to help a member of The 83.

"Yes, it is. ... Thanks ... Thanks for calling. I can"— he swallowed—"imagine how difficult this must be for you."

"No, you can't," she snapped, anger flooding through the words. "You killed my brother. Or are you claiming to be innocent?"

Kaine tried to calm his breathing, but speaking to Melanie over the phone wasn't the same as preparing to take a long-range shot with a sniper rifle. It was far more difficult. More difficult than he could have ever believed.

"No, Mrs Archer," he said, forcing out the words through reluctant lips, "I'm not claiming innocence. I did shoot down Flight BE1555, but—"

"You bastard! You animal. Why are you torturing me like this?"

"Please, Mrs Archer, you must listen to me—"

"Must I? Must I! You killed my brother and all those other poor people. Innocent people. You murdered them all. Why did you do it? Why?"

Kaine closed his eyes, unable to form an answer.

"Mrs Archer," Lara said, taking the phone from his sweating, trembling hand, "this is the woman you know as Emma Braithwaite. Please listen to us, things are not what they seem."

"You're with him, still? You bitch, I trusted you. Why are you helping a killer?"

"We can explain, but this is not the time. Yesterday, we lied about our identities, but told the truth about everything else. I swear."

"Why should I believe you? For God's sake, you're helping a murderer!"

"Mrs Archer," Lara said, "are you a murderer? Did you kill your husband?"

"No, of course I didn't. But—"

"Ryan isn't a murderer either, I swear it," Lara said, looking Kaine in the eye. "Things are complicated but, as we told you yesterday, all we want to do is help."

"Why?"

"Because I owe it to you," Kaine said, finally managing to give voice to his feelings. "I owe it to the families of all the victims. That's why we set up The 83 Trust. ... Mrs Archer, things aren't always the way they seem. One day, I'll explain everything and you'll understand what happened. I promise you."

"I don't believe you. Tell me now!"

Kaine swallowed again and Lara nodded her encouragement. "Powerful men tricked me, Mrs Archer. Although I did shoot down that plane, I have video and documentary proof of my innocence."

"Liar!" Melanie spat, her anger palpable, even down a phone line.

"It's true," Lara said. "Every word."

"Why don't you release this so-called evidence, then? Why allow the world to think you're a terrorist?"

"It's a long story. But if I cleared my name, the same powerful people who are really responsible for your brother's death would not be happy. You've seen what the legal process is like. You've seen how dangerous it can be in prison. Mrs Archer, you're the victim of a conspiracy for financial gain, the same as me."

Silence stretched out for what seemed like hours before Melanie spoke again, this time, slowly, more considered. "Say I believed you, what do you want from me? Forgiveness?"

Forgiveness?

How could he hope to earn forgiveness from her when he couldn't even forgive himself?

"No, Mrs Archer," he said, "I can't expect that. All I want is for you to let us help you. We want to keep you safe. That's all."

"How are you going to do that?"

"Since you have the phone, CM Thatcher must have talked to you."

"Yes, we spoke, but he didn't say much," she answered, the sibilance of her speech heightened by the disconnected voice.

"He's placing you in protective custody, though. Isn't he?"

"I have no idea how you managed to pressure him into it, but that's what he said. Soon as Dr Milliner gives me the all clear, I'm going to be locked up with sex offenders and corrupt police officers. The lowest of the low."

"Only until we can arrange bail, Melanie," Lara said. "And we're working on that right now. You can expect a call from a new team of solicitors this afternoon."

"Real ones this time?"

Lara smiled. "Yes, Melanie. These will be legitimate. I promise you."

"They'll have to be pretty damned good to get me bail after what you did yesterday. For some reason, the police think I'm working with you. No idea why they'd think that, do you?"

The accusation was clear. By entering Falston Manor under false pretences and by escaping in such a brazen manner, he and Lara had made Melanie's legal position even more precarious. No judge would ever release her on bail if they thought she was working with a terrorist.

Damn it. He'd screwed up again.

Bloody moron!

"Your new defence team, Lawson and Luscombe, LLP, will do all they can," Lara said. "They're going to brief a first-class barrister who'll work your defence when you finally do make it to court. We've looked at the police case against you and it's pretty circumstantial"—she looked at Kaine and he shrugged at her optimism—"but, in the meantime, we'll do everything in our power to keep you safe. And with that in mind, follow CM Thatcher's advice. You can trust him, from now on."

"A-Are you sure?" Melanie asked, doubt in every tentative word.

"Absolutely certain," Kaine said. "His career and his freedom depend upon keeping you safe and sound."

"You have something on him, don't you? Something forcing him to protect me."

"Yes, Mrs Archer. We do," Kaine answered. "Would you accept some further advice before we end this call?"

"Possibly," she answered, hesitantly.

"Keep that phone fully charged and safe. And don't tell anyone you have it. No one, not even your closest friends. Promise?"

After a delay, her cautious, "Okay, I promise," came as an immense relief.

"That phone is your lifeline, Mrs Archer. Keep it safe."

"I will," she said and disconnected.

Kaine stared at the silent phone for an age before slipping it back into his pocket.

"What do you think?" Mike asked, cupping his coffee in both hands. "Did she believe you?"

Kaine shrugged. "No idea. Hope so, but it doesn't

matter. The only thing that matters is that she stays safe and does what Thatcher tells her."

Mike slurped his drink. "Never thought I'd see the day when I'd be sheltering a fugitive who was blackmailing a prison officer into protecting an inmate accused of murder." He took another sip and slowly shook his head, smiling sadly. "Strange times."

Strange indeed, old friend.

"At least she'll be safe for a while. I really won't be long," Lara said and left the kitchen.

Kaine waited until her footsteps creaked on the staircase before turning to his old friend and current host.

"Mike, is everything okay?"

The former chief petty officer set his mug on the table before lowering himself carefully into one of his stiff-backed dining chairs. "Hunky-dory, thanks."

"Are you sure, Mike? I'm getting a bit of a vibe here. Have I done something wrong? Are we imposing too much on your hospitality?"

Mike swiped his hand through the air in front of him, narrowly missing the coffee mug and the risk of knocking it to the floor. "Don't be daft, man. I love having you and the doc here. Danny, too. You know that." He straightened his back and reached for the mug, but couldn't completely mask a grimace.

"Chief … Mike, what's up?"

"Nah, it's nothing, lad. Touch of indigestion. Heart-burn. Nothing to worry about. I'll pick up some antacids next time I'm in town."

"Stomach ache? You want me to call Lara, have her examine you?"

Mike jumped to his feet. "Don't be so bloody ridiculous! I'm not having that slip of a girl prod my belly and treat me as a patient." He pointed a gnarled index finger at Kaine. "Not one word, Captain Kaine. Do I make myself clear?"

Kaine raised both hands. "Take it easy, Mike. No need to get all het up. I'll keep quiet so long as you agree to take care of yourself."

"What do you mean by that?" Mike asked, his hackles raised in defence.

"For crying out loud, look at that stuff," Kaine said, jabbing a finger towards Mike's mug and the caustic brew it contained. "Four heaped spoons of coffee in that oversized bucket? No wonder you've got heartburn. You need to go easier on the caffeine."

"Nonsense," Mike countered, taking another deep slug, "I've been taking my coffee this way for decades."

"That's exactly what I mean, you old fool. Might be time to change your diet a little. I've noticed you've been developing a bit of a paunch lately."

Mike tightened his firm abdominals. "That's enough of your cheek, you puppy. I can still show you a thing or two."

"Yes, Chief. You're the boss."

"And don't you forget it!" Mike helped himself to another sip and smiled. "Elixir of life. I couldn't survive without my regular dose of medicine."

"That and your evening tot, eh, Chief?"

Mike's smile broadened. "You've got that dead right, lad. Coffee and rum, two of my five-a-day. A dietician's delight. Now, where are you and the doc going?"

"Well, Chief Petty Officer Procter," he said, adding a slight bow, "Lara and I will be heading to Nottinghamshire to chat with a general factotum."

"Generals," Mike said, sniffing into his drink. "Never trust a general. Want anything done, ask a sergeant any day of the week. Either a sergeant, or a CPO."

Kaine shook his head. Mike knew exactly what a general factotum was, and who they planned to meet. The joke was Mike's way of drawing a line under the subject of health and welfare, but Kaine considered himself too good a leader to ignore the pastoral care of his men, even if the man concerned was retired and their host.

Chapter Thirty

Wednesday 21st April - Daniel Pinkerton

Construction Site, Burton-on-Trent, Staffordshire, England

Danny glanced upwards through the dirty windscreen, unimpressed. What started out as a bright, spring morning had quickly deteriorated into a dull, grey afternoon. He'd left the farm by midday, having swapped the exciting Triumph Tiger for an underpowered and rust-spotted Ford Fiesta—one of a number of second-hand cars the captain stored in an outhouse on the farm—and headed to Burton-on-Trent. He found his target easily enough and parked in a side street, around the corner from the construction site, making sure he had a good view of the entrance gates.

Sitting in the compact car, watching Andrew Braemar's

less-than-stellar construction operation, gave Danny's mind plenty of time to wander.

What the hell are you doing with your life, man?

Working with the captain was pretty much a dream life for an unencumbered adventurer. He'd loved the past few months, but sometimes wondered where it would lead.

Mostly, Danny supported the captain's goals one hundred percent. Kaine happened to be a father figure to Danny—not that he'd ever admit it aloud. Ever since they'd first met in a grubby, back-street dive in Germany, Danny's fortunes had been almost totally intertwined with those of Ryan Kaine.

With the captain's support and encouragement, Danny had applied for a transfer to the Special Boat Service, where he'd met the team's quartermaster, Rollo, and had been well and truly beasted. He'd joined Kaine's highly regarded troop, and fought alongside some of the toughest and most skilful men alive. Men who'd gladly lay down their lives for each other, irrespective of the toe-curling cliché those words conjured up to the wider population.

But circumstances had changed. Danny had changed. His relationship with Bobbie had altered things more fundamentally than he'd ever thought possible. No longer a single man without a care in the world, Danny had new responsibilities.

With Bobbie, he had a future. One that was incompatible with his chosen profession—assuming it was legitimate to call what he was doing a profession. Many wouldn't. To some, Danny would be nothing more than a mercenary, a gun for hire, a vigilante. A man operating outside the law. In Danny's line of work, one mistake could lead to disaster. So many times in recent months they'd skirted the very edge of the abyss, avoiding catastrophe by a combination of judgement, skill, and plain luck.

As a loner, Danny had viewed the life as an exciting trip from one neat adventure to the next, but times had changed. And the clients had changed, too.

Normally, the captain's vow to protect The 83 fell in line with Danny's own set of values. Supporting the families of the innocent victims who died aboard Flight BE1555 was a task worthy of Danny, the men of Kaine's troop, and the other disparate volunteers. But, not everyone happened to be worthy of the captain's protection.

Melanie Archer seemed a case in point.

Danny couldn't agree with the captain's assessment of their new client, but he'd still have to support him all the way. It would be unthinkable for Danny to do anything else but, on this occasion, the captain was wrong.

So fucking wrong.

Archer had murdered her old man. No doubt about it. The cops had worked the investigation and made a case that even the Crown Prosecution Service agreed met their strict, "Full Code" tests. After so many high-profile cockups, the CPS was more reluctant than ever to bring sub-optimal cases to trial. Yes, Archer was guilty and would be punished accordingly. So why was the captain wasting so much time and so many resources on her when there were other, more deserving cases?

The thing that had finally soured Danny's mood, tilting his support away from the Archer woman, was her plan to play the old, "coercive control" card in her defence.

The lying bitch.

If she'd really been abused, there'd be records. Medical and police reports, but if Corky couldn't find any, they didn't exist. And if she really had been abused, she would have left. No self-respecting person would put up with that bullshit.

Doesn't make sense.

For Archer to claim spousal abuse and use it as the main plank in her defence was totally unacceptable. For her to cry wolf and use other people's suffering as a way to wriggle out from under a murder charge was a shitty thing to do. When she played that card and failed, she'd make it even more difficult for the people who'd *really* suffered spousal abuse to win justice. The same way women who falsely accused men of rape made it more difficult for real victims to be believed.

Isn't right. No way.

The rain clouds emptied their load, pummelling the Ford's roof. It ran down the windscreen, causing rivulets of muddy water to chase each other down the glass, smearing the grime that had collected on the dusty journey from Long Buckby. He keyed the ignition and flicked the stalk. The wipers juddered forwards and backwards across the windscreen three times, but the blades did little more than smear the dirt and reduce visibility even further.

Danny sighed. Time to move. He'd delayed his approach long enough. The working day would end soon and he'd promised the captain he'd make a start.

As usual, Corky had produced an impressive legend for him, which made Danny's job easier. The hacker hadn't even resorted to a name change, just an increase in rank to colour sergeant. Danny couldn't help smiling. Since leaving the service, his rate of promotion had exceeded all expectations. Whereas it had taken him six years to make corporal in the SBS, he'd climbed the ranks all the way to "Colour Sergeant" within a few months of hitting Civvy Street.

Nice one, Corky.

Danny waited another couple of minutes for the rain to

ease before cracking open the door and stepping out into the afternoon gloom.

The rusted security fencing ahead of him creaked in the stiffening breeze, showing its age and its lack of a firm bedding. A pair of gates topped with tarnished razor wire stood open, if not exactly inviting.

In the two hours since Danny's arrival, not a single vehicle had entered or exited the place. Midweek on a site whose once-impressive, but now faded and weatherworn, signage proclaimed it to be, "The Latest Luxury Development in the Braemar Property Ltd Portfolio", showed almost no activity. A second sign, located to the left of the first, offered the chance for investors to buy luxury homes with one, two, or three bedrooms, off-plan. "In the heart of the countryside, a dream for your future!"

Beneath the proclamation, a computerised, 3D rendering of the architect's drawings showed an impossibly perfect interpretation of the proposed finished development.

Danny didn't believe a single digitised line or brush-stroke. The place was a veritable bomb site. He'd seen more likely building plots in Helmand Province after a heavy bombardment.

The view through the open gates revealed an area littered with rubbish, the detritus accumulated from years of neglect. Soggy newspapers disintegrated under the rain's attack. Decayed leaves gathered in mounds in the corners in front of pre-formed concrete blocks. Oil drums were stacked in uneven piles. Off to one side, a derelict bulldozer rusted against one of the walls, the only hint of the place ever having been an active building site.

Penned on three sides by a two-metre-high, chain-link fence, again topped with tarnished razor wire, a row of four ancient warehouses stood tall and menacing—and perilously close to collapsing in on themselves.

The walls of the first storey were constructed of red brick, now crumbling and weatherworn. Sometime in the recent past, the large windows had been covered by weatherboard panels. Above the brickwork, the three upper storeys and the roofs were clad in corrugated iron, all pitted with rust and dotted with holes.

A battered, prefabricated hut took pride of place on one side of the open gate, guarding the site against unwanted visitors. Another sign proclaimed the area was, "Private Property", and told the world to "Keep Out". Not much of a welcome for prospective investors in Andrew Braemar's so-called Luxury Development.

Danny strode towards the cabin, dodging the puddles and piles of rubbish, and raised his hand in preparation to knock. But, before he could complete the action, the door juddered inwards and a black-bearded monster wearing the generic, dark blue uniform of a security guard filled the opening. A smidge shy of two metres tall, the man had to duck to avoid hitting his head on the door's wooden lintel. Behind him, three similarly dressed men sat around a table playing cards. One wore his dirty, blond hair in incongruous dreadlocks. They paused to scowl at him for a moment before resuming their game.

"You not read?" the monster asked, stabbing a chunky forefinger at the sign attached to the cabin wall.

His guttural voice boomed around the open, rubbish-strewn site, echoed off the corrugated-iron walls, and rebounded into Danny's ears. The accent was indistinct, but definitely not from Staffordshire. Possibly eastern-European.

Danny smiled. "Yeah, mate. I can read well enough." He sniffed and wiped his nose with the back of his hand.

"The signs are for the punters, right? Health and Safety bollocks, yeah?"

Monster's forehead crinkled and his dark eyes narrowed, focussing on Danny's words as though struggling to work through the translation.

"Read sign," the man said and reinforced his meaning by slapping the notice with a paw the size of a small shovel. "Go!"

The cabin wall deflected under Monster's heavy pummelling. Either the wall was made of paper, or the giant packed one hell of a wallop. Danny would prefer not to find out first hand, not yet.

"Can I speak to the gaffer, please?" he asked, smiling pleasantly. No point in upsetting such a big geezer. At least not until he needed to.

Monster stopped pounding on the unfortunate notice-board and dropped the shovel-for-a-hand to his side, clenching it into a fist the size of a small rock. The sinews at the side of his thick neck stood out and the muscles on his broad shoulders stiffened.

Need some Prozac, mate?

"Gaffer? What is 'gaffer'?"

Danny forced his smile to widen. "The foreman. The boss. The head honcho. The person who runs this site."

"Ah," Monster said, understanding finally taking place inside the slab of a head. "I boss here," he said at last, thumping his chest with the rock.

"No, you don't understand. I'm looking for work." Danny mirrored Monster's action and punched his own chest. "Sparky. Electrician. Work. Yes?" He followed up the sign language by pointing from the notice attached to the dilapidated buildings and back at his chest.

Monster shook his head again and pointed to the gates. "No work here. Go."

"What about a phone number? Is there anyone I can call?"

"You go. Now."

The big guy in the spotless-but-overstretched uniform stepped out of the hut's shadow and lingered over Danny, who would have preferred to stand his ground, but flinched instead. He'd faced down bigger opponents and wasn't intimidated by the man-mountain, but showing fear seemed more in keeping with his guise of innocent job hunter. He took a couple of paces backwards.

"This is a building site and I'm a sparky. C'mon, mate. Give us a break, eh? Times are hard. I need the work."

Monster lurched forwards and reached out a hand. He dropped it on Danny's shoulder and spun him around. The grip was strong, but Danny could have broken it easily enough. However, rather than struggling, he timidly allowed the large security guard to frogmarch him to the gates.

"Get off me," he shouted, making a deliberately ineffectual attempt to tear out of the big man's grasp.

Monster cuffed the back of Danny's head with enough force to concuss a man who didn't have the reactions to roll with the blow. He shoved Danny through the gates, and swung them closed behind him.

Danny staggered away, rubbing his head as though it actually hurt.

"That's assault, that is," Danny said, making it sound like a whimper. "I'll call the cops on you!"

Monster cracked a smile and waved a hand in the air around him. "Call them. It not matter. No cameras, see? No proof," he scoffed and started to secure the gates with the chain and padlock.

Danny smoothed out the creases in the shoulder of his denim jacket and staggered away. "You big arsehole. Good job you're behind that gate, safe and sound, or I'd smash your bloody face in!"

Monster growled and his dark eyes became slits.

"What you say?" he growled.

"You heard me, arsehole!"

Monster dropped both ends of the chain, pulled open the gates again, and made to step through.

Danny backed away, stumbled off the edge of the pavement, and into the empty road. He regained his balance and hustled back towards the "safety" of his Ford. With his back turned to the so-called building site, he smiled. Despite the apparent humiliation, he'd learned enough to file an interesting report back at base.

Andrew Braemar talked a good game and his website proclaimed him as the owner of a thriving business in the process of building a top-of-the-range, luxury apartment block.

Yeah, right.

Danny had seen all he needed in the flesh to know that Braemar Property Ltd's flagship development was nothing but a sham. Although why Andrew Braemar went to the expense of protecting the ghost site with a huge defender from Eastern Europe and three of his mates was, without doubt, worthy of further investigation. If Corky was going to be busy over the next few days, so was Danny.

Braemar Property Ltd claimed to have three other developments in the East Midlands. All of which Danny planned to visit in person, and very soon. First though, he needed to report in.

Danny rounded the corner, dived into the dry shelter of

the Ford, and pulled out his phone. He dialled the captain's mobile and waited.

Chapter Thirty-One

Wednesday 21st April – Terrance Elphick

Archer Heights, Papplewick, Nottinghamshire, England

"…we could always wait and take her out on the way to court, if you like." Terrance Elphick took a breath. He knew the fuckwit's likely answer but wanted to draw him in, for the recording.

"How soon's that likely to be?" Andrew Braemar's high-pitched whine trembled down the other end of the phone line.

The younger man's accent and the quality of his voice was so strikingly similar to James', Terrance couldn't listen to Braemar speak without conjuring up an image of the man he loved in the full vibrancy of his prime. But the voice was where all similarity ended. It was the only thing the first cousins had in common.

While James had been tall, athletically built, and devastatingly handsome before the illness took his vitality and his looks, Andrew Braemar was a bloated, unkempt, snivelling blob of a man. A creature with little going for him in the looks department and even less in the way of intellect. No, Andrew Braemar was nothing like the gorgeous James. Nothing at all.

"No way of telling," Terrance answered, biting back the snarled reply he'd rather have made. Best to keep the oily, rat-faced creep on side, at least for the time being. "It will probably take months."

How the fuck would he know how long it would take for the courts to get their act in gear and put the skinny cow on trial?

"But I can't wait months. It has to happen soon."

"Patience is a virtue, Andrew."

Keep priming the pump.

"Don't start hitting me with those fucking platitudes, Terry. It won't work."

Terrance. My name is Terrance, you ignorant fuckwit!

Only James had permission to call him Terry, and then only in private. How dare the ignorant creature call him that?

Careful, Terrance. Cool head, son.

Yes. He needed to keep calm for now. There'd be plenty of time for the cousin to answer for the many slights he'd levelled at Terrance over the years.

James and Terrance had been so careful to keep their secret. Only the two of them knew about their special relationship.

The two of them and the skinny bitch, of course. Melanie "Window Dressing" Bowman. The scrawny cow. But she didn't really count.

During the marriage, James had treated her with all the respect she deserved. Sure, he took her to parties. Dressed her in the finest clothes and jewels. He showed her off to the world, when he really wanted to walk out, arm in arm with Terrance. But that wasn't possible. The age of same sex marriage when husband could step out with husband and wife with wife, without loss of face—or fortune—came too late for Terrance and James. Thirty-seven years too pigging late.

Thanks to the archaic, family rules—rules set in stone even before Victoria ascended to her throne—James had been forced to marry the bitch to cement his inheritance. And the cow married him for money and status, nothing more. Nothing more.

Fucking bitch deserved everything she had coming to her.

A blind man could have seen how much she benefitted from James' death. She stood to inherit most of the money, but only if a jury found her innocent. On the other hand, if they found her guilty, Braemar would take a whole chunk, and that wouldn't do. Oh no.

Wouldn't do at all.

Terrance wanted more than his paltry share. Far more. He'd get it, too. All he needed was leverage over Braemar, and he was in the middle of getting just that.

Without pretty much near-instant access to the cow's share of the inheritance, Braemar would be finished, which meant the shithead was desperate. Terrance wasn't too proud to use that fact, neither.

In short, the miserable cow had to die, and the sooner the better.

Time to finesse the opportunity.

"Like I said, Andrew. A prison transfer will be the perfect opportunity to finish her off," Terrance continued. "She'll be near enough defenceless. A couple of guards in a van won't put up much of a fight."

"Prison guards? God, how many people will get hurt?"

"As though you give a damn about collateral damage," Terrance said, unable to stifle his disdainful snort.

"If too many people get hurt, it'll draw attention to us. Like you said, a simple fight in prison would have been easy to explain away. Prison inmates die in brawls all the time. Pity your plan went tits-up."

"Don't go there, Andrew."

"Sorry," the creep said, "sorry. Anyway, we'd need muscle for a hit on a prisoner transfer."

"You've got access to muscle, Andrew," Terrance said, calm and to the point. "Courtesy of Eastern Europe."

A gasp down the line made Terrance smile.

Got you, arsehole.

"What the hell are you talking about, Terry?"

"Christ, you think I didn't know about your side-line in off-book workers?"

A gargled cough confirmed that Braemar fully understood Terrance's message.

"How long have you—"

"James was such a canny man. He asked me to investigate your operation the first time you turned up at the hospital after so many years without a word."

Terrance smiled at the memory of James who, despite his illness, could still recognise a conman when he saw one.

"Don't know what you mean. I simply wanted to pay my respects. That's all."

"Yeah, right. Of course you did. And who could blame you?"

Sniffing around his sickbed like a pig searching for truffles, more like.

"How much are you making from employing all those illegals?"

"Barely enough to cover my overheads." Braemar mumbled his response.

"Bollocks," Terrance snapped.

Stupid fuckwit.

Who did he think he was talking to?

"No, no … it's true. The construction sector's still in deep recession, Terry. Obtaining planning permission is a total, bloody nightmare. Bribes don't go anywhere near as far as they used to. On top of all that, the government's cracking down on immigration, and I'm in desperate need of a skilled workforce."

"A skilled workforce that puts up with long hours and can't insist on minimum wage, you mean?"

Braemar cleared his throat again, an ugly, wet sound. "That's beside the point. Overheads are still crippling, and the people I hire my workers from take a huge chunk out of my bottom line."

"Shit happens when you get into bed with lowlifes, Andrew."

"I-I didn't have a choice. Anyway, I still can't afford to wait for it to go to trial. I … don't suppose …" Braemar's voice trailed off.

Terrance let the silence drag out, letting the arsehole squirm before relenting a little.

"What exactly are you asking, Andrew?"

"I'm looking for a partner. I don't suppose you have the money available for a buy-in?"

That did it. Terrance finally let loose and burst out laughing. "Are you fucking kidding me? I'm a valet, man. Where the hell would I get that kind of cash?"

"Well," Braemar started, "given that you and dear James were so very, very … close, I thought he might have made sure you'd be … comfortable in your later years."

He knows? How?

Terrance deepened his voice to a threatening growl. "James and I were, as you say, close. He was a generous man and did leave me well cared for financially, but that's all tied up in probate. And it will be until they find the cow guilty … or something untoward happens to her. If you see what I mean."

A breathless chuckle.

"Yeah, I see exactly what you mean. You're saying you have as much to gain from her … departure as I have."

Hit the nail on the head at last, you prick.

"You could say that, Andrew."

"Yeah, I just did, Terry. So, what are we going to do about it?"

Terrance let another pause stretch out the conversation. The only noise on the line was Braemar's heavy breathing. The man sounded like he was running for a bus—uphill and wearing a backpack loaded with bricks.

Useless, fat prick.

"What if I told you I could bring the schedule forwards?" Terrance said, after making the cretin stew for long enough.

"Your inside man again?"

"Yes, Andrew, that's right. My inside source."

"The same inside man who was responsible for organising that fuckup in the showers?"

Terrance grimaced.

"Yes, well. The cow got lucky. No one could have foreseen what happened."

"And you trust your man to get it right this time?"

Considering his contact would be organising the escort detail, yes, they would damn well get it right this time.

"Yes, I trust my contact. And I never said it was a 'he'."

"A female screw?"

"Didn't say that either, Andrew."

"You always were a close-mouthed bugger, Terry."

You got that right, fuckwit.

"So, are you in?"

Terrance fell silent, waiting for the fuckwit to piss or climb off the pot.

Braemar's laboured breathing sounded serious, bordering on terminal. Terrance could almost hear the wanker's blood pressure rising. Much higher and he'd stroke out.

"Okay," Braemar said, eventually. It had taken a little while, but he did sound calmer. "If we do decide to do it your way, how quickly can we move?"

"How about within the next couple of days?"

"Bloody hell!"

"Yes, Andrew. I thought you'd be pleased."

"Can your contact let us know the route and schedule of the prison van?" Braemar's excitement was clear in his hushed and rapid speech.

"Yes," Terrance answered, smiling even though he tried to keep it out of his voice. "I'll take care of the intel, Andrew. You just sort out the logistics and the muscle, okay?"

"Yeah, yeah. I can provide a team who won't charge the earth or ask too many questions."

"Thought so. I'll be in touch with the details."

Without letting Braemar say another word, Terrance ended the call and powered down the sound recorder.

He smiled.

Time to call Falston Manor.

Chapter Thirty-Two

Monday 3rd May - Evening

Mike's Farm, Long Buckby, Northants, England

Kaine checked the time. 20:12.

Twelve minutes late. Anything could have delayed her scheduled call and he had no real cause for concern, but he couldn't relax. Kaine had offered her his protection, but having no direct access did nothing but stretch his nerves.

Thatcher's afternoon text, a curt, "All clear", didn't offer much in the way of comfort, but Kaine could expect nothing more from a compelled man. Relying on individuals he had to force into action could hardly guarantee success.

Although this was their seventh scheduled call, Kaine

couldn't sit still. He began pacing the comms room, weaving in and out of the sparse office furniture and sidestepping between the server cabinets. Back in his military days, he'd been just as antsy when awaiting the return of a patrol, although he usually forced himself to show outward calm to the men—no one wanted to see the group leader pacing nervously around the ops room. However, alone in Mike's barn, he could vent his frustration and do whatever he damn well pleased.

If they'd been anywhere else but in the middle of the country—a place without streetlights—he'd have eased his growing tension by heading outside for a run. But yomping over rough terrain in the dark was a sure-fire route to a turned ankle or, worse still, a broken—

The mobile in his hand vibrated so suddenly, he nearly dropped the thing onto the wooden floorboards. He hit the green button with a fumbling right thumb.

"Hello?"

"It's me, Melanie Archer," she whispered.

"You're behind schedule. Any trouble?"

"Not really. Just had to wait for the screws to finish a search."

Bloody hell. Thatcher was supposed to inform them in advance of a unit screening. Any more demerits on his report card might just earn the bugger a severe, physical reprimand.

"The guards tossed your cell?"

"No, they left me alone. I think they found some drugs in the cell next door. I-I couldn't make a call while they were on the block. Sorry."

"No problem. I was concerned. Nothing more. How are you?"

"Pretty good, thanks. It's not been too bad a day, considering I'm banged up for murder." Unusually, he heard a smile in her delivery.

"You sound chipper," he said, aiming for chipper himself.

"Yes, I'm in a really good mood for once."

"Good to hear. Any particular reason?"

"They're sending me to Nottingham tomorrow."

What?

Warning bells started clanging in Kaine's head.

"They are?"

"Yes. My dentist has agreed to fit a replacement crown."

"Are you sure you're going to the dentist? He's not visiting you in prison?"

"That's right," she said. "A car is taking me to the Aspire Hospital in Nottingham, early tomorrow morning. PO Priestly told me this afternoon."

"That's … interesting."

"You sound worried, Mr Kaine."

"No … Not really. It's just that I don't like surprises."

Thatcher hadn't mentioned a day release for dental treatment during his report, and he should have done. Another demerit. Tension niggled at the base of Kaine's neck. During any operation, he didn't take kindly to the unexpected, and a lightning-fast, one-day parole for non-urgent medical treatment most definitely fell into the "unexpected" category.

"I wasn't anticipating it so soon, but … I am happy about it."

"Yes, I can imagine. It didn't take long for Governor Bancroft to sanction a day-release," Kaine said, trying to keep the caution from his voice.

"That's what I thought, but apparently," Melanie said, "if it doesn't cost the prison anything, they can do things quite quickly. Surprisingly, Dr Milliner kept her word and contacted my health insurance company last week. James, my husband, had us both covered for private healthcare and paid a year in advance. The insurance company has agreed to cover all the prison's expenses, including overtime for the prison escort personnel. The dentist has a cancelled appointment for tomorrow afternoon, and I'm first in line. I'm actually rather nervous, really."

"Nervous about the treatment?"

"No. I've never had a problem with dentistry. Never did mind someone digging around in my mouth with drills and stuff. I'm just a little nervous about going outside, you know?"

"Not to worry, Mrs Archer. We'll have your back."

"You will?"

"Wherever possible, I keep my promises. But I would like to know how your dentist can make a replacement crown so quickly."

"That's simple enough. The clinic has its own machine to create ceramic crowns, and they still have the scan from my original operation. It'll be a perfect match for size, shape, and colour—or so they claim."

"That really is great news," he said, absently. Part of his mind was already working through the logistics of a tailing operation with only Danny available to help him at such short notice. "You'll be happy to have your smile back, I imagine."

"Yes," she said, "I can't wait. The inside of my lip is torn to ribbons, and I hate speaking with this lisp. Not that I have many people to talk to in here."

"Sorry about that, but at least you're safe."

"Yes, at least I'm … safe. I-I didn't mean to make it sound like a complaint."

"Have they given you an itinerary for tomorrow?"

He listened intently, taking notes, as she gave him all the information she had on the "jaunt", including the approximate departure time from Falston Manor, the hospital appointment time and location, and the expected duration of the operation.

"Excellent. Thanks, Mrs Archer. Don't worry. You probably won't see us, but we will be there."

He signed off and immediately called the team together for an emergency briefing.

―――――

KAINE GATHERED them around the table in Mike's kitchen and opened by outlining his concerns. An unscheduled day trip to the dentist might well be innocent and nothing to worry about but, more than an hour after he'd learned of the dental visit, the tingling at the base of his neck still hadn't dissipated. His plan—to follow the prison car and be prepared for anything, just in case—met with approval from Danny and Mike, but not Lara.

Out of necessity, the operation had to be simple.

Danny would head straight to the hospital on scouting duty, while Kaine followed the prison vehicle at a discreet distance on the Africa Twin. Lara and Mike would stay on the farm, out of harm's way—although he didn't actually use that phrase with Lara listening so acutely.

As was her way, Lara waited for him to finish before pointing out—calmly and clearly—what she called a significant flaw in his thinking. Kaine spread out his hands, giving her the floor.

"So," she'd said, drawing the word into a long sigh. She looked at each of them in turn, finishing by locking eyes with Kaine. "You plan to roll up to Falston Manor in broad daylight, and then sit on a motorbike for who knows how long, pointing a pair of binoculars at a prison?"

A slow and patient headshake caused her recently darkened hair to dance around her shoulders. It wasn't the same. He couldn't wait for her natural hair colour to grow back.

"Why not?" Danny asked before Kaine had the chance to defend his case.

In answer, Lara reached for the laptop that sat open on the table in front of her, into which she'd been typing for the previous few minutes. She turned it to face the three former-military professionals.

The screen showed a satellite image of Falston Manor and the surrounding countryside, which spread out into open fields defined by low hedges and dotted with the occasional farm and even more occasional coppice. No decent cover for at least three miles in any direction. With that one screen image, Kaine knew exactly what Lara meant, but he kept silent while she made her case.

"We've been there, Ryan. You don't think a man on a motorbike is going to draw attention to himself?"

Danny frowned. "The captain doesn't have to make it obvious. If he times it right, he'll only need to be there for a few minutes."

"What if the car's delayed, or a prison officer spots Ryan and calls the police about a suspicious-looking character on a bike, casing the prison?"

Danny shrugged and gave her an impish grin. "You saw how long it took the cops to react when you broke out the other day. Bonnie and Clyde would have been proud of you both. By the time the Boys in Blue reached his obbo point, the captain would be long gone."

At first, Kaine couldn't work out whether Danny's answer was flippant or serious, but the twinkle in the younger man's eye gave him the answer. Like Kaine, he'd seen Lara's point the moment she'd spun the laptop.

"But what good would that do?" she asked. "The whole point of Ryan being there is to identify the vehicle they're using, confirm the time of departure, and follow it all the way to Nottingham. If he ends up racing through the green lanes to avoid the police, how's he going to do that?"

"Good point," Mike said from his chair at the head of the table. "You have an alternative suggestion, I suppose?"

"Why use a motorbike in the first place?" she asked. "Why not take a car? Maybe use two cars, even. It would be less noticeable, and—"

"You could come along as a spotter or drive one of the cars?" Kaine said, anticipating her obvious suggestion. He shook his head adamantly. "Forget it. That's not happening. We were lucky last time, and only escaped by the skin—"

"No," Lara snapped, taking her turn to interrupt, "we escaped because you had the forethought to plan things properly. You don't have time to do the same thing here. So, what's your answer?"

"To what question?"

"Why use a motorbike instead of a car?"

Kaine turned to Danny and waved a hand towards Lara. "Care to step in here, Sergeant?"

Danny cleared his throat and his dining chair creaked as he sat up straighter. Patch, the sheepdog with white markings around his left eye, lifted his head from where it lay on top of Mike's slippered foot. Mike dropped a hand from the arm of his well-used chair and scratched behind the dog's ear. The second animal, Petra, mewled and scrunched forwards to earn the same reward.

"For an effective, covert operation of this type," Danny explained, "we'd really need at least four trail vehicles of different types—cars, vans, bikes, you know? To avoid being spotted by the quarry, the tails would need to be coordinated and swap positions regularly. In heavy traffic, the bigger the team, the better. And don't forget, by the time the target reaches the outskirts of Nottingham, it'll be close to lunchtime rush hour and all the main arterial roads into the city will likely be choked.

"With only two in our team, the motorbike's a better alternative. It can flit in and out of traffic." Unnecessarily, he flicked his hand like a fish's tail to illustrate the action. "Meanwhile, I'll be at the hospital to make sure there's no reception committee waiting."

"What if this so-called reception committee chooses a different place to intercept the target?" Lara asked, again showing her inherent grasp of all the logistical challenges. "What if the car takes a different route?"

Kaine took over. "There aren't that many direct routes between Falston and the hospital, and we know the one they're planning to take. No reason to think they'll change it."

She nodded.

"Okay," Danny said, "let's assume there are no changes. At that time of day, there are only two obvious interception points. The hospital itself and the three-mile approach to the aerodrome."

"What if these same would-be attackers decide to run the prison car off the road? There's an opportunity every kilometre of the journey from start to finish—in both directions," Lara added.

Danny scrunched up his face and shook his head. "The rest of the route is too busy. Too risky for them. And we can't cover every possible variable. Besides, we're only being ultra-cautious. We've heard nothing on the grapevine about an attack. Mrs Archer's been safely tucked up in solitary for the better part of two weeks. And, according to Corky, Andrew Braemar's done nothing but scratch around trying to raise funding for that white elephant in Burton."

Danny took a breath and glanced at Kaine as though looking for permission to continue. Kaine nodded his consent.

"For the past few days, Braemar's been pushing the boat out, showing potential clients around that so-called development site of his. Last Friday, a couple of gents from the Middle East spent all of ten minutes at the place. Took one look around and couldn't leave quickly enough. They headed out so fast, the wheels of their Rolls Royce dug deep gouges into the gravel."

"That only shows how desperate he's getting," Lara said, evidently unimpressed with Danny's logic. "Look at it this way. Tomorrow will be the first time Melanie's been out in the open since being locked up. If Andrew Braemar really was responsible for the attack on Melanie, he's almost bound to make another attempt. The next opportunity won't happen until the bail hearing or the trial."

Danny scrunched up his face. "I really can't see it, Doc. As far as we can tell, Braemar's flat broke. I doubt he could raise the money to call in a decent hit team, and those people wouldn't work on credit. The way he organised the attack on Mrs Archer in the first place showed that clearly enough."

"But she nearly died!"

"Yeah, fair enough. But my point is, Braemar's method —assuming he did set those inmates on her, and we're only guessing here—proves he doesn't have the contacts or the cash to set up a professional hit." He opened out his hands as though to show he'd made his point effectively.

"Yes, well," she said, showing no signs of letting the matter drop, "we still haven't ruled out Terrance Elphick as a threat."

"No," Kaine said, adding what he hoped was a disarming smile, "and we haven't ruled him *in*, either."

Every attempt they'd made to investigate Elphick—both digitally and physically—had produced a big, fat zero. Not even a hugely frustrated Corky could find any dirt on the man. Elphick turned out to have an even smaller digital footprint than Kaine's technophobic police contact, DCI David Jones.

So far, all their low-tech methods had failed, too. The man hadn't acknowledged any of their "official" requests, by phone and letter, for a meeting. When Kaine and Lara— posing as researchers for Melanie Archer's defence team— turned up in person at the Archer's family home, Elphick hadn't even allowed them over the threshold. On top of everything else, apart from Braemar's obvious familial relationship to James Archer, Terrance Elphick had no direct association with the developer. At least, none they could identify.

No, they hadn't ruled out Terrance Elphick as a suspect or a threat.

Short of abducting the man and trying to sweat the information out of him—and Kaine had no intention of doing anything of the sort—the manservant and former professional boxer would remain an enigma.

Corky would keep digging, though. That much was certain but, so far, they'd hit a brick wall.

Even though they had the technology and good intentions, as far as criminal investigators were concerned, Kaine and his team could only ever be described as amateurs. Until that point, Kaine had been holding off, but at some stage, he'd have to hand all their research over to the professionals.

Yes, before long, Kaine would have to arrange a clandestine meeting with David Jones, who would know the best way to approach the investigation. Whether the somewhat stiff-shirted detective would be prepared to look into a case that fell way outside his jurisdiction was a separate matter. Kaine wasn't looking forward to broaching the subject with the detective chief inspector. No telling how he'd react.

"In that case," Lara countered, "if it's so safe and nothing's going to happen, why bother following the car in the first place?"

"That's easy," Danny returned, laying his trump card, "there's no harm in making certain. Isn't that right, Captain?"

"Okay, how about this," Kaine said, feeling the need to step in and pour the soothing oil. "Why don't I take a camera and film the whole thing surreptitiously? That way, I'll be less conspicuous, and you can monitor the whole event from the comms room."

Lara's stern expression softened, and Kaine took it as her tacit acceptance.

"Mike," he said, "did the handlebar camera arrive from Rollo, yet?"

Still scratching his dogs' ruffs, Mike nodded. "Yep. I accepted delivery this morning. It came with a whole bunch of other gizmos. I locked the packages away in the barn."

"Excellent," Kaine said, looking at Lara. "Will that suffice?"

"Suppose it'll have to," she said, looking down at the dogs, not at him.

Kaine suppressed a grin at finally winning a battle against her, but he'd have preferred it if she hadn't turned away from him.

When had life as a fugitive become so damned complicated?

Chapter Thirty-Three

Tuesday 4th May - Afternoon

The Overlook, HMP Falston Manor, Derbyshire, England

Kaine pulled the Africa Twin into the layby, kicked down the side stand, and killed the engine. The silence stretched out around him. From his slightly elevated position, he had a decent view of Falston Manor, which sat low in a picturesque valley nearly a mile distant. He'd parked the bike facing the prison so the handlebar-mounted camera had a clear and direct view of the prison estate in all its stone-built, Victorian splendour.

He removed the helmet and sucked in a refreshing lungful of the cool, country air. Although top-of-the-range and fully vented, the air inside the helmet could get a little warm when he wasn't moving.

Kaine pulled off his bike gloves, retrieved the mobile from his jacket pocket, turned his back to the prison estate, and studied the camera's field of vision through the phone's screen while pretending to read a text message. He zoomed in the camera and winced at the damage he'd inflicted on the prison's perimeter infrastructure. Although not one to relish causing wanton destruction to public property, it couldn't be helped. His and Lara's escape from Falston Manor had made the damage essential.

To assuage his conscience, and with Corky's assistance, Kaine had made an anonymous donation to the Prison Officers Association Welfare Fund in an attempt to offset any injuries the poorly paid civil servants might have sustained during their escape. As for the damage he'd inflicted upon the physical structure—two destroyed blast gates and the associated mechanics to open and close them —the UK Government had deep pockets. It could damn well stump up the funds for the renovation. After the way the authorities had treated him, they deserved nothing better, and he refused to make life any easier for the politi- cos, irrespective of which side of the political divide they sat on.

The authorities knew he was innocent—DCI Jones had seen to that—but the current Home Secretary in his infinite and politically correct wisdom had refused to quash the charges against him, insisting he take his chances in a public court of law. As far as Kaine was concerned, the UK government could rot in hell. The others, however, the hard-working and the innocent, the prison officers, deserved all the help he could provide. Hence the money to the POA Welfare Fund. A healthy donation Corky had taken from

Kaine's personal fund, not the money he'd earmarked for The 83.

As it turned out, the prison authorities had made a good start on the repairs, not that they had much choice in the matter. After all, how secure could a prison be if it was unable to close its front gates?

A team of engineers armed with heavy-lifting gear had cleared away the damaged metalwork. The same company had replaced them with temporary fencing—the sort used to prevent theft from building sites and thwart unauthorised entry to music festivals. In short, not particularly secure.

The presence of police vehicles and armed police officers in full riot gear added a degree of essential fortification and showed serious intent. Thankfully, none of the inmates would be able to take an unsanctioned sabbatical on account of Kaine's wanton destruction.

A clear case of trying to lock the stable doors after they'd been totally obliterated.

Again, Kaine found himself unable to prevent a smile forming.

Ryan Liam Kaine, you are a bad, bad man.

According to Corky, the new, bespoke doors were being fabricated by a company in Germany since no UK firm could handle the order at such short notice. Another sad indictment on the state of the UK's industrial sector, and one more reason for Kaine to reject the government's kind offer to incarcerate him while they worked out whether his video evidence stood up to forensic and legal examination.

Given the number of times he had to step in to help members of The 83, Kaine's reply to DCI Jones' offer to negotiate his surrender of, "No, thanks. I'll carry on as I am for the moment," seemed ever more justified. Difficult and sometimes dangerous, but justified all the same.

Seven minutes later, with his back firmly to the prison and staring at his mobile's screen the whole time, Kaine spotted movement.

An unexceptional, dark blue Vauxhall with tinted rear windows—the car he'd been waiting for—rolled towards the damaged gateway at little more than walking pace. The driver's window rolled down and a grey-haired man popped out his head and right arm. The hand attached to the arm held a sheet of paper, the temporary release warrant, Kaine assumed. The prison officer passed the letter to a uniformed security guard who'd stepped out of a makeshift sentry box the moment the Vauxhall had nosed its way out of the internal compound.

The guard studied the sheet of paper, ran his index finger down a form on his clipboard, and then bent to inspect the inside of the car. Apparently satisfied with its occupants, he returned the paper and waved the driver on his way.

Kaine tapped his earpiece twice to open the channel on his state-of-the-art comms. Recently provided by Rollo, and made even more secure with software designed and installed by Corky, the system was as close to failsafe as it was possible to acquire. Its specifications far exceeded anything available to even the best-equipped military organisation— it was far too expensive.

When time allowed, Kaine would ask Corky if there was any way they could roll out a similar system for commercial use. Given the many budgetary constraints, the Defence Procurement Agency could use all the help he could provide.

The system bleeped awake.

"Alpha One to Charlie One, are you receiving me? Over."

"*Charlie One to Alpha One, receiving you full strength. Over,*" Danny replied instantly, his voice as clear as if he was sitting on the pillion seat behind Kaine rather than over forty miles away in Nottingham.

"Target in view." Kaine gave the make, model, and licence number of the Vauxhall and ended the message by saying, "We'll be with you within the hour. Over."

"*Message received, Alpha One. Over.*"

"Anything happening your end? Over."

"*All quiet here, boss. No obvious bogey presence. Over.*"

"Will let you know of any variations to the planned route. Stay awake, Charlie One. Alpha One, out."

Kaine disconnected the comms before Danny could react to his insulting and unnecessary warning.

Below him at the damaged prison entrance, the driver slowly manoeuvred the Vauxhall past a chicane of obstacles, twice having to stop at police checkpoints, and twice having to show his pass to ever more efficient and eagle-eyed security personnel. The police took more time to inspect the car, opening all the doors and the boot, and passing a mirror attached to a pole under the floor pan.

It took a full ten minutes for the Vauxhall to make the three-hundred-metre journey before it finally reached the end of Woodland Spur and turned left onto Uttoxeter Road. On their current route, they would pass within touching distance of Kaine and his Honda.

He donned the helmet, snapped the visor closed, and tugged on his gloves. For once, the weather decided to play nice and a watery sun with little wind promised a reasonable day for a bike ride. The only thing missing to make it more pleasant was having Lara on the pillion. Still, she was on the farm with Mike, reluctantly monitoring his and Danny's progress in perfect safety.

Kaine keyed the Africa Twin and waited for the dash-board lights to scroll through their "pre-flight" ignition checks before hitting the starter button. The big bike growled into powerful but subdued life. A couple of light throttle twists confirmed the engine as raring to go. He depressed the clutch handle, kicked the bike into first, and waited in the layby for his target's arrival.

He didn't have to hang around for long.

The Vauxhall had picked up speed on the Uttoxeter Road. Red lights flared as the driver braked to negotiate the sharp right-hander leading to the slip road onto the A50.

Kaine allowed them to pass and gave them plenty of time to join the dual carriageway, initially leading west, before he checked over his shoulder and pulled onto the empty road.

He headed west for half a mile, joined the westbound carriageway of the A50, and the Vauxhall passed him on the opposite carriageway, heading east, towards Notting-ham. Everything was going according to plan.

Kaine slowed at the approach to the first roundabout, took the fourth exit, and joined the eastbound carriageway no more than two miles behind the Vauxhall. Another slight twist on the throttle caused the mighty bike to surge forwards, reaching and then breaking the speed limit in a few heartbeats. He throttled back to keep the bike below eighty and slowly reduced the gap between him and Melanie Archer.

Kaine spared a thought for her state of mind.

She'd been locked up in Falston Manor for more than a month. The world outside the prison had to look pretty good to her, even from behind the windows of a car.

As she'd told him on the illicit phone, the upcoming dental work didn't hold any fears for her. After all, she'd already been through the operation once. Fitting a new crown to an existing implant should be nothing to fret over. Nottingham's Aspire Hospital boasted a stellar reputation, and they certainly charged enough for their private health care to guard their reputation jealously.

It took less than five minutes to catch up with the Vauxhall, which cruised along in the inside lane, keeping well below the mandated seventy-mile-per-hour speed limit. No doubt the driver was enjoying his time on prison parole as much as his passengers—and at decent overtime rates.

Under duress, Thatcher had given Kaine a full briefing of the transportation detail, including the names and addresses of the two guards on escort duty—Supervising Officer Louis Grant and Prison Officer Saran Priestly. Each had a spotless work history and could be trusted to perform their duties with professional efficiency and calm, or so Kaine had been assured. He'd already seen Priestly in action and trusted her as much as he could trust any stranger. As for SO Grant, Corky hadn't unearthed anything suspicious so far.

Kaine and the sprightly Africa Twin roared past the Vauxhall, giving them plenty of room, and knowing they couldn't possibly recognise him behind his tinted visor. When operating solo, tailing a vehicle from a leading position worked as well as anything else.

Fifteen miles later, with the Vauxhall a distant blip in his mirrors, Kaine took a slip road off the dual carriageway and slowed enough to let the target vehicle pass below and to his right. Taking the second exit off the ensuing round-about enabled him to re-join the A50 well behind the Vauxhall. This time, he matched their speed and followed two hundred metres behind, keeping at least six cars between him and his target. If either Priestly or Grant in the Vauxhall were avid motorbike spotters, the bypass manoeuvre should have been more than enough to mask his intentions.

At the wheel of the Vauxhall, SO Grant obeyed all the rules of the road, indicating when necessary and giving the other road users plenty of advance warning of his intentions. In short, tailing the prison transport was a delight and left Kaine with plenty of spare capacity to enjoy the feel of the open road beneath his wheels and the warmth of the sun on his visor.

As they drew ever closer to Nottingham, the traffic increased in volume and slowed in pace. The road filled with vehicles, running nose-to-tail on the outside lane and bunching on the inner. He cracked the visor and allowed the cool, fresh air to blow away the cobwebs.

Wake up, Kaine. No such thing as a milk run in this game.

Over his right shoulder, the clouds, which had been thickening all morning, darkened and lowered, blocking out the southern sky and hiding the sun.

Ten miles from Nottingham, a sudden squall blew in from the southwest, hitting hard. The raised banks on either side of the road rotated the wind into a vortex and buffeted him from both sides. To increase traction and extend his safety envelope, Kaine eased off the throttle and slowed the Honda to below fifty.

A few minutes later, the heavens opened.

Rain hammered down.

It drummed into the shoulders of his leather jacket, bounced high off the handlebars and headlights, and formed a semi-opaque mist around him. Rainwater boomed against his helmet and ran in a torrent down his visor, reducing visibility even further. Before long, the road ran slick with oily runoff.

He lost sight of the Vauxhall.

Crap!

Kaine increased his speed, undertook a truck, and passed two cars on his inside.

There!

Five cars ahead.

He indicated left and muscled his way into a narrow gap between a Ford SUV and a small Toyota in the inner lane. The affronted driver in the Ford flashed his headlights, and Kaine raised his hand in apology. It never paid to antagonise other road users, especially without the protection of a car frame and the requisite number of airbags.

On the outskirts of the city, a logjam formed, and the traffic ground to a rapid and complete halt.

Kaine idled in traffic, right foot depressing the rear brake pedal, left foot on the tarmac, absorbing the wrath of nature—an untimely reminder of one major drawback of motorbiking.

He hunched his shoulders and sighed. Maybe he should have chosen a car after all.

No, things are good.

Although the conditions were uncomfortable, he'd suffered worse conditions on winter manoeuvres in Wales and Scotland. The bike would suit him well enough in the heavy traffic, assuming they ever started moving again.

Filtering between the lanes was tricky and potentially dangerous, but he'd just proved its value. He couldn't use the method often, though, since it drew so much attention.

He stayed put, leaving the five vehicles between himself and the Vauxhall.

The conditions were becoming ever more treacherous. When they finally started moving, traction would be an issue. Two wheels were never quite as stable as four.

A double-click in his earpiece announced an incoming message from Danny.

Ahead, brake lights glowed, diffused into a widespread and dimpled mass of red and grey by the rain running in a rippling, spotted wave down his visor. He ran a gloved index finger across the tinted plastic, but it didn't help much and he had to raise the visor a crack. Rainwater splashed into his eyes, driven by the growing gale. The traffic in front started pulling away, the blockage having finally eased. He opened the visor wider and blinked away the blinding rain.

The road ahead of the Vauxhall cleared and SO Grant pulled off. Kaine bided his time. He could close the gap between them quickly enough. No point in taking any risks at this stage.

"*Charlie One to Alpha One, are you receiving me? Over.*"

"Alpha One, here. Go ahead. Over."

"*How far out are you? Over.*"

"Five or six miles. Stuck in traffic. Why, is there a problem? Over."

"*That's an affirmative, Alpha One. A monster of a problem. Over.*"

A monster of a problem? What was going on? Danny didn't usually exaggerate.

The vehicle immediately in front of Kaine, a white van, pulled away. Kaine released the clutch, tweaked the twist-grip, and the Africa Twin leaped forwards.

Time to close on the target.

A huge, refrigerated lorry filled the outer lane, blocking his outlet. Kaine ground his teeth.

Ahead, the van in his lane picked up speed slowly and the lorry matched its pace, boxing Kaine in position.

"Charlie One, how serious is it? Over."

"*Deadly. Can you intercept the target? Over.*"

"No idea, but I'll try. Alpha One, out."

Kaine controlled his breathing. Concentration was key.

The white van indicated right, its driver in a hurry to pull into a non-existent gap. The lorry gave way and the van edged right. Kaine opened the throttle, jumped forwards, then hauled on the brakes to stop himself running into the back of a large, white box of a caravan. His rear wheel lost traction and the bike bucked beneath him, but the ABS took charge and helped to control the slide.

Kaine shook the error from his mind and the rain from the visor. He allowed the gap between him and the caravan to grow and edged closer to the white line running down the middle of the dual carriage way.

Up ahead, the Vauxhall had gone. Disappeared into the mist and rain.

The overall speed of the surrounding traffic grew to forty-five miles per hour. The spray thrown up around him by wheels running on inundated tarmac formed a dense curtain of mist, reducing visibility to a few metres.

Conditions were worsening by the second.

The end of the dual carriageway approached, forcing the traffic to slow once more as the vehicles in the outer lane merged into the inner lane, acting like a dealer riffle-shuffling a deck of cards.

Kaine swallowed hard.

While he fought the traffic, the Vauxhall was drawing further away, heading into who knew what sort of danger.

Finally their speed picked up and the road turned from dual carriageway into a twin-lane blacktop. In the oncoming lane, vehicles ploughed towards him at high speed, showering him with plumes of gritty water and pummelling him with storm-force blasts of wind.

Go for it, man.

He racked open the throttle, targeting a narrow gap between the white caravan and an oncoming truck. He sucked in a breath as the handlebars came within a few centimetres of becoming acquainted with the caravan's glossy paintwork. If he hadn't removed the side panniers that morning, his chase would have ended there and then. And ended badly.

Finally, the road ahead cleared and he increased speed, hoping for a sight of the dark blue Vauxhall.

Nothing.

The calm voice from the GPS bolted to his handlebar warned of an impending right turn, eight hundred metres ahead. Kaine maintained speed, weaving in and out of traffic, filtering, taking huge risks.

A central reservation grew out of nothing, and Kaine barely had time to jag left before the safety barrier cut him in half. He braked, ducked further left onto the hard shoulder to undertake a family saloon. In the rear window, the white face of a shocked child flashed past in a blur. Leaning to his right helped him race around another car, this one a Porsche. A turning lane formed on the outside, filled with traffic.

Kaine carried on, racing, filtering between waiting cars.

At the turning, amber traffic lights snapped off, turned red. He squeezed the handbrake and stamped on the foot pedal. The bike's rear end slid to a sideways stop in front of a bright red transit van. He revved the engine and waited for the lights to change or for a gap in the oncoming traffic —whichever came first.

All around him, horns blared angrily and headlights flashed. He'd made no friends that day and probably cemented a hatred for bikers in the minds of the other road users forevermore.

Kaine didn't give a hoot.

The Vauxhall was way out of sight, heading into potential danger. Heading straight for whatever had spooked Danny. Things were becoming desperate.

With the front brake locked down hard, he kicked the bike into first gear, revved the engine high, and slipped the clutch. The rear wheel spun, clearing the road of water, gaining traction, and burning lost heat into the rear tyre.

The traffic lights glowed stubbornly red and the westbound traffic roared towards him in a continuous line of flying spray and dazzling headlights.

Come on. Come on!

A tiny gap appeared in the oncoming line between a car and a truck. Miniscule. Impossible.

Doable.

Kaine opened the throttle wide.

The powerful Africa Twin shot forwards into the path of a container lorry. Headlights flared, turning muddy gloom into rain-splashed brilliance. An engine roared.

He'd misjudged the gap!

An angry air horn blared.

The front of the truck dipped and the cab shuddered as the driver stamped down on the airbrakes. Kaine twisted the throttle harder—wide open.

The truck's front bumper kissed the Africa Twin's tail light cluster, tore it loose. The bike's rear tyre skidded right, bounced, left the road.

The Honda became a bronco. It bucked, trying to shake him free.

Kaine's world transformed into a whirling, spinning, washing machine. Boots left the foot pegs and he parted company with the seat. Man and machine flew through the air, joined only by his hands locked tight to the grips.

The rain-washed tarmac rushed up to meet them.

Chapter Thirty-Four

Tuesday 4th May – Daniel Pinkerton

Car Park, Aspire Hospital, Nottinghamshire, England

Aspire Hospital gleamed in the sunlight, a shining example of private healthcare in the UK. At least that's what the lettering on the pale green sign gracing the plate-glass frontage of the modern building proclaimed.

Danny tried to remain unimpressed, but it wasn't easy. The facility reeked of money, and it did actually shine in the pale sunlight. The brilliance wouldn't last long though, not if the clouds building on the southern horizon had anything to do with it. The weather forecast promised heavy rain later that afternoon, but the cold front pushing up from the southeast hadn't learned to tell the time. The damned thing was at least two hours ahead of schedule. Already, the breeze had picked up, and the windsock hanging from the pole in the nearby airfield stood out straight and horizontal.

Like the oncoming weather front, Danny had arrived well ahead of time. He'd never visited that part of Nottingham and hadn't wanted to risk missing the target's arrival. Although not feeling the same way for Mrs Archer as the captain did, Danny wasn't about to let either of them down. He'd said his piece at the outset. Told the captain what he thought of a woman who used spousal abuse and coercive control as a defence for murder, and refused the captain's offer to step down. He'd volunteered to watch over her and would never consider going back on his solemn word. Not to the captain. Not to himself. Not to anyone.

Aspire Hospital sat in the middle of a brownfield, development site on the southern outskirts of Nottingham, built on land adjacent to the small, private airfield. Although the hospital itself had been completed and operational for a couple of years—with its brand-new access road standing out black and sharp against the mud of the surrounding earthworks—the area was still an active building site. The skeletal structures of commercial buildings in various stages of completion grew out of the mud like the fossilised bones of ancient animals exposed by erosion.

Flat land stretched for hundreds of acres around the site, no doubt set aside for future development. What was once seen as wasteland now offered itself up to the speculators and developers as prime, construction real estate.

On his arrival, Danny toured the site slowly in his beat-up Ford, scoping out the area as a potential, if improbable, battleground.

Unlike the so-called development site in Burton, which he'd been watching off and on for over a week, this place teemed with activity. Contractors from numerous firms, and sporting livery of different colours, swarmed over the diverse construction sites. On one plot behind where Danny eventually parked with a good view of the hospital entrance, concrete mixers rolled in one after the other, their loads churning away to keep from setting hard. They disgorged the concrete into pre-set foundation channels, while workers raked it flat before leaving the space clear for the next delivery.

Scaffolders bolted steel tubes together and slid wooden planks into place, offering at least the illusion of safety for future building crews. Dust, churned up by the growing wind, covered everything in a thick layer of russet.

A car park filled with vans, trucks, four-wheel-drive pickups, and cars all covered in multiple layers of grime, stood on the outskirts of the site, which was where Danny chose to set up his observation post.

By mid-morning, the place was buzzing with hard-working people, mostly men, building for the future. In his Ford, spattered with dirt from Mike's farm tracks, Danny blended in well enough. He sat behind the wheel, eating a sandwich, more for camouflage than to ward off hunger, although as the saying went, in the field, a soldier should never miss an opportunity to fuel up. And, looking around at the expanse of flat land, the term "in the field" couldn't have been much more appropriate.

He finished munching on one half of a cheese and pickle sarnie and cracked open a bottle of cola—recyclable plastic only. Danny prided himself on his environmental credentials. The minimum of single-use plastic for him. He valued the planet and, if his relationship with Bobbie progressed as he hoped, the planet needed to support human life for another few centuries yet. Especially since he planned to add at least two little ones, maybe three, to the next generation. Fingers crossed.

His earpiece clicked twice. He washed down the remains of his sandwich and tapped the device into activation.

"*Foxtrot One to Charlie One are you in position? Over.*" The comms unit's bone-conduction mechanism made the doc's voice clear and sharp.

"Charlie One to Foxtrot One. In position. Over."

"*Anything to report? Over.*"

"Not a thing. All quiet here, apart from the noise and the dirt, if you see what I mean. Any news from Alpha One? I've not heard from him yet. Over."

"*Alpha One is on the way. Should be in position shortly. Over.*"

"Copy that, Foxtrot One. I'll let you know if anything changes my end. Charlie One, out."

Danny tapped the earpiece again and it clicked into standby mode. The team's new-fangled comms unit was the best he'd ever used. If they'd had a system like it in Helmand, lives would've been saved. One of the best things about working with the captain was the availability of top-quality equipment and the enhanced software to run it. Having the services of a genius like Corky onside was, without doubt, essential.

The earpiece clicked twice and Danny activated the system again.

"*Alpha One to Charlie One, are you receiving me? Over.*"

Danny smiled. Talk of the Devil. It was almost as though the captain had been earwigging his conversation with the doc.

"Charlie One to Alpha One," Danny responded, "receiving you strength five. Over."

"*Target in view. They're in a blue Vauxhall Insignia, licence number Sierra, Tango, Five, Nine, Alpha, Charlie, Charlie. We'll be with you within the hour. Over.*

Danny repeated the licence number in his head a couple of times to lock it in place.

"Message received, Alpha One. Over."

"Anything happening your end? Over."

Danny reported that all was clear and put the system in standby mode after the captain's terse, *"Stay awake, Charlie One. Alpha One, out."*

As if he'd ever fall asleep in the middle of an op!

Bloody cheek.

Danny would have been royally pissed if he thought for one moment that the captain was being serious.

Stay awake?

Danny laughed and settled down to his vigil. Time enough to head for the main access road. As per standing orders, the captain would let him know when the target vehicle was within five minutes of their destination. Meanwhile, Danny had plenty of time to kill.

As he waited, the rain arrived, started gently, and picked up energy. In seconds, it turned into a deluge, hammering loudly on the Ford's roof.

———

MOVEMENT on the far side of the car park caught Danny's eye. A five-year-old, lime green, Fiat Ducato with white panels pulled through the barrier. It cruised the aisles at walking pace, the driver apparently searching for a free parking spot. Nothing unusual about that, as such, but the artwork on its side panels drew Danny's attention. Someone had covered the company name with red splurges of graffiti. Again, not unusual. In some of the neighbourhoods Danny had lived in, a pedestrian standing still long enough would end up being tagged by any of the local idiots who could steal a can of spray paint. However, these particular paint splurges obliterated the company name, but not the logo—a stylised oak tree that might well have been stolen from a political party's manifesto.

A thousand fine hairs on the nape of Danny's neck bristled. He'd seen the logo recently—very recently.

The van turned into Danny's row and approached, maintaining its walking pace. He followed its progress in the Ford's wing mirror. The bearded driver and his clean-shaven passenger stared straight ahead, not scanning for empty spaces. They both wore black beanies—a clear warning sign for anyone who'd watched a heist movie in the previous two decades—and only had eyes for the hospital's access road.

As the van drew alongside Danny's Ford, he scratched his forehead to hide his face from the dreadlocked man in the passenger seat, who passed so close, Danny could have reached out and shaken his hand through the van's open window.

The rain still pelted down.

Luckily, the height and position of the van hid Danny from the driver, who might well have recognised him. They'd met the same time Danny had first seen the oak tree logo—at Andrew Braemar's defunct building site in Burton-on-Trent. The giant security guard with the Eastern European accent—Monster!

Fucking hell!

Of course, Monster's appearance could be a total coincidence. After all, the man worked for a property developer and for him to be cruising a building site such as this one didn't lie too far outside the realms of plausibility. Monster might well have been pitching for work, as Danny had pretended to do during his first visit to Burton. However, for someone so closely associated with Mrs Archer to be in that particular place at that particular time stretched the bounds of probability beyond breaking point.

On top of everything else, Corky's deep dive into Andrew Braemar's business dealings had been comprehensive. If Braemar Property Ltd had any interest in the Teuton Road Development Corridor inside which Danny now sat, the hacker would have discovered it. Corky had found no such association. Therefore, Monster's appearance could not be interpreted as a coincidence.

The Ducato turned right at the end of the row and cruised another, keeping to the same speed.

Monster was doing what Danny had done on his arrival —scoping out the area and keeping on the move to avoid raising suspicion.

Danny keyed the Ford's ignition. The motor caught on the first turn. He engaged bottom gear, fed in a little more fuel, and pulled slowly out of his parking spot. He followed the Fiat but tried not to make it obvious.

He checked the dashboard clock. 11:23.

Jesus.

Mrs Archer's transport was due any moment. Where were they? Where was the captain?

He tapped the earpiece.

"Charlie One to Alpha One, are you receiving me? Over."

"*Alpha One, here. Go ahead. Over.*"

"How far out are you? Over."

"*Five or six miles. Stuck in traffic. Why, is there a problem? Over.*"

"That's an affirmative, Alpha One. A monster of a problem. Over."

"Charlie One, how serious is it? Over."

"Deadly. Can you intercept the target? Over."

"No idea, but I'll try. Alpha One, out."

The comms line clicked into silence and Danny was on his own, heart racing, mouth dry.

If anyone could intercept the Vauxhall and convince a couple of prison officers to abort, it was the captain. In the meantime, he'd keep eyes on Monster and his fair-skinned passenger, Dreadlocks. Danny prayed that he was being over cautious. Monster's appearance might well turn out to be innocent. If so, Danny had just cried wolf. Still, better crying wolf that leaving it too late and ending up crying for real.

Deep down, though, Danny knew he was right.

The Ducato pulled up to the car park's metal barrier, which stayed resolutely in place while Monster's huge arm snaked through the window and fed his ticket into the slot. Danny counted seventeen seconds before the machine bleeped and the barrier started climbing.

Until the captain arrived, Danny stood alone against Monster and Dreadlocks. Two against one. Fair odds. He'd seen Monster in action—slow and ponderous. Danny wasn't worried. He added a smidge of pressure to the accelerator pedal.

Game on.

Chapter Thirty-Five

Tuesday 4th May - Daniel Pinkerton

Car Park, Aspire Hospital, Nottinghamshire, England

Almost as though Monster could hear Danny's comms traffic—an impossibility, thanks to Corky's magic software—the Fiat jerked forwards and ducked under the lifting barrier. Monster mistimed his start in the driving rain and the spars of the Ducato's roof rack scraped the metal strut, causing it to creak and vibrate on its ascent. Behind the wheel, Monster ignored his error and carried on, without a care.

For a second, Danny considered tailgating the Fiat through the barrier, which hadn't quite reached the peak of its arc, but that would have drawn Monster's attention and he needed to keep a low profile. If it came to a fight, surprise would be a key factor. He hit the brakes and allowed the Fiat to pull away.

In the Ford, Danny waited for the automated barrier to descend and click into place, his impatience growing as each second passed with excruciating sluggishness. The machine took minutes to read his ticket, hours to calculate the charge, and a whole bloody day to count and accept the three pound coins he lobbed into the hopper. The machine flashed up the message, "No change offered", and thought about things for a moment.

So, what's taking so long? Get a bloody move on!

The Ducato turned left at the end of the feeder track and increased speed as it reached the road with the better surface, on a direct route to intercept the Vauxhall.

Shit, bloody shit.

Using a car park with the slowest barrier ever created had been a mistake. The seventeen seconds dragged into twenty, twenty-five. If it reached thirty, Danny would slip the clutch and floor the throttle. Who cared if he broke the barrier and damaged the Ford's pitted paintwork?

Finally, the barrier's lethargic, electric motor clicked into action and the metal arm started its laborious climb, moving even slower than it had before.

How's that fucking possible?

The Ducato rounded a corner and disappeared behind a half-built warehouse. Still the barrier creaked upwards, its angle less than thirty degrees from the horizontal. Twenty-seven seconds.

Hang it.

Danny stomped on the throttle and pulled his foot from the clutch. The Ford's front wheels spun, shooting dirt and gravel under his floor pan and into the grill and headlights of the Citroën kissing his arse. The Citroën's driver blared his horn, flashed his lights, and gave Danny the finger. The Ford's rear end sank as the front wheels finally gained traction, and the car shot forwards with all the speed of a tortoise on diazepam.

He slammed the top of the steering wheel with the heel of his hand. Next time he rated point duty, he'd ignore the need to blend in and rent a bloody Lamborghini.

Without lifting his foot from the throttle, Danny threw the Ford into the same sharp, right turn Monster's Ducato had taken what seemed like hours earlier. The Ford rolled and floundered on soft suspension and recovered enough to roll again as he straightened the wheel and gathered speed on the relatively smooth and straight road into Nottingham.

He negotiated a slow left-hander and the road stretched out for half a mile straight ahead. The Ford's wipers whipped back and forwards at full speed, but struggled to clear the deluge from the windscreen. The pummelling downpour, combined with the Ford's forwards momentum, reduced visibility to dangerous levels, but Danny kept his foot jammed down hard on the throttle. The rain bounced up from the tarmac in a metre-deep curtain.

Where the hell's that shitty Ducato?

There!

In the distance, some six hundred metres ahead, the Ducato's brake lights flashed seconds before it took a right turn. Danny lost sight of the van as it seemed to be swallowed by a thick hedgerow and a shroud of dirty rain.

He mashed his foot harder down on the accelerator, not that he expected it to do any good—the tachometer was already deep into the red numbers.

"Come on, damn it!"

The Ford's speed climbed steadily, topping eighty by the

time it reached the corner. Danny lifted his right foot, tapped the brake, and dropped down into fourth gear rather than risk leaving the road at the apex of the turn. He didn't relish the idea of careening into the high-security fencing that guarded the aerodrome. It wouldn't do the Ford any good and would do nothing to help protect Mrs Archer from whatever Monster and Dreadlocks intended.

Rotational forces pressed him into the seatbelt and threw him sideways, then lessened as the car crested the apex of the turn. It leaped forwards on the outer limit of the curve and Danny centred into the driver's seat.

The Ducato's brake light blazed again, the front dipped under the load of heavy braking, and the gap between it and Danny in the Ford shrank.

What the fuck?

Danny lifted his foot from the throttle, and the Ford's momentum slowed rapidly.

Without indicating, Monster pulled the Ducato onto the side of the road, its nearside wheels bouncing as the van mounted the soft verge.

Danny applied more pressure to the Ford's brake pedal and the ABS shuddered, shaking his teeth and forcing him hard against the locked seatbelt once again. The Ford's rear end slipped sideways, but the ABS did its work and Danny controlled the car's direction well enough to take a sharp left and dart down a narrow lane out of sight of the main road.

Danny dropped his chin to his chest and puffed out his cheeks, trying to regain his breathing. That had been close. If he'd been travelling any faster, or if the rain had been any heavier, he might have rear-ended the Ducato. What chance of flying below the radar then?

He performed a rapid, five-point turn on the narrow

track and edged the Ford closer to the junction with Teuton Road. The Fiat hadn't budged. It sat on the side of the road, hazard lights flashing amber in the gloom, hot bonnet steaming. The Citroën driver Danny had upset in the car park flashed his lights and sounded his horn as he passed. The poor chap was definitely not having a good driving day.

For the first time since it had started, Danny was grateful for the downpour. The reduced visibility hid him from the men in the Ducato and made his cockup less terminal. He wound down the side window and braved the inundation. Dark fumes billowed from the Fiat's exhaust pipe.

Monster and his buddy, Dreadlocks, were stopped, lying in wait.

Danny wiped his lips with the back of his hand. What the fuck was he going to do?

He clicked the earpiece once and waited a count of five before tapping once again. Silence. No response. The captain must've been having his own problems. Danny looked up at the unbroken range of black clouds above. He wouldn't have fancied the idea of riding a bike in such a deluge.

Rather you than me, Captain.

He tapped the earpiece twice and the comms unit clicked into life.

"Charlie One to Foxtrot One, are you receiving? Over."

"*Foxtrot One, here, Charlie One. Is everything okay? Over.*" She sounded breathless.

Danny outlined the situation with the Ducato, telling the doc only what he thought she needed to know. He ended with, "Any news from Alpha One? Over."

"*His comms are down, as is the camera feed. When he received your message, he was stuck at some road works and then the rain started. He lost sight of the target. I watched him race through the traffic like a madman. Then his comms unit failed. I'm terrified, Dan —sorry, Charlie One. Over."*

"Don't worry, Foxtrot One. Alpha One can handle a bike well enough. Over."

"I know, Charlie One. But that rain and then he cut in front of a big truck … damn it." Despite the rain hammering on the roof of the Ford, the comms system was sensitive enough to pick up a catch in the doc's voice and a sniffle as she blew her nose. Danny didn't mention it. No need to add to her anguish by outing her as a caring soul worrying about her partner.

"The target vehicle should be with you any moment," she added. *"What are you going to do? Over."*

No pigging idea, Doc.

Danny swiped rain out of his eyes. The Ducato's flashers still blinked brightly in the daytime gloom. Stopped at the side of the road, restricting the sparse traffic, the van looked predatory.

"I'll have to play it by ear. If you regain contact with Alpha One, let him know I have eyes on the Fiat and will hold off until they do something aggressive. I might have misread the situation. Charlie One, out."

In the distance, oncoming headlights cut through the rain, heading towards the hospital and travelling relatively slowly, the driver taking care in the adverse conditions. The headlights flashed twice in a warning to the waiting Ducato, and the approaching car slowed further as the distance between it and the van closed quickly.

What the fuck?

The Fiat's hazards cut out, its engine roared, and the

van jumped forwards, crossing the lanes. Monster ran the Fiat straight into the side of the car, a Vauxhall.

The Vauxhall.

Bonnet met offside, front wing in a crunching, grinding screech of tortured metal, stopping the Vauxhall dead and shunting it sideways off the road and onto the verge. The Ducato's engine roared and tyres screeched on waterlogged tarmac. Spray flew and the impaled Vauxhall buried itself into the hedge.

A woman screamed, her cries carrying through Danny's open window and over the roaring engines.

"Fuck!"

Danny glanced left, checking for traffic leaving the construction site.

Lane clear.

He threw the Ford into gear and stamped on the throttle. His car bounded out from the lane. Danny tweaked the wheel, aiming for the crash site, racing to close the two-hundred-metre gap.

As he gripped the wheel tight, teeth clamped together, eyes taking in the scene, the Ducato's rear doors flew apart. Two huge men wearing donkey jackets, faces hidden behind ski masks, burst out. Each carried an axe handle. They rumbled towards the Vauxhall. Almost simultaneously, the front, passenger door opened and Dreadlocks climbed out. In his right hand, something glinted in the Fiat's headlights. A knife. Big. The top edge of the shiny blade was serrated.

A hunting knife.

Clutch disengaged … third gear.

Clutch … fourth.

The Ford bounded forwards.

The gap between Ford and Ducato reduced, but not fast enough.

Where the hell was the captain?

The odds against Danny had widened. One versus two had become one against four.

Not so good.

What was Monster doing? With any luck, he'd been hurt in the shunt. If so, Danny had one less bad guy to contend with.

He leaned on his horn, its high-pitched, angry wail deafening through the open window. The two men from the back of the van stopped dead. Turned. Faced him. Recognition registered. Behind the dark ski masks, eyes grew wide and mouths gaped open.

One screamed, dived to his right, planting himself head first into the hedge. The second man wasn't as fast, or as lucky. The Ford caught him at hip height. It crushed him against the Ducato's open rear door, tearing it from its hinges, sending both man and metal flying through the rain-filled air.

The Ford crunched to a halt in the ditch running in front of the Vauxhall, engine racing, horn still blaring. Danny's chest slammed into the seatbelt.

Damn. That'll bruise.

Dreadlocks roared something in a language Danny couldn't understand and spun to face him.

Danny hit the button to release his seat belt, pushed open the driver's door, and scrambled out into the torrent. His booted feet sank into the slick, muddy turf. Rainwater sluiced over him.

The driver's door screeched open and Monster staggered out, shaking his head. His hands were empty. The freak didn't need a weapon. He probably thought he could rip metal apart with his bare hands. A cut on his forehead dripped blood into his right eye. The idiot had mistimed his attack on the Vauxhall.

Tough.

Monster canted his head upwards, allowing the rain to flush the blood from his eye. He looked at Danny in confusion for a moment before recognition lit his face. He smiled. Not a happy smile and not a pretty sight. Crooked and stained teeth filled his wide mouth.

"Hey, electrician," Monster said. "Dimitri knew you were lying." He punched his chest with the inside of his fist to confirm who he was talking about.

"Hi there, Dimitri," Danny said, adding a smile of his own. "Nice to see you again."

"You hurt my men!" Dimitri thundered, waving the hand at the scene of devastation. "I kill you for that!"

Rain hammered into Danny's shoulders. It soaked through his denim jacket and polo shirt, pasting them to his skin, making breathing difficult, restricting movement.

Danny ripped off the jacket and threw it to the ground behind him.

"Do you have a driving licence, buddy?" Danny asked, playing for time.

He shook out his arms and flexed warmth and mobility into his fingers. He needed them loose and supple.

To his right, the man buried deep inside the hedge groaned weakly. A leg spasmed, and the toe of a boot dug into the dirt. No danger from that quarter. The fourth man lay in the middle of the road, part hidden beneath the crumpled door. Unmoving. His crushed head spilled out brains, blood, and gore. Danny had seen enough wounds to recognise death when he stared at it.

The odds had returned to where they'd been before the crash.

Dreadlocks stood on the far side of the Ducato, near its undamaged, nearside, front wing. His gaze shifted from Dimitri to Danny and back again as though awaiting instructions.

In the Vauxhall, something moved. A painful sobbing cut into Danny's thoughts. A woman hurt.

"Help! I need a doctor," a second woman shouted over the weeping of the first.

Dimitri waved a hand at Dreadlocks, pointing him towards the Vauxhall. He spoke.

The words sent a chill through Danny's gut.

"Kill woman. I okay here."

Dreadlocks grunted and breathed deeply, apparently happy to have received his orders.

A huge and smiling Dimitri stood between Danny and the man with the dripping dreadlocks and the hunting knife as he picked his way through the debris, heading for the Vauxhall.

"Come, electrician," Dimitri taunted, raising his hands and beckoning with meaty fingers. "We dance, you and me."

Crap!

Behind the monster, half-obscured by a shoulder the size of a large hill, Dreadlocks reached the Vauxhall's crumpled rear door. He grabbed the handle and tore it open. The woman screamed again.

Danny launched himself forwards.

Chapter Thirty-Six

Tuesday 4th May – Daniel Pinkerton

Development Corridor, Teuton Road, Nottinghamshire, England

Danny flew, closing the gap between himself and the lumbering giant in an instant. He threw a right jab, faking an attack at the man's throat.

Dimitri lifted his tree-branch forearm to block the punch. Opened himself up. Danny bent at the knees, twisted his waist, and ducked inside the raised arm. He landed a clubbing, straight left to the giant's ribs. The monster grunted and staggered away.

Instead of following up his attack, Danny raced past Dimitri and shoulder-charged the Vauxhall's rear door, pinning Dreadlocks against the car's door frame. A woman's hand reached out from inside the car. Fingers grasped dreadlocks and tugged hard. The man's head slammed into the torn edge of the door. He howled in anger and pain.

Dimitri roared, signalling his attack.

Danny dived to his left. Dimitri's snap kick missed him by a whisker, but connected with the Vauxhall's half-open door. Glass shattered and Dreadlocks' howl cut short. Arms sagged to his sides. He slumped.

Danny's shoulder hit tarmac. He rolled through a full revolution and came up on the balls of his feet, in perfect balance.

Bloodshot eyes glared at Danny from out of a flushed and bearded face. Dimitri stood still, blowing hard, his massive chest rising and falling like bellows, nostrils flared. After taking a final deep breath, he opened his arms wide and round, leaned into a bearlike crouch, and advanced.

The woman in the car called out, "Help. She's hurt! I can't stop the bleeding."

Danny shot a glance at the car. Dimitri attacked, his huge mass a dark blur of movement. Danny turned sideways, ducked at the knees, avoiding the lunge easily. The giant flew over Danny's shoulder. He hit the road in a tangled mass of flailing arms and legs, and slammed into the Ducato's grill. The giant folded over the bonnet and bounced backwards, landing in the stodgy mess of the blood and brains oozing from the skull of the first would-be assailant.

Dimitri rolled onto his front and pushed himself onto hands and knees, shaking his head to clear the curly, black hair from his eyes. He howled.

Hitting the Ducato and the road that hard would have concussed most men, but Dimitri wasn't most men. He simply shook off the effects in moments.

The giant struggled to his feet and stood, swaying only slightly. The gash on his forehead had reopened. Blood flowed again. He wiped it away with the same forearm he'd used to block Danny's initial jab. A right-hander who only used his left for balance or picking his nose.

Relatively easy meat.

Danny tensed in preparation for another hulking and clumsy attack. This time, he'd finish it quickly. The cries from inside the Vauxhall demanded his attention, and demanded it fast.

Dimitri dropped the arm and spat a glob of blood. It landed on the road at his feet, mixing with the rain-diluted splatter from the deceased attacker number one.

The big man's right hand disappeared inside his jacket and came out holding a knife. Even in the man's shovel-like hand, the blade appeared enormous. In any other fist it might have passed for a small sword. Twenty centimetres long where it met the guard, the blade's cheek had to be at least eight centimetres wide. The spine was serrated and the curved tip flowed into the finest of points. The lower bevel took up a third of the blade's length and had been honed into a razor-sharp edge. A serious strike from that blade could take off a man's arm.

Dimitri aimed the glinting point at Danny's left eye and showed off his damaged teeth in a malicious snarl. The huge man's nose, broken many times before, skewed off to one side, making him even uglier.

"You die, fucker!"

Danny backed away. Blew out his cheeks. His heart raced, but not in fear. It had been a while since he'd tackled a man with a knife.

Braced for action, Danny waited.

This'll be interesting.

The gut-punching roar of a low-revving motorbike engine broke through Danny's thoughts. New headlights enveloped the crash scene.

Dimitri spun to face a fresh threat.

The bike stopped in a wet squeal of rubber on tarmac and gravel. The engine note dropped to a racing idle. The leather-clad biker jumped from the saddle, allowing his machine to topple slowly onto its side. The left side of the biker's jacket showed the inner lining, the sleeve a shredded mess, and the missing left, wing mirror revealed where biker and bike had made recent shredding contact with tarmac.

Before the Africa Twin's crash cage hit the road, the biker had removed his helmet and thrown it to the ground.

The captain's bearded face cracked into an exasperated smile.

"What a mess, Sergeant," he said, advancing on a stunned-looking Dimitri. "Can't I leave you alone for five minutes?"

Danny beamed. He'd never been so happy to see anyone in his life.

He shrugged, said, "Sorry, boss. This time, it's not my fault," and turned towards the crinkle-cut mess that used to be a prisoner transport vehicle. "Mind dealing with this fool while I play field medic?"

Danny didn't need to wait for an answer. The captain would have sized up the situation before leaping from the Honda and could handle the huge man with the big knife even better than Danny.

He turned and raced to the Vauxhall.

Chapter Thirty-Seven

Tuesday 4th May – Daniel Pinkerton

**Development Corridor, Teuton Road,
Nottinghamshire, England**

Danny grabbed Dreadlocks by the collar and tore him from the pincer grip of the twisted metal. Gravel-sized pieces of glass fell from the door's window frame, tumbling in a glinting shower of hail.

The rain stopped as suddenly as it started, replaced by a watery sunshine. Silence grew around the wreckage, broken only by Mrs Archer's cries and the grunts and thumps of the two-man battle behind him.

Inside the car, a blood-spattered mess was spread over torn and battered seating.

"Thank God!" Mrs Archer yelped, her voice a mix of desperation and relief.

Seemingly unhurt and held firmly in place by her seatbelt, she leaned sideways, arms outstretched, both hands clamped on top of the heavily bleeding thigh of another woman who lay on the seat beside her. The second woman's eyes were closed and her mouth lolled open.

Fuck.

Mrs Archer turned pleading eyes towards him. "Help her. I ... I can't stop the bleeding. I think she's dying."

Danny stretched past Mrs Archer, deeper into the carnage. The injured woman, younger and wearing the uniform of a prison officer, was covered in blood. Mrs Archer's thumbs dug into a gash on her lower thigh, a few centimetres above the knee.

"The man with the dreadlocks tried to stab me," Mrs Archer said, tears rolling down her pale cheeks. "Officer Priestly kicked him. Stopped him. Got in the way. She ... she saved my life. Help her. Please!" Her face carried old and partially healed bruises. A livid scar over her eye disfigured Mrs Archer's attractive face.

Danny's heart lurched.

He placed one hand over both hers, adding more pressure to the leg wound. Judging by the amount of blood covering Priestly's trouser leg and pooling in the footwell below, Dreadlocks' knife must have nicked an artery.

He pressed the tips of his index and middle fingers to Priestly's neck. The pulse was weak and fast, but present. With the same fingers, he tapped the comms link twice, then used the same hand to unfastened his belt and pull it through the loops of his jeans.

"Charlie One to Foxtrot One. Are you receiving? Over."

"I'm here, Charlie One. Over."

"I need an ambulance right now! Over." The comms system would give the doc his exact coordinates.

"*Already on their way, Charlie One,*" the doc replied. "*Over.*"

"How did that happen? Over."

"*Alpha One called them three minutes ago. The airport is dispatching an ambulance. Should be with you very soon. Over.*"

"Thanks, Foxtrot One. Charlie One, out."

With both hands, he looped his belt around Priestly's thigh, a couple of centimetres above the wound. Offering her a silent apology for the pain, he pulled as tight as he could and tied it in place, turning it into a tourniquet.

"Let go now, Mrs Archer. Let's see if that holds."

With her gazed fixed steadily on Priestly's leg, Mrs Archer didn't react.

"Mrs Archer … Melanie!" he shouted. "Let go!"

His words broke into her daze. She looked up at him from staring at the carnage and shook her head. "No, I-I can't. She'll die. She mustn't. She saved me."

Danny couldn't see the harm in letting her think she was helping.

"Okay, okay. Never mind."

He reached across Mrs Archer and checked for a pulse at Priestly's throat again. Couldn't find one. No movement at her chest.

Shit!

"She's stopped breathing," he said, trying to keep calm and remember his first aid. "Can you get out? I need some room to work."

"I … Yes, yes."

Mrs Archer finally released her hold of Priestly's leg and searched for the button to unfasten her seatbelt.

The lock clicked loud as it disengaged and the seatbelt recoiled into its holder.

"Please help her," Mrs Archer cried, shuffling sideways and scrambling out of the way.

Danny kneeled in Mrs Archer's vacated seat, his head and shoulders scraping the Vauxhall's roof. He leaned forwards then gently turned Priestly's head and lifted her chin. He pinched her nose, opened her mouth, and blew in a deep breath. Priestly's chest expanded as her lungs accepted his expelled air.

A good start.

He located the notch beneath her sternum, interlocked his hands and started compressions, keeping the rhythm high as he'd been taught and the way he'd seen medics do it on battlefields the world over.

Thirty compressions, two rescue breaths, thirty more. All the time, watching for signs of life, signs of recovery.

Nothing.

Priestly's face was pale, her lips blue. She'd lost a shedload of blood.

In his awkward position stretching across the seat, it was tough to keep going. He had to use strength more than leverage and bodyweight.

The heat inside the car built. Sweat poured out of him. It ran from his scalp, dripped into his eyes. Stung him into tears. He blinked hard. Facing Dimitri had been easier. Much easier.

…twenty-eight … twenty-nine … thirty.

He leaned closer, breathed for Priestly again, continued with the compressions. A rib cracked under the heel of his fist.

Fuck.

Such a hideous sound.

He kept going. Breaking ribs during CPR was normal, or so he'd been told.

Breathing in the confined space became more difficult. If the paramedics didn't arrive soon …

No, you won't stop. You damn well won't stop!

Close to his head, someone spoke.

Incoherent, mumbled words broke through Danny's thoughts. Still maintaining his count and his compressions, Danny looked up.

Outside, a yowl of agony quickly followed by another churned Danny's stomach, momentarily interrupting his tempo. Dimitri had felt the full force of the captain's skill. Danny almost felt sorry for the giant.

Almost, but not quite.

To his right, a large-bodied, grey-haired and balding man—SO Grant—lay slumped in the driver's seat. He bled heavily from a nasty-looking wound to the side of his head. The man drooped to one side, held in place by his seatbelt. The deflated pillow of an airbag covered his forearms and hands, which apparently still held onto the wheel in a death grip.

"Why? Why do that? Not the plan," Grant said, slurring his words and seemingly talking to himself. "They … they were only supposed to pull us over. Not the … plan. Not … Why?"

What the fuck?

A shadow loomed over Danny's shoulder. He twisted at the waist, turned his head. The captain peered in, studying Priestly. Frowning.

Apart from flattened helmet hair and a little colour in his cheeks, the captain didn't look to have expended too much energy. He wasn't even blowing. In the road behind him, Dimitri lay in a heap, his right elbow bent awkwardly, clearly dislocated. Face bruised and bleeding, nose spread across his face, eyes glazed, the giant stared into space. Dimitri wasn't going to cause anyone grief for a while.

"Can I help, Danny?" the captain asked, leaning close and keeping his voice low.

In the distance, sirens wailed. Blue lights flashed.

Thank fuck.

The happy sound and colour gave Danny a boost. Relief flooded through his system, making the compressions seem easier, less demanding.

"No, boss. I've got this," Danny said, breathing hard, but happy to continue. "Get Mrs Archer away from here. Keep her safe. Take my Ford. I'll make my own way home."

The captain glanced over his shoulder, winced, and shook his head. Danny followed the captain's gaze. The Ford's offside, front wing was buckled, and steam billowed up from the front grille. The radiator might have been holed.

"Your car's seen better days, Sergeant. Is it a runner?"

"Yes, sir. It's a goer—probably. Wouldn't bet on it being able to outrun a milk float, but it'll get you away from here well enough."

Ten ... eleven ... twelve ...

The noise from the sirens grew louder as the ambulances raced to the scene. In the background, not too far away, onlookers stood and stared, but kept their distance. Half a dozen cars from the direction of the construction site filled the lane, parked bumper to bumper. Most had their sidelights on and their hazards flashing. They partially blocked the road but, thankfully, left enough space for the emergency responders.

Twenty ... twenty-one ... twenty-two ...

Small groups of civilians in work clothes looked at them. None stepped up. None offered to help. One or two held up mobile phones, filming the scene for posterity or possible sale to the news channels.

Useless bastards.

Danny kept pumping Priestly's chest, kept counting, kept checking her responses, but she showed no signs of improvement. In the front, SO Grant still mumbled to himself incoherently and more quietly.

What a fucking mess.

"The damage to your car is coming out of your pay, Sergeant."

"That's a little harsh, Captain," Danny said, speaking in time with his arm thrusts.

"Suck it up, Sergeant," he said, adding a wink. "Got to go. You happy to play the Good Samaritan with the authorities?"

"If I have to, boss."

The captain clapped Danny on the shoulder and backed away.

Phone cameras flashed as the captain tried to drag a reluctant Mrs Archer to the damaged Ford.

"Let go of me," she yelled, trying to tug her wrist free of his grip. "You set this all up, didn't you! I'm not going anywhere with you."

Panting hard, Danny glanced at the growing crowd. None of them made a move to interfere with what must have looked like an abduction.

"Mrs Archer, Melanie," the captain hissed, "you're in danger. Can't you see that? There may be others. Other attackers. Please come with me. I'll keep you safe. I promise."

He released her wrist, and the arm dropped to her side. Keeping his face shielded from the audience, he pleaded again. "Melanie, please."

She shot a desperate, uncertain glance at Danny, who managed a sharp nod, which forced more sweat to drip into his eyes.

"Go with him, Melanie," Danny said between panted breaths. "It might not be safe here. I'll be with you as soon as I can."

Twenty-nine … thirty. Breath.

The captain ushered Mrs Archer towards the Ford once again. She hesitated for one more moment, glancing all around before the tension finally broke, and she allowed the captain to help her into the back of the Ford. After encouraging her to lie flat, he jumped behind the wheel, started the engine, revved hard to extract it from the ditch, and took off.

Although relieved their client was finally under the captain's protection, Danny couldn't afford to relax. He redoubled his efforts, maintaining the rhythm of the compressions and the breaths.

Minutes—hours—later, something touched his back. He snapped his head around. A middle-aged paramedic with a serious expression leaned through the open door.

"We'll take over now, sir," she said firmly.

Thank fuck for that.

Danny clambered out of her way. He'd never been happier to vacate a car in his life.

The paramedic ducked into his space. "How long has the patient been unresponsive?"

"No idea, I'm afraid. A few minutes? Half an hour?"

Danny stood on shaky legs, leaned back, and drank in deep breaths of cool, refreshing, moisture-filled air. He stared at his hands. They trembled and were covered in Priestly's sticky blood. He wiped them on his soaked and mud-splattered jeans. Sometime during the fight and scramble in the dirt, he'd torn them at the knees. Accidental damage, not a fashion statement. Blood, Danny's blood, had seeped from shallow grazes and stained the frayed edges.

As yet, his wounds didn't hurt. Adrenaline was keeping any pain at bay. It would come, but not for a while and not much. He'd suffered worse injuries during training.

A second paramedic stood close by, surveying the damage. Looking as though he wanted to scratch his head. He was tall, dark, and wore a bushy, black beard. He slipped a heavy-looking backpack from his shoulder and lowered it to the grass.

"Bloody hell," he said. "What happened here? Looks like a bloody war zone."

Danny shook his head. "A skirmish perhaps. Not a war. What took you so long to get here, mate? The hospital's only a couple of miles away."

The paramedic, Richard Bickerstaff according to the name stitched into the pocket of his green jacket, stiffened and shot Danny a look he could only interpret as a mix of anger and disappointment. He read the time from his watch. "We received the emergency call eight minutes ago, mate."

"Eight minutes? Are you kidding?"

If the captain had made the emergency call just before he arrived, Danny had been performing compressions for less than five minutes.

Is that all? Bloody hell.

Judging from the trembling exhaustion in his arms, legs, and stomach, it felt as though he'd been working away at Officer Priestly for bloody hours.

"No, mate," Bickerstaff answered, "I'm not."

"Sorry, I didn't—"

"That's okay. I understand."

At the request of his partner, Bickerstaff unpacked a defibrillator unit from his pack. After he'd passed it through the buckled, rear opening, he tugged open the driver's door and checked the pulse at SO Grant's throat. He nodded, apparently satisfied.

"Can you give me any details of the patients?" Bickerstaff asked, pulling out of the Vauxhall and staring hard at Danny.

"No idea, mate," he lied, wiping some rain from his hair and flicking it to the ground while doing so. "This shit had already happened when I arrived. Just trying to help. By the way, the driver's been babbling. Incoherent nonsense about the crash. Got a nasty knock to the side of his head, but I thought he could wait. The woman looked in more danger."

"Anyone else in the car?" Bickerstaff asked. "Are you sure no one staggered away in a daze? We aren't going to find someone wandering around the fields in a state of confusion?"

"There was a woman. She got out of the car as I arrived, but she buggered off with some bloke in a knackered, old car. Skoda, I think. Or maybe it was a Peugeot. Small hatchback, at any rate. Dunno much about cars, me. Definitely grey, though. Took off that way."

Danny pointed in the general direction of Nottingham. There were only so many lies he could tell in one day. He could only muddy the waters so much and the other witnesses would have their own stories to tell.

Witnesses! Crap!

Thinking about the rubberneckers and their goddamned phone cameras sent a warning tremor through him.

"Thanks for that, mate," Bickerstaff said, looking

doubtful. "The cops are gonna find that information highly useful, I'm sure. Now, if you'll excuse me …"

Danny backed away, allowing the bearded paramedic easier access to his patients and his colleague. He headed towards the watching crowd, listening to their excited conversations, trying to blend in.

Within seconds, three other ambulances arrived, joining the first. Two came from the direction of Nottingham, the third from the hospital. They disgorged their payload of paramedics, who studied the scene for a moment as though trying to decide which injured attacker to deal with first.

An estate car arrived next, its paintwork the same as the ambulances, and its blue lights adding to the sweeping wash of the others. Lettering along its side read, "Serious Incident Command Unit". A dark-haired man climbed out and took control. He waved his arms, barked orders, and jotted notes into a pad attached to a clipboard.

The new arrivals in paramedic uniforms jumped into action. One pair headed for the man in the hedge, another gathered around Dimitri, and the third took charge of Dreadlocks, who still hadn't come to his senses. No one bothered to check on the man with the crushed head lying beneath the Ducato's dislocated, rear door. The coroner's people would deal with the corpse. Everyone could see there was no point wasting time on him.

More blue lights and sirens announced the imminent arrival of the fire engines and the police.

Time for Danny to make tracks. But first, he had the delicate matter of the witnesses and their phone cameras to deal with.

Chapter Thirty-Eight

Tuesday 4th May - Daniel Pinkerton

Development Corridor, Teuton Road, Nottinghamshire, England

Danny found himself standing alongside a particularly vocal trio—a group wearing jackets from the same Nottingham plumbing wholesalers. One of them, a scraggy-haired man of indeterminate age, with dirt ingrained under his fingernails, held up a phone with a large screen. Beneath his purple work jacket, he wore a filthy, Nottingham Forest jersey, but his wobbly jowls and huge belly confirmed him as an armchair fan rather than any sort of player. The phone pointed at the first responders and followed them at their tasks. Then, he turned the phone to face Danny, who shook his head and held up a bloodstained hand to hide his face.

"Don't like my picture taken, mate."

The man's eyes opened wide, stretching the saddlebags and wrinkling his forehead. "Kidding, right? I saw it all. You're an 'ero, buddy. Someone should give you a medal, y'know?"

Footie Fan's mates gathered around, turning their backs to the scene, earwigging closely.

The man himself lifted his camera again. Danny shook his head. "Sorry, mate. That's enough. There's plenty going on over there for you to snap. Not me!" He nodded towards the scene.

"Suit yourself, man," Footie Fan said, shrugging his fleshy shoulders. "You got it. Don't understand, but things is cool. I got plenty of shots of that biker bloke. Way 'e took care of that huge arsehole with the knife. Never seen nuffink like it. The film's going straight onto my Facebook page. It's going viral."

Shit. No way that'll happen.

"Mind if I take a look?" Danny asked, holding out the same grubby hand he used to block the photo.

Footie Fan looked dubious, and he pulled his phone away. "With them 'ands?"

"Just a sec."

Danny squatted, scrubbed his hands through the wet grass at his feet, wiped them on his polo shirt, and held one out again for inspection. Even covered in part-dried blood, his hands were a damned sight cleaner than Footie Fan's filthy mitts. But who was he to argue with a man of such poor taste in football teams? The deluded fool had enough trouble on his plate.

"Please?" Danny begged. "I'd love to see how he did it. I mean the big bugger attacked me first with that knife, and he was huge. The biker saved me a gutting and he was only a short-arse."

Sorry, Captain.

"Are you bloody kidding?" Footie Fan spluttered, his eyes bulging. "You fought that mountain, too? Is you a soldier?"

"Something like that," Danny said, adding the tweak of a shrug.

Footie Fan and his mates gaped at Danny, a mixture of awe and disbelief on their rain-washed faces.

"You didn't see that part?" he asked them all.

"Nah," one of them answered, shaking his head. He shot a furtive glance towards the fallen Dimitri, then turned his rheumy eyes on Danny. "We got here same time as the biker. Didn't see what happened afore that. We was the first ones here, too. Wasn't we, Harry?"

Harry, a short, older man with an unlit cigarette stuck behind his ear and protected from the weather by a wide-brimmed hat, sniffed. "S'right, Ticker," he said, answering his mate, but studying Danny carefully. He looked as though he didn't believe a word Danny said. "You was just about to get into the car, to start that kiss-of-life thing. You done it good, too."

"Didn't think of giving me any help?"

"Nah," Ticker said, the twitch in his left eye showing how he'd earned his nickname, "weren't none of our business."

"You what! It's everyone's business, you bloody—"

"Don't listen to Ticker," Footie Fan interrupted, saving Ticker from an ear-bashing at the very least. "What 'e means is, you and the biker bloke 'ad it under control and we'd 'ave only gotten in the way. Ain't that right, Ticker?"

"Huh?" the twitching man asked, now concentrating on what was happening with Dimitri. "What you say?"

The paramedics had tied Dimitri's damaged arm to his side, clearly unwilling to risk further injury to the elbow by straightening it. Standing on either side, they tried helping the big man to his feet, but he let out a huge howl the moment he put any weight on his left leg. The smaller of the two medics buckled under his weight and Dimitri crumpled to the ground once more.

Danny's new friends hooted in delight.

"'E's a big bugger, all right," Footie Fan chortled, but still refused to give Danny his mobile.

"How'd that little biker beat such a freak?" Danny asked, even though he more or less knew how it must have gone down. "What did he use? A baseball bat? A tyre lever?"

"Nah, man. That were the thing. Biker didn't 'ave nuffink. Unarmed, 'e was. Bloody brilliant. Like watching one of them 'Ollywood blockbuster movies."

"Yeah," Ticker said, nodding vigorously, but still watching the medics working on Dimitri, "like Jason Statham only smaller and faster, he was."

Harry elbowed Footie Fan's arm. "Go on, Giggsy. Show him the film. Bloke deserves it, after what he done in the car. Wouldn't mind seeing the fight again mesself."

Giggsy tilted his head and looked at Danny. Suspicion glinted in his narrowed eyes. "You know the bloke on the bike?"

"Why d'you ask?"

"The way you and 'im was talking, seemed like you was best buddies."

"Nope," Danny lied, and shook his head doing it. "Never seen him before in my life, Officer."

Ticker and Harry snorted. Giggsy's shoulders relaxed and he even showed Danny a gap-toothed smile.

"Yeah, nice one, man. I get you. 'Ang on a sec." He worked the touchscreen with the grimy fingers. "'Ere you go. Film's ready to run," he said and handed his precious mobile across.

Danny hit the start triangle. The action playing out on the small screen was shaky and difficult to follow, canted as it was at a sharp, Art House angle. Giggsy wouldn't make it as a film director. He'd be better off keeping his day job delivering plumbing supplies.

As expected, the fight didn't last overly long. It only took up thirty-nine seconds of screen time. He'd seen the captain in action often enough to know how he worked, especially with people who attacked defenceless women. Ryan Kaine was a bit of a throwback. An old-school hero.

For a few seconds, Dimitri tried the old side-to-side, soft shoe shuffle, trying to work out the captain's weaknesses.

Yeah. Good luck with that, buddy boy!

A bob, a weave, a half-hearted thrust. All the while, the captain waited, barely moving, studying the gargantuan's skill with the blade. Or rather, his lack of it.

Dimitri screamed and lunged again.

The captain sidestepped the wild knife lunge, and ducked beneath a flailing, straightened arm. He grabbed Dimitri's wrist in both hands and locked the giant's elbow against his shoulder. Using his own shoulder as a fulcrum, the captain stood tall and simultaneously heaved down on the wrist.

Dimitri's elbow cracked and bent the wrong way. The huge man's blood-curdling scream would have made the perfect addition to the soundtrack of a horror flick. The knife dropped from a lifeless hand and bounced up from the tarmac almost as high as the rain.

The captain ended things with a heel strike to the outside of Dimitri's left knee.

The would-be assailant screamed again as his knee bent inwards. He collapsed, falling backwards and slamming into the side of the Ducato. His boots slipped on the slick tarmac, and he slid to the deck, cracking his head against the van's corrugated wing on the way down.

With his back to the camera, the captain loomed over the downed man for a moment, making sure he was finished. Then he turned and headed towards the Vauxhall. The imaged stopped—the final frame focused entirely on Dimitri.

Not once during the whole video, did the captain's face appear as anything but a pale and blurred, unrecognisable blob.

Danny swiped through the phone's recent memory, searching for more videos or clear photos of the captain. He found none and relaxed a little.

"Great video," Danny said, smiling his encouragement. "Might be worth something. Do you have film of him leaving in the car?"

"Nah," Giggsy said, shaking his head. "Wish I did. Reckon it'd be worth a mint. Got carried away with what you was up to in the Vauxhall."

Danny returned the mobile.

"What about you guys?" he asked the others.

Harry shook his head. "My mobile don't have a camera. Don't need one of them fancy smartphones."

"Ticker?"

"Nah, battery's dead."

"Yeah," Giggsy said, "idiot keeps forgetting to plug it in. Don't you, Ticker?"

Danny left it at that. Since Giggsy and his mates had been first on scene, the other spectators were unlikely to have any pics of the captain worth fretting over. Whenever possible, he'd been careful to keep his back to the spectators.

As for pictures of Danny in action, if anyone less inept behind the lens than Giggsy had managed to capture a picture that would identify him to the police, so be it. At worst, they'd be able to charge him with leaving the scene of an accident. A minor offence punishable by a slap on the wrist. But considering how hard he'd worked to save PO Priestly, they'd probably let him off with nothing more serious than a warning. Definitely no medal, though.

Shame. His mother would have been so proud. Dad, on the other hand, wouldn't have given a toss, wherever the useless article hung his hat these days.

More sirens and more blue lights announced the arrival of the next set of responders.

"That's my signal to bugger off. See ya, guys."

Danny turned his back on his new best mates, heading away from the bright lights, the battered vehicles, and the even more damaged bodies.

"You ain't 'anging around?" Giggsy called to his back. "Thing like this will make you famous. Put you on the telly."

Danny ignored the guy in the Nottingham Forest top, turned up the collar of his polo shirt, and kept on walking.

Me on the telly? No, thanks.

Chapter Thirty-Nine

Tuesday 4th May – Daniel Pinkerton

Development Corridor, Teuton Road, Nottinghamshire, England

Shivering against the chill wind's pitiless blasts, Danny hurried past a growing queue of cars, trying to blot out the angry looks and angrier shouts of increasingly impatient drivers. Although Danny had no idea why they were giving him the evil eye. It wasn't like he'd caused the traffic jam, but maybe he just looked as though he had.

No, all he'd done was stop a slaughter.

He smiled, allowing himself to bask in some credit. He'd done well.

Danny picked up the pace, marching out, trying to exercise some warmth into his chilled bones. Suffering from the cold *was* his fault, though. He'd forgotten his jacket and wasn't about to reverse course to collect it.

His immediate intention was to pick up a taxi at the hospital and let the two-mile walk-jog give him time to think. However, the cold made it difficult to string a coherent series of thoughts together. Added to that, strolling along a country road wearing a pair of ripped jeans and a thin, bloodstained polo shirt didn't exactly lend itself to keeping a low profile.

Danny ducked behind a tree in the hedgerow, stripped off the polo shirt, and turned it inside-out before tugging the cold and sodden thing on again. Back on the side of the road, and looking only slightly less disreputable, Danny picked up his pace.

Think, Danny. Think!

A question had been bugging him from the first moment the shit started hitting the fan. In the gloom, the driving rain, and with oncoming headlights so dazzling, how did Monster know he was about to T-bone the correct car?

The answer hit Danny like a physical blow.

SO Grant had flashed his lights in a prearranged signal!

A signal.

Had to be.

SO Grant had been in on it, but Dimitri and his chums had double-crossed him. Apart from a Hollywood stuntman, who else would willingly subject himself to being part of a head-on car crash? In his delirium, Grant had said something about it not being part of the plan.

No doubt about it, something sus was going on and Danny needed to run the whole story past the captain, sharpish.

Second thing—he needed to work out a way to make it up to Mrs Archer for thinking she'd killed her abusive, old man and planned to fake the coercive control defence. No one who'd worked so hard to save a prison officer could be a murderer, could they? And her reluctance to leave the car confirmed it as far as Danny was concerned.

Compassion, empathy, and honesty.

Each emotion had been revealed in Mrs Archer's eyes.

The woman didn't have it in her to kill anyone. No way. Danny had never been more certain of anything in his life.

How could he have been so wrong about her? Prejudice, pure and simple. The way Aunt Trina had treated poor Uncle Howard had soured Danny's mind. Yep, he'd have to make it up to Mrs Archer in his own way. Question was, how?

An idea started to work its way into his head. Danny smiled. Maybe the march had finally started pumping some blood around his brain, some warmth. He passed vehicle after vehicle, the queue had stretched out for more than half a mile, reaching all the way back to the junction.

He passed a white Range Rover. The passenger, a woman with her nose hidden beneath a silver splint and her eyes darkly bruised, shot him a frightened glance before looking away. His reflection in the window wasn't pretty—soaked and muddy jeans, torn at the knees, and the inverted shirt. He could understand why she wouldn't want to make eye contact.

Sorry, love. Didn't mean to scare you.

Or was her nervousness down to something else?

His recent bout of self-reflection might have heightened his sensibilities, but something about the woman's manner struck him hard. Sure, her facial injury might just have been the result of a medical nose job, a rhinoplasty. Not a rarity these days—at least in some circles. After all, Aspire Hospital did have a decent rep for cosmetic surgery and the Range Rover had come from that direction, but …

Danny stopped and retraced his steps.

He smiled at the woman with the metal nose splint and made a signal for her to wind down her window—a signal she studiously ignored. After another furtive glance, she turned her head away, pretending not to have seen his signal.

No. That's not happening.

Danny leaned forwards and tapped on the window.

"I'm afraid it's chaos up there, miss," he said, using his poshest accent and speaking loud enough for both passenger and driver to hear through the slightly tinted glass. "You could be here for quite some time."

One of them relented and the window lowered. Not for the first time in his life, posh accent number one had worked a treat.

"You okay?" the driver asked, leaning roughly past the woman, who jerked back her head and raised her hands to protect her face.

Jesus.

Danny's hackles rose.

The driver's evident lack of concern for the woman's condition and her reaction to his close proximity told Danny all he needed to know.

He tried to make out the man's face, to gauge the look in his eyes, but the darkness inside the car and the man's long hair obscured his features. Danny leaned closer, peered harder, but the driver backed away, further out of sight.

"Yes, sir, I'm fine," Danny said. "This isn't my blood, but thanks for asking."

Driver pointed towards the blue lights. "What the fuck is happening up there?"

Language!

"Massive pile-up. There are quite a few vehicles involved. I would imagine it'll take the police rather a long time to clear it away. The fire service has only just arrived. In my opinion," he continued, laying the accent on thick, "you'd be better off retracing your route and finding another way."

"Yeah."

Driver hit a switch on his central console and the window started rolling up. The woman looked at Danny. Fear showed on her heavily damaged face. Pleading filled her bloodshot eyes.

"One moment, my friend."

The window stopped halfway up.

"What?"

"You're going my way. Any chance of a lift?"

Driver snorted. "With you dressed like that? Fuck off!"

Charming

The window finished its climb. Driver revved the engine, reversed far enough to give him room to manoeuvre, and executed a sharp U-turn. Both nearside wheels mounted the verge on the far side of the road, and the big car roared back towards the hospital.

Bastard!

Danny's hackles kept high. He'd just seen the action of a man with an evil heart and it had little to do with his refusal to offer a cold, wet stranger a lift.

During the U-turn, Danny made a point of catching sight of the Range Rover's number plate. He had a good memory for license numbers.

He watched the Range Rover shrink into the distance in a cloud of grey mist and a blossom of brake lights.

Later, buddy. Later.

The comms unit in his ear clicked twice. In his chilled distraction, Danny had almost forgotten he was wearing it. He tapped it into life.

"*Alpha One to Charlie One. Receiving? Over.*" The system's noise-cancelling element worked well, but it couldn't completely mask the rattle and clatter of the Ford's over-worked and battle-damaged engine.

"I'm here, Alpha One. Everything okay with you? How's your passenger? Over."

"*I'm fine, but the passenger is angry and confused. She's unhappy because I've refused to answer her questions so far. By the way, I've given her a spare earpiece. Over.*"

"She's not the only one who's confused," Danny said. "Mrs Archer, can you hear me? Over."

Since the captain hadn't given her a radio designation, Danny used her real name. Breaking radio protocol would make things easier for her and would enable him to speak normally. He wanted to put her at ease.

She didn't respond.

"Mrs Archer … Melanie," Danny said, speaking quietly and increasing his walking pace, "if you can hear me, I'm the man from the Vauxhall. My name's Danny. Over."

"*Danny? Y-You can hear what I'm saying?*"

Danny waited a moment before realising Mrs Archer had no idea about correct radio protocol. As a civilian, why should she?

"Yes, Melanie, I can hear you. By the way, say 'over' when you've finished talking. Works better that way. Over."

"*Oh, sorry. Not done this before. … Over.*"

"Not to worry. You'll get the hang of it. Over."

"*How is Officer Priestly? Did she … well, you know. Over.*"

"She's still alive. They were extracting her from the car as I was leaving, but her eyes were open. You did a great job there, Melanie. Saved her life. You should be proud of your-self. Over."

"You're the one who saved her. I didn't do much. Who are you? … Over."

What the hell? Didn't she know?

"You don't recognise Alpha One? Over."

"Yes, of course I know who he is," she snapped, the anger building in her voice, *"but who are you, and why are you helping Ryan Kaine? Over."*

She was obviously trying to come to terms with what had happened in the Vauxhall. And, even though she'd been in contact with the captain via the smuggled mobile, being within touching distance of a man she'd probably grown to hate couldn't have been easy. Danny could hardly blame her for the anger, or the name dropping.

"Melanie," he said, "please listen. Alpha One will explain everything when you reach the far—your destina-tion. Until then, please be patient. You can trust him, trust us all. We will keep you safe. I promise. You saw what happened earlier. Over."

"Who were those men? Were they really trying to kill me? Over."

"No idea who they were," Danny said, although this time, it was only half a lie, "but they were definitely trying to kill you, which is why we had to get you away from there. There was no telling who else might have turned up. As for who sent them, we'll discuss that later. You might be able to help us with it. Alpha One, where are you now? Over."

"Twenty miles from base. Did you pick up the Honda? Over."

"That's a negative, Alpha One. The cops arrived, and I thought it best to clear the area. Over."

"That's a pity. Rather liked that big beastie. Can't beat Hondas. They're bulletproof. That one saved my bacon today. Over."

Danny smiled. There he was again with his, "Hondas

are bulletproof," bullshit. Triumphs were much better. They had more class, more style, and more grunt.

"Understood, Alpha One. Last time I saw it, the engine was still running, despite the damage and the way you let it drop. Dreadful way to treat a motorbike. Can it be traced back to you? Over."

"Not a chance, Charlie One. I pocketed the camera before ditching the bike. Over."

"What took you so long, anyway? Did you have a shunt? Over."

"Let's just say the bike and I parted company at one stage and leave it at that, eh? By the way, it sounds as though you're breathing heavily. Any problems your end? Over."

"Just started jogging, boss. Perishing cold here and I left my jacket at the scene. Over."

"Dreadfully remiss of you, Charlie One. However, a little exercise will do you good. Over."

"Yeah. I thought that's what you'd say. Over."

Danny smiled as an old military saying raced through his head, "No sympathy in this man's navy."

"You should ask Foxtrot One to send you a taxi. Over."

"No point, boss. I'm little more than a mile from the hospital. I'll pick up a cab from there. It'll be quicker in the end. Over."

"Okay, Charlie One. I'll expect to see you back at base in a couple of hours. Over."

"Might take a little longer than that, boss. I have an errand to run first. Over."

"An errand? Care to elaborate, Charlie One? Over."

"Not at the moment, boss. Charlie One, out."

Danny tapped the earpiece and cut the connection before the captain ordered him to explain his intentions. Danny had only ever disobeyed an order once, and that hadn't ended too well for him. He had no intention of repeating the offence with the captain. He had far too much respect for him to disobey a direct order.

He jabbed the earpiece twice.

"Charlie One to Foxtrot One, come in. Over."

"*Foxtrot One here. Over,*" the doc responded immediately.

"I take it you've been listening in? Over."

"*That is correct, Charlie One. Are you going to sue me? Over.*"

Danny smiled. "Wouldn't dream of it, Foxtrot One. Especially since I need a favour. Over."

"*How can I help? Over.*"

Danny asked one question, listened to the answer, made his request, and explained his immediate intention. After that, he ended the comms without further discussion. The doc understood what he wanted and why, wished him luck, and didn't ask any awkward questions.

Good on her.

The road stretched out ahead and Danny increased his pace from jog to run. Cars passed him on the other side of the road, heading back towards the building site. What had started with the solitary Range Rover, increased to a trickle, and ended in a flood as drivers abandoned their place in the queue and went in search of an alternative route.

The long, straight road ended at a T-junction. Danny turned left, and hugged the verge tight to the side of the road. The clouds had returned, bringing more rain. An early dusk had set in.

Good.

Darkness was his friend. It suited his purposes.

The distant hospital lights brightened the gloomy evening. Danny slowed to a fast march. His polo shirt steamed at the shoulders. To the passing drivers, he must have looked a sorry sight, but no one took enough pity on him to stop and offer a lift. Danny couldn't blame them. He wouldn't have picked up a rain-and-blood-soaked man in the near dark, either.

On top of which, he wouldn't have accepted a lift anyway. He didn't need anyone eavesdropping on his next comms chat, not even his immediate circle of military friends.

He reached a hand up to his earpiece, pressed the activation button, and held it for a two count. He received the quick response he was hoping for.

"Whatcha, Mr P. How you diddling? What do you want from Corky this fine night?"

In the growing darkness, Danny grinned. No point waiting for the irreverent hacker to say, "Over". Although the little man knew the correct radio protocols well enough, he mostly refused to use them.

"Hi, Corky. Thanks for answering so quickly. Can we keep this chat between the two of us, please? Over."

A click confirmed that Corky had isolated their conversation.

"Done, Mr P," the hacker said. *"Only you and Corky can earwig this dialogue. What's up?"*

"How are you fixed for an off-the-books task this evening? Over."

Corky let loose one of his notorious, high-pitched chuckles. *"Off-the-books is* all *Corky's fixed for, Mr P. What d'you have in mind?"*

Danny explained what had happened with the Vauxhall and outlined his upcoming objective.

"Aw," Corky said when he'd finished, *"that's real sweet, Mr P. You are such a charmer. Give Corky a mo' and let's see what he can find."*

Danny rubbed his hands together, trying to generate some much-needed warmth.

Cold hands led to stiff fingers, and stiff fingers wouldn't be any use to him that evening. Neither would strolling into a brightly lit hospital looking like a drowned rat who'd rolled around in a pool of someone else's gore.

On a building site as large as the one he was approaching, he was bound to find something warm and dry to wear. If not, the hospital laundry would probably oblige with some clean, dry scrubs.

Once again, Danny increased his pace.

Chapter Forty

Mike's Farm, Long Buckby, Northants, England

Kaine paced the lounge. He'd done quite a bit of pacing recently and it didn't get any easier. He hated being out of the loop of anything that related to the people he'd chosen to protect.

Although the approach had worked with Angela Shafer, somehow, letting Lara take Melanie Archer through the video evidence that cleared his name seemed cowardly but, as Lara explained, coming from him an explanation might have seemed self-serving. Reluctantly, he'd submitted to her suggestion.

"Take a seat, lad," Mike said, his resonant voice drowning out the crackle of the logs in the grate and the dream-inspired yips of Patch at his feet, "the video is powerful stuff. She'll forgive you."

Kaine ran a hand through his unruly mop of hair. "I'm not looking for forgiveness, Mike. Can't even forgive myself. I just want her to understand what happened. She needs to know why I have to protect her. She'll never trust me completely if she thinks I actually intended to kill her brother."

Mike's eyes glinted in the orange light of the fire. "I know, lad. The doc will explain everything. Trust her."

"I do trust Lara," Kaine said. He changed the direction of his pacing, ended up near the fire, and collapsed into the sofa. "It's just that I hate feeling so damned helpless. Waiting is a bloody nightmare. Always has been."

"Tell me about it, Captain. While you and the boys are off galivanting around the world, righting wrongs and saving the day, this poor, old, retired CPO is left alone on his farm, worried to death, not knowing what's going—"

"Yeah, yeah. Okay, Mike," Kaine said, flapping his hand in the air between them. "Point taken. Lara uses the same argument to wheedle herself onto ops. You saw what she was like when I tried to talk her out of going to Falston Manor the other week. Bloody relentless, she was. And you know what a disaster that turned into."

Mike had the good grace to look uncomfortable. "You made it out all right in the end though, eh? You're more than capable of dealing with a few poorly trained prison officers. The doc and I have every faith in you."

The old man hacked out a dry cough, turning pale and gritting his teeth from the effort.

"You okay, Mike?"

Mike clapped his chest a couple of times and held up a

hand until the colour returned to his cheeks. "It's nothing, lad. Something went down the wrong way."

"Are you sure we're not imposing on your hospitality too much?"

Mike snapped up his head and stared at Kaine. "Don't be daft, Captain. Like I said the other day, it would get terrible quiet here without your regular visits. As for the doc, she's a breath of fresh air. In fact, I'd be really upset if you bypassed this knackered, old man entirely."

"Old and knackered?" Kaine scoffed. "You could probably still beat me in an arm-wrestle."

The twinkle-eyed smile was a throwback to the Mike of old and, through his worry, Kaine returned it as best he could.

"So, changing the subject," Mike said after the silence started to grow uncomfortable. "Given what happened today, I'm guessing a visit to CM Thatcher's on the cards?"

"Damned right it is. I'll be having words with the evil bugger as soon as I'm done here. He sanctioned the dental visit, and must have had a hand in organising the transport. If he hadn't kept quiet about it, we'd have had more time to prepare for the attack. Marcus Thatcher has been a very naughty boy."

"But you have him over a barrel. Why would he set up a hit?"

Kaine sighed. "Not sure he did, but I am going to find out once and for all."

"Is that another reason why you were acting like an expectant father just now?"

"Sorry?"

"All that pacing. It's not like you to be so tense."

Kaine took a moment to pull warm air into his lungs

and come up with a decent answer. "It's been a few hours since I heard from Danny."

Mike scratched his beard. As usual, he'd taken time to trim it since Lara's arrival. The old man thought they didn't notice, but the transformation couldn't have been more obvious. Once again Kaine wondered when the grey flecks that had already started appearing in his own beard would take over and turn him into a Santa lookalike—albeit a thin one.

"Danny's missing?"

Kaine grimaced and wagged his head from side to side. "Said he had something important to do and dropped out of contact."

Mike perked up. "He's wearing one of those fancy earpieces, isn't he?"

Kaine nodded and absent-mindedly dropped his hand to ruffle the soft fur behind Patch's ear. Petra's plaintive whimper forced him to attend to her needs, and he soon had both his hands full of dog fur.

"Yes. At least he was the last time we spoke."

"If you're that worried about him, why don't you ask Corky to run a location check?"

This time, Kaine shook his head. "Danny can take care of himself, and I don't want to appear like a mother hen. Besides, I'm not worried about Danny. Not in the slightest." He jumped to his feet, stood with his back to the fire, and allowed its warmth to permeate his jeans and toast the backs of his legs. "I'm just annoyed at being kept in the dark. Anyway"—he shot Mike a sly glance and added a wry grin—"Corky's not answering his comms unit."

"Ah," Mike said, chuckling, "you're just being nosey. And impatient. Sit down, Ryan. You making the place look untid—"

"Nope, that's it. Sorry, Mike, but I've had enough. I'm heading for the barn."

Mike straightened in his chair. He winced at the sudden movement, but tried to hide it with a cough. "Captain, leave them be. Lara knows what she's doing. You'll only make things more difficult for her."

The old CPO was dead right. Kaine knew it well enough, but acknowledging it did nothing to improve his mood. He spun around and returned to his chair by the fire. The second his backside touched the seat, the outside door to the boot room squeaked open. Female voices, talking quietly, filtered through the solid kitchen door, which opened and Lara led the way, her eyes red and puffy, as were Melanie's. They'd both been crying.

Mike stared pointedly at him in an unspoken, "Told you so."

After a lifetime of marriage to the patient and empathetic Ellie, Mike had learned more about women than Kaine would ever hope to. He should have listened to the old man. In future, he would.

Yep, definitely.

Kaine stood and opened his mouth to ask something inane, like whether anyone wanted a cup of tea, but Mike raised a finger to his lips and made an almost imperceptible shake of the head, which neither Lara nor Melanie would have seen. As a trial run, Kaine took Mike's advice and shut his mouth.

That's it, Kaine. Good start.

Melanie wiped her eyes with a tissue and fully entered the lounge. She paused by the coffee table and took a deep breath before continuing towards the fireplace. Tears fell again, but this time, she didn't wipe them away.

She drew closer and stopped in front of Kaine, standing

within easy touching distance. She held her arms down at her sides, hands balled into white-knuckled fists.

"I-I'm so sorry." Melanie spoke so quietly, Kaine could barely make out the words.

He kept silent, unable to think of a response.

"All this time, I hated you, but I had no idea. What that man, Sir Malcolm, did ... what he put you through ... it was monstrous. The beating, it was—"

"Nothing," Kaine interrupted gently. "As you can see" —he waved a hand in front of his face—"I recovered well enough."

"Lara told me everything. You're ... you're as much a victim as I am in all this. I'm so sorry for the way I acted before. I was horrible to you."

Kaine tried to swallow, but the constriction in his throat made it impossible.

"Don't worry," he croaked, "it's not an issue. Sir Malcolm's rotting in jail, and you know how comfortable a prison cell can be. He's doing his fair share of suffering."

Melanie inhaled, her breath catching. "Lara also told me why you haven't published the evidence. She said you were doing more good with the money than the government ever would. But ..."

"But?"

"You have to clear your name, Mr Kaine. People think you're a mass murderer. I did. But it's not fair on you."

Kaine glanced at Lara and smiled. He silently thanked her for explaining everything so well and turned back to their client once again.

"The government already has the evidence you've just seen, and more. A friend of mine—a senior police officer— delivered it within days of the ... incident."

Kaine had never been able to call the intentional

destruction of Flight BE1555 an "accident". To call it that would be an insult to the victims.

Melanie nodded and reached out to take hold of his forearm. "I know, Lara told me. Why are you still a fugitive? Do they think you faked the video?"

"No, it's nothing like that. They believe it, or so they say. They've seen all the data, the decrypted emails, and the bank transactions. They have the full audit trail showing how Sir Malcolm funded the attack and set me up."

"So why don't they make it public? Why don't they say you're innocent?"

"The current Home Secretary is a former solicitor. Wants me to stand trial. Mrs Archer," he said, resting a hand on top of hers and giving it a gentle squeeze, "for show, the authorities will put me on remand while the Crown makes the case against Sir Malcolm and his co-conspirators. I can't set foot in prison, at least not under my real name. It would be far too dangerous."

"Dangerous? For a man like you? I saw the way you dealt with that huge man at the crash site. You surely can't be afraid of anyone?"

"There's a price on my head. Serious money. Powerful men would rather I didn't live to tell any tales, and prisons are dangerous places." He studied the partly healed cut over her eye. "You know what it's like inside. Even I wouldn't be safe."

She lowered her gaze. "Yes, I think I understand. But what's going to happen now? I can't spend the rest of my life on the run."

Why not? Works for me.

Lara skirted the coffee table and drew closer.

"We'll keep you safe, Melanie," she said. "We can give you a new identity. The 83 Trust can set you up anywhere in the world. That's what we use Sir Malcom's money for. You could disappear forever."

"No, no. You don't understand. If I run, people would think I *did* kill James, but I didn't. I didn't. Mr Kaine, the police's case is rubbish. There can't be any real evidence against me. There can't be!"

Melanie's grip on his forearm tightened. Fingernails pressed through the sleeve of his cotton shirt, digging into his skin and threatening to draw blood. Her eyes shone with emotion and glistened with unshed tears.

"Instead of spending the money on sending me away, can you use it to help me prove my innocence? Please?"

"Mrs Archer … Melanie," Kaine said, exasperated, "you're not making sense."

"Please help me. I couldn't stand it if people thought I was guilty. Let me go back to prison and stand trial. I'm innocent. Somehow, I'll prove I didn't kill James!"

Gently, Kaine prised her hand from his arm, but refused to rub the damage which was probably going to leave a bruise. He couldn't help admiring her determination to prove her innocence. She was an impressive woman. Naïve but impressive.

"Melanie, I'm not a detective. None of us is. We have no idea how to conduct a proper criminal investigation. And if you go back to Falston, we won't be able to guarantee your safety."

Melanie crossed her arms. Her lips thinned in a gesture of determination. "What about that policeman friend of yours. Can't he help?"

For pity's sake.

She wouldn't let it go.

"No. I've already spoken to him. He can't help."

"Why not?" she asked, plaintive and close to tears again.

Kaine hesitated. How could he tell a desperate woman the truth? How could he tell her that DCI Jones had already seen the evidence against her but had refused to intervene? It would likely break her. He hated the idea of lying, but if it was for her own good …

"Nottingham's out of his jurisdiction. Although he's seen the case notes, the locals wouldn't let him interview you, and without that he won't—"

The moment the words tumbled from his mouth, the light of hope exploded behind Melanie's eyes, and Kaine knew he'd messed up. Lara's slow facepalm confirmed it. He'd just dug himself a monstrous big hole and couldn't see a way to climb out. Maybe he'd sealed Melanie's fate, too.

"But, I'm here now!" she said, excitement overtaking her. "Let him interview me here. I can convince him I'm innocent. I know I can!"

Kaine was beaten. A tiny woman with a missing front tooth had beaten him to an emotional pulp, and he knew it. He looked from Lara to Mike and back again. They both knew it, too.

He only had one more card to play.

"And if you can't convince him to take up your case, what then?"

"But I will."

"If you don't," he insisted, "will you let us set you up with a new identity?"

Melanie hesitated a moment before mumbling, "Yes."

She lowered her eyes and rolled the damp tissue into a tight ball. Lara stepped closer and put an arm around her shoulders.

"You promise?" Kaine pressed, wanting to drive the message home.

She looked up at Lara, who nodded her encouragement.

"Yes," she said with more conviction. "If your policeman doesn't want to help after I've met him, I'll let you send me anywhere. Send me to Timbuktu, if you like."

Mike, who'd been sitting in silence taking everything in, decided it was time to enter the conversation.

"Nope, that won't work," he said. "A pretty, blonde lass like you suddenly appearing in the middle of Mali would stand out a mile. Hardly the best idea I've ever heard. We'd as likely send you to Siberia."

His intervention worked as intended and Melanie smiled.

"No way," Lara said. "I'll make sure he sends you somewhere warm. How does the Caribbean sound? There are plenty of European expats in the West Indies. You'll blend in a treat. And there's no reason you have to stay blonde, is there?"

Melanie ran a hand through her long, wavy hair. "Colour it like a rainbow if you want, I don't care. It's not going to happen. I'm staying in England. Ryan's ... sorry, the captain's friend is going to believe me, and he's going to help prove my innocence."

Kaine sighed. Again, he couldn't prevent himself admiring her optimism and her tenacity, if not her logic, but he held his immediate comment in check. "It's okay. You can call me Ryan, unless I'm undercover, of course."

Patch jumped up from his place at Mike's feet, in front of the fire. He barked in excitement, raced into the kitchen, and sat patiently, tail wagging ferociously. Petra, the tired and elderly matriarch, did nothing more than raise her head, yawn, and settle back down on the rug.

Mike heaved himself out of his chair. "That'll be the

lad. Cold outside this time of night. I expect he'll fancy a coffee. Anyone else like a brew?"

"I'll help," Lara said, following Mike to the kitchen.

"The lad?" Melanie asked, shaking her head, no doubt thrown by the sudden activity.

"I expect he's talking about Danny. Patch has taken a particular shine to him," Kaine explained and gently ushered her into the kitchen.

Seconds later, a rain-soaked Danny, dressed in sodden, green hospital scrubs, pushed through the boot room door. Patch jumped into his outstretched arms and started licking Danny's face while accepting a vigorous petting for his troubles.

Even before he could step over the threshold, dog in arms, Danny had to field questions fired at him from both Lara and Mike. Although fired in unison, he handled the inquisition in order of importance.

"Yes, please, Mike. A coffee would be great. Any of that chicken pie left? I'm starving."

"Take a shower before coming in here," Mike said, already at the sink, filling the kettle. "Lara and I spent hours cleaning this kitchen while you were out playing in the mud and rescuing damsels in distress."

"Use the shower in the boot room," Lara added. "I put a clean set of your clothes in there earlier."

"Thanks, Doc."

"Just one minute," Kaine said, "this is all very domestic and touching, but where the hell have you been, Sergeant?"

Danny grinned and carefully lowered Patch to the floor. He dropped to his haunches and carried on rubbing the dog's head.

"Me, boss?" he asked, the wide-eyed picture of innocence.

"Yes, Sergeant. You!"

"I've been to hospital, boss," he said, a grin forming on his youthful face. "Had to wait ages for an appointment."

Lara rounded on Kaine.

"Captain Kaine," she said, so firm and commanding, he almost shot to attention, "the debrief can wait. Melanie"—she nodded to the paroled prisoner—"this mud-encased idiot is Danny Pinkerton. I believe you've already met."

"Hi, Mrs Archer," Danny said, his infectious smile blossoming into its full wattage. "Glad you survived the trip in a car with the captain." He shook his head slowly. "Worst driver I've ever seen. Just be grateful you didn't have to jump on the pillion of his motorbike. It would have been a truly terrifying experience for you."

Melanie approached him. She ignored the mud and held out a hand. They shook formally. "Happy to meet you properly, Danny. Thanks for … everything. And the captain's driving isn't that bad. At least he didn't run anyone over on the way here. Not like some in the room."

Danny exchanged the grin for a wince. "Touché, Mrs Archer. Guess I deserved that."

Lara reached a hand up to Danny's shoulder and spun him around. "Shower, now! Debrief later. No excuses."

———

DANNY TOOK twenty minutes to scrape himself clean enough for Lara to allow him entrance to the kitchen. Dressed in clean chinos, a plaid shirt, and thick socks, he presented himself for inspection and was given permission to attack Mike's hastily prepared supper.

All five sat around the table together, four of them finishing before Danny, who was working through his second huge slice of chicken pie and three veg all swimming in a thick, rich gravy.

Kaine's impatience stretched towards breaking point, but Lara's regular warning glances and headshakes made him keep his serious questions to himself. Instead, the conversation revolved around the quality of the food, the drinks, and the inclement nature of the weather. The frivolity around the table made it clear that everyone was finding great amusement at Kaine's expense.

Finally, Danny set down his knife and fork, pushed his plate into the centre of the table, and wiped his mouth with a cloth napkin.

"Thanks, Mike," he said, grinning. "That really hit the spot."

"Finished?" Kaine asked, trying not to growl.

"Yes thanks, boss."

"Tasty?"

"Delicious. The village baker really knows how to make a chicken pie."

"Cheeky, little sod," Mike said, grinning so much, his beard looked as though it might explode, "I made that pie, as you damned well know."

"You made it?" Melanie asked, her expression showing surprise and joy, which was a definite improvement on her mood when she first returned to the kitchen.

Lara and Mike were dead right. A good meal with normal, pleasant conversation could work wonders to reduce the levels of stress in the room.

"Yep. I enrolled in a cookery course after my Ellie passed away. Didn't take me long to get tired of frozen pizzas and chilled ready meals. No one delivers takeaways this far out of town and I couldn't stand the idea of a housekeeper getting under my feet."

Melanie nodded and beamed. "It was delicious. Thank you."

"You're welcome. But compared with your diet for the past few weeks, you'd probably have said that if I'd served you a toasted cheese sandwich, yes?"

Kaine waited for Melanie's mood to darken but, again, Mike had judged the change of direction well.

"Oh yes. Cheddar cheese on toast, drizzled with Worcestershire sauce. Nothing better." Her quiet laugh was music that made everyone smile, even a highly irritated Kaine.

"No way," Danny said, shaking his head, "tomato ketchup. Can't beat a dollop of tommie sauce on a cheese toasty."

"Snap!" Kaine said, sharply enough to make everyone look at him and stop talking except Danny.

"Snap? Does that mean you prefer tommie sauce on your toasted cheese as well, Captain?"

"No, Sergeant. That was the sound of my patience going 'twang'." He dropped his napkin on his empty side plate and leaned forwards, preparing to stand. "I take it your report is too sensitive for public discussion? If so, let's step out of the room, shall we?"

"Sorry, Captain," Danny answered, looking anything but apologetic. "We were having such a nice chat, I forgot all about it."

"Sergeant Pinkerton, with me, now!" He stood, pushing his chair away with the backs of his legs.

The annoying youngster with the goofy smile, who was heading for a long spell in the brig and a demotion back to Corporal if he didn't smarten his ideas pretty damn quick, winked at a grinning Lara. He leaned to one side and dug a hand into the front pocket of his chinos. When the hand reappeared, it held a sealed, plastic box big enough to house an engagement ring.

"Here you go, Doc. I'm sure you can find a home for this."

He passed the box to Lara.

Why the hell was Danny handing Lara a ring? Had she asked him to collect it for her? Wasn't a bloody leap year, was it?

Lara held the box up to the nearest light to read the label which contained a typed ident and a barcode.

No. Not a ring.

Kaine didn't know whether to be relieved or disappointed. The fact he leaned towards disappointment surprised him.

Snap out of it, Kaine.

"Danny, if you don't tell me what's going on, I swear to God!"

Lara's nod of recognition was almost as annoying as Danny's was smug. As for Mike and Melanie, if their confused expressions were anything to go by, neither had a clue what was going on either. At least Kaine wasn't the only one scrambling around in the dark.

"Have much trouble obtaining this?" Lara asked, not glancing in Kaine's direction.

Danny and Lara were having great fun at his expense. Kaine dropped down into his chair, slumped against its back, and deliberately unclenched his jaw. He refused to let them wind him up any further. The angrier he became, the longer they would take dragging it out. Damn it, he'd show everyone how well he could take a joke.

And … breathe.

"Piece of cake," Danny said, finally making eye contact

with Kaine. "Security in Aspire Hospital's dental clinic is a joke. Especially when the burglar has a Corky on his side."

Enlightenment dawned, and Kaine put Danny's momentary flirtation with the brig on hold. Mike's expression mutated from confusion to understanding. He'd worked it out, too.

"You broke into Aspire's dental clinic?" the retired CPO asked. "Is that what I think it is?" He pointed a gnarled and work-damaged finger at the box.

"Not sure, Mike," Kaine said, finally joining in on the joke, "if you think it's an engagement ring, or my missing motorbike, you'd be dead wrong. That right, Danny?"

"Yep. That there box happens to contain the dental crown they were going to fit this afternoon."

Danny checked the time on his watch. Kaine did the same with his.

00:03.

"Correction," Danny said. "Make that yesterday afternoon."

"Really? That's my replacement crown?" Melanie's surprise and excitement improved Kaine's mood even further.

Danny's delayed return from Nottingham had moved up the scale from intriguing to heroic and the Sergeant's prospective entanglement with the brig receded into the far distance.

Lara leaned forwards and patted Melanie's hand. "Danny thought it would be a real shame to let this go to waste."

"Everybody keeps calling you 'Doc'. Are you a dentist? Is that why you looked in my mouth earlier during the examination?"

"No, I'm actually a veterinarian."

"You're a what?"

"Long story," Kaine said, "but you can trust Lara with your health. We all do."

"So," Melanie said, sighing heavily and slumping back in her chair, mirroring Kaine, "this is what my life's come to? A vet's going to fit my dental crown?"

The smile she added at the end of the complaint made Kaine smile and Danny laugh.

"Don't be silly," Lara said, gently scolding her latest patient, "that's a job for a skilled orthodontist. Although I've removed impacted teeth from horses, I'm not prepared to perform delicate dental work on a human. Assuming you're okay with it, we'll visit the man who saved Ryan's smile. Believe it or not, under that gruff and rugged exterior, he has a lovely smile—when he deigns to grace us with it."

Melanie looked from Lara to Kaine and back. "Sorry, I'm really not following you."

Kaine played his part, finally putting the imaginary brig's key back in its pocket. Danny had well and truly redeemed himself.

"Mrs Archer," Kaine said, facing Melanie once again, "apart from an obvious distaste for the inside of a prison, and a deep hatred of Sir Malcolm Sampson, you and I have something else in common."

Melanie's frown deepened, and her shoulders sagged in defeat. "And what might that be?"

Kaine peeled back his upper lip to expose his teeth and tapped his upper right canine. "We both have dental implants. You can trust the dentist Lara's talking about. He's a total genius."

"Okay," she said, even though she shook her head. "I can go along with that."

"There's a slight problem, however," Lara said.

"Which is?"

"Unfortunately, the dentist can't see you until early next week. Right now, he's on a ship in the middle of the Adriatic."

"He's a sailor?"

"A senior officer in the Royal Navy," Kaine answered for Lara.

"I had no idea the Royal Navy employed dentists."

"A ship's crew suffers from toothache the same as any other population. And military injuries aren't only confined to arms and legs."

"He'd be prepared to work on an escaped prisoner?"

Kaine grinned. "Good question, and the answer is yes. If I asked him, he'd see you. So, the question is, are you happy to stay here for a week?"

"Yes," she answered without hesitation. "Assuming Mr Procter is okay with it."

"My name's Mike, lass. And you can stay as long as you like. In fact, I'd be delighted for the company."

"I can cook and help around the house, but the livestock …"

"As my guest, you'll do no such thing. You need to recover from those injuries. I've seen how you wince when you bend. Wouldn't hear of it."

"But I need to help. Hate being idle."

"How about we let the doc decide when you're fit to do some chores?"

"Okay, you have a deal. But what about you? Aren't you worried about sheltering an escaped prisoner?"

Mike arched his bushy eyebrows. "You're kidding, right?" He pointed at Kaine. "I'm currently harbouring one of the most wanted men in Europe. What's the problem with adding one more to the list?"

"Excellent," Kaine said, standing and beckoning to Danny, who wiped his mouth with the napkin again, "that's settled. Sergeant, with me, please. You and I have things to do."

"Yes, boss. Right with you."

Danny stood and waited.

"Where are you two going at this time of night?" Lara asked.

"To begin with, we're heading for the comms room," Kaine said.

"We are?" Danny asked, wincing, but trying to hide it.

Something's up.

Kaine shot Danny a sideways glance. The sergeant had something else on his mind, but evidently didn't want to discuss it in public. He'd find out when they were alone. He turned to Lara.

"Now that Melanie has decided to accept Mike's generous hospitality," Kaine continued, "she has to meet DCI Jones. But before that can happen, Danny and I have some organising to do."

"Can't it wait until morning?" Lara asked.

He leaned down and kissed her cheek. "Sorry, love. This is important. Mike, Melanie, see you later." Kaine headed towards the door. "Sergeant."

Danny smiled at Lara and winked at Melanie.

"Yes, boss," he said. "*Normally*, I'd follow you anywhere, anytime, boss."

Normally? What's this?

Kaine barged through the kitchen door, into the boot room, and waited for an unusually reluctant Danny to follow.

Maybe he'd need that key to the brig after all.

The END.

Next in the Ryan Kaine series

vinci-books.com/onthehunt

When trust is all they have, can they survive?

Danny Pinkerton's fight against a ruthless crime family sends him across Europe, with only his loyal friend, Ryan Kaine, by his side. Survival is a battle, but betrayal could be deadly.

Turn the page for a free preview…

On The Hunt: Chapter One

Wednesday 5th May - Daniel Pinkerton

Chequer Way, Amber Valley, Derbyshire, England

Danny had only seen the woman for a few seconds. At the time, he didn't know her name or anything about her, but her bruised and bloodshot eyes, and the fear expressed in them, had drawn his attention.

She'd been in the front passenger seat of a white Range Rover stuck in traffic, two miles from the Aspire Hospital, Nottingham—a traffic jam caused by the failed attempt on Melanie Archer's life.

In those few, brief moments, the injured woman's plight had touched Danny's heart.

He'd been trudging along the side of the road, dressed like a vagrant in ripped jeans and a grubby polo shirt, covered in someone else's blood, but when she'd looked at him through those damaged eyes, he couldn't let it go. The metal splint taped to her nose confirmed her as a woman in serious pain.

At first, he assumed she'd just left the hospital following a nose job, but the way she reacted to her driver's aggressive proximity fired off warning bells in Danny's head. Then, after a brief exchange of words, the driver had raced away in the Range Rover, ignoring Danny's request for a lift and leaving him standing in the driving rain. But as the driver made the turn, he showed Danny the SUV's tailgate and the cherished licence number it carried, "RNP 111".

During his sodden jog to the hospital, Danny contacted Corky, and it had taken the talented hacker seconds to identify the SUV's registered owner—one Robert Neil Prentiss. Corky also provided the man's home address and the name of his wife, Marian Jennifer Prentiss.

Danny had to act. He couldn't help himself.

———

DEEP IN THE AMBER VALLEY, twenty miles northwest of Derby, Chequer Way stood pretty much in the middle of nowhere, but Danny's slow, overnight drive-by had shown him plenty.

The security wall running along the front of the pretentiously named "Prentiss House" stretched out for a little over one hundred and fifty metres. The only gap in the brickwork allowed for a grand entrance, flanked by stone pillars that were crowned with prancing horses, carved from what looked like white marble. Recessed from the road by a short, gravel driveway, a pair of electrically operated, wrought-iron gates protected the opening, defending the floodlit home from whatever rampaging hordes the owners most feared.

Behind the gates, Prentiss House—more private mansion than working farmhouse—stood in all its glory. Sandstone walls shone bright under the orange floodlights. Imposing and expensive.

Pompous or what?

Danny didn't need to be hit over the head with a lump of sandstone to recognise valuable real estate when he saw it. No doubt about it, Robert Prentiss was loaded.

Didn't give him the right to beat his wife, though.

No bloody way.

So, since he'd made the trip, what was he going to do?

He couldn't exactly breach the fortress, knock on the front door, and ask the householder how long he'd been beating his wife. No way. There could only be one response to such a question.

Prentiss would refute the charge and dismiss Danny from the grounds. The bugger might even call the police and try to have Danny arrested. And where would that leave the possible victim? No, such a bumbling, half-arsed approach might even make the situation worse for Marian Prentiss.

Danny needed proof.

Not the same level of proof required by the UK's stodgy legal system. Oh no. He just needed enough to convince himself of the rich man's guilt. Then, and only then, would Prentiss receive his lesson.

Only then would the bastard learn what it felt like to be on the receiving end of a thumping.

Danny parked his leased, mid-range, BMW 3 Series in a lay-by two miles to the north, returned on foot under the cover of darkness, and completed a surreptitious circuit of the defensive wall. He found another opening at the rear, barred by a pair of solid, wooden gates, which he scaled with ease. Keeping to the deep shadow, Danny skirted around to the front of the house and found a row of rhododendron bushes where the wall formed a corner, then dropped to his haunches.

Inside the wall, landscaped gardens to the front, rear, and sides showed the intensive work of someone with green fingers. Mainly set to lawns and with well-stocked herbaceous borders, the grounds at the rear contained numerous outbuildings, including a detached triple garage, a large greenhouse, and two small, wooden sheds.

Danny's hiding spot gave him a good view of the house's frontage and most of the rear. He settled in for the long haul, his back propped against the cold brickwork. He grew colder by the minute, but the memory of Marian Prentiss' battered face warmed him and drove him on. What was a little discomfort compared to her injuries?

He rolled his shoulders, stretched his neck, and trained the Zeiss Victory SF 8x42 binoculars—the only piece of surveillance equipment he'd found in the "borrowed" grab-bag, apart from the "special" comms glasses—on the front of the house, making the most of the floodlights' illumination.

Danny sighed and shook his head in disgust. He'd screwed up big time. During his rush from Mike's farm, he'd liberated a fully packed grab-bag from the stores only to arrive and find it loaded with the wrong equipment. He'd found a torch and spare batteries, a compass, a fire-starting kit, flares, and some compact climbing equipment. The kit would be useful for some operations. Unfortunately though, not for this one.

Focus, Danny. Focus.

The entrance portico—two white columns supporting a triangular canopy—aimed for impressive but only hit excessive and ostentatious. Two steps led up to a semi-circular floor covered in black-and-white tiles laid out in a chessboard pattern. Double doors— panelled and painted black in a high-gloss finish—wore black, wrought-iron furniture. Two huge lionheads with thick, metal rings in their mouths acted as knockers. Two more formed the handles. Raised iron rivets fastened enormous, wrought-iron hinges into the woodwork, trying to give the impression of a drawbridge.

Fuck's sake, what a mess.

Danny raked the binoculars across the façade, looking for security cameras or motion-activated spots, but found none. He returned the binoculars to his small rucksack and settled back to wait.

———

AT 01:30 the floodlights powered off, plunging Danny's world into inky blackness. It left him blind and immobile until his natural night vision took over. While waiting for the house to sleep and before venturing out of his obbo point to take a closer gander, Danny replayed his most recent conversation with Corky—carried out while driving to Amber Valley—in his head.

"Hi there, Mr P. How you diddling?"

Danny grinned at the memory. If he hung around for Corky to comply with correct comms protocol, he'd be waiting forever.

"Hello, Control. What do you have for me? Over."

"Plenty, Mr P. Plenty. Whatcha need first?"

"Names and bios will do for a start. Over."

"Corky sent them to your mobile half an hour ago."

422

"I'm driving. Can you give me the bullet points, please? Over."

"Yeah, okay. Sure. Like, why not. After all, it ain't as though Corky don't got a million other things to do, is it?"

"Sorry, Corky," Danny had said, slapping some life into his cheeks. "I appreciate all your efforts, mate. I really do. Hoped you'd save me a little time, is all—"

"Nah, just joshing, Mr P. Corky's happy to oblige. Just a sec."

To Danny's surprise, the active map on the dashboard's GPS screen had shrunk into a corner, and Corky's round and wispy-bearded face took its place.

He nearly lost control of the BMW.

How the tech genius had achieved the trick, Danny would never know. Corky was able to do things beyond the scope of even the most gifted, military techies.

Apart from the small-scale map, the screen behind Corky showed nothing but a white wall, which made a change from the usual panoramic view of sea and sky he preferred.

"Whatcha, Mr P," Corky said, his cheeks fattening into a cheeky grin. "Much better speaking face to face, yeah?"

Danny returned the grin. "Sure is."

"This way, we don't need none of that 'over and out' bullshit, neither."

"If you say so, Corky."

"Didn't know these consoles had built-in cameras."

"You'd be surprised what the manufacturers hide inside their 'infotainment systems', Mr P. These days, Big Brother is always watching you."

"Okay," Danny said, "so who exactly is our target?"

"Robert Neil Prentiss. Aged thirty-six. Owns Prentiss Haulage Limited and operates from a distribution centre on the outskirts of Derby. Likes to call himself 'Robbie P'. That's the geezer on the screen right now."

Corky then pointed over his shoulder and a colour headshot of a man emerged on the white background. Strong face, square jaw, light brown eyes. Some might say good looking. Danny had tried to match the image with the driver of the Range Rover from the previous afternoon, but it didn't really work.

In the headshot, Robbie P had short hair, was clean shaven, and the smile reached his eyes. The headshot made him seem warm and friendly, but looks could be deceptive.

"How old's that picture?"

Corky shrugged. "Dunno when the pic was taken, but it was uploaded to the company's website six months back. Why?"

Danny sniffed. "The bloke I saw driving the Range Rover had long, dark hair and a beard. Didn't get a clear sight of him due to the floppy hair and the darkness inside the car, though. Might be the same guy, I guess. You couldn't find anything more recent?"

Corky pinched his lips together and shook his head. "Nah, not really. Corky found a few publicity shots of Robbie P from when he opened a distribution centre in Hungary eighteen months back, but the quality's poor and there ain't any pics newer than that online. By the way, his hair was short in those pics, too. And he didn't have a beard."

"Find anything interesting on the wife?"

"Nothing much. Marian Jennifer Prentiss. Maiden name, Turvey. Aged twenty-eight. They've been married round about five years. No kids yet. She's got herself a degree in Fine Arts from Nottingham Trent University."

"Anything worrying in her medical history?"

"Didn't find nothing in her NHS records."

"No emergency admissions for unexplained injuries? Broken bones? Facial trauma?"

"Er, nope." Another headshake.

"What about the damage I saw to her face yesterday? No record of that in the Aspire's records?"

Corky scrunched his mobile face into a wince. He'd almost seemed embarrassed. "Yeah, now that's where Corky's had a little bit of bother. As you know, for some reason, the Aspire's computer systems fell over last night."

"You don't say." Danny couldn't prevent the irony invading his voice.

Danny knew all about the Aspire's computer troubles. He knew, because he'd asked Corky to disable their IT infrastructure long enough for him to break into its dental clinic and "liberate" Melanie Archer's replacement ceramic crown. The same ceramic crown she'd been paroled from prison for the day to have fitted.

"What happened, Corky? You didn't break their IT system, did you?"

"What? Corky? Nah, 'course not. It's got nothing to do with Corky, and it ain't permanent, neither. The hospital's IT service provider is running a system-wide, diagnostic sweep on account of the unplanned shutdown. It means that Corky can't interrogate the system right now. At least, not safely."

"How long are you going to be locked out?"

Corky's wince transformed into a deep scowl. "Now listen here, Mr P. What part of that explanation said Corky were locked out? Corky hasn't never been locked out of a computer system in his life! Bloody insulting, that is."

Keeping a straight face and concentrating on the road

ahead, Danny had raised a hand in apology. "Sorry, Corky. Didn't mean to upset you."

"Locked out! There's no way Corky's locked out. He's keeping his distance for security purposes, that's all. Get it? Any outside interference on the Aspire's systems at this stage will lead to questions Corky doesn't want anyone asking. Is that clear?"

"Yes, Corky. It's clear. I get it. And again, I am sorry. Any idea how long the systems are likely to be inaccessible?"

"The idiots are taking their time over the security scan. They say it'll be down 'til at least midday. Typical. If Corky were running the systems check, it would already be done."

Danny nodded. "I understand. Can't be helped. Until then we're blind, yes?"

The chubby hacker's cheeky grin returned. "On the other hand, Corky did discover who provides Mr and Mrs Prentiss with their medical insurance."

"Brilliant."

"Too right it is. The company's called Notts Private Health Services. Seems they agreed to cover the costs of 'emergency treatment' at the Aspire Hospital under Robbie P's account. Apparently, two nights ago, she tripped and fell down the stairs. Broke her nose and her right cheekbone."

Yeah, right.

Danny had gripped the wheel tighter and tried not to grind his teeth.

"Tripped and fell down the stairs, my arse," he scoffed. "The bastard hit her."

Corky tilted his head to one side in agreement. "Looks that way. What you gonna do? Corky hates wifebeaters, just as much as you do, Mr P. You gonna give the guy a good thumping?" the hacker asked, excitement shining bright in his eyes.

"Probably, but I need to do some obbo first. I want to be certain of my facts."

"The facts seem clear enough."

"Maybe, but I'm not in the habit of turning people over without proof. Before doing anything serious, I'll try to get Marian on her own. It would be good to hear her side of the story. You never know, her injuries might well have been accidental." Danny had tried to sound convincing, but failed miserably. He happened to be as certain as Corky of Robbie P's guilt.

"So, anything else you need from ol' Corky?"

"A layout of the house would be useful?"

"More 'bullet points'?"

"Yes, please."

"Okay, here you go." His gaze slid to the left and he'd started reading, probably from another monitor. "The architect's plans are online, and Corky's been taking a shufti. Robbie P started renovating the house six years ago, right after they moved in and renamed the place. The house has two storeys and an attic. Ground floor's got three receptions, a home office, a sun room, and a kitchen with utility room. First floor has four bedrooms, two with en suites, and one large, family bathroom. The attic has planning permission for a granny annex, but the work stopped three years ago. Dunno why. Maybe the vicious bugger ran out of money."

"Can you find out?"

Corky winked. "Next thing on the to-do list, Mr P. Corky reckons Prentiss Haulage Limited might have stretched their finances a bit thin when they opened that satellite hub in Hungary. Seems to be something fishy going on there. Like, who chooses chuffing Hungary for their base of operations? Hardly the epicentre of the European haulage trade. There aren't all that many routes to and from the major agriculture or manufacturing centres, you know."

"You'll keep searching, I imagine?"

"If there's anything iffy going on, Corky's gonna find it."

"Don't suppose Prentiss House has a burglar alarm or surveillance system you can break into?"

Corky shook his head and his expression had turned glum. "Nah, 'fraid not. They got an alarm and a CCTV setup, but it ain't hooked up to the web, at least not yet. Corky can't give you ears or eyes inside the house without splicing directly into the system. And there ain't no way that's happening any time soon."

"Okay, mate. I'll have to do it the old-fashioned way. Thanks for everything. I'll find a spot inside the grounds and lie doggo for a while. If and when Robbie P heads out to work in the morning, it'll give me a chance to ask Marian about his behaviour. Assuming he leaves her home alone."

"Good luck with that, Mr P. Corky's off now." He chuckled, faded away, and the GPS map expanded to fill the screen again.

———

SLOWLY, one by one, the stars blinked out and a pale dawn washed away the darkness of night.

Danny shivered. The morning dew had long since soaked through his clothes, and the chill had worked its way into every joint of his body.

Bugger it.

He should have come better prepared. A groundsheet would have helped, but no point crying about that now. It wasn't as though he could call on anyone for help, either.

For the first time in years, he was operating solo, which felt both good and bad. Good, to have no one questioning his actions or monitoring his performance. Bad, to have no one to bounce ideas off, not even the captain.

What had originally seemed like the most obvious thing in the world—save the girl, punish the vicious arsehole—had turned into hours of waiting in the perishing cold. Hours of double-guessing and doubt.

Earlier, his post-floodlight searches hadn't added to his small pool of knowledge. Peering through windows and pressing his ear to the glass achieved nothing. Heavy curtains hid the view inside, and triple-glazed windows on the ground level prevented all sounds filtering through into the night. A complete bust.

He'd been deaf and blind to whatever was going on inside Prentiss House and had failed to add to Corky's intel.

A thermal-imaging camera might have told him how many people were in the house and where they slept, but he hadn't found one in the grab-bag he'd borrowed and hadn't checked in his haste to "save the damsel in distress". Another bloody mistake. One of many. No groundsheet, no parabolic microphone, no infrared or night vision glasses, no nothing. Damn it, he wasn't even armed.

What was it Uncle Cuddles used to say? "Fail to prepare and you might as well join the SAS." Yep, dear old Rollo wasn't averse to mangling the odd platitude in his search for a hilarious put down.

And anyway, why the hell would he need a weapon?

Danny faced nothing but a wifebeater. A bully and a coward, not a Taliban insurgent, and Danny knew how to handle bullies.

Around him, the dawn chorus welcomed the onset of day and the temperature rose with the sun. With the minimum of movement, Danny loosened his joints and warmed his muscles in preparation for whatever the morning would bring.

Before him, Prentiss House remained silent. The curtains hid what went on behind the ground-floor windows, and shutters covered those on the upper two floors.

Once again, Danny waited.

———

THE MIDDLE of the three high-security garage doors rolled up to expose the gleaming, white, and ludicrously expensive Range Rover 5.0L V8. Brand new, the top-of-the-range beastie would have set Robbie P back more than £130,000. The powerful monster's engine growled in smooth anger. White condensation spewing from the tailpipe, the SUV pulled slowly out of the garage and into the daylight some thirty-five metres from where Danny concealed himself amongst the rhododendrons.

Finally, after damn near seven hours of freezing his nuts off, Danny had movement.

He allowed himself a little fist pump.

Here we go!

The Range Rover rolled forwards and stopped outside the grand front entrance, purring, waiting for release. Behind it, the garage door rolled down and clunked into place. The driver's door popped open and a swarthy man with long, wavy hair and a well-trimmed beard climbed out. Slightly below-average height but powerfully built, the man wore a dark business suit, white shirt, muted brown tie, and polished-leather shoes. He bore a striking resemblance to the driver from the previous day.

Robbie P?

Danny raised the binoculars, focused them on the man. Pale blue eyes shone out of a weather-beaten face.

Blue eyes?

Can't be right.

Danny tweaked the knurled nut of the binoculars' focus adjuster to sharpen the image further. Yep, the driver's eyes were definitely blue.

Shit!

Definitely not Prentiss.

The headshot Corky had thrown up on the BMW's info-tainment screen showed Robbie P with light brown eyes, not blue, and Corky's detailed bio confirmed it. The bio also stated that Robbie P stood at around one hundred and eighty-eight centimetres, but the driver was at least eight centimetres shorter.

What the hell was going on?

The swarthy man, Driver, glowered at the closed front doors and peeled back the sleeve of his jacket to reveal a heavy, gold watch. He all but tapped his foot on the gravel in his impatience.

Driver waited another thirty seconds before shouting something guttural in a language Danny didn't understand. Moments later, one of the front doors opened and a second man in a business suit, his short hair thinning on top, stumbled out, propelled by the stiff-armed punch of a third man.

The man in the suit bunted into one of the columns supporting the portico's canopy and fell to his hands and knees.

The third man stayed in the open doorway. He wore blue jeans and a white T-shirt under a sleeveless, denim vest. Squat with a shaved head, his muscular arms and thick neck were covered in black ink—prison tats.

Tats shouted, "*Idióta,*" and coughed out a harsh laugh.

With his back to Danny, the fallen man scrambled to his feet. He raised his hands to Tats, shouted, "Don't hurt her. Please don't hurt her again!" and spun towards Driver, finally showing his face to Danny.

Robbie P!

Fuck.

In that instant, Danny realised his mistake. Robbie P was no more a wifebeater than Ryan Kaine was a murdering terrorist.

What the bloody hell had he stumbled into?

On The Hunt: Chapter Two

Wednesday 5th May - Daniel Pinkerton

Prentiss House, Amber Valley, Derbyshire, England

From his hiding place in the shrubbery, Danny watched an evil grin split Driver's face. "Follow my instructions and no more violence will be necessary," he called, his accent thick.

Robbie P wiped his mouth with the back of his hand. "Y-Yes. I promise. But, please don't hurt my wife again."

Driver beckoned with a flick of his fingers. "Come!"

Robbie P rushed from the shade of the portico into the sunlight and hurried towards the Range Rover, dusting himself off and smoothing out the creases in his suit along the way.

Danny kneeled, silent and helpless as Robbie P dived into the Range Rover's rear passenger compartment. Driver pushed the door, which closed with an expensive-sounding clunk, and swaggered, still smiling, to his position behind the steering wheel.

Seconds later, the SUV pulled away. It rolled sedately along the gravel driveway to the open security gates, and turned right, heading towards Derby.

In the doorway, Tats waited, arms folded and biceps bulging, until the Range Rover moved out of sight behind the wall and the gates started closing. Then, laughing, he turned and headed back inside the house.

The moment the front door closed behind Tats, Danny took off. Crouching low, he used the bushes and mature trees for cover and hugged the wall.

Tats' laugh had been ominous. Danny didn't need to be a mind reader to know what was going on inside the tattooed thug's shaved head.

Still on the move, Danny dug into the breast pocket of his boiler suit, took the special comms glasses from their protective case, flipped the "activate" switch, and slipped them on. Rather than risk losing it, Danny left the earpiece in place but tapped it inert.

"Charlie One to Control," he panted, keeping his voice low. "Are you there? Over?"

Three seconds of silence drew out forever.

"Hey there, Mr P. Corky's listening. What's up?"

"Hang on a minute. Be right with you. Over."

Danny reached the place where the wall arced inwards to form the gated entrance and kneeled in the shade of the column. On the other side of the wall's arm, the wrought-iron gates met with a metallic clang, and the hum of electric motors fell silent.

Breathing heavily and keeping to the shadows, Danny stood and lowered the zip of his boiler suit and struggled out of the grubby workwear. He rolled it up tight, hid it at the base of the wall, and faced the house again.

"*With you moving about like that, Corky's getting seasick,*" the hacker said. "*Why were you running?*"

"Shit's hit the fan here. Over."

"*In what way?*"

"Tell you later. I'm about to make the approach. How's the picture? Over."

"*It'd be clear and sharp, if you didn't move your head so much.*"

"Sorry, mate. Needs must. I'll try my best, but things have to look natural. Okay, here I go. Please keep your eyes and ears open. I'm going in blind. No idea what I'll find in there. Over."

"*Yes you do. Corky sent you the plans.*"

"Not what I meant. Heading in now. Over."

Danny took a settling breath, stepped around the wall into the middle of the gravel driveway, and started walking. He glanced down at his freshly revealed clothes. Work boots, chinos, polo shirt, leather jacket. All dark, all chosen to look reasonable even when heavily creased and slightly damp. Hopefully, he'd be acceptable enough to pass muster.

Time to dial up the charm, Danny-boy.

Not that he expected charm to get him far with someone like Tats. He plastered a pleasant smile to his face and stepped up his pace, aiming straight for the entrance portico.

Danny had been staring at the entrance for most of the night. From his hideout in the grounds some sixty metres away, the portico looked ridiculously overblown. Moving up close did nothing to change his impression. This was a large house trying its best to be imposing. Trying and failing. The phrase "mutton dressed as lamb" came to mind.

Here goes.

Still smiling, Danny bounded up the steps, marched across the chessboard surface and grabbed one of the iron rings. It was heavier than he expected. Might have even been a real antique.

That's a surprise.

He smashed the ring against its raised strike plate twice—the thuds echoed loudly through the interior—and stepped back.

C'mon, Tats. Where are you?

When nothing happened for thirty seconds, Danny repeated the knocking. This time, he used even more force.

Behind the door, footsteps clacked on a hard floor, growing louder. The spyhole on the middle of the left-hand door darkened. Danny looked straight at it, maintaining the smile.

A black handle turned, and the same right-hand door opened to reveal a scowling Tats. His shaved head exposed the white, spiral-flex cable running from an old-fashioned earpiece into the front pocket of his denim jacket. A suspicious bulge near the jacket's left armpit told Danny two things. Tats carried a gun and was most likely right-handed. He filed the information away in case he needed it later.

As tall and broad as Danny, Tats filled the part-open doorway, blocking Danny's view of the interior.

Danny pricked up his ears, but the inside of the house remained ominously silent. No screaming. No crying. No one else's footsteps.

Where was Marian Prentiss? Had Tats finished her off already?

"Corky here, Mr P. Running facial recognition. Get back to you real soon."

Danny smiled inwardly, but didn't let the reaction show

on his face. Corky was a Godsend. The man certainly knew his stuff.

"How you get here?" Tats asked, his heavily accented voice booming beneath the canopy. He glanced towards the front gates.

While keeping a close eye on the dark man's right hand, Danny gave him the benefit of his most engaging smile. For all the response it generated, he might as well not have bothered.

"Simple enough," Danny said, pointing over his shoulder to the pathway. "I walked."

Tats opened the door a little wider, squeezed through the gap, and pulled it shut behind him. He leaned closer, trying to threaten. Not usually prone to intimidation, Danny was neither impressed nor daunted.

"How you get through gates, asshole?"

Danny let his smile drop, but maintained his position, refusing to back down.

"They were open."

"No. Gates always locked."

"Not this time, my friend. But I have to say, you're much quicker than most," he said.

Tats frowned. "Huh?"

"Didn't take you very long to sum me up," Danny said, playing for time.

"What you say?" Tats asked, his frown deepening.

"Normally, it takes even the most discerning of individuals a little time to determine that I am, in fact, an arsehole." Danny nodded and reprised the smile.

"Fucking smartass!"

Tats leaned even closer to Danny. He clenched his fists, cracking his knuckles.

Unfazed, Danny maintained his position.

"Yes, I'm one of those, too. You're very good, you know. Really quick on the uptake. Do you have any more insults, or are you going to ask who I am and who sent me?"

Tats bristled. The flat muscles attaching his neck to his shoulders tensed. His fists tightened, and his forearms rippled. He looked ready to attack, but something stopped him. Some doubt. Tats clearly wasn't used to this sort of response from an unexpected and unannounced visitor. More to the point, he didn't seem accustomed to visitors at all. Tats glanced behind Danny, looking for... what? Backup? The return of Driver?

"Well?" Danny demanded.

"Huh?"

"Oh dear. You're obviously not as bright as I initially gave you credit for. Ask me who I am, fool!"

Tats took half a pace forwards. "You fuckin—"

"No, no," Danny said, raising his index finger for silence. "Wrong move. The boss won't give you any credit for attacking a visitor whom you've not fully vetted. My God, man. You've not even asked my name or what I'm doing here."

Danny's interruption struck home. Tats stopped advancing and peered hard at him, sticking out his chin in the process.

"What your name?"

Danny shook his head. "Not telling you now. You've been too rude. Let me speak to Mrs Prentiss."

Tats frowned in confusion again.

"*Got him*," Corky said, finally.

Keeping his hands raised in case Tats attacked, Danny took a backwards step. "About time. I couldn't delay this clown much longer. What do you have? Over."

"What you say?" Tats demanded. "You go now before I—"

"Will you be quiet for just one moment? I'm talking to the boss," Danny said, and half turned away. "Please carry on, sir. Over."

Tats blinked, raised a hand to the side of his head, and used his index finger to press the earpiece more firmly in place. He blinked again, then stared hard at Danny who watched him through the corner of his eye.

"*There's an Interpol Red Notice on this nasty geezer,*" Corky said. "*Name's Csaba Nemeth. Hungarian. Real nasty piece of work. Escaped prisoner. Doin' twenty-five to life for some real bad stuff. Multiple rape. People trafficking. Worst charge was the extended abuse of a minor. Suspected of murder, too. Take care, Mr P.*"

Keeping eye contact with Tats—Csaba Nemeth—Danny held a hand to his ear and nodded. "Okay, sir. I'll tell him. Over."

Nemeth tapped his ear a couple of times and shook his head again. "My radio not work."

"That's okay, Csaba," Danny said, stepping closer and holding out his hand. "The boss told me to introduce myself. I'm Danny, latest member of the team. How you doing?"

"Yes?" Nemeth said. Confusion still raked his face, but he took Danny's hand. "No one told me about new—"

Danny yanked hard, straightening Nemeth's right arm and tugging him off-balance. He shot a left jab into the Hungarian's exposed ribs. At least one bone cracked. Maybe two.

Nemeth grunted. Crumpled. Folded in on himself. His knees buckled.

Danny punched him again. Another rib snapped. He released his grip and shot the webbing between his thumb and forefinger into the Hungarian's throat. Nemeth collapsed to his knees in a gasping, gargling, coughing heap. His hands reached up to his throat, fingers scrabbling, fighting for air.

In Danny's ear, Corky chuckled. "*Nice one, Mr P. Them fists are lethal. Mr K couldn't have done it better. Corky's glad we're on the same side.*"

"Me too. Over."

Slowly, Nemeth toppled to the chessboard tiles, gagging, eyes streaming, floundering. Helpless. He lay on his back, one arm held tight around his chest to protect his damaged ribs, the other bent, its hand clutching at his throat. Danny swung his foot and kicked Nemeth in the nuts, hard, merciless. Nemeth howled.

Danny repeated the crippling attack, his boot's steel toecap delivering untold, maybe permanent, damage.

Two vicious, pitiless blows, and Danny didn't give a shit.

"*Ouch. That's a bit nasty.*"

"Multiple rape and the abuse of a minor, you said. Over."

"*Okay. Gotcha. Understandable. Do it again for all Corky cares.*"

"Nemeth won't be messing with kids again in a hurry. Over."

"*Fair enough. Want Corky to call Interpol or the National Crime Agency for you? They've been hunting the arsehole for the past eight months.*"

"Not yet," Danny said, keeping his voice down. "Something's fucked up here, mate. I need to find Marian Prentiss first. Over."

Keeping an eye on the spyhole in the door and an ear open for noises inside the house, Danny dropped to one knee. He relieved the quivering, rapist-paedophile-murderer of his weapon—a Beretta PX4 Storm—and checked the load. A full, nineteen-round magazine. What the hell was all the firepower in aid of?

Danny told Corky what happened between Robbie P and Driver, while patting down the still groaning, still sputtering Nemeth. He found a wallet bulging with notes, a spare mag for the Beretta, a smart phone, and loose change. Danny pocketed the wallet and mag, powered down the phone—Corky might find a use for it later—and slipped it into the same pocket.

"We must have missed something. Over."

"Whatcha mean, Mr P?"

"I mean, what's Robbie P gotten himself into? What's a shit-for-brains thug like Csaba Nemeth doing here, and what's the story with Driver? Robbie P *is* just a businessman, yeah? Over."

"You know what Corky knows. Maybe he's pissed off the Magyars somehow. After you've found Mrs Prentiss, Corky's gonna dig deeper into Prentiss Haulage. Loads deeper, but that ain't happening 'til later. Okay? Corky can't leave you without backup."

"Aw, does that mean you're worried about me? I didn't know you cared. Over."

"Nah. Just means Corky don't want the blame if you get hurt. Mr K and the doc will be upset, and Corky wouldn't want that."

Nemeth continued to twitch and groan. A dark, wet stain had spread across the front of his jeans and down the legs, but Danny couldn't tell whether it was blood or urine. Maybe a mixture of the two.

Danny ripped out the miserable creature's earpiece. He yanked the Hungarian's right hand away from his groin and the left from his throat, turned him onto his front, and used the spiral-flex cable to tie them behind his back. Nemeth put up no resistance, but turned onto his side and curled into a foetal ball, mouth open and flapping for air. His face had turned a nasty shade of purple.

"There's something serious going on here, Corky. Driver ordered Nemeth around. He sounded like the boss. Must have a hell of a lot of juice to spring Nemeth from a Hungarian prison and transport him all the way to the UK. A hired hand like Nemeth wouldn't be able to manage it on his own. As for how the bugger ended up at Prentiss House … Anyway, that's for another time. I'm going in. Over."

Danny wiped his feet on a welcome mat that actually said "Welcome" and reached for the lionhead handle on the door Nemeth used. He twisted the handle and leaned against the door. It opened as quietly as before. A wave of warmth wafted into his face. It smelled of lavender air freshener.

Inside, the large entrance hall almost made Danny's jaw drop. Straight ahead, a wide, central staircase with marble treads split in two halfway up to the first floor. The walls were painted a cream so deep it might have been clotted Devon, and the flooring matched the one in the portico in both material and pattern.

Oversized chess pieces, hip height, lined the walls. Major pieces only, no pawns. The four rooks—one in each corner—doubled as plant pots and contained what looked like plastic ferns. The knights had been converted into low-level lampstands complete with silk shades.

The décor said something about the owners' taste and about the designers who pandered to the whims of their clients, and nothing it said happened to be complimentary. The entrance hall could have made the set of *Love Island*.

He grabbed Nemeth by the collar of his sleeveless jacket and quickly dragged him into the house and across the hall. The groaning man's leather shoes squeaked and left black scuffmarks on the chessboard tiles. He also left a thin trail of blood. If Robbie P and his missus employed a housekeeper or a cleaner, they'd have their work cut out to polish the floor back to a shine. Danny hauled Nemeth all the way around to the back of the hall and deposited him behind the staircase, out of sight.

Danny stopped, listened. Heard nothing but the creaking of a big old house being warmed by the rising sun. The entrance hall stood empty. All seven internal doors were shut tight. Above him, the house remained quiet. No footfalls, no quiet conversations, no TV or radio.

Silent and breathless.

Focusing on the ground floor, Danny used the memorised architect's plans to picture what lay behind each closed door. From left to right in a circle: staircase, kitchen, dining room, lounge—the double doors of the entrance—toilet, cloakroom, office and, finally, the sunroom which overlooked the rear gardens.

He hesitated, trying to decide where to go first.

Fuck's sake, Danny. Move!

The lounge would be as good a place as any.

He hurried across the hall, skirted the staircase, and paused outside the door. He pressed an ear to the panel and held his breath. A quiet whimpering.

He knocked gently. The whimpering stopped.

Silence trundled through the house once more. Even Nemeth had stopped his pitiful and evermore feeble whining.

On The Hunt: Chapter Three

Wednesday 5th May - Daniel Pinkerton

Prentiss House, Amber Valley, Derbyshire, England

After receiving no answer, Danny knocked again and entered a room large enough to house a five-a-side footie pitch. Every piece of furniture in the room faced a curved TV the size of a multiplex cinema screen. The overarching colour pallet was green—subtle tones a-plenty. Throw rugs, soft furnishings, upholstery, walls. If the entrance hall held all the charm and comfort of a modern railway station, this room was tasteful and homely by comparison.

Bright sunlight flooded through a triple row of bifold doors, one of which was open, allowing the sage-green curtains to billow into the chilly room.

An enormous, six-seater sofa dominated the space in front of the TV. Cowering in the far corner, surrounded by half a dozen throw cushions and hugging a stuffed toy—a brown-and-yellow-spotted giraffe—Marian Prentiss turned towards him. Long, dark, brown hair, brown eyes, rail thin, she looked frail and helpless.

The dark bruises beneath her bloodshot eyes still looked angry and painful, the metal splint still protected her nose. She looked at Danny with disinterest. Her reaction to a total stranger entering her lounge couldn't have been more surprising, or disconcerting.

Rather than shout and scream at his intrusion, she returned her eyes to the TV's muted screen. The programme—a man and a woman sitting on a red sofa, chatting—typified the blandness that could only be daytime scheduling.

Danny stepped further into the room, but kept a decent separation between them for fear of spooking her.

"Mrs Prentiss?" he asked quietly.

She turned her head to study him once more. Confusion on her damaged face turned to vague recognition.

"Who … Do I know you?" The husky and nasal tone to her voice confirmed that her injury still had quite some healing to do.

"No," he said, shaking his head. "At least, we've not actually been formally introduced."

"What … do you want now?" Although she tried to hide it, the poor woman couldn't mask the fear tainting her voice.

"Nothing, I'm here to help."

"That's what *he* said. At first."

"Who?"

Marian shot a frightened glance at the door before lowering her eyes. She hugged the giraffe tighter as though seeking its comfort and protection. Another gust of chill wind billowed the curtains and raised goosepimples on her bare arms. She didn't seem to notice.

"Vadik."

"The one driving the Range Rover?"

Slowly, suspicion in her eyes, she dipped her head in a nod. "Yes."

"Who is he?"

"Don't you know? You work for him!"

"No, Mrs Prentiss. No, I don't."

She frowned and her lower lip trembled. Tears dripped from the bloodshot eyes and ran down the outside of the splint. She licked them away from her chapped lips.

"Are you okay?"

"As if you care!"

Finally, an appropriate reaction. Anger. Fitting, but misdirected.

"I do care, Mrs Prentiss. Which is why I'm here."

She looked past Danny and towards the open door he'd entered through. "Where's ... where's the other one?"

"Csaba Nemeth?"

She frowned and sucked air through her teeth, wincing at the movement. "No one told me his name. Evil man. An animal."

"Big guy. Ugly, covered in tattoos?"

Again, she shot a glance at the open door.

"Y-Yes. Him."

"Did he do that to you?" Danny slowly raised a hand to indicate her injuries.

The breath caught in her throat. She pressed her lips together, nodded.

"You know he did."

I know for definite now.

The wind blew another blast of cold air into the lounge. Danny rushed to the other side of the room and pushed the central hinge on the bifold doors. They swished on pneumatic tracks and closed with a satisfying click. He drew back the curtains and the room brightened even more. All the while, he felt Marian's eyes boring into the back of his head. Yet, still she didn't move. She seemed resigned to his presence.

"That's better," he said, rubbing his hands together. "Bitter in here."

He returned to his original place near the door, giving her a wide berth. No crowding. At any moment, she could start screaming. The last thing Danny needed.

"Nemeth and I had a 'free and frank exchange of views'," Danny said. "He won't hurt you again."

She clamped her jaw closed and grimaced. The injury wasn't confined to her nose and eyes, but extended to the side of her face. The swelling, too.

"I don't believe you."

"Nemeth's out of action. I promise."

"Vadik said that, too. He's a liar."

She jumped to her feet and scrambled away, keeping the sofa between them, another line of defence to augment the protection offered by the little, brown-and-yellow giraffe.

"Who are you?" she demanded, her voice raised, almost shouting.

Danny lifted his arms, hands open in an attempt to placate. "I'm a friend, Mrs Prentiss. Here to help. Really."

She pointed to the open doorway. "And him?"

"I told you, there's no need to worry about Nemeth.

He's not going to hurt you again. Won't be able to hurt anyone for a while."

She lowered the giraffe slightly. "Really?"

Danny dipped his head. "He's behind the staircase in the hall, tied up and in no condition to go anywhere. I really do promise." He smiled gently, encouragingly. "Go see for yourself if you like."

Her knees buckled. She grabbed the back of the sofa, teetering on the edge of collapse for a moment before straightening.

"You're lying! I-I don't believe you. This is some sort of trick. A sick joke."

Still smiling, Danny shook his head. "No tricks. No jokes. Stay there a sec. I'll be right back. I need to check on our tattooed 'friend', anyway."

He took the phone from his pocket, hurried out of the room, which was just as well. Csaba Nemeth had made something of a miraculous recovery. Danny found him sitting upright and leaning against the wall behind the staircase, struggling to push himself to his feet.

On seeing Danny, the Hungarian redoubled his efforts to stand. The soles of his leather shoes squeaked on the tiles, and he slid up the wall and onto his feet. A stream of words spewed from his bloodied and battered mouth. Danny didn't need to speak Hungarian to understand their meaning. He raced towards the bound man and kicked him in the nuts again.

Third time's a dream.

Nemeth's rant ended abruptly. The tattooed man doubled up, collapsed to his knees, and bent forwards, forehead connecting with the tiles. Danny's follow-up boot to the temple ended all resistance. It probably ended Nemeth, too. Not that it mattered. Although kicking a man in the head when he was bound and helpless might have offended the Marquess of Queensberry, Danny didn't give a shit. Given the opportunity, he'd have offered every paedophile on the planet the same treatment. Men who beat up women, too. It happened to be the reason he'd ended up at Prentiss House in the first place.

Without bothering to check the pulse at the downed man's throat—dead or alive, it didn't matter—Danny raised his phone.

"Say 'cheese', paedo." He pressed the button and the image of the pathetic, curled blob of a man saved to the camera roll. "Oh, not to worry. A smile won't improve the picture a whole lot."

He returned to Marian and showed her the photo. She burst into tears—these seemed like tears of relief. Danny again stepped back to his spot by the door and waited for her to recover. It didn't take more than a few seconds before she'd quietened enough to look up at him again.

"Are … are you from the police?" she asked, a tremble in her voice.

Danny shook his head and offered his most encouraging smile.

"No, Mrs Prentiss. I'm just here to help."

"One of Robbie's friends?" Again, she frowned. This time, a grimace didn't follow it. Adrenaline must have been masking the discomfort.

"Again, no. Your husband and I have never met."

"You're not one of them? Really?"

"I swear to God. Is there anyone else in the house besides the two of us and the cretin with the tattoos?"

"No." She showed him the ghost of a smile.

He took a speculative step forwards, watching for a response. She didn't flinch. He moved closer. Again, she held her place behind the sofa.

"Would you mind?" he asked and pointed to the cushion closest to him. "You and I need to talk."

She shuffled to the front of the sofa but made no move to sit.

"It'll be more comfortable if we sit," Danny said quietly. "You stay on that side. I'll keep my distance waaaaay over here." He added a cheesy grin.

The injured woman, who turned out not to be a battered wife, tugged a sweater from the arm of the sofa and draped it over her bare shoulders before lowering herself tentatively into the corner of the leather unit. Once surrounded by the comforting cushions, she crossed her long legs at the ankles.

Questions raced through his head, demanding answers, but she needed time to settle. Pushing her too hard too soon would most likely be counterproductive.

Marian Prentiss took a deep, stuttering breath and looked him up and down, studying hard.

"I-I've seen you somewhere before. I ... know it. If you're not one of Robbie's friends or ... one of *them*"—she shot a frightened glance towards the entrance hallway—"who are you?"

"My name is Danny," he said, happy to start with an easy one. "Danny Pinkerton, but if you ever call me Pinkie, I'll be most upset." Again, he smiled. "If I look familiar, it's because you saw me ... yesterday afternoon. Outside the Aspire Hospital. Remember the accident? The traffic jam?"

He paused to give her time to remember.

"My God!" Her hand reached up to her throat. "The

hitchhiker covered in mud and … blood. We barely spoke. What are you doing here?"

Danny took a deep breath before launching into the story. This part could easily become a little sticky.

"I saw your injuries and your terrified reaction when the driver reached across you. You were really scared. I thought the driver was your husband." He shrugged and grimaced in apology. "When you drove away, I memorised your car's number plate. A particular mate of mine has access to the DVLA database and—"

"You thought Robbie was driving the car?"

This time, Danny tried an apologetic smile. He was going through the whole range.

"A reasonable assumption at the time. Your husband's the registered owner and the Range Rover is really … Well, I didn't think he'd let anyone borrow such an expensive piece of machinery. I put two and two together and came up with—"

"Five," she said, almost as a sigh. "You assumed I was a battered wife? Well you were wrong. Dead wrong. Robbie wasn't driving, and he didn't hit me. He would never hit me. Not ever."

Danny cast his mind back to the previous day. It had been raining heavily, and the Range Rover's dark interior had made it difficult to see the driver.

He'd so misread the situation.

"An easy mistake," he said. "I'll apologise to your husband when you introduce me, but …. can you tell me what's happening here?"

"You won't believe me. This is a nightmare. It … It's going to sound like the plot of a gangster movie."

Danny shook his head.

"Try me."

"Robbie and I are being held against our will."

"That," Danny said, registering the weight of the Beretta and the spare mag in his jacket pocket, "I'd already gathered."

"Right, yes, of course. Erm, well ... two nights ago," she began, speaking to the giraffe, "Robbie returned from ... from work with two armed men. I'd never seen either of them before. R-Robbie told me they intercepted him on the way from the depot." She stopped talking, swallowed, and looked up at Danny. "Robbie runs a haulage company. It's based in Derby."

Danny nodded but didn't tell her that he probably knew as much about her husband's business as she did.

She took another deep breath and continued, her voice growing stronger all the time. "Robbie said they forced him into the back of his car and drove him here. When they arrived, we thought they were going to rob and maybe kill us, but they just kept us here ... in this room ... at gunpoint. At first, they said nothing. Wouldn't answer any of our questions. Just stood there"—she pointed to where Danny had stood when he'd entered the room—"aiming their guns at us. It was terrifying. I-I ... soiled myself." Her chin trembled and she lowered her eyes to the soft toy again.

"That's natural. Nothing to be ashamed of," he spoke quietly, trying to offer comfort.

Marian nodded. "I know, but ... the one outside ... Nemeth ... he laughed at me. Humiliated me. Robbie wanted to fight them, but they had the guns. It was useless."

She broke off. A tissue appeared in her hand, and she dabbed gently at the tears.

"Is that when Nemeth hit you?"

"No. No. I asked ... b-begged the other one, the one who introduced himself as Vadik Pataki. The one who took

Robbie away this morning. I-I asked him if I could have a shower and get changed. He said no. Then his mobile phone rang. He left the room to take it while the other one, Nemeth, guarded us. Five minutes later, he returned and said I could change. Nemeth took me upstairs to my room. The way he l-looked at me … I-I thought he was going to … to … I-I …"

She broke down again. This time, wracking sobs accompanied the tears. Danny wanted to reach out in comfort, but it didn't seem appropriate. He waited, giving her more time.

He checked his watch. 08:47. Still early. Wherever Robbie P had gone, wherever Vadik Pataki had forced him to go, they wouldn't be away forever—hopefully. Danny needed to speed things along, but definitely couldn't force the issue.

Slowly the sobs quietened. Eventually, they stopped. Watery eyes found Danny's.

"Sorry," she said, "it's embarrassing. I never cry. Not ever. But this is … this situation is …" She took another deep but fragmented breath.

"Are you okay to continue?"

Although she nodded and said, "Y-Yes, I think so," she fell silent again.

"Nemeth took you upstairs?" Danny prompted.

"Yes. Yes, that's right."

"Did he touch you?"

She shook her head, lowered her eyes to the giraffe. "Only to grab my arm and push me into the bathroom. He let me take some fresh clothes from the closet first."

"After that?"

"I showered and changed, and we came back downstairs."

"And your injuries?"

Again, she shook her head. "Th-That happened later. When we came back here, the other man, Vadik, was asking Robbie questions, but Robbie was refusing to answer."

"What sort of questions?"

"Work stuff. Dates and schedules. Bank account passwords. I-I don't have anything to do with Robbie's business. That financial stuff goes right over my head." She swallowed, and the accompanying grimace suggested it hurt. "I just take care of the house and the gardens. I'm doing an online course on interior design." Distractedly, she waved her hand around the room. "This is my work."

"Very nice," Danny said, not knowing what else to say, but meaning it. "So, your husband refused to answer the man's questions?"

"Yes, he claimed to have no idea what Vadik was talking about. That's when … that's when the man, Nemeth, started … started hitting me."

Danny ground his teeth together and clenched his hands into fists. If he hadn't already done so, he would have returned to the entrance hall and introduced Nemeth to the steel toecaps on his boots.

"I was a mess. Screaming. Blood everywhere. Robbie begged them to stop. Promised to tell them everything. Then I must have passed out."

"You lost consciousness?"

"Y-Yes. Woke up in bed, panicking. Could hardly breathe. Robbie was with me. They'd locked us in our bedroom. He was crying. Telling me how sorry he was for what they'd done. I tried to … to tell him it wasn't his fault, but I-I couldn't catch my breath. My nose wouldn't stop bleeding. I was gagging. Had a blinding headache. I-I've never been so … so scared."